Lemon Seas

Neil Beardmore

To Bruce
Good wishes
Neil B

PNEUMA SPRINGS PUBLISHING UK

First Published in 2016 by:
Pneuma Springs Publishing

Lemon Seas

ISBN13: 9781782284239

British Library Cataloguing in Publication Data. A catalogue record for this book is available from the British Library.

Pneuma Springs Publishing
A Subsidiary of Pneuma Springs Ltd.
7 Groveherst Road, Dartford Kent, DA1 5JD.
E: admin@pneumasprings.co.uk
W: www.pneumasprings.co.uk

Cover illustration from 'Indian Dancer', an original painting by Neil Beardmore

ACKNOWLEDGEMENTS

A novel is never the product of one person alone but of many. Thanks firstly therefore go to my wife Ashra Kumari Burman without whose inspiration, wisdom and support this book would not have been possible and to my close family, Paul and Linda. I wish to remember here also my late parents, and my brother Alan and his partner Jane, all of whom have given unfailing love and encouragement from as early as I can remember. Guy Russell's meticulous editing skills helped hone the piece into a novel of quality, and his work along with Judi Moore's helped me develop as a writer. Apu Bagchi's guidance was invaluable, as was Richie Beale's. Novelists Sue Hampton and Leslie Tate have never been far away when I needed help. In Goa my good friend Rupesh was an unfailing source of information and detail. Tricia Cunningham has championed my writing for well over twenty five years and has consistently given me hope and practical suggestions. Two fond friends going back many years passed away while I was writing Lemon Seas - Lance Taylor and Andy McMaster - writers and artists themselves, both gave years of mentoring, advice and encouragement especially at low moments. Likewise Sabiha, who is no longer with us.

Other family members have offered encouragement, including Sue, Michael, Wendy and family, as well as my brothers-in-law Billy and Seany, the Burman family and the Fitzgerald family.

Many others have directly or indirectly contributed to my writing life who deserve mention and thanks: Martin Brocklebank and Speakeasy Writers, Carol Barac, Caroline Davies, John Thynne, Rosemary Hill, Mike Elliston, John & Penny Best, Lisa & Arun Gupta and family, The New Bradwell Writing Group, Lubna Haq, Ronny & Brian, Richard Hancock, Merryn Williams, Toddington Poetry Society, Bob Devereux, Ian McEwen and Ouse Muse.

BBC Documentary maker Michael Yorke sent me much detail, while writer and campaigner Catherine Rubin Kermorgant has only been an email away with information and support.

Finally, Mrs Vivian Akinpelu of Pneuma Springs Publishing has been ever supportive and patient, seeking perfection over deadline. Lemon Seas could only have been written with the belief of all the above mentioned: my thanks to all.

Dedication

For young Laxmi and her mother in Goa who inspired the writing of Lemon Seas

1

The sun was losing its brilliance over the beach. Her eyes were open. Like in a painting on a wall where the eyes follow you, stare in yours wherever you go. He had seen one dead body before: his mother. Rich shuddered. A woman in a blue sari leaned forward and covered the girl's left breast, then retreated with her fingers to her mouth. The girl of about thirteen lay in the remains of an orange and green salwar kameez, one earring held on to her right ear, the other was lost in the sea or in the forest. Chatter had lulled, now it was a group gaze, mostly men. Fishermen in baseball caps sniffed, women in saris with wide midriffs edged in with elbows. The hiss of words was asking who she was, who she belonged to, whether she came from Bagolem. A man raised a handkerchief to his sweating brow, his wrist with a red tattoo.

Palm trees frilled the fringe of forest leaning the arms of their trunks out over the sands. Rich's bag seemed to gain in weight by the minute.

The sea tried to creep up to her hair, pulling the dupatta, her long scarf, but fell away.

'Who is she?' Rich asked a man with a broad grin. There was a mark on her forearm like a faint circle with a figure inside.

'Not from here.' The man pointed at the mauve-blue hills behind. 'They say her name is Sunita.'

Men in uniform were shouting, pushing people back.

'How did she die?' A sliver of fear suddenly coursed up through Rich.

The man shrugged and looked away.

'Bruises on the neck?' Rich said.

The man with the grin shrugged again, then smiled: 'No one asks question.'

The police were cordoning her off. Rich thought she might smile, then straightened himself, pushing away the tiredness of his journey. A big man with wide waist bawled for the people to give his men space and pushed a smaller thin man ahead. People stared silently now.

'You want a place to stay? I have a very nice hut.' Rich's new friend broadened his grin again revealing two lines of teeth browned at the edges.

Rich suppressed a sudden feeling of sickness in his stomach. They should close her eyes so she would not keep staring at him. 'Where?' He had to move.

The men in khaki were shouting for people to go home; no one shifted.

'This is your first time in Goa? You have holiday? Not dead people every week.' He laughed: 'Dinesh.'

The bus driver had assured Rich he would easily find a cheap chalet to stay in along the beach front. He shook the extended hand, 'Rich.' Dinesh was about the same age as him, he guessed – late twenties, with thick black hair combed back on top and short at the sides. Rich's hair was a fainter brown, his nose shorter and straighter than Dinesh's, and Rich's skin was sallow and untanned, his eyes brown, but not the rich black-brown of the man who was leading him now.

Dinesh laughed again: 'You are Rich, very rich. I like.' And led him on to a white-washed brickwork chalet with an unevenly tiled roof that steeply came down over the short veranda, it was the end property of a terrace of six.

Rich wiped his brow with his sleeve, pushed his fingers through his hair. This was not the start he had wanted. The white ball of sun pounded its afternoon rays on the back of his head, and he could not take the image of the dead girl's face from his mind.

Having pushed the door back, Dinesh held out his arm for Rich to enter the darkness. Another girl – a thirteen or fourteen-year-old like the dead girl – bounded out. This girl, with uncombed hair and wearing a dirt-worn salwar kameez of purple and green braved a cheeky grin at them, throwing Dinesh off balance and making Rich flinch. Their attempts at recovery were arrested by her abrupt smile, but it wasn't enough to curb Dinesh's anger and he yelled something at her causing her to step back. But quickly regaining her balance she held an open palm under Rich's chin, a fragile hand of thin fingers pointed together in a delicate cone. Henna lines crawled over the skin of her palm and wrist.

Dinesh yelled again and she smiled before scuttling away and disappearing into spaces between palm trunks.

'Who was that?' Rich said.

'Nobody.'

'Does she work for you?'

Dinesh motioned for him to enter, and seeing the ruffled bed clothes darted ahead and smoothed them. Rich's eyes took time to search the sudden blackness he had entered, take in the bed with faded green and gold covering, the wardrobe-cum-cupboard, the bedside table and wicker chair. It could have been a hundred years ago. A fan – dark brown painted – beat overhead, clunking in its fixture and a bare light bulb swung in time with it.

'Her name?'

'Dead girl?'

'No. The other. The one in here. Does she sleep here?'

'Lalima.' Dinesh sneered. 'Beg. Dance.'

Rich liked the sense of daring in her eyes, of excitement and lack of fear.

'She's like a cat – look round – then fall asleep.' Dinesh curled up his lips in disgust. 'We must lock the door always.'

When Dinesh had gone Rich lay on the bed staring up at the helicopter blade swinging overhead. Ten hours on a plane, three on a bus. Sleep. Nothing else mattered: no Tina, no little Jeanette, no girl with the smile of death on her lips, no begging girl lying where he was now.

*****

'Frank -'

Rich estimated he was in his late fifties, his thin grey hair barely covering his now tanned crown, his nose slightly out of alignment as though it had been broken in his youth, and his browned arms sprouted sun whitened hairs. Rich leaned forward from his wicker chair and held out his hand to his neighbour, uttering his own name through the groggy end of sleep.

'Lemon Seas.' Frank threw his arm out towards the turquoise line. 'Beautiful isn't it?'

'Lemon?'

'It's what they say. See. Right now. Before the sun falls to a pink ball over the horizon and sinks under waves, it glows suddenly - only for a quick time - from white to lemon.' Frank laughed. 'Very poetic. Making a long wide line of lemon across the sea. You can see it now, look.'

Rich followed his finger to the broad reflection that fanned out to the shore. The reds and blues, orange and white and green of wooden boats dragged beyond the tidal line added colour to the bleach of sunlight. Some had slipped out with tourists, their outboards leaving trails of surf.

'I got out of it for a while.' Frank pushed a line of grey hair from his eyes. 'And you?'

'Had to get away.'

'Relationships, eh?'

Before he had stepped on the plane Rich had promised himself not to talk about Tina and Jeanette, and the breakdown. Leave it all behind. Start again.

'Kids involved?'

'Who's that girl, Frank?'

'Always worse when there's kids to sort out.'

'That dead girl. Up the beach. Sunita – is that her name?'

'They're all the same, Rich. You watch them. Don't give in to begging. You'll never get rid of them.'

'You don't know?'

Frank held his gaze out to sea: 'Beautiful.'

Rich noticed his shoulders stiffen.

'Don't get involved. Some begging tart.' Frank spoke out towards the ocean. 'There's so many of them. Police don't care. They *say* her name's Sunita.' Frank paused for breath, then let out: 'Just another dead whore.'

'She was bruised, Frank. They must do something.'

'She fell. Or done herself in. She wouldn't be the first.'

'The police . . . ?'

'Don't mess with them.' Frank was stern. 'It was an accident.'

'And Lalima?'

'They're trouble, Rich.'

'Lalima should be in school.'

'Spoken like a true teacher.'

'How did you know?'

'Written all over you.' Frank beamed again. 'Listen mate, there's plenty of fish in the sea as they say. And anything you want. Anything. I'm talking to this widow. Piles she's got mate. Not those piles, you jerk. Money. Loaded. German. Very Teutonic. You can find anything you want here, Rich. If you've got the cash. Come on Rich. Food . . . I know a good place along the front . . .'

They stuffed themselves in the Pink City restaurant, facing out to the black sea.

When he got back to his chalet the night's heaviness had pulled itself between palms into crevices behind buildings, had soaked the air with its damp void and clamped itself around figures on the beach.

Rich had drunk too much and stumbled up the steps laughing with his new friend, but inside the blackness of his room Rich regretted the ramblings of his tongue, silvered by alcohol: telling a stranger about a messy relationship with a four-year-old in the middle. He should unpack before bed, but found he could not stand. The special extra thick plastic bag with its soft chalky contents would have to wait until morning.

He thought he was woken in the night by the whisper of men's voices next door, but couldn't remember his dreams in the morning.

*****

After swimming in the sea next day, he carried on dreaming in the shade of a boat most of the afternoon, but was quickly woken by the sounds of shifting feet in sand. The cone shaped hand was a few feet from his chest, the little worn fingers still with traces of henna, as though a vine had wrapped itself round her arm and hand. He allowed his gaze to follow up the length of Lalima's body: from her ankles with thin metal chains, through her narrow hips to her lips curled in a smile. At around thirteen, perhaps, she was about the age he was when he had drawn pictures for his mother.

He waved her away empty handed and she was light footed over sand to another girl in red by the trees and they laughed together and tripped away, Lalima calling her friend's name: 'Babita, Babita.'

Up the north end of the beach mountain giants bent to the sea's viridian reach and under their shadowy heads the specks of hut dwellers moved along strips of grey muslin sands. For a time a Brahminy Kite circled, eagle-like, as if it would swoop with bared talons and scoop a being from its attachment to nets, tear him away into the lemon sky. Where Sunita's body had been the footprints of onlookers and police had faded with surf, and the sea had smoothed her imprint in the sand glossy white and yellow in reflected sunlight, as though she had never been there.

Setting up near his chalet, he let his pencil scour lines over paper of cliffs, specks of people and boats, trying to let go feelings of how he thought the picture should be and allowing it to form itself. That's what his mother had taught him, yet it seemed to be the hardest thing of all to learn when drawing and painting.

Nothing was beyond Rich's mother's capabilities in drawing: when she sketched a tiger it had individuality; not just a simple side view, but she could outline its head so it was turning towards you. Yet strangely, she had never pursued it as a career – always dead-end office jobs, and even bar work.

'I can't draw like that.' Rich had told her many times.

'You can. Observe things like I do. Look at pictures.'

The pencil dithered in his fingers.

'Lisa will keep an eye on you.'

Lisa gave him cakes; in between men callers. She was a tall woman, overweight, with a good smile and always wearing thick red lipstick. He remembered thinking Lisa knew a lot of blokes. But she was always good to him, never angry, just smiling with fat spongy cakes with mountains of cream while mum was away at the bar. That's where mum said she was.

'You're not trying.' Mum regarded his previous sketch of a tiger with legs of different lengths. 'Do it again tonight. Observe and really concentrate. That's what real art is all about.'

He looked up at her then looked away: it was hard each time to let her go.

'We need the extra, Richard. Lisa will pop in with cakes.' Mum eked out a smile: 'Five pounds for a good likeness.' She had on a grey pencil skirt that suited her slim lines, and a little dark jacket over a purple blouse. Her lipstick was softer than Lisa's.

'You look good, Mum,' he said then, hoping it would make her feel all right about leaving him, even though she looked the same each night, and even though it was only one of two good outfits his mother had.

Money added an angle to the task, but however hard he scribbled the tiger would not emerge from the undergrowth in any correct or realistic way.

When she came back she snatched the pencil and with a few careful lines brought the creature to life.

For weeks misshapen animals grew from his pencil lines, and the ghost-like spectres of people; each time his hands ended up as empty as her looks. One night she nodded at his cows, but no money changed hands.

Several nights later he decided he would never be good enough to get the fiver, so it was not worth trying. He waited for the cakes and while munching one placed the other on a plate with a rose pattern round the edge and drew it slapdash as quickly as he could.

This time when she got back she scowled at the cream around his lips while he suppressed feelings of fear and laughter. If she felt like smiling, she didn't. 'There's something here, I can see that. All right. Next time there's five pounds for a great likeness, ten for distinction . . .'

'Observe. Concentrate. Allow the brush to go its way,' her voice still harangued him as he challenged himself to let something go inside and allow his drawing of cliffs and sea to evolve.

'Just like the Brahminy Kite,' he told himself as he watched it explore air currents effortlessly over the specks of fishermen below, 'it does not think how to fly, it does not try to fly – it just – flies . . .'

Girls in grey school uniform came with fresh laughter and watched him working, but it was hard for him to get used to the idea of being looked at and he shooed them away, their pigtails tied with little white ribbons at the end and the hems of their grey pleated skirts rocking round their knees, satchels bouncing on their backs. It reminded him of school back home: life was still new and special for teenage kids and there was something pure about their laughter.

'Very good,' Dinesh observed his cliffs.

Back then his sketches were not detailed enough for mother.

'If you need anything, tell to me. Or Rita,' Dinesh gestured to a middle aged woman in blue sari who was half bending with her broom of bound up feathered branches and swishing dust and sand and bits of plastic into a heap on the veranda. Rich watched her push forward rhythmically, hips swaying as her brush teased into corners, wheedling out the odd plastic bottle top.

'Mmm,' Frank considered the picture, the sides of his mouth down. 'You've got a snore. You know that, Rich?'

Rich laughed: 'Walls are thin.'

'Like them pigs out the back,' Frank laughed, nodding his head to the area behind the huts where a brood of small black boars snorted through the wreck of meals. 'Just remember,' Frank chuckled over juice on the veranda, 'that everyone here is trying to make the distance between you and your money as wide as possible. Never trust a beggar. Why would you? Part of some clan – paying some man with a big car in the shadows. It's everywhere, Rich. Rip-off is a way of life.'

Rita finished by wiping the round table.

'Make sure you do under the bed, Rita,' Frank sniffed. 'Right under. Not like last time. And you didn't do the toilet yesterday. It stinks. The Pink City again tonight, Rich?'

While he pulled on a long sleeved shirt and trousers Rich considered his picture, his scorn for it making him curse his mother and question why he was here.

It was Red Snapper, well cooked, with bright peppers and tomatoes with red wine. Frank filled him with banter about surviving in Bagolem, and how all the restaurants and chalets were temporary builds which had to be taken down before the monsoon – except the old converted fishermen's huts they stayed in. Then it was instructions about Rich's painting skills: 'You've got a talent, you've got to use it. It's your duty. Look at the rest of us. Useless. Don't know one end of a pencil from another. Here's you, with something, and you don't want to be bothered. The world's not fair, Rich.'

Rich left early: Frank had someone to meet. The sea bent into the land, pushing it back, flowing over its glass flat sands in long reaches. He walked awhile splashing his feet in its warmness, black now in the night except where it surfed, then he cut back through a gap between shacks and headed for a track inland that would lead him to his abode. Night filled spaces between palm trunks and the sides of shacks, drew him into its grim hold. Bare electric light bulbs hung here and there masked by mists of insects mesmerised by false moons. As his eyes adjusted he could find a trail through the dirty sand but was inhibited suddenly by the appearance of a hump ahead: a black hog lifted her eyes, squealed and led her fleeing flock into nothingness.

The sound of a man's voice came out of the oblivion. Rich was getting closer to the backs of houses and he was now in the range of a swinging light bulb. A smallish woman in a sari was waving her finger at a taller figure in shadows. Rich was ten metres away in darkness watching a strange film playing out before him. The figure in shadows shook the woman causing her to drop a metal bowl that clanged in a circle until it stopped with a pop. She shouted back and he whacked her across the face, but she did not fall, muttering something. He swiped again and she rolled away into pools of light. Rich held his breath wondering what the man's next move would be. The silhouette of the attacker stood over the reclining shape for long seconds, the shadow of his body cast by the lightly swinging bare light bulb swaying in sharply defined lines across her body. Rich could not work out what to do. The man could kick her, or grab a knife. The light bulb rolled to an unsteady halt. The man went in the inner darkness of a doorway.

Rich stepped forward, realising he was now in the light. She was leaning on one thin arm, propping herself up, staring at Rich. A locomotive howled a couple of kilometres away, a diesel wail that evaporated in the jungle parted by the train. She held him firm in her stare.

2

In the hospice his mother had told him to go to India and kept making him promise to do it: 'It will open up your life, Richard. We should have gone together and drawn and painted.' He had hushed her and listened to the rattle of her cough, turned away from the sweet green bile she brought up. His childhood drawings did not mean anything to her: they were just a device to keep him quiet while she was away, he had thought then. Yet now that he was here and had accomplished a good drawing he realised how much she had taught him, and how much it was beginning to mean to him.

In the night when the incessant chug of the fan kept sleep away and promoted images of Jeanette playing, Tina shouting, and mother trying to explain herself, he stepped out naked from his mosquito net and confronted what was left of his mother. All that remained of life in the end was misty white stuff you could sink your hands in and stir about. The urn was too big and awkward to carry. There she was in a bag, ready to blow away.

'I want a box,' Rich told Dinesh after his morning swim. 'Something big.' Dinesh leaned against a pillar while Rich went inside, coming back with a pack of ashes. 'She made me come here.' Dinesh looked puzzled. 'Mother. She came to India.'

'Nice,' Dinesh seemed to understand. 'You can buy at the shop. You can get a nice box.'

'It's clear now,' Rich dumped the package on the table. 'She wanted some of her ashes spread here,' he paused, 'to make me come.'

'English people say,' Dinesh began, 'India changes your life.'

'How do you know these things, Dinesh?' Rich laughed, rubbing his hair with a towel.

'You and your mother were close?'

'It was a ploy to get me here,' Rich faced the pile of ashes. 'It's so obvious, now I'm here.'

'What is ploy?'

'Oh,' Rich was impatient: 'something you do to make someone do something.'

'Today I'll ploy.'

'That was it. A ploy to get me here,' Rich was so absorbed he didn't correct him, the corners of his eyes beginning to water. 'Mum. We never really saw eye to eye. But you were always so clever in your ways,' he said as though she was in front of him.

'You need a boat,' Dinesh was looking down the beach. Fishing boats were basking like huge insects under the sun, their lumbering hulls with trail lines in the sand where they had been pulled up to dry themselves.

'Boat?'

Dinesh nodded at the bundle in Rich's hands: 'Take to the sea.'

'Where to let her go, that was always - yes, Dinesh, the sea. Have you got a boat?'

'Milit. He's got a red and blue boat,' Dinesh waved along the beach to a craft with an orange and green and white flag.

'You can get it?'

'I can ploy.'

'We don't say it quite like that,' Rich let out a quick laugh. 'When?'

'If you've got rupees - tomorrow. Milit can take you round the island,' Dinesh waved casually at the hump of jungle at the edge of the bay. 'Dolphin beach. You can only get there in a boat. Special.'

'You're a genius, Dinesh.'

Dinesh was grinning again: 'I will get it tomorrow. I will go ploying.'

'Not like that Dinesh. Ploy is a noun. You have to say something like: "it was a good ploy." - a good plan. I must get a box, Dinesh. A nice painted one.'

Frank arrived, his body dripping: 'Painted box?' he grabbed a towel and rubbed. 'I know just the place you can get a good bargain.'

'Something special,' Rich pointed at his bag. 'For my mother.'

'Right,' Frank headed inside to change.

The way his mother always corrected Rich's work made him feel inadequate. One day she put all of it together and scanned the development from the first tiger to the last human being. She overdrew, lengthening limbs, broadening torsos, until there was something of a smile on her lips. He was expecting the usual detailed criticism, but it might have been that her intuition told her he had worked hard these months and deserved a reward for he got a fiver. That day stood out now for him, as he remembered feeling as through he had gone through an apprenticeship and earned the beginnings of a skill; she would always be better at it than him, but he had something he could use now.

'They rip you off here, given the chance,' Frank hustled him up the main street. 'One price for locals, one for tourists . . .'

The village street led down through a wide clearing in palms and came to a halt at a taxi park overseen by a tall lamp. Each shop had a stall with myriads of colourful fabrics, spiritual icons and animals modelled in bronze and wood.

Frank led him down a short alley to a place bedecked with dried palm leaves and sheets of blue plastic. A small woman in red and green sari came from the back and smiled. At first he was not sure, but it was her: the woman he had seen beaten. Turning away sharply from his gaze, she observed the things they were handling: 'You want a box? This is a nice box.' She picked up a wooden thing decorated with elephants, but would not look him in the face and he could not stop looking at her, then turning away he cursed himself for standing there last night, doing nothing.

'That's too big for him, Chanda,' Frank said.

'You must have shopped here a lot Frank?' Rich watched how familiar Frank was with the shopkeeper who was now looking over her range of wooden boxes and paper knives, her thin arms waving over the little city of wooden structures, her fingers touching things lightly with a respect for each object. He admired how her business-like dignity obscured any feelings she may have had in his presence. Red and gold earrings swayed as she moved her head, keeping her right side carefully towards them, Rich noted, so the pale purple flower on her cheek bone was not obvious.

'This one. How much is this one?' Rich held up an enamelled box decorated with a peacock with turquoise wings spread out in a fan.

'Two thousand.'

He sniffed the piece, drawing in its sweet fumes.

'Too much,' Frank was in quick with the line it seemed he had at the ready and used often. 'That's over twenty quid.'

'Peacock,' Chanda pointed. 'It will bring good luck.'

'It's not worth two thousand. You know that, Chanda.'

Her thin fingers caressed it: 'It's a very good box. In Punjab they say-'

'Not even one thousand, Chanda–'

'What do they say?' Rich covered his momentary irritation of Frank: 'In Punjab, Chanda . . .?'

'The peacock is a good bird.'

'Yes. A beautiful bird,' Rich studied the imitation.

'Five hundred is more like it. Come on Chanda. Give my friend a really good deal.'

'They say in Punjab, when an old lady dies, she will come back as a peacock,' Chanda smiled, then looked down.

That was it for Rich: 'It's got to be this box.'

Frank scowled at him.

'One thousand and eight hundred.'

'Chanda,' Frank yelled.

'The peacock jumps on a wall and shouts,' Chanda held cupped hands to her mouth: 'Coo, coo, coo – the old lady has come back and cries on the wall. People in the village know she is here again.'

'Don't believe all that sales tosh, Rich, it's all a game to get your money.'

Chanda nodded.

Rich could not keep his eyes from her: 'Is it true?'

She rocked her head gently.

'Will my mother come back as a peacock?'

For a moment she dropped her business manner and looked down at the bird on the box: 'For your mother?'

'It's got to be a good box,' Frank said. 'For her–'

Rich gazed: 'I want to set her free now.'

Chanda was quiet for a moment, took the box from him gently and stared at the kaleidoscopic span of its wings. 'Nine hundred,' she turned as if embarrassed and went to a pile of paper to wrap it, her ankle bells tinkling as she moved. His vision fell on her narrow hips hidden under tucked in material, and the thin line of her midriff above the red and green.

'Here,' he said, offering her two thousand, and she rooted for change as he shook his head.

Frank scowled again: 'What are you doing?'

'Keep it. Two thousand is good.'

'Rich?'

Without smiling she wrapped the box niftily and handed it to him.

'It's not worth that at all,' Frank scoffed.

Chanda seemed embarrassed again, turning over artefacts and dusting as though her customers had gone.

'It's worth that. For my mother. She is a peacock, and I'm going to set her free in the sea–'

'You don't believe that.'

Rich glanced at Chanda working over her objects, her little hands flitting the cloth over invisible dust on elephants and tigers in advancing rows and little figures of Siva and Buddha dancing and meditating, all things she held in little herds and tribes in a display which she had probably dusted three times that day.

For a moment her eyes lifted to Rich, reminding him of his inaction the previous night, but she let a brief smile touch her lips. He replied with a smile too, enjoying the fine exchange of eye contact behind Frank's back.

The clang of rickshaw traffic and scooters outside nearly drowned Frank's cries: 'You can't carry on like this, Rich. Really, you've got to play the game.'

A cow was heading across the road towards them, saliva hanging from its jaw, one horn in a crescent up to the sky, the other a bloody stump.

Frank paused and wiped his brow with the back of his hand: 'It is a game you know. This India thing. A big game. And everybody plays it. They want money off us and we give as little as we can. That way the world goes round and we're all happy. We all know where we are.'

'I like her story,' Rich chuckled his weak response.

Frank's face showed horror and disgust at the hole in the animal's head as it stopped ahead of him, and turning back quickly he nearly careered into a passing motorbike.

'Steady, Frank.'

With a quick turn Frank had headed for the path to the chalets. Rich was about to follow and placate him, but the noise of flute music and drum arrested him. Slipping his way through a small group of tourists and a few Indian men and women, he nudged the shoulder of a European woman, tattooed with clinging ivy. Her friend had tied back her black hair under a large brimmed sun hat.

A girl was dancing in the sand: her feet stamping and shifting nimbly, ankle bells jingling, her hands clapping and her hips shaking. Wearing a green salwar kameez, Lalima swung her body lightly. A woman in long brown and dirty gold and pink sari with torn edges stood in shadows. Her hair was tied back, but loose strands were unruly and dry ended. She had a straight set mouth and flat cheeks and was probably in her forties, Rich imagined, although a hard life may have brought more lines on to a thirty-year-old face. A child of around five held her hand; a be-frocked little thing with laughing eyes and flake white teeth she banged a hand drum. Next to her a teenage girl in red, Lalima's friend Babita, played a wooden flute.

Lalima span in green and purple, fingers flipping, face alight with smiles. Her feet thumping down sand, she pumped her body round, rattling ankle bells, her dupatta scarf rippled and flowed with her moves. Waving her arms, she circled, clicking her tongue, and rolled her hips invoking the earth to urge her body in convolutions of turning, leaning, dipping and bowing. When she turned again she held out her hands to her watchers as she swung round in an arc to them, and the whistle-flute sounds pushed her on until the music slowed and she allowed the machinery of her body to close down as she crumpled in a ball to the applause of onlookers. The little girl went around with a basket the size of a cradle big enough for her to sleep in, collecting coins and notes. Rich left.

The blade on the ceiling comforted him when he was alone staring up from his bed, as the dozing Lalima had done so before she had jumped out on him. Jeanette would be Lalima's age in about ten years - less. Tina was never the same after Jeanette was born - up and down, desultory, blaming, accusing, and keeping touch out of the relationship. He had tried many times to get close but was butted away, and then the new man arrived in her life with talk and tools who could put up shelves, had a big smile and some cash in his back pocket, while Rich's career dived, he had lost his job and been forced into any supply work he could get.

Worse was to come, the big betrayal from his mother: you don't just die suddenly like that leaving your only child to survive. At least, not without paying them ten quid for a drawing.

He was sure there had been a trace of a smile on Chanda's lips and that they had shared a special gaze.

*****

'Ready?' Dinesh urged him with a smile.

'I'll get my things,' he would be all right in T shirt and swim shorts, but Rich darted inside the blackness of his room, grabbed the peacock box and locked up. He had to run over sands that were already scorching his soles. Dinesh had stopped and was waving to him and he looked down at a thin line of white that was leaking from the peacock: mother's ashes were spreading in a trail behind him. He slammed the thing tighter.

Two men stood with their backs to sunlight, their figures in silhouette. One was shortish and thin, the other taller, a policeman with a bulging stomach held up by a belt gripping khaki trousers. As Rich got closer and their figures were illumined, he took in the taller one with thin moustache and eyes scouring the scene as if searching for a target to fix on.

'Milit's boat,' Dinesh introduced the smaller figure in red shirt.

Rich offered his hand and they shook; there was a familiarity about him.

'Big Police Chief,' Dinesh nodded to the other.

'Not a policeman,' Rich laughed, offering his hand. 'Do we need protection on a boat?' It was meant to be bonding banter in jokey ironic style, but the man in uniform dropped his hand, eyeballed Rich for over long, then turned away.

'Push,' Dinesh tried to dismiss the confusion by nodding at the boat.

The long wooden hull had wings with floats on one side to stabilise it. Men grabbed the struts and heaved, arms taut, their feet pushing deep in sand as they wound themselves like springs ready to uncoil with the motion of the sliding hull.

Milit's little body strained with the weight and a couple of passing lads helped Dinesh. Rich slammed his teeth together and heaved while the Police Chief watched with folded arms.

'He's not playing then?' Rich observed to Dinesh with a joking nod at the bystander. Saying nothing, Dinesh shoved as the reluctant creature urged itself seawards, lazily easing itself down black wooden rollers damp and oily with lubricant.

'We could do with help,' Rich raised his nose in a nod to the uniformed man. 'A big man like you.'

'Get in boat,' Dinesh was short with him.

Rich swung his leg over the side of the hull and jumped in as the craft punched headlong into waves, breaking them into white. When he looked up the Police Chief was already up the beach, heading for the darkness of palm trees. Stiff in gait, tall but not bowed or with hunched shoulders, he carried himself powerfully over the roughness of sand and moved into the gloom of shade with a graceful stride.

'Police,' Dinesh shouted to Rich: 'Always we are friends. His name is Lakshya. Police Inspector.'

'I didn't upset him, did I?'

'Always friends,' Dinesh nodded out to the horizon as it rolled up and down and the boat's outboard chugged into action and thrust them deeper through waves.

Rich was looking back and thought he could see Lalima in the shadows of palm trees, and beyond he could just make out the speck of a man in khaki shirt. Was the Police Inspector nearby, looking on? Everything's small in the end, he told himself as he held the specks of his mother closely and was conscious of his heart pumping. This wasn't going to be as easy as he had thought.

Dinesh pointed at the sea, the ball of a head bobbing.

'Frank. Frank.'

They hauled his trunk in like a flapping fish. Rich threw him a towel as they left behind a rim of palms, huts and restaurants that receded beneath the weight of haze-blue hills behind.

Frank nodded at Milit.

A couple of fishing trawlers had grouped themselves on the tightrope of horizon like birds on a wire, their purple-blue misty shapes two dimensional against the blast of sky.

Milit motioned Frank over, pointing at his shirt. Frank took cigarettes from Milit's pocket, lit one for the driver and one for himself, guarding the flame with cupped hands then letting blue smoke escape in a gush.

Rich felt the sudden need for Jeanette by him, but he was no longer sure whether he still loved Tina.

When his mother was in the hospice she had called him over and whispered to him: 'Draw those flowers,' as she pointed her withered finger at a vase of blue irises with long stems. She was pushing him again. If he had listened to her more in the past, the days when his right hand just wouldn't put pencil to paper unless it was motivated by some intrinsic prize, he might have achieved what she secretly desired: 'I wanted to illustrate children's books,' she said, 'never quite got round to it. You've got more talent. You never use it. Draw those irises will you.'

Working swiftly he outlined the shape of the flowers and stems, shading them a fine deep blue with touches of violet while her eyes followed his fingers, then his eyes, and back to his fingers in a sort of dazed awe. The room smelled of sickness and flowers. Using pastels from a box by the side of her bed, he worked colour in with his fingers, smudging lines carefully but deliberately, adding more pencil, and smudging a little again, so the small picture began to shine.

'Over there,' she wagged her finger at an envelope.

He picked it up and opened it: a ten pound note. Pushing down tears he leaned and kissed her. Fame at last.

The green and brown island floated past them as they came to a bay. The underworld of rock had forced its way upwards and outwards to the sea and cracked itself open in blunt cliffs, graduated here and there by narrow drainage valleys. Dinesh nodded to Milit and the boat bobbed, the outboard quieting, until only the lapping of water could be heard. The men were strangely silent. A Brahminy Kite slipped out of the edges of blue, the white headed bird broadened its great winged body like an eagle over shallows of sky.

They looked at Rich. Dinesh smiled at him, letting his gaze fall to the peacock box in Rich's clutch.

Against the glare of reflected sun on the water a dolphin pounced out and back without a splash. Another glossy grey was up sleekly in the wink of an eye, and the men were silenced as the fish put on a show, ecstatically nosing up and out and down playfully.

It seemed like a new awareness of life suddenly throbbed through Rich, an intuitive understanding of how things worked, but it had no words, for it welled out of the unconscious in darting flows and could not be expressed, could only be glimpsed at with intuition and allowed to flow into the world. The water of tears at the edge of his eyes was as salty as the sea as he remembered his mother drawing pictures of tigers and Jeanette kicking waves.

The Brahminy Kite moved its head occasionally in search, allowing currents to decide its destiny.

The men sat, each with his own thoughts.

Rich stared at the box, tracing the outline of the peacock with his finger. Dinesh shuffled near and whispered: 'You must do it now.'

Rich could not move, trapped in tears. Dinesh put his hand on his shoulder. The other men were quiet still: 'You must let her go.'

Rich's hands were frozen.

'It's what she wants,' Dinesh cooed in his ear. Still he could not, grasping the last of her.

The boat rocked. The bird was drifting.

Dinesh said: 'I swim in the sea one day, me and little Nikhil. So much fun we had, splashing and laughing,' Dinesh smiled at

Rich. 'There was a bird in the sky. Then my little brother is gone. I can't see him. I look and look. Panic. For an hour. Nowhere. What can I do? What can I tell mother? He has gone nowhere. Dolphins were coming. One of them go down deep and come up and Nikhil is there swimming on its back with big smiles. I took him home, Rich. "Where did you go?" I said. "With dolphin," he said, "under the sea with fishes. Dolphin."' Dinesh bent to Rich: 'I thought he was dead for an hour.' He paused, then: 'You must let your mother go.'

The bird was sucked back in the sky's silence, as though suddenly invisible. The water was flat. Two trawlers dragged themselves over the line of horizon.

'Rich?' Dinesh whispered.

Rich looked in his eyes: Dinesh never read or took degrees - how come he knew how to do these things?

Taking the peacock box, Rich opened it, held it up to the sun and tipped, pouring the last void of her into the air and sea, so she blustered a little on wind eddies and trailed softly in white like a departing ghost, flattening herself on wavelets and dissolving in air and sea with a silent swish. She was free, back again in the turning wheel of an egoless universe.

His tears dripped in with her. Dinesh held one shoulder and Frank the other while Milit steadied the boat and they stared at the abyss, powdered now with the dust of her entrails, its meniscus brightened by her last flash and his last tear.

3

He seemed incapable of doing much for the rest of the day, closing in on himself in his room for a couple of hours in semi darkness and then reading on the veranda. Frank and Dinesh were good to him, leaving him except for the odd gesture: 'All right?' And he would nod back unsmiling. The letting go of the umbilical cord was slow and cumbersome and Frank's suggestion that they get blotto that night so he could blow it all away began to seem purposeful.

Later he took himself to a deserted area of beach: having a swim cleared his mind, but coming up out of the sea he felt a nick to his right big toe, followed by the sight of a stream of crimson flowing like watercolour through the shallows. Frank had told him careless drinkers still came along the beach at night - even though it was against the beach rules -- discarding beer bottles that then got broken. The anger of his bereavement came out in a yelled curse, and falling cross legged to the sand he nursed the cut, trying to squeeze the lips of it together. A shadow was over him, observing, then another. Lalima and her flute playing friend bent to him like nurses, pulling his foot around for better viewing, but he was in no mood for begging and angrily motioned them to scat. The girls looked at each other, turned and ran towards the trees.

He hobbled a few hundred metres, swearing, the blood still pulsing into the sea like a bleeding pipeline. Lalima was back with a wide green banana leaf and a piece of blue plastic string she had salvaged from a small pile of jetsam. Quickly tearing the leaf into strips, she urged him to sit but he roared at her again. Her friend stood nervously a few feet away. Stooping quickly Lalima lifted the wounded foot, causing him to jerk sideways and fall awkwardly onto the wet sand. The other girl laughed, Lalima giggled, and Rich could not hold back a yelp at the ridiculousness of the situation.

'Challo - Come Babita.' Lalima called her friend over – a shy girl with thick brown eyebrows and thin lips. They worked with the green banana leaf, pulling his foot roughly to them and binding a strip of the tough frond around it and he watched them, enjoying for a moment his own feelings of vulnerability - he had to lie back and allow her to take charge. Lalima took another piece and wrapped it round with the rhythm and firmness of a qualified nurse who was used to squealing patients, then secured the banana strips with the blue string, causing him to wince at the squeeze of the knot. Lalima stood looking at him a moment, a smile on her lips and he found himself smiling back, having found new depths to her. 'Cousin.' She smiled at her accomplice: 'Cousin Babita.'

She turned and ran, Babita following.

'Hey. Hey.' They deserved a reward – he must arrange to pay them some rupees -- but they were gone in shadows between palms.

When he got back to the chalet Frank chided: 'God, Rich. What the hell -'

Dinesh took him to a doctor who sniffed at it, refused to use stitches, but bound him tightly with proper bandages, smirking as he did so at the banana leaf improvisation.

Later Rich sat on a low stool in the shade of a fishing boat to make sketches. Fishermen nearby poured smoke from their lungs, coughed, their gravelly voices soaked with last night's alcohol fermented in their gullets. Only late in the day when the sun had no mercy were they quiet, letting their voices recover: in the shade of draped plastic roofs, usually of standard cerulean blue, they played cards as if in a silent movie, their quick hands embracing the winners they coveted, their crooked smiles with gleaming eyes.

Rich wanted to find Lalima and Babita, and occasionally glanced around to see if they were about but only saw Milit heading for the fishermen's huts and put it out of mind. A couple of German lads were skimming a Frisbee along the beach, and a girl in her twenties in black bikini was experimenting with a hula hoop, wiggling her hips and bottom in vain attempts to keep it orbiting round her. A tattoo in the shape of leaves on a rising stalk clung round the back of her silver neck. Her mate was laughing at her efforts. Shorter, with straightened dark hair, she clasped her hands now and again imploring her friend to try. Her attempts were equally useless. They laughed and moved on.

Watercolours evaporated rapidly in sun and breeze and then they were immovable. You could paint over, if you were to risk a muddy mess: it was an anomaly that all the colours of the rainbow distilled into white, whereas all the colours of the watercolour pallet distilled to a shabby brown, sometimes reddish or purplish depending on how much of a particular primary colour had gone into it. But mud all the same. You had to be quick with it; and bold.

The one horned cow was curious, watching him with deep black eyes – a stare that went into him and disturbed something of his complacency. Edging close, it nudged his side and Rich let out a cry. This was not a creature that wanted to leer over his shoulder and admire, this was a cow that owned territories. Sidling to him again, she pushed him and he balanced only by putting a hand down on the sand. Her glassy eyed stare held him and he saw there fear and chaos. She shook her head, waving the single horn, the gory fly trap of the stump of the other, sticky red. Fear struck through him and he pushed frantically, but she bleated and prodded him. Other eyes were on him, and he knew in a Hindu world it was not cool to aggravate sacred cows, but his ridiculous fear must be evident. The cow was unafraid, bellowing as if parted from a child and penetrating his animal defences.

Fishermen were laughing under blue plastic awnings and he did not know whether it was at him, but it might as well have been. The laughter and the bellowing would not stop. Hairs on the back of his head were tingling and the thing was breathing heavily as though excited about gaining ground.

'Challo! Challo!' The high pitched voice pierced his dream world. 'Jeldi. Jeldi.' Babita, who he had thought was timid, slapped the cow's backside, and Lalima yelled: 'Challo. Jeldi.' With a snort of discontent and a look of humility, the cow retreated.

'Cow not like art,' Babita laughed.

'Not your art,' Lalima joined her.

'You must teach cow,' Babita persisted.

Rich enjoyed their laughter, and held out his paint brush in the direction of the cow's backside: 'You want to have a go then? Is that what you want?' he joined in their jokes.

'Teach cow to paint picture,' Lalima couldn't control her hysterics.

'No,' he was still chuckling, 'I've got a better idea,' he turned to them. 'I will teach you.'

The girls could not stop their giggles.

'Can you write English? Read it?' His words made no difference to their mirth.

There were other eyes on the trio.

'Here,' he fumbled in his bag, pulled out several notes: 'You deserve this. Looking after me–'

Lalima calmed and counted. It was a lot. Too much. The girls looked at each other and smiled, Lalima tucked the notes in a small cloth bag and seeing Milit in shadows, they ran.

'I mean it. Teach you English,' he yelled after them; only Lalima turned. Jeanette would be that age one day.

At night he could not separate the image of Lalima now and the projected view he had of Jeanette at thirteen. He must find a present for his daughter, something long lasting - an elephant, in bronze or silver, nothing big, but something she would always remember her dad by. Jeanette loved elephants, the last time he saw her she was wearing a little blouse with patterns of little pink ones on it.

'Best with trunk up,' Dinesh told him outside the chalet. 'An elephant with its trunk up will bring good luck. Always.'

They chatted in the doorway beneath a light bulb whose empty glare and fiery red lines of filament attracted a fat moth.

'Chanda always has good elephants –' Dinesh had to go to his daughter he said, and tripped off out of the bulb's range. The sound of laughter peeled out from next door: 'He does tell 'em,' Frank came out rubbing wet strands of hair with his towel, naked but for red swim shorts. 'I've heard them all, but never that one - elephants with their trunks up. You can't believe anything anyone around here says, you know.'

'I've got to get one like that now, haven't I?'

'Always doing what you're told. You'll never get anywhere like that. Don't let that Chanda rip you off again. Just because you've got the hots for her.'

'Come on Frank.'

'I've seen that twinkle in your eye,' Frank paused, flicking his towel at imaginary insects. 'Got to get some clothes on. These pesky mozzies. No, I mean Rich, you've got to get wise.'

'When am I going to meet this German woman then?'

'I'm serious. You can't afford to like anybody round here. You don't do that. It's not part of the game.'

'Game?'

The dark night heat pressed the last embers of old sunlight beneath the horizon and the moth flapped its brown body around the silver light bulb uselessly.

'It's all a game, I've told you,' Frank called out from the glowing gold lamp in his room. 'Them and us. Ever since the Brits come here and built everything up.' He coughed a second. 'Let's face it, it would have been nothing without us. We built roads, and the biggest railway network in the world.'

'Why, though?' Rich watched the pathetic struggles of the creature attempting to fly into its moon. He did not know where the question had come from; the answer should have been apparent to him, yet it came to his lips anyway: 'Why did they do all that?' he pushed his mate.

'The Brits wanted to improve the world in those days – white man's burden and all that –' Frank flew his answer out quickly, '– improve the natives' lot and all that. That's what we gave. You must know that.'

Rich was sorry for the flapping thing and turned the light off. 'Those ideas are very old now, Frank.'

'Old?'

The moth relaxed, cured a moment of its addiction.

'India's growing. It doesn't need us. Those days are over.'

Stuck to the wall with its wings at the ready it contemplated its next move.

'You don't know what you're talking about,' Frank laughed out to him. 'They need us all right. We have to show them the way of democracy, we have to help them develop their industries. Them or us.' The man was in the doorway, his hair still spiky and damp. He scrubbed his scalp again as if trying to rub up better replies: 'It always has been and always will be. They'd have the shirt off your back if you let 'em, Rich. You've got to wise up. Play the game. Can't get too close, Rich.'

Needing another fix, the moth was attracted now to the lamp in Frank's room.

'Contaminate the genes, eh?' Rich let his sarcasm fly.

'Look what you've done: you've turned your light off out there and now the thing's gone in my room. I'll never get rid of it now.'

Rich smirked in the doorway, watching as Frank went for a swatter. It would be dead in seconds under the swinging biceps of the man as he lunged like a drunk this way and that, finally falling on the bed, the moth fluttering tantalisingly close but out of range.

'Turn your light off, Frank.'

The man swam around on the bed flapping indiscriminately.

'Turn it off and I'll turn mine back on. Lure it out.'

Frank lolled over the bed, flipped a switch and brought himself and his adversary into darkness. It took a while for it to sink into the creature – the three of them frozen for seconds – before it leapt ecstatically for the door way and fixed itself up with the outside bulb, burring and flapping.

Frank rolled himself off the bed, throwing the swatter aside, while Rich chortled in shadows.

'He didn't mean it you know,' Frank was brushing himself down as he came out. Rich watched him, puzzled; Frank looked as if he knew he had his man on the hook. 'Dinesh. He didn't mean it. All that about dolphins rescuing his brother. You didn't believe it Rich? Never. All stories. We had to get back, Rich. That boat was booked out again after us. Somebody had to find a way of getting you to do it. Dinesh is good at that sort of thing. We left him to it.'

Rich hovered, letting it sink in, wondering if Frank was getting his own back for Rich's defiant stance towards him moments earlier.

'Come on, if you're coming,' Frank headed into dark sands, 'If you're going to eat –'

'Don't you ever eat with your German lady?' Rich left the moth to the delights of his outside light bulb, thinking it better to leave it on for security.

'With friends,' Frank cursed the existence of biting insects.

Rich stared at the grey rim of foam along the black sea and a couple of dogs in silhouette.

The moth flew towards the moon.

*****

Slivers of sunlight burst through his ragged curtains making triangular stilettos, and as he watched their sun-dial arc over the covers he was reminded of his mother's delight at her only grandchild: they had played all day on Long Rock beach as the tide slipped out leaving glossy undressed sands with the medieval mount of St Michael behind like a huge moored ship. Rich had managed to have Jeanette for a week and this had been mother's last long outing with her son and granddaughter.

Today he would get the elephant.

'You never had kids, Frank?' he asked his mate after morning coffee on the veranda.

Frank shrugged: 'Boy and girl.'

'Ever want them to join you over here?'

Waiters were serving breakfast in restaurants nearby.

'Grown up. Got their own lives,' he swallowed. 'You know what it's like these days. Families. What are they?' he waved to a couple of waiters for more coffee. 'Sided with her when I left. Funny really. You could say it was her fault more than mine - she found somebody else, I didn't.' Rich nodded. 'They told me to stick it out. It would all burn out and blow away. What was there to wait for when all this is here–' he laughed throwing his arms wide. 'Paradise.'

Rich nodded again, but his acknowledgement of 'I know' was lost under piles of Frank's enthusiasm.

'Or hell,' Frank blustered. 'It can be. Just watch yourself. We're all vulnerable here, you know. You don't want to end up on the wrong side of the law - in some dingy prison cell. I've seen it before. You think the embassy'll help you - by the time they get their back sides in gear you might be at death's door. And it'll all be some pretty accident. I've seen it Rich. Drugs and prostitution, all on the dark side of the curtain. You watch what you're putting in your mouth and where you put that thing –' A waiter brought him another coffee and left. 'He knows that's not how I like it - far too much milk. These Goan Christian boys haven't got a clue. And the Christian Indian girls in long frocks - it's all out of place. Upside down. They all smile. Always a sign of someone trying to get something from you. But when in Rome, and all that. And watch that Lakshya. Have you met the Police Chief yet?'

Rich nodded: 'On the beach yesterday – he wouldn't help us push the boat out.'

'He's got pockets deeper than a cow's bum. Likes them lined now and again with silky rupees,' Frank hacked a false smile, holding back his lips a moment with a finger each side. 'See. Like that. Go on. Practise. Go on, Rich. Do it.'

They stood, pulling false smiles to each other like clowns, twisting their faces and jerking their heads and leaning from the hips. Two boys pointed and laughed, and turning to each other copied them. The men joined the boys and had a whooping time for a few moments, drawing a crowd of kids, several old men, and women with fishing baskets. When the performers could no longer keep up the act due to the irresistible urge to corpse, they fell about laughing, lighting up the audience further with yelps and hoots. It was a good day to buy an elephant.

'Why did your kids side with her, Frank?' he asked as they went back to their seats.

'Frank glanced at him: 'They're doing their own thing, they don't need me now. Anyway I've got all I need here.'

'Jeanette's all I've got.'

'Lucky you.'

'Tina gets in the way.'

'No one can get in the way of love.'

'Profound, mate. Deep.'

'True,' Frank let the words trail as he headed into the dark doorway. 'Never let her forget. Not like me . . .' Light chiselled in his chalet in a quick blade across the floor and bent up the side of the wall, the shadow of the man flat and awkward like cardboard against it.

'Have the police found out about the dead girl, Sunita?' Rich threw in Frank's room, but there was no answer, as he got his bag ready to go to the village. A slight hobble on Rich's right foot was still necessary, although by turning his ankle a little he could take the weight off the injury. He would need to change some money soon, although he had got a few notes left, but not enough to cover something big.

The opening of the path into the main street was blocked by a group crowded round Lalima, drum beats echoed through palms swaying in breeze. An older woman stood in shadows holding the hand of the child with the drum. Lalima stamped sand and threw up her hands, twirling to the claps and cries of an enthusiastic audience of tourists. There was no flute music so Babita must be missing.

Lalima bowed to applause at the end and the little girl exchanged the drum for a cradle-like basket, collecting cash. Rich stepped forward, notes in hand, ignoring the urchin officially collecting. Lalima, not even a little breathless - as though the dance had merely been a warm up for something more urgent - smiled at him. Her hair was tied back with a dirty orange band, strands of it hung dryly round her face, he tried to imagine her scrubbed up in a new silk kameez.

As the crowd was dispersing a woman came out of the shade. Her left eye was damaged: where the pupil should have been dark brown to black was a mark of grey like a sliver of metal. He had to look, while she glared suspiciously at him though her good eye. Rummaging for notes, he handed them over and she took them without smile or comment.

'My mother, Jyothi,' Lalima introduced her to him. 'And little sister - Aditya.' Lalima put her arm round the infant.

'She saved me,' Rich laughed to the mother, holding up his bandaged foot, 'and Babita. Where is Babita?'

'It's good?' Lalima nodded at his foot.

'Oh yes. Just a scratch really,' he turned back to her mother: 'I want to teach them English. Give them something. Where is Babita?'

Lalima scowled and looked down.

'She's gone?'

Lalima looked away and her mother pulled her arm.

Aditya riddled her fingers through coins as though it was sand.

'Tomorrow. We'll do an English lesson. I will come here, to this same place near the juice stall. You bring Babita,' he could not get Lalima to look him in the face. 'Thank you.'

Her mother watched him, the silvered eye seeming to look inward. Aditya came to him with a banana and he held it stupidly for a moment, until Lalima eased it from his fingers, unzipped it, broke bits and handed them around to him and her family.

'You live here – in Bagolem?'

'We travel,' Lalima traced crescents in the sand with her toe: 'Beach to beach.'

'You've been to school though,' the teacher in him spoke, 'I mean, you speak well . . . in English, I mean.'

'I'm no good,' she laughed, hands on hips, swinging from side to side. He hoped Jeanette would be like her.

'Twelve o'clock. Tomorrow,' he turned to Jyothi's blank look. 'And Babita.' Shoving his hand in his open shoulder bag he came out with his final notes and stuffed them in her hand, thinking his altruism would save the poor. She took them and tucked them deep in her cotton purse, while he wandered off with his shoulder bag unzipped.

The stall at the front of Chanda's shop displayed boxes and icons, and inside soft purple-red-yellow-green fabrics blasted their colours around brass statuettes of Siva, Laxmi, Ganesh, Hanuman, Buddha, that paraded themselves along shelves and tables. Sandalwood incense sticks burned in the corner, their firefly tips sending out snake-wriggling lines of smoke. 'More like a grotto than a shop,' he mused to himself, smiling as he came to Chanda. Wearing a purple and red sari, a little worn but bright, she was sitting head down behind a small table cleaning a brass Buddha with a cloth.

'Hi Chanda,' he called to her. Without looking up she carried on vigorously and he was unnerved a moment. There was a line of red in the parting of her gloss black hair, oiled and tied back. She would not give him her eyes. Her ear was perfect, beautiful to him – a little foetus round and supple, the curls and shapes of it unblemished. 'Look up and smile,' his mind insisted, but she chugged on rubbing. It reminded him of when Tina was angry – she would do something while she yelled, preferably banging pots about and throwing bands of cutlery in a drawer as if to say: 'I do things round here. You don't. And this noise proves it.'

He was considering he had upset her and decided it wasn't the right day to be going after elephants so made to leave. Turning, he found himself facing a small silver elephant with its trunk curled upwards. Bringing it down, he enjoyed its roundness and sandalwood smell, and turning towards her their eyes met before she looked away. She might still be sore that he did nothing to intervene when he saw her beaten but her eyes did not show that, only quick traces of fear. She had the red smudge of a tikka in her forehead between her eyes.

He was thinking how he could show some warmth to her: 'I like the elephant,' was all he could manage in clumsy tones, as he returned it to its position on the shelf.

She had abandoned the polishing and was now on the phone, urgently pipping out a text. A shiver ran through him and he felt something was not right but shrugged it off as his imagination.

Now his attention was caught by another elephant a few feet away to the left, a larger one with a patterned face that he had to reach up to and he was aware of Chanda's movement behind him in light dance-like steps, seeing a flicker of her reflection in a mirror framed with a wooden Islamic arch. His bag was slung over his right shoulder and pushed behind his back and she seemed to lean against it pressing it against him. He expected to turn and find her ready to assist him, but as he did so he was surprised to find her back in her seat again, head down to the

Buddha which now shone with illustrious enlightenment. Cupping the larger model he smiled, but her head was down while she rubbed, and he put it back, forgetting the smaller model he had first admired.

'I'll get money,' he was distracted by her lack of response: 'I'll go and get some change.'

She glared up at him, lips and brow set.

He was heading through the narrow exit towards the glare of the street when he heard her call; her second utterance was clear.

'Steal,' she shouted. 'Steal.'

He faced her quizzically, the light still blinding his eyes.

'You took it. You steal it,' she pointed at his shoulder bag.

'Chanda?'

'You took the elephant,' her eyes glared.

He glanced back at the shelf by the front of the shop: there was a space where the little elephant had been.

'I wouldn't steal from you, Chanda.'

'You steal the elephant,' her body shook and pointing her fingers wildly, she pushed past him and was out in the sunshine calling for the police.

Other shopkeepers were quickly at their doorways and passing workers and carriers began to assemble.

'It's a mistake, Chanda.'

Rickshaws stopped and taxi drivers ambled over. Without realising, he was hemmed in the entrance by a crescent of inquiring eyes.

'He steal my elephant,' she enjoyed the stage she had suddenly improvised.

'No, Chanda.'

Shouts came from the crowd and the angry waving of arms.

'Thief,' she roared at him. 'It's not there. You touched it and you took it.'

The audience swayed, eyes searching, fingers pointing, and their power suddenly drew up over him.

'Get police, Chanda,' a woman was shouting.

'Cheat,' another.

'Thief.'

'Robber,' a man was waving a stick.

Rich had no money in his wallet to show he intended to pay and no way to buy himself out.

The crowd were waved aside leaving a gap for the Police Inspector to fill and he strode through, thin moustache over the firm line of his mouth. They were silenced. Milit ran behind.

Chanda approached the leader as though he was royalty: 'He steal. Elephant. He steal,' her voice cracking, and she followed as the police chief came up to Rich.

'I don't know what's going on. I'm no thief,' Rich shrugged his shoulders.

Some members of the small crowd looked from one to the other, expecting much from this sudden show of street theatre.

Police Chief Lakshya snatched Rich's bag and dived his hand in, wriggling it around a moment as if stirring a pudding. The crowd's eyes were on the bag, then up to Rich for reaction. Lakshya's face became animated, a sudden deliberate look of shock expressed itself in his eyes, his thin firm mouth turning from lines to a circle with a thin black line around the top. Rich found it difficult to take it seriously – this was getting like a Bollywood movie with all the melodramatic acting skills, and pushed back a smirk that insisted on forcing itself to his lips. Pulling out the wooden elephant like a rabbit from a hat, Lakshya held it up for the crowd's approval, drawing gasps and mocking cheers. Chanda's nervous gaze rested for a time on Milit, then the Police Chief, never on Rich. It was something out of a film, but as Lakshya grabbed him by the arm he knew the song and dance part was over. Hell was about to begin.

4

The fan in the police station was cranky and ineffective, a white thing with creamy blades flaked with months of dust that squeaked every few moments as the whole mounting swayed with the propeller's enthusiastic spin.

'What do you think would happen if I left you to them?' Lakshya jerked his head in the direction of the shops.

The interview room was musty even though the blade above tried to stir its contents. The single window had rusty iron struts. Rich was sitting; the smirk had gone. Lakshya stood over him, Milit at his side, hands trembling.

'Pull you apart. Every one of them. They may do that anyway,' the police chief's enunciation was precise, 'in the dark shadows at night between palm trees. Out with the pigs.'

A bit of body odour came over to Rich. Milit laughed.

'I didn't do it,' Rich's firmness was received with a sideways shout so unexpected that he was knocked sideways and stunned.

'Thief.'

Milit laughed again.

Rich was about to leap up and swing at him but Milit pulled him back down. Lakshya's finger was centimetres from his nose: 'I find an elephant in your bag and you say you're not a thief? Tell me you are a thief. Tell me.'

Rich bunched up his lips in protest, head down.

'Tell me. Say it: thief. I am a thief.' Lakshya pulled Rich's jaw with thumb and forefinger so he faced him again. There was a smirk from Milit and a growl from Lakshya. 'You English. You don't understand, do you?' Lakshya leaned back a moment. 'We run the place now. You come here and you think your money can buy us. Only *our* money can buy us, you understand?' Lakshya exchanged smiles with Milit. 'Only our money. You think you can talk how you like to our women. You look at them. And look at you. Look at your women. They walk around in underclothes. Like prostitutes. You think this is still a colony, a playground where you come and do what you like? You think you can lie about on the beach and a waiter will bring you drinks all day – and shout at them.' He straightened. 'My nephew is a waiter in restaurant. One day off in thirty. He works until eleven at night with only two hours off in the afternoon. Do you see that, Mister Englishman?' he smiled again at his partner.

Rich's impulse was to punch out, but he held back: they would hold him down and pulp him. 'I need a lawyer. You can't keep me here.'

Waving his request aside, Lakshya leaned forward to him again: 'Waiters work long hours, and they die too young.' Milit and his boss laughed: 'And you lie about and disrespect us. And steal. Thief. My nephew will never be able to lie on a beach and do nothing for month on month. Never. If he saves up all his money all his life. Never. He has a scooter, and soon he will be married. But never lie on a beach trying to get the same colour as us –' The men laughed, poking him about in their own language. The police chief became serious: 'I am the power here, Mister Lomas, Mister Richard Lomas. Now *we* do it for ourselves. Without me you would all be fighting each other – like a football crowd – if I don't have power, this town is dead. You know that. I have balance. The little god you fear and hate –'

'Is that what you want?'

'Yes. Fear and hate. I want to see it in your eyes. I don't want to see your greed anymore.'

'What are you doing about the dead girl, Sunita? What are you doing about that?' Rich flared.

He was slapped down with grunts.

'I want a lawyer. My rights.' It was hard to know a way out, and his pride was making invisible bars too.

'Give me fear and hate in your eyes, thief.'

'I didn't steal a thing.'

'We can play all night,' Lakshya smiled at Milit. 'Get us tea, Mil.' The assistant was on his feet as though propelled by a spring.

'You don't see, do you Mister Lomas. Like your fellow men you have that, how shall we say, *arrogance*. You seem to make an art out of being rude. Then with pride you tell the world it is wrong and it is rude and you are not.' He paused. 'You steal from us.'

'It was not me.'

'Your father and your grandfathers turned Hindu against Muslim, in a killing frenzy. You know about Partition. You think we forget about that.' The police chief took his time now. 'Do you know about Amritsar?' Rich held up half-closed eyes, 'You see you do not know your history, Mister Lomas. 1919, Mister Lomas - hundreds of Sikhs were shot down by troops - women and children and old men - unarmed civilians, Mister Lomas, by a certain General Dyer. You do not know your own history. Nothing. Your ignorance is astounding. Dyer with his red dye. You are a thief. Say it.'

'What can I do to get out?' Rich was almost thinking out loud.

The police chief laughed under his breath, glanced at his assistant and sighed: 'You want to get out? How does my nephew get out - as you say? There is no get out for him - a life of struggle and maybe a day off now and again to see his children. Where did all your money come from, Mister Lomas? You know I think some of it came from India. You cannot have factories and science without money. I wonder what was taken, Mister Richard Lomas, all those years ago when Queen Victoria was Empress of India and owned every grain of every person in Bharat. Did India finance Britain's Industrial Revolution? I wonder when I stare up at that old fan struggling its way around like the world struggles round and round. Isn't that right, Mister Lomas?'

'I don't need a history lesson.'

Milit brought a mug of tea for Lakshya and one for himself, nothing for Rich.

'I want water.'

The police chief nodded at his lackey and Milit was off and back with a small glass with fingerprints around the edges and tide marks at the bottom.

'You don't bother about real crimes,' Rich yelled again, 'a little elephant is more important than a dead girl on your beach?'

'So,' Lakshya whispered close to Rich's ear, 'we find an elephant in your bag. All the evidence. I'm sure we could find other things too. There might be drugs hiding in your bag – we should check again.' Rich made a lunge forward but Milit pulled his tired body back easily. 'Violence against police officers . . . attempted murder even . . . There's a range of things could keep you here, Mister Lomas, but not in the style you're accustomed to. You'd get your meals every day, and shelter. All free for you. But bars all round, and no sun and sea and sand for you, Mister Lomas.'

'You can't keep me here. I haven't done anything.'

Lakshya raised his hand ready to strike, Rich flinched, but the standing man withdrew laughing.

'You can't make me pay for crimes I didn't commit.'

'Can't I? Doesn't your religion say: "the sins of the father will come upon the children"? You have to pay, Mister Lomas. We all have to pay in the end. All of us. It's karma, Mister Lomas. Simple karma. As you say in your country: "There's no such thing as a free lunch."' He belly laughed. 'And: "You make your bed and you lie in it." You're lying, Mister Lomas.' He rubbed his hands. 'Vedic writings say not just individual karma, karma of nations. We share the karma of nations and of their wars. Our slavery belongs to us - our nation - down to individuals - we all own a share of national karma.' He hushed again. 'You are a thief, Mister Lomas. The son and grandson of thieves. I have taken the elephant back. Now. What to do with you-' He nodded at Milit, who disappeared out a door and returned with another uniformed police officer. Milit seemed like some sort of servant in civilian clothes, someone Lakshya liked to boss around - the one owing something to the other, the one owning the other in some way.

'This is a scam and a shambles,' Rich hissed.

Lakshya held him back and eyed him: 'We have our suspects for the dead girl. And you could be one of them.' He nodded to the men to take him away.

The cell stank of urine. There was a blanket and a low wooden bed that collapsed with his weight when he lay on it due to a broken leg. They gave him dhal and rice which he gorged as the space between the bars of the trunks of palms outside the metal bars and grills on the inside mellowed to grey and brown in the thickness of night, and he allowed sleep to take him from his new troubles.

He was woken by a call to the dirty plastic bucket, already covered by the dried faeces of previous inmates, and splattered his fast contents inside, as faint glows flowed through undergrowth outside and filtered into his own private abode. Through heavy eyelids and murky ear drums he confused his dreams with the sound of voices arguing down a long passage beyond doors.

He heard the clank of keys followed by the door flying open as if electrically operated.

'Get him up.'

'Frank,' Rich found himself mumbling. 'Frank. You're here?'

Frank urged his friend to his feet, but he was unsteady and had to be supported. The shadowy shape of Lakshya loomed behind the freedom-maker shouting: 'Get him out of here. Jeldi.'

'This cost, Rich,' Frank helped Rich through the cell door. 'My god, you cost me, Rich.'

'You bought me out, Frank?' Rich looked at his saviour.

'You're all yellow face and - What else do you expect me to do? I told you, didn't I? You don't mess with things.'

'I didn't do anything, Frank. Someone put that there. The elephant thing– ' Rich was reluctant to blame Chanda out loud, and anyway it might infuriate his captors more and their eyes were on him as he struggled out, but he remembered her hovering behind him in the shop and nudging his bag when his back was turned. A guard was waiting to open the door at the end of the corridor.

'I told you Rich. You stupid-'

'It wasn't me.'

'They all say that,' Frank shuffled his man on past another occupied cell, and as they rolled down the corridor Lakshya went in Rich's cell and inspected the bed.

An Indian man came forward to the bars of his cell and hissed to Frank and Rich: 'They got me. I didn't do it.'

The guard stepped forward and banged the man's cage with a truncheon.

'I didn't. Not a girl –'

'Broken,' the police chief nodded to the guard to halt them. 'Broken bed. Five thousand.'

'Get me a lawyer,' the man in the other cell reached through bars and tugged Rich's shirt.

'What?' Frank bellowed behind him.

'Broken bed. He has to pay: five thousand.'

'You could get hundreds of beds for that,' Frank laughed cynically.

The guard began to push them back, stopped and whacked the imprisoned man's hands.

'All right. All right. Tomorrow Lakshya.'

'You know the police chief, Frank,' Rich said. 'You call him by his name.'

'Done this before, you idiot. Tomorrow. I'll take you to the ATM,' Frank made reassuring noises that echoed down the corridor and encouraged the man blocking their path to stand aside. 'I told you, Rich. I told you. Don't trust any of them. They're all on the make,' Frank whispered again in his mate's ear.

'Get me a lawyer. I didn't do it,' the prisoner's cold shout echoed from his cell down the windowless corridor.

*****

To the south end of the beach was an outcrop of rock – a favourite place Rich retreated to when he wanted to think and draw. Mother told him not to be too precise, let the picture evolve – like a sculptor with a lump of rock: somewhere inside was a work of art, he just had to keep chipping until he found it. 'Allow your pencil to drift your ideas along,' she had said. It was a good way at the moment of blocking out what had happened in the cells that night.

A path led up between two glorious boulders the size of small houses – as though ancient gods had thrown them there like dice and they waited under wind and sun and monsoon for the next roll in some future millennia. In front of and below the structures a restaurant hung out tentatively to the sea, and from that vantage point Rich had clambered so he could look over the dried palm and plastic roof.

The perch on the rock held a perfect view: the beach spread out in a crescent up away northwards, the sickle shape three or so kilometres of sand petering out at a river estuary. Near there rocks led out to the island hump, cut off at high tide but joined at low. The platform he occupied on one of the flat boulders was a little difficult for the less intrepid to get to, it requiring legging it up and hauling the trunk over and rolling on; blokes didn't bring their girls here. They would gather in groups instead on Sundays, a clutter of men with bottles, laughing loudly and pushing each other playfully, young Indian men from villages. On the beach they wore loose fitting trunks, or swam in over-sized white-grey Y-fronts.

Here he let his pencil drift over paper, sketching the bay and hump of green island up the north end with a sailing ship moored, the sun beginning to dip to it.

Occasionally at the back of the restaurant where the kitchen was, a waiter would appear under the makeshift roof with a bowl of dirty water and sling it out to sea, the sliver of silver liquid in a slick line broke up into droplets and smacked back down. The bowl slinging exercise had one real purpose it seemed: having gone through the ritual, a twenty-year-old, tall with well developed arms, lit up a cigarette and gazed out over the horizon.

Rich guessed at his thoughts: at least that snatched fag gave him a moment of meditation, a gap between the bustle of chat and orders. Had he, like some of them – according to what Dinesh had told him – come down from the Punjab, or even the mountains – left his home and snowy peaks, dried his mother's tears as she wailed the loss of her firstborn son, the hope of her life. Had he told her he had to go and she persuaded him with tears not to, but there was work there and money and a fortune to be had. Had she wanted him to marry the little girl he grew up with down the road who he loved, but had told to wait. Had he found the thighs of English and German women inviting?

Did he dream of Bollywood, or being discovered out of nowhere, or dancing with some Indian Queen with long shiny hair who danced and danced and sang her heart out for the beloved boy she could not have, until three and a half hours of conflict and more song and dance had transpired? Was he the boy she danced with as he drew blue smoke in his body and stared out to the little trawlers on the horizon that hovered like faint blue insects as they inched their way across the expanse. Dance and dance and dance and sing. What was life? There was no gold here, no great sums of money to be bagged. Slog. More slog and only a few days off.

A shout from inside the restaurant made the shirker automatically throw his dog-end out to sea like he'd done a thousand times already that season, and its little light snipped out with a fizz as he ran back to the world.

The sun sent lemon yellow streams across the ocean and for five minutes, perhaps ten, all things were tinged with the colour – palm trees, huts, restaurants, hills. Then sudden pink: the time when piles of stuff out the back of palm trees combusted – the burning of rubbish. From Rich's vantage trails of blue-grey hung around branches, slow drifting pools reshaped themselves to ever newly sculptured forms, sometimes elephants, or monkeys, camels . . . a one horned cow . . . or briefly a figure something like Siva with piles of dreadlocked hair on top of his head smiling out to Rich from billows lumped in air. Strands of smoke rode behind palms along the tide drained river. Land thirsted and cloud cover would not crack. Fires sent stagnant signals of smoke slowly up like incense in perfect lines to fizzle in haze and flatten out like volcanic dust.

Bagolem, having busied itself all day with tourist centred activity settled back into the openings of twilight. Cries from the shoreline faded as beach games slowly ended with the imperceptible encroachment of darkness. Vendors came with toys they fired elastically in the sky like mini propellers that burnished up in purple and yellow halos and feathered their way back down.

He headed into it.

5

Lalima was sitting in the shade of a beached boat when he stumbled on her the next day. Leaning back on the hull, her head down, she pushed her finger through sand. He stood over her, but she did not look up.

'Lalima.'

She kept poking sand.

'Lalima,' he stooped but she would not move. 'What's the matter? Where's Babita?'

'Gone.'

'Where?'

Lalima shrugged.

'She can't go far, she lives here?'

'Nowhere.'

'When was the last time you saw her?'

'We dance. Yesterday. She say she go to auntie.'

'We'll go there. Together.'

She looked up at him.

'We can. Tell me where.'

She was rising, pointing towards the hills, and grabbing his hand began to drag him along. As they reached the end of the fishing craft's hull and were about to turn Jyothi stood in their way, Aditya holding on. Mother-and-daughter words were exchanged, Jyothi pulling Lalima close and showing her the back of her hand. Lalima shut her expression down and looked at the sand.

'Where's Babita?' Rich demanded of Jyothi. The mother glared suspiciously at him through her good eye, the silvered one seeming to look inward and pulled her children from him.

'You've got to find her,' Rich called. 'I'll help. Tell me–' Jyothi was leaving, but Lalima turned appealingly to him before disappearing with her family behind huts.

He was still wondering how he could help them find Babita, and whether she would just turn up very soon anyway with a story about her adventure when Frank found him walking through low waves as the sun was setting.

'Going for an evening swim?' Frank came out of the darkness of late evening.

'German widow last night, was it?'

They dipped under surf lines in the dark sea as the sun set and a sliver of moon rose, drying themselves on sand sparkling with the reflected lights of restaurants and bars.

'Mozzies, insects, kill 'em,' Frank whacked the air with his towel as they were walking back. 'That's the only thing about this place.'

'Like god created this paradise,' Rich laughed, 'but threw a devil in to stir things up.'

'There's more than one devil around here – you can't have heaven without hell, Rich. Neither functions without the other.'

'It was planted, Frank – the elephant -- '

The smell of fish cooked in coconut sauce streamed past them.

'They'll do anything,' Frank said.

The lads in the Golden Sphere restaurant nearby dashed back and forth, moving food and plates and people about.

'It could only have been Chanda,' Rich was reluctant to give her name up. 'She must have got behind me and slipped it in my bag. Why, though?'

'Little tart.'

'I thought she was–'

'Don't,' Frank cut in. 'You think too much. Too deeply. That's your problem.' He laughed at himself, 'Most of us don't think about anything we do, that's why we're surprised at the consequences. Have fun. Forget yourself. Find yourself an English rose – '

'I had one,' Rich spat.

Frank handed him cream and he took it and smeared his face and arms, 'Get yourself another.' Couples were walking the darkness along the rim of surf towards eating places. 'And another. And another, another, another – at your age.'

'What about this German widow, Frank? When do we get–'

'Not an Indian woman. Of course. Untouchable.' Frank laughed at his own pun, 'You can't touch them.' He paused, waving insects aside. 'They are available of course. At a price – which reminds me – yes – you would like that. Later. That's another side of India –'

'The girl dragged from the sea?'

The moon was high now, its crescent with horns pointing upwards.

'It's all controlled, Rich – drugs, porn, prostitution. Just like everywhere in the world. Big-wigs with big cars and paid-off people in all sorts of lines.'

'And that's the result: a girl's body in the sea?'

'They've got someone banged up. You saw –'

'He didn't look very guilty.'

'Anyone's guilty after a good beating, Rich. It's in the local paper,' he looked out at the sea and sighed: 'And if it doesn't stick they'll have to let him go – say she took her own life –'

'Bad.'

Frank shrugged his shoulders: 'Some young bloke I knew got caught up in it. Suicide. Gerry – and I quite liked him. Well, that's what they said – or OD. You know what I'm saying? It's best not to know about these things. Live a quiet clean life with people you know and trust. "And always know where you're dipping your wick," as my dad used to say. He was never wrong, Rich. Stick with me and you won't go wrong. Now, it's the ATM isn't it? I'll take you on the back.'

Frank led Rich out to a dusty blue scooter in the night at the back of the chalets. The black trunks of palms surrounded it, their heavy winged branches holding back the moon.

'I've never done this before, Frank.'

'Hold my waist. Not too hard, I'm not in love with you.'

The men arched themselves over the thing, Frank charged it into action and they bumped off following the triangle of light that fanned out from the headlamp through trunks and clumps. The tyres skimmed and slid through sand ridges up to a short concrete bridge over a stream clogged with plastic and paper waste. There was a gap of about a foot between the end of the run-up to the flat concrete over the water, forcing Frank to bang the scooter down, then up and over, shaking Rich's confidence in his driving, but Frank pulled it round quickly and pushed out to the streetlights of the road out of town.

Shops were still open and ambling tourists became the main target of scooters, rickshaws, motorbikes and the occasional bus blundering down with blasting horns. Frank's route along the tarmac refused to be straight: instead he weaved left and right, and sometimes over the wrong side of the road, wafting around walkers and talkers and buyers and kids running and a cow with one horn that stood in the middle baying, always following the national tradition of sounding and sustaining the horn for as long as was bearable. Rich shut his eyes.

'Blow this, Frank,' Rich cursed at the ATM for the time it took to process, a little building with security doors that looked like the entrance to a shower or sauna. Funds from supply teaching were sinking. Money would come from mum eventually, but he would have to go back home to sort that out.

'You saved me, Frank,' Rich handed over the money in a small café in the village of Chawjim several kilometres inland.

They ate dosas in a tiny room with tables browned by years of use on bench seats near a chatting family, the mother in a cerise sari lit up the windowless cave they sat in.

While they chewed on their dinners waiters brought in thalis for the family.

'God knows where you would be now,' Frank let out the words between mouthfuls.

'You know him.'

'Oh. Lakshya. You've got to get on the good side of him, Rich, you started on the wrong foot. We've got to change that somehow.'

'What's with him?'

'You've got to get to know him. That nosey look on your gob tells me you want to know how and why. The guy who they say topped himself – Gerry. I knew him, well, for a few days anyway, like I know you, nothing too close, like. I found him.'

'That isn't good, Frank.'

A waiter was in and out, chatting and laughing with the family. The father ate quietly, leaving the rest of his tribe to make up the talking time.

'It wasn't. What a mess. Down the south end of the beach in a wooden chalet-hut. I had to kick the door down, I knew he was in there. When I got in he was sitting on his bed leaning forward, his body grey, hardened like stone. You don't want to know. And the stench. You wouldn't think all this stuff we carry about with us could stink like that – all the aftershave and cologne we put on, and none of it will get rid of that. And the flies, my god the flies and the cockroaches, all in for a feed. We're all made up of the same stuff, Rich. All the genes and atoms – same as cockroaches and scorpions and hell, man . . . the stench . . . the look in his eyes. Anymore time and the maggots would have set in . . .'

The café was hushed.

'Shut up, Frank.'

Frank looked about him, smiled at the family who smiled back in strained chorus and carried on eating, and whispered back: 'It's life. You can't turn away from it. Death is always in the middle of life. It's just more obvious here than at home. All part of how it works out. Dinesh reckons the mystics say your body is just a vehicle for the soul – a bit of meat to carry you through. Hah. What do you think of that, Rich?' he slapped his new pal on the shoulder. 'Your bit of meat keeping your real self cooped up inside the dirty smelly flesh. Yours is all right. Not diseased. Not like Gerry. All messed up with coke and booze and god knows what–'

The woman was glaring at Frank as the waiter brought in puri for the children. 'Get them a bottle of something nice,' Frank shoved notes in the waiter's hand.

'What?' Rich whispered.

'It's not just the Russian mafia, you know. Oh, they're here all right – up the coast. There's others. Keep your nose clean. Don't give anybody a reason to put things on you.'

'Was it suicide?'

The waiter was back with glasses of Lassi for the family, the mother at first protesting she had not ordered them, but the waiter explained and the family turned smiling faces to the Rich and Frank as though posing for a group photograph.

'Nobody ever knows with suicide, do they? Nobody with any sense asks any questions. Like with the girl, Sunita . . . You know about Siva? Dinesh told me strange things about him. He's a god of death and destruction with skulls around his belt. Dinesh showed me a picture. You don't mess with Siva. He dances through a circle of flames – the dance of death, and resurrection – everything comes up new through him, so the Hindus say. He's the one who decides – him with the crescent moon on his forehead. You tremble when you see him, the young god Siva who brings death –'

'You had some sort of vision of Siva when you found Gerry?'

'No, stupid - I prayed to him. Said a silent word. Like you do: thanks for going to his door, not mine. We're all glad when our pants are saved. Give some offerings. Buy a garland of flowers from the man who sells newspapers in the morning to hang over your door for protection, and hope Siva and his like will only touch you with kindness. It's what Dinesh says.'

'Nah.' Rich sighed, laughing.

'Siva is a good god,' Frank addressed the family.

'Very good,' the mother in pink said.

'A terrible god.'

'Terrible,' she nodded, 'very terrible.'

'See,' Frank turned back. 'Not scared of Siva? Then you're scared of Lakshya, I can see it in your eyes. Karma's about staying alive. In the best way possible. With as much stuff around you as you can. That's it, isn't it? You're here, then you die. That's what scientists in the West say. We're all one big accident. Here, and then die young. Ping. That's it. Have a good time while you are – nothing else matters. For you end up a stinking heap forgotten in a chalet along a beach in paradise –'

'Let's go,' Rich wanted to pull out of the messy talk they'd got themselves into.

Fishermen were huddled in shadows mellowed by the sentinels of four candles surrounding a pile of playing cards. As Rich and Frank passed they heard grunts but no discernible words, but then a roar from one of them and an outpouring of rage. Milit was on his feet, body stiff with anger, haranguing a group of bobbing heads. Another stood with him, pulling him back down until the two seemed to be one creature in the blackness that bled into the wider blackness of the beach.

The following morning Milit was lying in the sun, shirt torn, his face turned aside into sand. Dinesh went to him with water and patted his cheeks until the man's eyes flickered, and supporting him with his arm, raised his body enough for the man to drink, his pink dry lips cracked and torn.

Rich was passing them on his way for a morning swim but stopped. Together they raised him to his feet, dragging his limp limbs along and leaving a deep groove etched in sand, to the three steps up to the platform in front of the chalets.

'You don't bother with him,' Frank waved his hand as the helpers motioned Milit's feet into automatic in order to make him step up to the sandy flatness. Then they dragged him past Frank's scowl, to Rich's veranda and dumped him in a wicker chair.

'Idiot–' Frank cawed again at Milit as Dinesh and Rich fussed the man with water, pouring it over his face and in between the parched gap. 'Cleaned out again.'

Rich regarded the man with the hangover, then up at Frank.

'Milit blows all his money gambling every week with the local fishermen. Or the big boys in Chawjim he plays with. His poor wife, and he's got a baby boy as well. Is Lakshya jealous of that. Lakshya wanted a boy and what did he get: three girls. The cutest you've ever seen –'

'You know a lot about what goes on–' Rich was trying to sound vague but his friend did not pick up on it.

'He drinks too much,' Dinesh whispered. A crow with a soft grey circle round its neck sated its curiosity a quick moment by sitting on a wall nearby, then flew off to its mates with the latest. 'Every week he plays cards,' Dinesh shook his head. 'It's no good.'

'Another of life's wasters,' Frank put his hands on his hips enjoying his authority. 'You can't do anything for people like that. Always up Lakshya's backside. No wonder why. Better wind up on the beach in the morning and be cared for than in a dirty cell. He's got to stay in with them.'

Rita was back, brushing out Frank's room, the muscles of her arm rippling with the waving motion of the sweeps.

'That's not very good under the bed, Rita,' Frank was calling. She scowled and scooped under. 'Can you do a bit more than that, Rita. You've got to go right down.' He waved his palm and she got to her knees pushing dust to the posts of the bed in piles, then urging them towards the door to sweep back into the wider world of detritus. 'And the toilet needs doing again, Rita - you haven't been round for a few days - I was saying to Dinesh, he must replace you if you don't do your job properly –' he said and turning to Rich: 'Don't have the same standards of cleanliness, you see. They just don't see it. Get themselves up in fancy dress - all those dazzling colours - but dirty houses, dirty toilets. You have to get on to them, Rich.' Poking his nose in the dark empty space where the woman roamed he hissed again: 'I can't give you any rupees today, Rita –'

'That's a bit hard, Frank,' Rich said. 'She's doing what she can.'

'Too right, mate. She'll do my room properly if it's the last thing she does. You can't be too soft in this world, I'm telling you. If I'm paying for a service I want it done properly.'

'Things are no good at home for Rita,' Dinesh spoke for his silent worker. 'You must speak quietly to her. If anything wrong - tell me, I will do.'

Frank turned to Rich: 'Sometimes I think: "Are you telling me what I want to know, or what you want me to know?"' Frank tried to shrug it off laughing.

'I'm sure she's trying, Frank.'

Rita slipped out like a Cinderella, shoulders tense in her sky blue sari, rattling rubbish out of the bin into a plastic bag. As Frank went in to inspect she scuttled to the end of the block and turned the corner. Rich caught a look of concern from Dinesh and went after Rita.

She was huddled near the concrete wall of the back of the chalets. Piglets were snorting happily near her.

'Rita,' he called but she turned away. 'Rita. I'm sorry, my friend, he - Rita?'

As he came to her she was dabbing her eyes, her cheeks with shiny rivulets. He stared. A villager was over the back watching, a bowl in his hand. 'Rita?' And in shadows another figure was at the edge of his vision.

Rich knew nothing of this fragile world. Looking briefly up at him, Rita ran. Palm leaves eased themselves together in breeze above him and crows cawed. Pigs were ecstatically pawing over discarded pineapple pieces. Fragments of sky appeared briefly among palm fronds. The village man watched and turned away.

Rita had gone.

A figure was moving through the shadows cast by the trunks of palm trees.

'Lalima,' he called. She walked on and he had to run to her. 'Babita? You have found her?'

Lalima looked down as she shook her head.

'Your auntie?'

She stared at the sand.

'How long is it now?'

'Two night.'

'You must go to the police.'

She looked at him.

'Come on,' he nodded towards the road and she walked behind him all the way.

*****

Milit was drinking tea from a mug with finger marks round the side, his eyes bloodshot.

'Lalima's cousin is missing,' Rich began. He could hear voices in a back room.

'Police Chief is not here,' Milit flicked his arm for them to go.

'Then you can write it down,' Rich pointed at a notebook with curled edges.

'Lakshya is in charge.'

'A girl has gone, Milit. Police have to do something.'

'Girls go every week,' Milit had his left hand on his hip.

'Yes. And one died. You do something. Babita has been gone for two nights.'

'Girls come here, and girls go–'

'Get somebody – the police chief–' Rich was losing his patience.

On cue, the big man opened the door of the back room and strode in.

'Ah. Mister Lomas. Good to see you again. In such good health this time,' Lakshya extended his hand. Rich hesitated, and thinking the better, allowed his own to be gripped and shaken roughly while Lakshya's glower extended to Lalima.

'Her friend has gone missing.'

Lalima looked down.

'They usually turn up. But you know, Mister Lomas, you really shouldn't trouble yourself. This is routine, as you say. Many girls come here selling. We try to keep them safe, you understand, but there are always darker forces than the police. We keep ourselves alert and vigilant. I learned this word from an English policeman,' he laughed. 'He came for a holiday. "Be vigilant is our slogan", he said.'

'But one girl has already been found dead –'

'It happens. My men can't be everywhere.'

'You don't sound very concerned.'

'We caught him,' Lakshya shrugged, smoothing his moustache with the index finger of his left hand.

'What if you've got the wrong man?'

'He confessed.'

'It must have been beaten out of him,' Rich pushed him. None of the policemen or their assistants seemed to be taking it very seriously it seemed to Rich.

'We are the law, Mister Lomas. We catch criminals. And we have caught him.'

'And another girl goes missing.'

'She will turn up.'

Lalima was looking the police chief in the eye.

'Tell her,' Lakshya boomed, 'that in time, the girl will appear.' And pulling Rich aside he whispered in his ear: 'Sometimes a bad man or gang will take a young girl for two or three days. They come back.'

Rich could not get the image of Jeanette grown up from this mind: 'What do you do about that?'

Lakshya nodded at the cells.

'You need to search.'

'Where?'

'You have contacts. Informers.'

'This isn't a Hollywood movie, Mister Lomas. I have few men. I can only look in places I know of.'

'Then do that. At least show you are concerned.'

'Mister Lomas. We have the murderer. This girl you say – what's her name?'

'Babita.'

'This Babita. There will be no more killing,' Lakshya smoothed his moustache again and glanced at Milit: 'If it makes you happy, Mister Lomas. Open the book, Milit.'

The assistant pulled the worn covered exercise book over and picked up the stump of a pencil.

'Where do you live?' Lakshya addressed Lalima.

Her lips rippled but words were imperceptible.

'Come on girl. Milit needs to write it down.'

She went to Milit and instructed him.

'Oh, that place,' Lakshya sniffed. 'That camp. Huts. Near the road builders–' He turned to Rich and screwed up his mouth, nodding: 'These are very poor people.'

'They need help.'

'Of course. Of course. We will find her. Now tell Milit your auntie's address.'

'You know her auntie?' Rich was bemused.

'They are all related,' Lakshya waved his hand, laughing.

Lalima gave all her details.

'There, Mister Lomas. It is good to do business with you on such good terms. We can redeem ourselves, can't we, Mister Lomas, through our good deeds. That is something we can do: redemption. You see, Mister Lomas, it is part of the Hindu religion - to redeem. The Christian is born in sin, and Jesus saves him. All done. But for a Hindu - if he does wrong, he can come back, reincarnate - he will have a chance to redeem. That is good, isn't it, Mister Lomas?'

Rich shook the extended hand again. Lalima's fingers were trembling.

'Come,' her mother Jyothi was in the doorway. 'Lalima.'

Jyothi's eyes met the chief of police's and they both looked away.

'Come.'

Lalima ran to her. Her mother's words were admonishing, reinforced by the pointing of her hand at Lalima's face. The girl was dragged out.

'You see what you have done, Mister Lomas,' Lakshya chuckled. 'Good deeds are not always wanted.'

6

'You don't do this every night?' Rich pointed an alcohol weary finger at his friend over the discarded remains of two plates of calamari. The buzz of talk in the restaurant surrounded them.

'It's Friday night, Rich,' Frank emphasised. Get plastered. Forget the world. You can't do anything about it anyway. It's what everyone does. Ever since I was a kid on a council estate on the bad side of Watford. I'm telling you, I was dragged up. My first job was in the local electrics factory. Electrics it was in those days. None of your electronics. Way before the digital age - you know - centuries ago when a volume control was a knob that said on and off in big letters even an idiot without his reading glasses on could read -'

Rich laughed.

'Those were the days when people did the unthinkable -'

'What, Frank?'

'Cleaned their shoes. I'm telling you. When I was a kid my dad inspected my shoes. Spit and polish. Well, when he was around - which wasn't often. You had to see your face in the tips. Mind you they banned girls from shining their shoes in my school. And patent leather was a no-no. They had to have scuffed and dirty shoes-'

'What are you talking about, Frank?'

'School rules, wasn't it. They wore skirts. You'd see the reflection of their knickers in shiny shoes -'

Rich's guffaws were so loud Frank scowled at him in case he drew too much attention in the restaurant and got them evicted. Buck's Fizz was a bit more upmarket than the Pink City, with waiters in black and white with little bow ties.

'Where was I?' Frank composed himself. 'Yes. Friday nights – a working class thing. Work all week in a boring mindless factory making boring mindless products and all you've got to look forward to is getting blasted on Friday night. In the end it gets taken over, doesn't it – the middle classes start doing it, then the upper lot. We start it. They copy. Now everyone gets blathered at the weekend and there's no more style to it. In the old days it was a flash in the patent leather. Now tarts get boggled on the street and fall over and it's all skirts and knickers. No mystery, no intrigue. That's what I like about Indian women – full of mystery. Deep dark eastern promise. That sexuality – delicious –'

'So you go for the German?' Rich said sardonically.

Frank shrugged, tucking into ice cream, and washing it down with a gulp of Cobra beer.

'Don't you miss your daughter?' Rich caught him in a moment of thought.

'Of course I do. Like you. We all miss our daughters – all our kids. Kids make the boredom nothing, they fill everything with meaning. You know that.' He looked as though he was grimacing back tears. 'They've got it all now. Everything. They don't need the likes of me with my shined up shoes. That's the trouble with the world today, Rich. Without us noticing, it's changed. Now, you make piles of money and you're a hero. Make it any way you can, and you're made into some kind of celebrity. It doesn't matter how you do it – legal or scam. So they all want to do it – all the kids – make a quick million on the internet and sit pretty, be famous. Nothing else matters. No boredom in that –'

'You?'

'Got out while I could. Nasty business. I should have set something of my own up. You have to be able to sell anything anywhere to anybody and not think about it – whether it works or it doesn't, whether it's ethical, moral, recyclable, environmentally sound, whether anybody needs it even – just sell it whatever. I got to the stage where I realised it was easier to sell trash than something worthwhile. And that lot bought me off. It wasn't a bad deal as things go. Then a manager in a security firm – that was the last job, slogging for years, then stabbed in the back. Got a good deal though, too as it happens. The golden handshake for me – and you move on. You should see what the overnight security guys get up to. You wouldn't believe it – women of ill repute sneaked in, porn on the net, coke parties, the lot. It becomes a culture that's hard to stamp out – talk about back-handers – I mean, what could I do about that?' Frank leaned back on his arms, 'Oh well, it all goes further over here of course.' Frank's talk trailed into muffled blows of words. People were straggling through darkness along the white sea crest; it could be Lalima and her mother. Rich wondered where Babita was, and how safe.

'Listen,' Frank flicked his finger in Rich's face to bring him round again. 'I know a place. Somewhere.'

'What place?'

'A bit of booze and all that.'

'And?' Rich searched the darkness for his teenager friend, but they had faded.

'A drinking hole – late into the night. You need that right now after what you've been through. Let your hair down.' Frank got up, settled the bill and led him out into the floodlit street. Most shops were still open, although some had shuttered their fronts, and a few tourists were window shopping. Taxi fellas were chatting in a bundle near the beach resort. The one horned cow was lying in the corner.

Frank nodded to a lone man leaning against his yellow scooter rickshaw, smoking; quickly he threw down his butt end, dived inside his machine and cranked it to life. Frank nodded for Rich to get in and the two big men pushed their calves side by side in the narrow back of the machine. The lights of closing shops skimmed past as they headed out of town into the dark hole of night and then into almost total blindness as the rickshaw cut through blades of darkness. The ripping blurt of the machine bumped down palm groves, round old brick buildings, along potholed tracks as they pushed into the muddle of jungle.

At one point Rich thought he might be sick, but they stopped at the end of a narrow track in front of a house with a dimly lit veranda and Frank pushed him out.

'Leave me here,' Rich joked, his tongue silvered with alcohol, 'and I'd never find my way back home.'

Myriads of stars were silent overhead: galaxies and constellations were stagnant for him for a moment of staring, and the blackness between their pinhole brightness was lighter than the blackness between the trees and shrubs that hugged the house.

'Damn mozzies,' Frank slapped with his palm at a spot that no longer seemed visible.

Rich's eyes were on the stars still, searching, missing Jeanette.

'Come on, Rich, shape up a bit,' the leader prodded him, 'you've got room for plenty more.' He laughed, whacking Rich's belly. 'You young blokes – can't take your booze.'

Dropping his gaze from the mysteries of the sky, Rich viewed the murky light along the veranda which seemed as sticky as the night, musty and misty. Frank led him to it and it swirled round him as though sucking him in its grip.

They entered the inner darkness of the place, darker it seemed than the spaces between palm trunks outside. The smell of jasmine punctured the air, then sandalwood and other sweet juiced aromas. He heard the movement of women's feet faintly, their ankle bells with distant tinkles, then silence. The mutter of male talk wafted from behind bamboo walls.

Rich followed Frank's bulk along a corridor among the sounds of men and the sniff of cigarettes. There was a blast of light to the left as they passed the beaded-off room of men and smoke and hands on table and playing cards and glasses and a bottle of half-drunk whisky. Rich thought he saw the police chief, but checked himself, knowing it could not be.

'Frank?'

'Keep it down,' the leader hissed.

'That was him,' Rich buzzed in a loud whisper, 'I saw him there. The police chief – what's his name-'

'Don't be daft,' Frank carried himself ahead, 'Lakshya wouldn't be in a thousand miles of this place.'

'What is this place?' Rich pushed his mind through an alcoholic haze. A passing man put a cigarette to his mouth, his hand and wrist decorated with patterns.

'A Speakeasy, or whatever. Nobody talks about it. A place for cheap booze and all that, a bit of music and what you like –'

'What you like?' Rich wanted to be back outside with the stars. Then, rubbing his eyes: 'I thought it was him.'

'They all look the same: them with moustaches,' Frank half laughed. 'Think they're right cool. Look daft to me. Come on –' He turned into a room on the right, heavily candled and pervaded with jasmine. The soft light illuminated throw-overs with bright Paisley patterns and elephants. Frank motioned him to sit and he lowered himself slowly into the comfort of deep cushions while Frank sat on a long couch.

A man was with them, holding his hand out, which Frank shook.

'Frank?' Rich looked to them both. 'What is this?'

'You know Milit. Get us the usual, Mil.'

Milit left obediently.

'He's–'

'I know all that, Rich. Trust me. He's all right. He just got himself into a spot, that's all. He's all right. He's on our side.'

'I might quote you on that.'

The flames of candles were unmoved in the stillness.

'He is. Just trust me now, Rich.'

Rich bit his lip and looked around for exits. None. Just night.

'We're here to enjoy ourselves and have a laugh. It's what the world lacks at the moment: a good laugh. Don't worry about it.'

Milit was back with a bottle and three glasses on a tray. Clumping it down on the red and green and yellow carpet in front of them, Milit unscrewed the top of the Johnny Walker bottle and poured three portions.

'Cheers,' Frank clinked glasses with Rich, then Milit.

'Good health,' Milit beamed.

'You've got it Mil,' Frank laughed. 'We'll make an Englishman out of you yet. Would you like to go to England?'

'My dream,' Milit bared his teeth with a grin.

Two women slipped through the beaded curtain, heads covered. Moving with the agility of silent dancers, ghostlike, they placed little trays of biscuits and sweets and cashew nuts in silver bowls for the men to dip into.

'You see Rich,' Frank leaned back, his face beaming with self satisfaction, 'you can have anything, if you know where to go and how much to pay.'

Milt nodded but Rich was unsure of him.

The shape and smell of the women was familiar: one smiled, the other held her head down with shyness.

A cheer went up from the men in the room down the corridor and the candles flickered. The sound of laughter followed.

'You don't have to be rich to have everything,' Frank smiled.

The women sat in half-darkness where the light of candles faded to grey. He noticed now through the haziness that the smaller one was in an orange and green salwar kameez, and although her brown and gold dupatta was pulled down to her eyes she must be young: a twelve-year-old with legs crossed. The other, a woman in purple and red sari with her head down in shadow muttered to the younger one who would not move.

The woman pushed the girl, growling and nodding at the door, but the girl resisted, wrestling the woman's hands. Rich observed through half open eyelids as the woman roughly threw the girl out to mutterings and yelps, and the image lost itself like drunken dreams fade in daylight.

He could not shake off the drowsiness and time dissolved in a filmic drift of ideas in which he could not pin down reality. The night was sticky. There were cries in the corridor followed by a further vision of another girl in pink and red and green salwar kameez being bundled along. It sounded like Babita's voice, and he found himself jumping up and calling her name, to no reply, and sleep took him again.

'Frank? Frank?' he found the roughness of his tongue could only just shape the word. One candle burned, spreading its light up the wall like the fan of a peacock's tail. Rich searched the void beyond light but found no shapes. A woman was sitting, half in shadow, her head and shoulders covered.

'Where's Frank?'

'All right.'

'Chanda? That's you?'

As she leaned forward to pour him another whisky the pallu, the head cover of her sari, fell away from her cowered face and the mellow light from the candle coloured her cheeks and nose and she did not move to cover her head again. He knew it was foolish to have more, but he needed it, and made her top up with lots of water.

'Chanda?' he spoke through the mists of alcohol. 'That was you pushing the girl out, just then?'

Silence hung between candle and incense stick, and beyond the range of the stiff flame's reach the void of night gripped covers and corners.

'You did push a girl out? And Babita, I heard her in the passage?'

'Babita is not here.'

'It sounded like Babita, Chanda. What's going on?'

Chanda shook her head: 'Babita disappeared. She is not here.'

'I thought I saw her.' He rubbed his eyes as if the motion would bring him to reality.

'Many girls look like Babita. You were dreaming.'

'Her voice seemed real. Like when she called to the cows: "Challo", something like that.' Rich garbled, not understanding fully what was whirling round him. 'I didn't take it,' he spluttered. 'The elephant, Chanda. I didn't take it. You put it there, didn't you? Why?'

Still she would not look at him. Then she said quietly: 'An elephant with a trunk up will bring good luck.'

'Then I'll have good luck,' he muttered with the aid of whisky. 'But I must find Babita, she ran down the passage. I've got to get home. Has Frank gone?'

She was watching him now, traces of a smile on her lips. Her eyes were deeply blackened along the rims and her hair, pulled back in a bun at the back, was bundled up with saffron flowers. Gold earrings hung in globes from her ears. Her nose was pierced with a red and gold jewel. Her chest heaved lightly with each breath.

A cheer went up from the room nearby, he could hear men's voices in a strange discordant song of rivalry.

She reached forward and held his hand.

'Chanda?'

Her wrist was encased by bangles in a long tube of colours turning and moving with her arm.

He let his mind drift to images of courtesans in Mughal palaces dancing like on painted screens he had seen.

'Pakeezah was a dancer,' she seemed to read his thoughts. 'She danced on glass. Broken –'

'Glass?' His words were nonsense in the blur.

She stood slowly, then curling her hands above her head she wriggled her hips in slow gyration for him, her body moving in and out of light. And stamping her feet, she moved over the floor to the sound of invisible music, stomping and twisting. Her ankle bells jingled with each stamp and her hands circled round her, fingers sometimes clipped in gesture, her face acting out of character.

The smell of incense was driving him crazy.

She rounded him as though he was a boy; a goddess with many hands, she circled him, bowing to him sometimes, gesturing to him, holding her open palm to him.

The distant hoot of a diesel train split the night.

Allowing the dance to trail into everyday movement she took his hand gently and raised him, and light footed - without the sound of trinket or bell - she led him through the beaded curtain into the darkness of the corridor and up and away from the sounds of the lighted doorway where men scrambled over their takings.

In the darkened room, the faint glow of a candle set aside shape and shadow.

When she had unbuttoned his shirt and he was bare for her, he felt her nipples pert on his lower chest. The cords of her clothes fell away and as she held his arms candlelight quivered over the edges of faint lines of hair along her arms, along the side of her face, in her hair. She took his cotton trousers away, letting the belt slither off like a snake, and in the faintness of candlelight he saw the dark triangle at the top of her legs.

Gripping his middle finger lightly and after sucking it awhile with play-bites, she led it there and gasped inwardly as he found the mysterious beginnings of her, lush and ready.

She pecked at his chest and torso, smiling little kisses, not too wet, like a nipping fish.

This was drunken madness. But it had been so long since a woman came to him.

A man's laughter rang out down the corridor.

She held his gaze with hers. It was her country, she had to lead.

She made no noise, on her back, bringing him down to her without tension, with no panic, but easily and with dance-like motions, drawing him into herself easily.

She did not yell, uttered little gasps, like a bird and let his breath cover her cheeks. Gasping, he let go the core. It could not be stopped, the flow of him. When he was loud she put her finger to his lip, for he found he was repeating her name. He felt like a kid holding onto its mother, and for a few timeless moments managed to shut out the filth of the world with its inhabitants fighting for survival, and be held by female force.

As dawn's orange seeped through cracks in curtains and under doors she knelt, coaxing him, encouraging his tongue to find her reflexes, and he was pushing fresh life in her again, cosy with her, as though they had known each other for years.

Then it was quiet. He said to himself that he loved her. Light poured in through gaps.

She lay next to him naked on her back, her head to one side in sleep, one leg bent up sideways.

A movement to the side caught his eye and he searched, then heard a chortle. The baby in ruffles of material wanted food and the sun was coming up.

7

He knew things were not right. Something should have held him back, but didn't. Tears – of joy, ecstasy or pain, he didn't know which – she had dried. And if something was wrong, it was a good wrong. He dreamed of Babita running and when he woke for a moment he could not tell whether his memory of the night before was real or imagined, whether it was Babita's voice he had heard raised in the corridor afterwards.

The howl of a diesel locomotive parted the forest and the baby shifted. As darkness receded and light washed itself through crevices he fumbled back into sleep. His eyes were open seconds or hours later. A figure in the residue of his dreams was standing over the bed.

'You must pay now.' A man's voice hissed through the darkness at him.

Rich was upright in a stroke: 'Get out.' He used his teacher's voice. There was something sacred and spiritual about a bed used for love and he did not want the ritual to be shattered by the senseless materialism of the outside world. He wanted it to be poetic, but knew it wasn't.

'Pay.' Milit's form leaned ineffectually forward towards him, his facial features becoming alive in slow light.

This was not how it should be.

Rich rolled out of bed, Milit observing his nakedness – the clump of an ugly thing hanging, like all men.

'Get out now,' Rich tried teacher talk again as he pulled cotton bags on and yanked the drawstring. 'Where's Frank?' The godfather would sort it out. Rich buttoned his shirt.

He felt Chanda half awake, but feigning sleep. The baby would cry in a moment.

Everything had to be complicated – sex most of all. Pushing Milit aside and cursing under his breath he went for the door. Chanda's eyes were on him, and Milit's were on her.

As Rich passed an open door he saw that the men had gone away from their game: the room was empty but for one person.

'Ah. Mister Lomas.' The police inspector did not raise his head as Rich was passing the beaded curtain. A pack of cards was neatly stacked on the table in front of the man, along with a half empty bottle of whisky. 'We meet again, it seems.'

Rich knew he should walk on. They had nothing on him. They would try, but he had no elephants for them, they all had their trunks up for him.

'One for the road?' Lakshya raised an empty glass to him. 'It's been a hard night, Mister Lomas. I'm sure you'll join me for a last one.'

Rich did not part the beads or give him thanks.

'I think you will, Mister Lomas – if you want to enjoy all the sensations Goa has to offer. As you can see it is a place of many excitements: the sun, the sand, the –'

Milit prodded Rich's back so his head pushed through the beads.

'I thought you would change your mind, Mister Lomas. You know what's good for you. You know we all have to pay our way in life. Every little thing is accounted for. A bit like karma eh, Mister Lomas? Every little thing we do is noted down – in the Akashi records so the rishis say – and replayed back to us at the end of our earthly life. Every tiny itsy bitsy bit has to be accounted for and paid up. I think you will pay this man–' Lakshya nodded at the figure of Milit behind Rich, who lunged, pushing him through the curtain.

'Get off,' Rich howled at the goading man.

Birds were beginning to sing in the trees.

'Nothing is free in this life, Mister Lomas. And nothing is

free in India. Not now. Do have a drink.' He poured two whiskies, sloshing half a cup full in each, then raising one to his face chanted: 'Cheers.'

Rich yearned to go back to bed and enjoy a long sleep with Chanda.

'You see, Mister Lomas. If you sleep with whores, you have to pay for them.'

'Whores?' Anger took Rich from nowhere.

'Courtesans, if you prefer. It's all in a name. What does it matter what you call them, they're all the same.'

'Chanda–' he began defending his new love.

'Sit down, Mister Lomas. Have a drink. We can talk amicably. We're not enemies, you and I. We had our differences – but you can see I am not one to hold a grudge – we are looking for Babita at this time. But I am a professional man, Mister Lomas. When I get a complaint I have to act on it. You see, too many of you people come over here and take things from us. I have to act on that. And when a client fails to pay for the services of a professional lady, then she must have someone to look out for her, you must agree –'

'A pimp as well as a policeman, then,' Rich muttered.

'Everyone needs someone to protect them. Women more than men, don't you think?' Lakshya glared, pushing back his anger, it seemed to Rich as he glared back.

'We can talk this through, Mister Lomas. If you will only sit down.'

As Rich pulled a chair out Lakshya motioned Milit away with a scowl, then smiling at Rich urged a glass of whisky on him.

'We've got a lot in common, Mister Lomas. More than you think. We all like to dip into Chanda now and again. Even married men like a dip-' Lakshya laughed, pushing his moustache upwards, irritating Rich. 'And she seems to like it.' Rich was bunching his fists. 'Marriage is meant for women, as you know. They provide the mystery of creation. It is for men to provide that creation, and they cannot be confined to women who are always tired. We understand that. Men do. So a service is provided.'

'You're a police chief.'

'Don't get me wrong. I couldn't possibly be involved. It's against the law. But I'm a practical man, Mister Lomas. How am I to run this town? Everything has to make a living – even those more powerful and influential than me. Do you understand? Everywhere there are powers that we have to obey. You know that, don't you. Everyone has to do what they're told in the end – even a police chief. So what can I do? Milit has to earn a living. I have to oversee the chaos.' He shook his head. 'Chaos. All town is chaos. Some own this bit of chaos, some own that bit. But chaos. So they appoint me to organise the chaos. Manage it. My job is not to dispose of it – I leave that in the capable hands of politicians and judges – no, my job is to keep it in check – keep the boundaries intact – arbitrate in disputes, make sure all are happy and that all bits of chaos are oiled and maintained and run smoothly. That way it works. All of it. That way everyone is happy. I only come in if there's some dispute, or someone's ripped off. I'm not a moralist, Mister Lomas. It is not my job to tell the world how to live.'

'I haven't done anything wrong.' Rich refused the whisky. 'Where's Frank?'

'Wrong? Like I said, Mister Lomas, I'm not here to decide what's right and wrong in the world. I let others do that. We all write our own history. The one thing we take out with us, is our karma.'

'Chanda–'

'I think you'll pay up, Mister Lomas–' Lakshya cut off his proclamations.

'You can't make me do anything.'

Lakshya looked up at him slowly: 'I think you will find that we can.'

Rich took a gulp of the fluid.

'We're all given certain power. There's always a bigger power above us. Right up to god. You know life can be easy or difficult for you here in Bagolem. Drink up, Mister Lomas. I have nothing personal against you, you understand. You seem a decent young man, as you would say in England. Let me put it this way: we are all human. All of us. Even the poor little ineffectual and inefficient Milit. He has his gambling ways. We all have our vices.' He looked accusingly at Rich a moment, then: 'But he has to get on with life. We do not have social benefits here Mister Lomas, or free hospitals, or great pensions – we do it for ourselves until we die – day in, day out – we all have to find ourselves a cog in some great wheel in order to survive. I think you have forgotten that in the West. But we have more of what the world scorns than you do: beggars. The world hates a beggar, more than anything. A rich man is god, a beggar, the devil. We fear them, they contaminate us with the knowledge of poverty. They challenge our ignorance. We have our share. Even they, the barefoot ones with nothing, even they must come under the umbrella of the law – even those low lives have rights, their chaos must be managed by what you call – the long arm of the law – isn't it, Mister Lomas?'

Rich stared at his drink as it brightened slowly with the colours of the morning and a baby cried out back and a mother tended to it, and dragging himself from the mugginess of sleep challenged the police chief. 'Instead of bullying me then and giving me useless lectures about your hardships, you can go and find Babita.'

'Tell me anything you cannot agree with, Mister Lomas? I will be generous with you now. One day you are in my custody as a criminal, the next you are redeemed, and the next you drink with me and we are friends–'

Rich scowled at him: 'Babita was here last night, wasn't she?'

'We are friends, aren't we?'

'I want to see Frank.' Rich was getting up. 'None of this is real, it's–'

'He is not the man you think he is. But we will not deal with that here. The point is: you don't believe me, do you? Our friendship? How can I convince you? Underneath we are all the same, we have all suffered, Rich. All of us. Not just you. It's not just the ashes of your mother and the dead marriage you have back home, and the child you love so dearly–'

'Where did you get all that?'

'It is my business to know,' Lakshya snapped in his police man's voice.

'So Frank is not the man I think he is? He's certainly given you lots of stuff about me.'

'Like you: he is our friend.'

'Friendship?' Rich spat the word out.

Lakshya sounded calm and sweet again: 'We are all fathers, us men, fathers to our children. People do not know. Women scoff at us. But inside our hearts we men, we cannot show it like women, but we love and hurt like them. More than them. They do not know that. That's their mystery, their ignorance. They do not know how much men love their children. Men are out at work all the time. I cannot be a policeman with a child hanging around me, a woman in a shop or kitchen can. If that is wrong, let god change it. Or women. Like they did in your country Mister Lomas, and ended up doing the housework, bringing up the children *and* doing a job.' He laughed. 'Here woman can be more free.'

'I don't see it.'

'Because you see with Western eyes.'

Rich shook his head.

'You've been hurt by women, Richard Lomas. A man cannot love a woman properly until his mother has died - you know that from your heart, like me. While your mother was alive your wife left you for another. You have a daughter you never see. I sympathise. All men have it, Mister Rich, yet they think they are alone.' He felt for his moustache a moment and smoothed its already smooth ends down against his skin. 'I was a handsome young man. This beautiful young girl was to be my wife. We met at street corners at dusk. There is nothing like the love of youth, is there Mister Rich? You are fearless and innocent – before the chaos – along a beach on Saturday afternoons with palm trees and crumbling Portuguese mansions. We played there. Her lips were a dream world for me. She was my purpose for living. And I hers. You know this, Mister Rich,' he smiled. 'You know that love don't you, only in youth, the first love, a gift more precious than all the gold in the world – you have it in your hand.' Tears welled at the corners of his eyes. 'You have it in your hand. And it is smashed.'

Rich watched him, 'So what happened?' his anger still lurking.

'We all lose in this life, Richard Lomas. Those with the most power lose the most. Those who beg have lost already. She was Christian, Rich. A beautiful Christian girl. An angel, sweet and sugary, all that a man wants. He would move mountains for her. She would give him sons. Their lovemaking would be sacred. Love is holy, is it not, Mister Lomas?'

Rich agreed with his eyes.

'She could not marry me. Christian with Hindu. You think her parents would be happy?' He stroked his moustache again: 'Have you seen your beloved with another man? Have you seen her, Mister Rich. In a car with a man richer than you could be. A man who owns her. And she's pregnant. She's got everything. And because you love her so much some part of you is stupidly glad she has everything while the other part of you rages. And that thing is spoiled: she suddenly spies you staring, your eyes meet. And what do you get, Rich? She longs for you. In that long gaze, it's you she wants, not this rich life. You know, don't you Rich – you have to live on. Oh, I'm happily married – three daughters–' He pulled himself together.

'But really you want sons, don't you?' Rich added an edge of his own.

Lakshya was quiet a moment, contemplating his drink and regretting his confession perhaps. Then he barked and Rich shook with the force of it: 'You will pay, Mister Lomas. You will pay.'

8

He slept into the afternoon, coming out to the glare with eyelids stuck together, parched mouth and head with a fist inside trying to punch its way out.

'I wondered where you got to–' Frank looked up from his newspaper, and leaning back in his wicker chair on the veranda, he sniggered at the stumbling figure.

Two women in their late twenties were scanning the back of the beach near a cow, baskets under their arms, the one in bright blue sari with shabby gold, the other in green. Their clothes had been rubbed by a thousand day's use, so the faded brightness reflected half of the newness and freshness of the dyes.

'You disappeared–' Rich's mouth could not seem to bring the words out coherently, they stuck in the back of his throat, got caught up on his dry tongue and came out of his lips skewed.

The women moved easily, one with ankle chains and bare feet, the other with flip flops, as if they were searching for hidden gold. One would lean forward, bend and pick an object and toss it casually in her basket. Then the other would see something and her body would lighten as she hastened to retrieve it. Rich's thoughts of Jeanette rippled on to musings about Lalima and her lost friend.

'Left you in capable hands,' Frank laughed. 'I knew they'd look after you.'

'Where did you go?' The sun was too much for his eyes.

Frank looked out to sea, the rim of the horizon faintly lined off sky from ocean: 'You got what you wanted.' He smirked.

'Set me up and went off with your German widow I suppose,' Rich could not hold back a sarcastic tone. 'Or some little tart of your own in that place.'

The sun was making the women's shadows longer, but he still could not make out what they were collecting.

Rich sat. 'You knew.'

'What?'

The one horned cow bellowed, shaking him in his seat, its shape black in shadows as it waddled indolently, kicking through sand.

'Lakshya. That mob.' A couple of crows hovered down the edge of roof tiles, cawing him mockingly, as though they had taken on the job of jeering at him and pricking his conscience. 'They want money, Frank.'

'I'll talk to them.'

'Frank.'

'I'll talk to them.'

'They'll bleed me dry,' Rich blurted. 'And you're so deep in with them. What's going on?'

The women moved in and out of shadows as though dancing - moving, bending, picking.

'You will get yourself in these situations, Rich. You've got to have the cash to back it up.'

'*You* took me there,' Rich downed a glass of water, the silvery liquid lubricating his tract. 'You set me up. Somebody put something in my drink. I - Babita was there, and–'

'All in your imagination. Anyway you wanted Chanda. It's so obvious. I can read you like a book. I just, well, oiled the cogs a little bit for you–'

Rich leaned forwards, palm over brow. The woman with ankle bells looked up at him and turned away.

'It's not like that. Chanda–'

'All whores are beautiful. Especially when you're tanked up.

Don't go soft in the head on me, Rich. And don't tell me you didn't know. Everybody knows what Chanda gets up to,' Frank laughed to himself. 'You have your fun and move on. I'm sure she catered fully for your needs - they say she's a good actress - you were becoming such a miserable nerd - needed some local tail, something a bit exotic. It does wonders–'

'Police run it, do they? They know where Babita is.'

'You've never paid for it before? So handsome you get it on a plate, eh?' Frank sneered into his paper.

'Your mate, eh?' Rich was trying to put down his anger. The cow's doleful cry was ignored by the surrounding world.

'They have to work with what they're got,' Frank snapped. 'They manage a situation. Like police do everywhere. Girls have been on the game ever since men set up brothels in caves and painted pictures on the walls–' He guffawed. 'That's what cave paintings were: pictures to cheer up waiting clients–'

Rich tried to laugh, but the edges of his mouth wouldn't curl up, so it came as a snort through his nose.

'Lakshya works with what he's got, that's all. You don't have to worry about him. I'll have a chat –'

'You two seem very good pals. What else do you get up to? Where were you, Frank, and what was that all about? What were they doing with Babita?'

'I'm going for a swim now. You coming?' he looked Rich up and down and then let out a cynical: 'Perhaps not then.' Frank folded the paper carefully and put it on the wicker chair, chuckled at the headline and addressed Rich again: 'You want to read? The Times of India: "Nasty Crook Caught by Local Cops. Christopher Da Silva, on the run for two months from cops was caught at Langa Crossing, trying to board a train to Kerala . . . Wanted for murder and robbery, Da Silva was known as the Red Handed killer because he was often seen with Henna patterns on his hand. This is thought to be part of his disguise - he is known to dress up as a woman for many of his robberies, and is thought to be part of a big gang called The Red Hand. –" All interesting stuff, buddy boy –'

'I saw that somewhere –'

'Who?'

'The hand.'

'Journalists always call them "cops" – funny, isn't it.'

'I'm sure I saw a man with a hennaed hand,' Rich pondered, unsure of what he had dreamed.

'Perhaps not then. Don't want to know what makes India tick? Maybe you're wise. I'll put the paper inside then. Leave it out here and who knows who'll pinch it–' Tossing it through the door, he locked up. 'Hey. Tonight. A band at the Rocking Globe. False Pretences, or something. Hope they're not going to live up to their name. Get yourself sober for that. And put her out of your mind.' He jogged off.

If it was really Babita last night, he should have done something. She was yelling.

The island was a hazy green lump at the end of the beach. Monkeys were there, they said.

The two women chatted and moved ahead.

'They get money,' Dinesh nodded at the women, answering his unspoken question.

He thought again about Babita, then about Jeanette as she might be as a teenager.

'Hi Dinesh. What?'

'Women–' he nodded again at the circling pair with baskets.

The more the night receded for Rich, the more Babita became a dream.

'They get money for their work,' Dinesh said again about the women but still he did not understand.

Chanda must have conned him. Milit was a police lackey, so perhaps she was too. He ran to the loo at the back and as stuff came up from inside his guts he felt the purge. He had been set up with the elephant business, and at the so called 'speakeasy', but the motive was not clear to Rich. He reappeared in the doorway, hair on end. The women were passing his little home, their baskets piled with empty plastic bottles.

'They get money for plastic,' Dinesh said. 'Recycle.' Laughing, he observed Rich: 'You look like a ghost. Yes, ghost. Sit. You need water. I will get you water.'

'Why are you such a good bloke, Dinesh?'

'My ploy.'

Rich laughed.

'Come Rich. I will take you –'

'Where?'

'Comb your hair.'

Rich patted the top of his head but the disjointed strands popped up again.

'Come and have a nice drink,' Dinesh motioned Rich on, leading him over hot sands, past stray dogs and a couple of cows, then turning under the arch at the end of the street that opened out to shops, he brought him to a stall near the taxi stand. They had caught up the women and Dinesh called to them, they turned and he went over and talked with them, then he was back with Rich: 'They have not seen her.'

'What Dinesh?'

'Babita.'

'Babita?'

'She disappeared. Go.' Dinesh rolled his lips in.

'The police are looking?' Rich could not help sounding cynical.

'They have not found her,' he shook his head.

'She would run away?'

Dinesh shook his head again.

'You know her?'

'My cousin.'

Rich hated his dreams. He should do something about them though. 'Babita is your cousin?'

'Come–' Dinesh nodded and pulled him along.

The women were lost in haze.

The stall was a rickety wooden thing on four over large thin wheels, its vendors a boy of fifteen and one of around ten who stood indolently around waiting for trade surrounded by piles of oranges and pineapples.

'I didn't know,' Rich whispered.

'She came from Mumbai to live with a friend of her auntie. She and Lalima meet and make friends.'

'She's gone back to Mumbai, Dinesh, without telling anyone, I bet you,' Rich lied to his friend in the hope that positive words would set Dinesh's mind at rest. 'Kids are like that - they don't tell you what they're doing. You'll hear from her in a day or two - wait and see.' After the confusion of the previous night Rich was less sure of Babita's safety but would not let on.

On seeing customers approaching, the vendors' body language changed, the taller lad standing to attention and kicking the smaller one in the leg as though inspection of troops was imminent, and the little one hopped dramatically.

'Orange?' Dinesh said. 'Pineapple? Sore head?'

'Pineapple.'

The elder boy poked through a pile of fruit, chose one, which Dinesh challenged, pointing out a bruise on the side and picking a different one. The bigger boy handed it to the smaller one, who took up a sword like knife which looked longer than the boy's legs and executed the pineapple with the panache of a chef relishing the death of a thing in order to create another.

Chunks and limbs and outer coating were rammed into a manual grinding machine with metal mashers that urged the stuff through its bending and expanding jaws like a wringer, the juice whittling down to a jug with three or four tide-lines of previous juices round the inside, the sign of a good pedigree Dinesh assured him: 'Drink.'

Under the watch of the two boys whose biceps had been developed through months of training on the pulping masher, Rich and Dinesh raised glasses pre-primed with earlier customers' fingerprints and scoffed, looking at the happy vendors. The juice sweetened Rich, filling vacuous spaces on the parched tongue, it seeped into him coolly, rejuvenating his will, and brought a smile to his face that the boys, smiling back, appreciated.

Turning and looking across the road, glass still at his mouth, Rich's gaze met another's. Chanda was standing inside her shop, watching him while nearby Milit was lifting boxes. She broke away when Milit shouted for help and guided him with a huge box. She was in blue today. For someone small she had great strength, manipulating the box and lowering it carefully with him. He could hate her, if he tried, but felt weak.

Dinesh was watching him: 'She has to do what he says.'

'Milit?'

'Cousin.'

'Milit is your cousin too?' Rich did not cover the shock.

'Cousin-brother. Mil.'

'You pull him out of the sun.'

'He drinks. Gamble. He owes money. Big money.'

'And her?' He found himself saying, hands trembling, hoping his face would betray nothing.

'Does everything he says. Everything. She must do what he tells her.'

'Why?'

'Wife. Chanda is his wife.'

Rich's face must have revealed his surprise for he nearly choked on his drink, and spluttering held his glass at arm's length.

'She must do things for him, whatever he asks. He owes big money. Big, big money - and a little baby–' Even when he was serious Dinesh wore a half grin, trying to hold his teeth back with his lips. 'Big money, little baby. All the same. Same for everyone, all round the world. All same.'

'He makes her work for him?' it came to Rich in a flow: 'Him? He makes her pay it off whatever way she can?'

Dinesh nodded, holding his dirty glass back into the young boy's dirty grip. Rich put his face in his hands, and letting his fingers create spaces he spied Chanda again dusting the little city of wares in her shop.

'And he beats her,' Rich whispered through his fingers, watching his lover move and wanting to console her.

'Maybe Lalima knows,' Dinesh pointed at several people surrounding a figure.

Twirling like Chanda had done, Lalima clicked her fingers, and her feet jangling ankle bells, she stamped sand and threw her arms up with controlled wildness.

'Babita. Maybe Lalima knows now.'

A small group was gathering.

She moved her body lithely as though electric motions up from earth were firing and propelling her, its inner urges charging her inner urges to move and flow and smile.

Dinesh moved him closer: 'Goddess Laxmi has many hands. She gives wealth to the poor and takes from the greedy. Laxmi helps the poor to make good business. Lalima dances for money. The dance of the world is the dance of money–'

The tambourine rattled its beat for her as she tossed her head and her long black hair trailed in the air. The crowd clapped along. A young woman with tattooed pictures of leaves rounding her shoulders was tapping her foot, along with a friend with a large sun hat who quickly put money in Aditya's basket.

Dinesh talked with Lalima, but they were shaking their heads when Rich joined them.

'Mumbai?' Rich asked her, but she bowed and shook her head again. 'Milit works with the police. Can't he do something?'

'They don't know where to look,' Dinesh answered for her: 'They try houses in the village. Many houses. They put out picture, but nothing.'

'Lalima,' Rich found a smile for her: 'Come tomorrow. I will teach you English and we can talk.'

She glanced at her mother with Aditya – they were busy collecting money – and back to him and nodded.

He was unsure whether he could feel Chanda's quick gaze on his back as he was going and dared himself to turn. He was only one of many. She looked away from him. Actress – entertainer of men.

9

The small stationery shop at the outer edge of the village was still open and he was able to purchase a folder of A4 writing paper and a couple of pens, and as he was going out he noticed a small doll in the window – the cute figure was dressed as an Indian dancer in reds and golds with black hair brightened with flowers, ear lobes hanging with plastic gold. He had to get it, and going back urged the assistant to take it out of the window. She slid it in its original box, the transparent frontage displaying the figure. As he headed back to his chalet dusk was drawing in and he was pleased with what he had bought.

Lights were coming up on beach restaurants and bars, some of which had extended their ramparts almost to the high tide line in efforts to reach out to tourist cash. As night took over the green and blue and white trailing lights around the trunks of palm trees came alive, signs popped on, waiters prepared tables and chefs sent tantalising smells through open doors and windows. Stars, stolen in daylight, opened as though a switch had been turned on until the blackness of the universe was heralded with a million grains. The sea folded itself in with slips of surf and the moon came up like a cradle, a U shape crescent it hung basket-like in the void.

At his chalet he rubbed cream on his arms and legs to keep mosquitoes away, but their leering motors were never far off, teasing their victim beforehand with a threatening hum – you knew when it stopped you had been had.

He wasn't going to pay up.

'Out of that chair, you,' Frank came up from the purple murk of shadows.

'I need a quiet night, Frank,' Rich moaned uselessly.

'No you don't. You'll come and see this band with me.'

'Under false pretences,' Rich played with the pun.

'Get your togs on. It's a good restaurant. If you don't like it you can clear off early. But this is India, Richie boy, there's no such thing as an early night,' He paused looking at Rich. 'You're not still thinking about her, Rich – a trollop, a floosy, whatever you want to call them. You can't have an Indian woman forever. You're too romantic and naïve. That's your problem. You need a good blow out tonight to get you back on your feet, get rid of those bags under your eyes with a splash of whisky.'

'Where did you go last night, Frank?'

'Scared I'll leave you again?'

'Did you see Babita?'

'The first drink's on me,' Frank piped up pressure, 'I can't be fairer than that.'

Rich did not move: 'I was dreaming. Babita, did you see her there?'

'Miserable so-and-so. Sit here and be moody and love sick then and feel sorry for yourself–' Frank went inside his chalet, turned the light on and combed his hair. 'You know you've got a maudlin side to you, Rich, and it doesn't do your friendships any good. You've got to learn to snap out of it.'

'Okay,' Rich was on his feet, exasperated. 'Get your point.' And going inside pulled on a dirty pair of beach trousers.

'You're not going like that, you pillock. Get something decent on. This is a big night.'

'Take it or leave it.'

'Please yourself. Awkward - Let's go.'

They headed into thick darkness between trunks along a route that edged its way through undergrowth and past the back of houses with washing still hung on walls and branches, and along a dark path parallel to the black waters of the river on its way to the sea. The Rocking Globe looked out to the estuary, a clump of wooden chalet huts hung with flowers and fabrics surrounding a bar with a small stage on which amplifiers, drums, mics, guitars and stands had been set up. The black river hung over the back of trees, silvered here and there by the moon. Stars punctured the sky.

It was Red Snapper again for Frank, garnished with shrimps and green salad – most of which he left. While Rich had tandoori vegetables speared on a stick with lumps of white cheese, the band assembled on stage, fiddling with instruments. The drummer tested as guitarists tuned. After a few drumstick beats they burst into 'Satisfaction' and the audience, having already been wined, were ready for entertainment and applauded warmly. There was a mixture of age and background – most were English, German or Russian, with a few Indian couples. Many were Frank's generation, but a good half were around Rich's age. Relaxing in candle light at small tables on the sand, they sat with their backs to the sea.

False Pretences had two guitarists Rich reckoned were English – one a bony faced pony tail man, the other with cropped hair – along with an oversized and smiling Indian lad on bass disturbing the cool outlook they were trying to portray, and an Indian drummer relishing the bash of skins with wood, sweating away under palms. The bassist sang, but without flavour. Rich said nothing to Frank, but thought they lacked vocal energy, and doubted his own ability to see the night through.

When they had finished eating and discarded plates of broken fish bones and wooden skewers, they leaned back and sipped red wine, the make of which for Rich tasted like untreated vinegar.

False Pretences stopped for a moment. They had been on a roll of Stones' numbers, a couple of Beatles' rockers, but the bassist now appeared to be appealing to someone in the audience and there was loud chat on a table up front. Rich leaned sideways to see through the grouping of silhouetted heads. Two women in their twenties were in the middle of an amicable squabble, one playfully resisting the other while the band leader leaned into the crowd supplicating with his right hand. After some cheers and slow hand clapping the reluctant one stood, and coming clearly into the light the ivy green leaf work on her lower neck was visible. Her friend - now hatless in the sticky night - was playfully but firmly urging her onstage.

The pony tail guitarist held his hand out to her and yanked her up with him, trying to relax her with easy body language and smiles. When the space of silence was getting too long he nodded to her to introduce herself over the mic, but she turned aside.

'She's doing an Amy Winehouse thing–' The bassist fumbled, and his efforts did nothing to allay the pretender's fears.

'I don't look nothin' like her–' the new singer tugged at her white-blond hair self mockingly. 'Got black on though.' She tittered smoothing down her black top and black tights. '"Back to Black," i'n'it–' She looked to the bassist for help and the drummer counted them in.

The mutterings of the audience mellowed to nothingness, allowing her bluesy voice to let itself flow out over the dark sea. At the end they roared with the vigour of one united animal.

'Fanks.' She was about to go but the bassist held her arm and she tottered, her body a little drunk. 'Not that one,' she told him audibly, but he insisted.

She did 'Rehab.' The crowd was in uproar.

'Nina,' the bassist chimed over demands for more. 'Nina Shaw.'

She slipped back into the darkness of crowds, the band broke up and some guy got up and put sounds on.

'Frank,' a voice came out of groups of heads around a table, surrounding darkness mellowed by candle light. 'That's you, Frank–' A female figure was heading for him. 'You didn't come,

Frank. Yoga–' She was in their light now, the young woman who had pushed her singer friend onstage.

'Got caught up,' Frank smiled, 'you know how it is in India.'

'Aarti is so good, Frank,' the other persisted with a grin. 'She's on again tomorrow. You should come–'

'What? And get some of this flab off, you mean?' he playfully patted the mound of his belly.

'She's such a good teacher – so much knowledge –'

'This is Angie–' Frank nodded to Rich. 'And Rich–'

Rich held his hand out to her and they shook lightly. Moving flame-light traced paths over her facial features: he liked her smile and the shy way she looked away from his eyes.

'You like yoga, Rich?'

'Well, you know. Never been there, Angie.'

Her deep brown eyes were warm and sparkled when she laughed. Her straightened black hair was not held under a hat now but was tied back with a strip of Indian material, and she had carefully trimmed eyebrows. Silver Indian earrings swayed as she moved her head when talking. Rich thought she looked good, would be great to have as a mate, and wondered to himself which side of her family was African.

'Aarti is so good,' Angie praised her guru again. 'It's not just yoga, it's all the other interesting stuff she brings–'

'Yeah?' Rich encouraged conversation.

'Knows about mystics and history and all that stuff about getting your mind and body balanced.'

'She needs a bottle of whisky,' Frank blurted, 'that'll get her balanced all right.' He bellowed and Angie smiled without acknowledgement.

'Yoga's good for relaxation,' she went on, 'but as Aarti will tell you, it's not all about that, and getting your body in shape – the original idea of yoga was to get your body and mind prepared for meditation – to keep body and mind supple –'

'You don't say,' Frank humphed.

'She works near the beach, in a hut. Round near where the estuary opens to the sea. You know, where they do boat rides–' Angie kept her eyes on Rich a moment while he let his gaze wander towards the black sea and grey froth.

'She ain't sellin' her to you is she?' Nina was behind her suddenly, a glass of coke in hand, 'Aarti farty – always goin' on about her –' She pulled a chair through sand for a metre and joined them at table. 'I've got to tell you Angie, you're a bit obsessed with that woman and that stuff–' Nina clutched the glass with her right hand, flicking her index finger to point at her friend.

'Good songs,' Rich addressed the artiste.

'She can only do them when she's drunk,' Angie got her own back.

'Go for it girl,' Frank said.

'Got to steel your nerves before you get up there, don't you?' Nina stared at Rich, the sides of her mouth down. 'What's your name anyway?'

'Rich,' he held out his hand.

'Hope you live up to your name, Rich,' Nina laughed to herself, 'could do with a bloke with some cash. Not like the losers I'm used to. Nina-' she yelled at him. 'Nobody introduces people no more. You have to do it yourself.'

'You don't need any introduction,' Angie was tart.

'You see, Rich,' Nina leaned towards him, 'it's hard up there. If they don't like you – it's bad – you know what I mean – they can kill your confidence with a knife in a matter of seconds – and you never know when it will happen–'

'So what do you do?' Rich tried to keep the conversation going.

'A bit of Dutch courage. Couple of whisky and cokes and you're there. Everything's rosy. Everybody does it, Rich. All the top singers – they're scared inside – they won't be liked, it'll all go wrong, they'll look stupid. Look at Amy–'

'It's just you carry it on,' her friend added.

'The problem with you Angie,' Nina was sharp, 'is you don't know how to enjoy yourself. All this yoga stuff - get yourself pissed one night, get yourself laid - it would do you more good than that woman-'

'I guess we like different things,' Angie tried to smile her way out.

'Maybe we should all try it,' Rich let out without thinking.

'What?' Nina smiled cynically, 'Yoga? Eight o'clock in the morning. I don't know any singer that knows what the world looks like at that time of day - or any sensible right thinking person even. The hours of eight a.m. to midday are the hours of slumber and hangover, blurred vision and silence. Talk at that time cracks the soul. And anyone dare ask a question - worse even than death-'

'You should hear her in the mornings,' Angie was light. 'A bear with a sore head.'

'That's the price you pay for creativity. For being an artist. It can't be up all the time.'

'Up and down, down and up, then is it?' Angie smirked.

'I'm more up than down.'

'Not from where I am,' Angie carried on her tease.

'You're too busy with your body balance and your mind stuff. You can't live on that.'

'Maybe Angie's right,' Rich said, 'we should give it a go.'

'That's including you, Nina,' Frank scoffed.' You're all front. Underneath we all know there's a real person lurking, someone with actual feelings in fact -' He laughed, and Angie laughed with him while Rich observed.

'Listen, I'll tell you-' Nina began her drunken diatribe, 'I'll tell you. What this place needs is a real band. Not covers. Anyone can do that. Not the same old songs over and over again copied from the original as close as possible. New songs. Singer-songwriter songs. I can do that -'

'You've never been the same since Dave left –'

'You find my buttons, Angie, all the time.'

'I was just saying, you need a new partnership.'

'They're all nob-heads, these guys,' Nina nodded at the stage.

'Rob on guitar seems okay.'

'Can he write music? I doubt it. He's just a strummer, Angie. You don't know anything about the business.'

'And you don't know anything about yoga.'

'Then we're quits. You keep off my turf and I'll keep off yours.' Nina shook her head, turning away from them in her chair.

'You up for it Frank, or what?' Rich challenged.

'If I must –'

'I'm going to find someone who can actually compose real music,' Nina stood, wobbled, then launched herself into darkness.

'She can't help it,' Angie laughed nervously, 'she can't help who she is –'

Rich watched her go, her shape quickly becoming another silhouette in the gallery of silhouetted bodies eating and drinking and talking.

'She's got something–' Rich said, unaware of Angie's glance at him, and then her quick withdrawal of the look.

He made his apologies: he was tired, he said, and needed to head back, and shaking a limp hand with Angie he moved away from candlelight and way off into the jungle path along the river. Dark silence enveloped him under palms, the grey of the river still to his left reflecting the upturned slice of moon that hung in the abyss of sky. He thought he heard movement behind – someone following, but brushed aside the thought, although now his senses had been triggered and his instinct was to be alert for danger. Howling dogs on the distant beach –

a canine chorus, he mused, of prancing leaders cockily pronouncing their ego intentions. The shrubs got denser – he had somehow lost the main path and was caught up in a narrow route through thickets and away from the little star-lights in cabins and wooden chalet huts.

Dog calling intensified distantly. It was too dark for him to see the hound a few feet ahead of him, but the growling bark threw him off balance and he stumbled sideways, slipping in the muddy remains of the river at low tide. As the dog yelled, Rich could see it only feet from him, in the way of his exit. Back to the river, he somehow had to pass the animal. He cursed the sucking pull at his trainers of the gluey mud that drew him back riverwards. The dog would not give up. Rich swore. He could get in the river and let its current take him to the sea and walk back soaked along the beach, but scoffed at how scared he had become of the barking shape in darkness. Or he could find a way along the muddy edges – if the dog did not follow him.

Trudging up river he sucked each trainer up one by one, sliding here and there, the moon's reflection following him. The dog was quiet a moment, but he could feel it breathing in the thicket. There was a log ahead, lying from shore and down to the water's edge – he could get to that and walk along it back into the palm trees and off home. Motivated by the new objective, he spurted towards it, noticing as he got closer how curious and almost human it was in shape. The dog was whimpering. Nearing the torso of the dead tree he could make out the branches of arms, hair trailing in mud. The dog was crying in darkness. There was the profile of a face in the log, he mused. A girl's face. He ran ahead. A teenage girl, face up in mud, trails of clothing muddy round her. He held her wrist: nothing. On her forearm a little circle with a dancing shape in the middle.

The moon came out of clouds. Babita.

10

'You found her face up,' Lakshya's eyes wandered from Rich's face to his hands folded on the table. 'You did not move her?'

The fan cut air above Milit who was scribbling in a notebook.

'I told you,' Rich yawned.

'You did not move her at all?' Lakshya was leaning on a copy of The Times of India.

'She had no pulse – I tried. Thought I might be able to revive her. When are you going to do something about this?'

'Her clothes were not disarranged?'

'I didn't touch her. You found her how I found her. You can't have bodies all around Bagolem, it's bad for business.'

'I appreciate your concern, Mister Lomas, but you must not tell me my job,' he sniffed, pulling his shoulders back.

'Red marks around her neck,' Rich observed. 'Like the first one –'

'You can leave the detective work to us, Mister Lomas.'

'That means the man you are holding could not have done it.'

'I'd like to remind you, Mister Richard Lomas – however much we have become friends – that you owe my associate here–' he nodded towards Milit, who carried on writing.

'And you think I'll pay.'

'I know you will pay, Mister Lomas, you are a man of honour.'

'Sounds like an old boy's club.'

'You were the person who found the girl. You must be considered a suspect,' Lakshya's elbow was resting on the headline.

'You've got to be joking. I was at the Rocking Globe all night and on my way home. People saw me.'

'In the darkness, walking home? Through a thicket?' Lakshya rumbled a laugh. 'Your chalet is along the front – the old fishermen's huts – with Dinesh?'

Rich tensed with the knowledge of Lakshya's intelligence about him: 'You know where I live, you know all that stuff. You know I wouldn't harm a girl. I'm a teacher.'

'In your country I am informed – although I have never been – I am sure I could learn a lot from your police force – I have heard there are many tales now of police corruption there, your newspapers glory in it from time to time. And sometimes the shooting without warning of a suspect. And yet, and yet, Mister Lomas, we suffer here from Europeans telling us we are corrupt.' He laughed. 'It is an odd upside down world. There will always be – what is it you call them – "bent coppers", but that does not mean the whole thing is bad.'

'Doesn't it?'

'If you are meaning there is corruption here, Richard Lomas, that is a very serious allegation, and we might ask you to prove it – or get out of town.'

'Huh,' Rich shrugged his shoulders: 'Are you going to find the teenage girl murderer, or not?'

'You say you are a teacher, Mister Lomas, and I am supposed to take it that because of that you are above corruption of young girls.'

Rich raised his body from his seat and screwed up his lips.

'Sit down, Richard Lomas. I have to tell you, you are – what is the expression – "sailing close to the wind" – whatever that means,' he laughed. 'You see, I learn a lot of English – English teacher.'

'I have a daughter–'

'Many men wait until their daughters are the right age–'

Milit pulled Rich back in his chair, grabbing his fist and unravelling it; Rich found him strong for his slight frame.

'Mister Lomas. You know as well as I that men who – what shall we say – have a taste for young girls – come from many classes. They are not just working men – they are everywhere in business, in teaching–'

'Even the police – the judiciary, politicians –'

'Mister Lomas,' Lakshya steamed, his face lightly pinked, 'you are a witness, and for that reason you must stay in Bagolem. Go now.' Lakshya moved his arm from the headline: 'Red Hand Man Escapes Jail. Members of the Red Hand Gang broke into jail early in the morning and escaped with the wanted criminal . . .'

Rich got up.

'Mister Lomas. You are in debt. Please remember.'

'I don't owe you anything.'

'I think you do. And I think you will pay.'

'Or what?'

'It will not be the last time you see the inside of this police station with its rusty old fan. You are becoming a regular, are you not? Perhaps you would like a longer stay here.'

Milit laughed.

Rich left them.

*****

'My room hasn't been done again, Dinesh,' Frank was railing. White light of morning was flooding the beach, pouring through palm leaves, bleaching roads and rooftops. Rich's nightmare had been of logs coming alive along a muddy river of baying dogs. And all logs were Babita. He wondered if Lalima knew yet and wanted to go and find her.

'This is the third day Rita hasn't done her job. Tell her, Dinesh.'

Dinesh's grin had gone: 'I will get someone.'

'You know, Dinesh?' Rich was instinctively awake on the veranda. 'Dinesh?'

Dinesh sat, bowed, as though about to fall off the low wall.

'Dinesh?'

'It's not good, Dinesh,' Frank fussed with a wet towel.

'Leave him, Frank.'

'Sucking up to the manager then are we?'

'His cousin, Frank.'

Frank shrugged his shoulders bewildered, as a man with a bundle of newspapers appeared at the step up to the veranda, garlands of stringed saffron flowers for sale on his arm – bundles of marigolds swinging from him with each step.

'Newspaper –' Frank exchanged cash for newsprint. The vendor smiled at the purchaser but got no response.

'Babita, Frank,' Rich said as his friend gazed at the headline: "Second Girl Dumped on Beach." 'You all right, Dinesh?' Rich put his hand on the shaking man's shoulder. 'You got any whisky in there, Frank?'

Frank went inside and came out with half a bottle and a glass, splashing in the golden liquid. Rich made Dinesh gulp. Dinesh screwed up his face with pain, eyes watering. Frank's hands were shaking as he swigged from the bottle, then handed it to Rich, who did the same. They breathed out together.

'You all right, Din?' Frank offered. 'Have another.' He half filled his glass and Dinesh downed it.

'They'll find him,' Rich said feebly.

'Yeah, Din. They'll get him.'

Dinesh drained the glass, threw it aside and grasped his head in his hands: 'I hold her. When she was a baby. I hold. She cry. I rock. I hold. I hold. Babita. Babita. My baby–'

Rich put his arm round him and looked up at Frank: 'That lot will get him, won't they?'

'They get him. I kill him,' Dinesh jumped up. 'Kill him, kill him.'

'You've got to keep calm now, Dinesh,' Rich tried to lead him back to his chair, but he railed, fisting the door, the wall. 'Dinesh. You go home now. You be with your wife and kid. Dinesh.'

He howled for a time, head in hands, then turned and went.

'There's one way to find the killer,' Frank watched him go.

'What?'

'Pay them.'

'Who?'

'The woodentops. Who do you think I mean? Lakshya and his mob.'

'Why don't you Frank?' Rich was forward.

'More money than I could put together.'

'You know them, Frank. Surely you've got influence there. Or,' Rich looked down at the paper: 'you get the press in.'

'You don't want to do that. Lakshya'll sort it, you'll see.'

'How far in with them are you, Frank?'

'I told you – that guy who died, Gerry – I had to tie things up with them – that's all –'

'The press can put the heat on, Frank – you can't have dead girls all over your tourist beach, nobody will want to come anymore.'

'It's not got to that stage,' Frank let out a nervous laugh, but Rich noticed his fingers still trembling. 'You'll see. Lakshya's a better cop than you put him down for – he's got a good detection rate–'

'But got the wrong bloke banged up.'

'You don't know that, Rich. That guy inside might be connected.'

Rich poured some of his whisky back in the bottle – it was too early in the day and he was still missing a lot of sleep. He sat for a moment staring out at the beach while Frank went inside. Two elderly women were sweeping with brooms made of switches of brushwood. Dumpy shaped, wearing broad straw hats with wide brims, long shirts and skirts down to flip flops, they swayed across sand half stooping, half swinging, as though in some sort of ritual, brushing this way and that, so the sand was charred with neat strokes. Little bits of paper, plastic and wood they scooped up in round wicker baskets and took away. Beach sweepers, like road sweepers, they rolled along shore as though on castors, older than the recycling team, they brushed away the detritus of tourism without sound, their shadows in tow. A grey headed crow sat on a rock watching them, cockily twitching its neck one way, then another.

Fishermen were untangling nets, little men with spindly legs they stood around boats, fingers unpicking knots, and some with fags hanging from lips, and some coughing – little men who somehow looked tall as they pawed through white plastic gossamer lines heaped on long dark brown hulled boats with orange and white and green flags, great creatures leaning ashore on floats on one side.

'They're coming for us, Frank,' Rich remembered. 'The girls.' He almost whispered. The island at the end of the beach seemed to have pumped itself higher in the night, its round animal-like hump perched on the light of the Arabian Sea.

'Blow the yoga,' Frank snapped, coming out, 'I'm going for coffee.' Rich's neighbour slammed his door, locked up and charged off, paper under his arm.

Waiters were washing down floors, serving early breakfasts and coffee to drowsy tourists with half open papers and half open eyes.

Three scraggy Indian kids were trawling the beach: a tallish girl of about Lalima's age, a boy of around seven and a girl of five. He must search for Lalima, give her the book and pencils and get her writing – maybe that was a way of helping her through her bereavement. Also, he wanted to see Aditya's face when he gave her the doll. He might even persuade her mother to let them go to school. The three he had spied drifted by the swirling beach cleaners, Rich reckoned none of them had seen a comb for a week at least, their hair as knotted and dishevelled as the nets the men were trying to disentangle. Rich could not hear the words, but the tall girl was holding out her open palm to passers-by, all ignoring her. She had on a faded green salwar kameez and bright green plastic earrings. Her begging was restrained, not urgent or pushy, more pleading.

The women brushed round them like silent slow motion machines as the children trod on in search of a benefactor. There was always one, Rich mused: a woman in her early twenties with straightened black hair tied back under a big sun hat: Angie. She'd got a small garland of saffron flowers on her arm and smiling, she searched her bag while the children grouped round her excitedly like a teacher they had known for years. She was having trouble finding her purse and when she got to it had to rummage to find coins. The boy was on tip toes trying to look in, eyes aflame with glee, and the little girl was jumping up and down, while the leader had the cool smile of someone who had provided for her flock. Coins were pressed in hands, and notes for the elder. It was a bonanza, and the little children danced ahead of their upright leader, the women described circles in the sand round them and the sea lapped up and washed the edges of the circle clean as the sun moved higher from white to deeper white and shadows diminished.

'Angie,' he called as she approached the steps up to the sandy platform outside his hut. With a hint of a shy smile, she glanced quickly at him then away.

'She couldn't make it,' Angie laughed. 'Couldn't get out of bed.'

'Just you and me then?' Rich smiled. 'Frank's gone off grumpy for coffee.'

Holding out the garland of flowers to Rich, she said: 'You'll come though?'

He found himself taking the yellow petals; he had wanted to see Nina. 'You gave to those kids.'

'They come from out the back somewhere. I know I'm soft but –'

'Too soft,' he laughed.

'Yeah. Yeah. I am,' Angie smiled unashamed, then becoming more shyly serious with him: 'The flowers. You hang them round your door. They bring good luck.' And finding a space near his door frame she threaded the string of the garland around a couple of rusty nails and let the flowers hang. 'You will come though?' she stepped back to see if the composition was balanced.

'We need something to bring us luck.' Pausing, he drew breath: 'You've heard?'

Angie shook her head a little and grinned: 'Yoga and meditation. It just doesn't match up to beer and football does it?'

'Babita?'

'I can go on my own.'

'Her body by the river.'

'No. Just a kid wasn't she? It's terrible.' She sat, shaking. 'What happened?'

'I found her on my way home last night.'

'Poor thing, you,' her eyes were dimmed in shade under the brim of her hat. 'It's terrible. Was she–'

'I reckon. Didn't seem natural.'

'Babita. Not her. Poor girl. Are the police any good round here?'

'If they think you've stolen an elephant–'

'What?'

'Nothing. They're just – I'm not sure they care. This is the second, after all.'

'Poor you, finding her there. Poor thing.'

'She's Dinesh's cousin, or niece or something. He's devastated.'

'Of course,' Angie's fingers were shaking. 'How are you?'

'Nightmares all night,' he laughed it off.

'That's horrible. How did she look, Rich, I mean–'

'Thought she was a log at first, lying on the river bank in the mud. When I got closer she was lying on her back, just like she was asleep, eyes closed, a slight smile on her lips – as though you could shake her and wake her up–'

'I've never seen a dead body – Poor boy. Are you all right?'

'A bit shaken, but, you know – life goes on.'

'And the police?'

'Statements down the cop shop. They don't like me, Angie.' Rich liked her.

'They must get somebody. It puts everyone on edge.'

She would make a good mate.

'Lalima. You know the dancer – she was her friend – '

'God, Rich. It's awful.'

'I've got to find her –'

'I can go on my own,' she stood. 'You need to stay here and relax. Then go and look for her -'

She was stocky in structure with wide hips in loose fitting cotton white trousers. Her breasts were packed securely in a low cut T-shirt of purple, the cleavage a three inch valley. Her purple trimmed straw hat matched her lipstick of mauve-ish red hue. He would have liked to see what Nina looked like in the morning light, but this girl had made an effort. He had not even washed – fallen out of a mosquito net and fallen into shorts and pulled them up and rubbed his eyes and headed for the torture room of daylight.

'Give me a minute,' he dived back in darkness, dragged a flannel across his face, under his armpit and around his loins and a toothbrush over his front teeth, pulled on a clean T-shirt and clean shorts and dived out a new man to the floodlit world.

She was sitting in a wicker chair, one leg crossed over the other, waving her sun hat in swings beside her and concentrating her gaze on the horizon, and jumping up when he came out said how good he looked, but he knew she had been thinking about Babita. He told her to lead the way.

Dinesh had brought out a bin of rubbish from a room at the end of the block, and Rich was surprised to see him back working: 'You should be at home – with family.'

'My boss wants me always at work,' Dinesh gave him a half smile. Rich had not seen this room before – a narrow place more like a short corridor than a place to stay. There was a bed to the right and a washbasin slung under a mirror with one corner broken away. On a shelf were a hair brush and jars of ointment and colour, and hanging on a crude hook some shawls and the remains of a blue sari.

Rich stopped, Angie trod on but backtracked when she saw him poke himself inside: 'What's this place, Dinesh? You don't rent it out, do you?'

'Not for tourists,' Dinesh forced a smile.

'Someone lives here?'

'Not now.'

'Used to?'

'Rita. Rita lived here.'

'Here, Dinesh?' It did not seem possible for someone to inhabit a room no bigger than a large cupboard.

Angie was on the side lines.

Dinesh nodded.

'This is home?'

'Not now. She's gone.'

'You're not sacking her?' Rich was suddenly worried about the power he and Frank wielded.

'Her daughter's in big trouble. She had a baby and her husband go off. Nobody knows where. Off.'

'That's bad, Dinesh.'

Angie stood, hat in hand in front of her.

'Where does her daughter live?'

'Mumbai. Rita's gone to her. Her daughter has nothing, no money. Rita must go–' he glanced in the cave-like dwelling.

Rich shared a look of sympathy with Angie. 'When's she back?'

Dinesh shrugged his shoulders.

'She's not coming back?'

Dinesh shook his head: 'Daughter cannot pay rent - soon she will have no house. Rita must help and find a place to live. In Mumbai - not easy. And baby –'

'The hidden India,' Rich heard Angie whisper as if to palm trees and the laughing crows who tricked their way through branches.

'Daughter can't come here. Not Rita and daughter and baby,' Dinesh nodded again to the corridor of the cabin he was cleaning, 'No room. Who's got room? Nobody's got room. They must find a place in Mumbai.'

Rita's broom was leaning against a corner under the sink, the spliced handle, the switches, tools of the trade useless.

'Rita has not had a good life,' Dinesh muttered, his face serious. 'Rita had a husband, then her baby daughter. Then Rita's husband go and nobody knows where. He just disappeared. Same thing. She can't pay rent. Same thing Rita, same thing daughter.'

'What the mother feared most for her own daughter, happened to her–' Angie was thinking out loud.

'What can you do?' Rich said.

'What can do?' Dinesh shrugged his shoulders. 'What can do?' Like the repeated sound of a strange bird: 'What can do? What can do? What can do?'

Rich took Angie away.

'Behind each hut there's a story,' Angie said and he looked at her, his mind churning, 'stories we don't know about, suffering we don't see. We tread on sand and they tread on eggshells.'

The three begging children were sauntering up the beach, each child with a fat ice cream covering its mouth. Tongues lurched around pink and white and chocolate stuff as the heat melted it down cones. Laughing faces slurped at the buttery mass and delighted eyes shone big over their trophies. The elder girl glided along contentedly having fulfilled a promise to her minions of bounties throughout the day.

'They bought ice creams,' Rich edgily laughed. 'You gave them money and they bought –'

'Ice creams,' Angie yelped. 'Kids. Having fun. It was worth it – parting with a few rupees for their daily treat.'

He was silent, taking it in.

Angie led him along the beach northwards toward the estuary. A couple of joggers eased past a woman in bikini meditating in lotus position among palm trees as the sun whitened landscapes. The sea was pushing itself up the estuary, rolling boats and lapping quietly around rocks covered in limpet creatures as the tide's fingers crawled over flats filling hollows, pouring itself back on the land. Each day and night it encroached, surging itself over the earth and into it, finding ways to creatively swell itself along river banks where palm trees held close.

Angie said nothing, her eyes in pale shadow under the rim of her sun hat as she led him over sands, by heaps of rubbished paper and plastic debris guarded by a couple of half sleeping dogs with one eye open for accosting strangers. One raised its head and let its pink tongue poke itself out of its mouth limply in anticipation of friendship and food. A warm breeze was exercising palms.

A track opened, leading through the back of chalet huts, then wood and concrete houses in the village that supplied labour for restaurants and bars and shops and stalls. Washing hung on lines, pastel colours of fabrics and clothes intermingling in breeze. Small huts and houses in various stages of crumbling disrepair, some held together with strung up sheets of blue plastic and dried palm leaves, cluttered near where barefoot children played.

A family of hogs was grazing through a pile of peelings, their grey-brown bodies fleshy pink underneath a line of fur, their faces pointed for searching, they gave out grunts of delight.

Children ran squealing through alleys, a few helpful girls looked up from their chores of washing, scrubbing, getting water, looking after little ones. The smell of women cooking with spices drifted to them as they wandered through. Old men and old women sat in shade. A stray dog cowered, a cow chewed and a monkey watched them from a tree.

'And all this behind the scenes, eh?' Angie observed. 'Makes you realise we've got it made.'

Rich nodded.

The track evened out to a road with bigger houses. Restaurant owners and successful local business people had built themselves small town houses with enough room out front to park a car. Red painted iron gates, satellite dishes, a cross for a Christian, a shrine to Siva for a Hindu.

They passed a house with a small flagpole, a tricolour of orange, white and green rippled in light breeze. A rather modest place compared to others along the street, its windows were barred with iron fittings like a cage, and shutters hung open over them.

Angie led him down a track by the side of the building – a family was finishing breakfast in the garden and a girl was playing with her little sister on the short lawn, while mother was bringing out orange juice and putting it on a breakfast table in the shade. A man with his back to Rich and Angie was bouncing a girl on his knee - a child of about three - and holding her arms gently in thick fists, he tossed her lightly, clicking horse noises from his mouth so she giggled back. Cooing to his child and dancing her up and down, he stopped to kiss her head, muttering words of affection, then back bouncing her again, exciting her with chuckles as he pulled her about easily but with the tenderness of a marionette operator as she wobbled and danced to his management of her strings.

The other girls came to him and pulled him up onto the lawn, insisting he play with all of them, and the eldest got an orange ball and tossed it to the man, his back still to Rich and Angie, and they played a minute, but the toddler was not going to be neglected and moaned for her dad to pick her up again. He bent, scooped her up with a kiss to her forehead and carried on tossing the ball to the other girls.

Angie was going ahead as Rich slowed. The man turned with the baby in his arms. Lakshya's gaze met Rich's and Rich shuffled on.

He was not going to pay.

The end of the track opened out into a grove of palms with a view over the river. A hut made of bamboo and dried woven palm leaves huddled itself in their shade, its shape off balance, leaning away from the rectangular towards a parallelogram. They passed through a gap in a low brick wall guarded by a seated Buddha in meditation, his right hand touching earth, a small bowl in his left.

'Although he's meditating and his mind is in the cosmos,' stated the young Indian woman standing by, 'he's still touching earth - in touch with the goings on of the world, however trivial-'

'This is Aarti,' Angie said with a short smile, and Rich smiled and said he was pleased to meet her.

A little shorter than Angie, Aarti had a pointed jaw and darting eyes. Her flat black hair hung straight down her shoulders and beyond. She had on an orange top with tight sleeves and black tracksuit bottoms. He reckoned she was in her early thirties.

'Maybe we wouldn't know so much about the Buddha - and his passion for non-violence -' she chatted on, 'if it wasn't for a great deal of violence-'

Rich and Angie looked on. A couple of grey ringed crows were looking down on them. A cow in purple-green distance over an emerald paddy field mooed.

'A great massacre – in history –'

They let her be host.

'Asoka. Oh, Buddhism had been going for centuries, but he popularised it, made it a national religion in the third century before the Christian era. You see, to extend his empire into Kalinga – the east coast, which is now Orissa, he's said to have massacred hundreds of thousands in battle. And then, surveying the dead, he was moved to regret by the bloodshed and converted to the non-violence of Buddhism. Like all good converts, he sees his mission as spreading the word. He builds thousands of stupas – pagodas – and columns and carvings; creates the famous four guarding lions back to back – the archetypal image of India you see on stamps and coins. The lion ruled India once, and Asoka makes him the king of religions – but I'm sure you didn't come here for a history lesson,' she laughed, suddenly aware of her tirade. 'Come inside.'

She led the couple into the shade of the hut where the ground was covered with interwoven dried palm leaves. Cotton rugs were scattered here and there. In the corner were stacked cushions of Indian Red and Indian Yellow, and others with large Paisley patterns. Lines of smoke twirled from a bunch of incense sticks, and spiralling upwards the lines could not hold, meandering into clouds that melted. Shards of sunlight pierced the matted walls and pricked his arms. Another seated Buddha commanded the back end of the hut, a smaller fellow than the first in faded brass. To the left Siva was dancing through a circle of flames. To the right a goddess with four arms stood, two of her hands holding lotus flowers, and in a dark corner another four-armed goddess grasping a sword and the remains of a giant's head lurked.

Aarti motioned them to sit on the matting. Angie could manage a lotus pose, Rich tried but could not put his limbs entirely where he wanted them. Smiling, Aarti put her hands together in a prayer position and bowed to her students. Angie did the same back to her, and Rich copied.

'The Om is the sound and the shape and symbolic form of the universe,' Aarti spoke with eyes closed. 'You allow a low hum to rise from your lungs, through your vocal chords and up through the nasal passage. Follow me–'

Angie followed Aarti's lead with a long low hum and Rich joined in tentatively, allowing a sound to emit from his chest, up the throat, and through the nasal passage in an effort to be in tune with them, and stifling an urge which came up through his belly to laugh.

The trio let the sound vibrate through them.

He felt nothing at first, only a charge of energy propelling itself from his nose into the air, and his mind rambled on over a myriad banal thought cycles: what would he have for breakfast; why hadn't he intervened when Chanda was beaten; why had he let himself be trapped by her; anger towards Lakshya and how he wouldn't pay; and Lakshya playing tenderly in his garden with his daughters while Babita lay at a riverside; and Jeanette laughing–

'Desire,' Aarti said, as if his thoughts had dribbled out into words, she had heard them and was answering: 'is the cause of all suffering. The Buddha tells us–'

'But we're born in a world of desire,' Rich rebelled. 'We cannot live without desire. It propels us to seek shelter and food and to look after loved ones. Desire is who we are–'

He found himself on the road but not convinced. The Buddha seemed to look at him wherever he wandered in the room, and Siva and the goddesses boxed him in. Nirvana was getting drunk: you couldn't carry all this in your mind, or the hurt that the world insisted on dishing out to you. Everyone hurt – it could be seen in everyone's eyes, or at least behind their eyes. You got your heart broken once, saw death amongst loved ones, left people behind – a daughter. Getting rid of desire didn't do it for Rich.

There was squawking outside, a rustle of branches and a thud on the roof. The creature jumped up and down, bending in the dried palm roofing. More squawking – an argument.

'Monkeys,' Aarti laughed.

Yelling continued a moment and they were gone; clumsily swinging away hooting. The three held silence. It was good to have space to let your thoughts roll out without feeling the obligation to converse and toss out small talk.

'Patanjali, the great pioneer of Raja Yoga two thousand years ago said: "Yoga is the practice of quieting the mind," Aarti whispered. 'Let us quiet our minds–'

Rich was amused at the all-fours pose she got them in: 'Place your hands below your shoulders and slowly arch your spine upwards – yes, slowly upwards,' Aarti was almost whispering. 'Next, gently lower your head towards your chest and look down. That's it. Now, draw a slow breath in and a slow breath out as you hold the pose.'

A stiffness in his joints prevented Rich from fully realising her instructions at first, but he pushed on.

'On your next breath out,' Aarti's voice was still quiet, 'slowly lower your back and lift your head upwards gently . . . and taking your time, breathe in . . . and taking your time, breathe out . . .' She waited for them to complete their move and then said: 'Let's do that again, now–'

Aarti's body was as supple as a child's, her joints loose and well lubricated, her limbs apparently turning whichever way she willed. She stopped a moment to tie back her hair, which she did in a business-like manner, keeping her eyes ahead on her students, and seeing Rich was not pushing up enough, came over and gently held her hands on his back to encourage him to lift it, her touch almost imperceptible to him: 'Fully up. As far as it will go – without strain or pain. There is no strain or pain in yoga. Or meditation – or life even– ' She ended laughing at her own epigram.

'You kidding or what?' Angie smirked. And Rich pushed his backside outwards with the downwards swoop of his spine and the upwards thrust of his head. 'No strain and pain in life?' Rich echoed, 'That must be Nirvana–'

They all laughed.

'You're probably right–' Aarti finished. 'Now. Downward Facing Dog–'

'You've got to be kidding,' Rich smirked. Angie already knew the position and was ahead of them.

'Kneeling on all fours,' Aarti directed, 'and now lift your knees from the floor, straighten your legs out. That's right, Angie. A bit more, Rich. Stretch your heels towards the floor. Keep your spine straight and relax your neck. Relax into the posture and breathe–'

He was finding the positions easy to follow so Aarti kept nodding a smile at his progress, ignoring her older pupil Angie who hissed a laugh through her teeth: 'How come you find it so easy?'

'Supple body and supple mind–' Aarti complimented him.

'Meaning mine's too big and stuff – this bum, these boobs–'

'We work with what we've got. And anyway, everything changes with time–'

'Flattery won't pay your fees,' Angie laughed, puffing to a standstill. 'All I can do properly is the lotus position – even then my right leg pings out sometimes–'

'Relax now, 'Aarti led them, 'we'll go into Upward Facing Dog. So now carefully start to lower your hips towards the floor – slowly now, with control – arms still supporting your upper body. That's it. Lift the chest, chin and look ahead. Feel a sense of lengthening through the legs, spine and neck, and still pushing up through the arms. Feel the Chi, the life force, flowing through each muscle and tendon – the life-energy that moves you, going through you freely – imagine it all unblocked – And breathe . . . relax . . . enjoy . . . smile . . .'

They ended up in what Aarti called the 'Corpse Position' – one Angie said she enjoyed – on her back, all muscles and limbs relaxed, eyes staring at the ceiling – and wondering whether the monkeys would come back.

It only took a few moments for his nirvana to turn to snores.

The sound of a distant tambourine caught his attention: he was up, and making apologies headed for the beach.

11

Lalima's mother Jyothi was bashing out a rhythm, while little Aditya pirouetted when Rich arrived. He spotted Lalima seconds later sitting under a tree, arms folded and head bowed. It was as though they were practising, there being no audience, and after a time Jyothi went to Lalima, shouted and gesticulated and tried to haul her up – nothing was going to happen without the star of the show. His eyes met Jyothi's and she turned away with an angry wave of the back of her hand at Lalima.

He sat with the girl, imagining her grief. A couple of crows were cawing in trees. The sea was a surge of distant surf noise. Pulling a nearby stick close he fiddled with it. Lalima still had her head bent towards the sandy floor, but he left her alone. After a time he found himself playing with the stick in the sand, writing out his full name in capital letters. Then next to that he wrote LALIMA in capitals. Jyothi sat Aditya in the shade and fed her the remains of a banana. Rich wrote her name again and again. Then he nudged her but she shook her head. 'Lalima,' he whispered, 'Lalima. Your name.' He wrote it again and nudged her again. 'Look. Lalima. Your name. Means 'Beauty'.' He wrote 'Beauty' next to it.

She looked up slowly at the letters, cheeks stained with tears. Then he rubbed it all out and started again – his name, Lalima, and Beauty, nudged her with his arm, and handed her the stick. She took so long to move he thought she was never going to take it up, but took it from him and scribed her own name out three times. When she had finished he applauded her.

'Now: "My name is Lalima"– ' He wrote it out in lower case. 'You try. Say it and write it.'

She would not talk, but she tried writing. Her script was jerky and juvenile and he had to hold her arm while she tried it again, and made her mouth the words without sounds. 'You've missed the 'e' off 'name'.' He wiped a tear from her cheek with a tissue. 'Try it. Write it. Say it: My name is Lalima.'

He waited. Aditya stuffed a large section of banana in her mouth and turned it over. Jyothi let a smile escape, her teeth browned as if smeared with chocolate. Lalima said it again louder, and again, and suddenly rushing over to her mother, stick in hand, wrote it out several times, each time, saying it aloud.

He watched her going over it dozens of times and then laughing. Her mother looked on while Aditya played with a banana skin. Standing to go he told them he would continue the lesson tomorrow.

'She marry,' her mother was erect, pulling them away. 'She marry.'

Lalima replied with: 'My name is Lalima.'

*****

When he got back to his chalet in the afternoon he found Dinesh instructing a boy of around twelve on cleaning procedure. With mop and bucket the kid was pushing the long pole under Rich's bed, wiggling it about and withdrawing while Dinesh, unsatisfied, nodded for him to do it again and the boy complied smiling.

'Kids working for you now, eh, Dinesh?' Rich greeted the pair.

'I look for someone now Rita's gone. Nikhil will do it for a few days,' Dinesh was serious.

Rich wanted to find something to say that would ease Dinesh's loss: 'Police will find who did it, Dinesh.'

'Milit.' Dinesh shook his head.

'He'll help?'

'Drink too much.'

'You don't trust the police?'

Dinesh roughly grabbed the mop from the boy and showed him to squeeze it out with all his weight so there wasn't too much water in it when he swished it across the tiles.

'How can we find out?'

Dinesh shrugged his shoulders.

'Is everyone afraid of Lakshya?'

'No one likes him.'

'He has to do something. This will be big international news.'

'That. Do that,' Dinesh half yelled at his new employee. 'You watch the man next door - Frank - he wants everything very clean. Very clean.' Nikhil stood to attention with his broom and saluted. Rich needed the long laugh he got from his pose.

Dinesh managed to join in: 'Dolphin boy.'

The sea turned yellow, slowly easing out of the white-sparkling turquoise colours of midday to a pale acidic yellow, not the intense colour of mangoes but subtle diamond spots of whitish yellow sunlight.

Dinesh's phone went, and he wandered down the veranda with it pressed to his head.

'What happened?' Rich filled in time with the boy, who was swinging one handed on the edge of one of the columns.

'Happen?'

'Dolphins.'

'I was swimming,' he spoke clearly.

'How old?'

Nikhil shrugged.

'Five? Six - Eight?'

'Yes.'

'Which?'

'Swimming. Then suddenly all goes black. Like the inside of a whale,' he put words together thoughtfully. 'No air. I'm choking.' He gestured like an actor convincing the world around his stage he actually knew what the inside of a whale was like. 'Choke, choke.' He flung his hands to his throat. 'Blackness. All.' He paused for dramatic reaction. 'Then I can see a path home, my mother is there and my friends - some I've not seen for years - and the day we went hunting and nearly got bitten by a snake–'

'Yeah?' Rich tried not to sound sceptical.

'And dolphins. Loads of them. Swimming with me, pushing me along - like surfing - their noses pushing, their bodies riding me - and then Dinesh was there, calling my name–'

'You're a good storyteller, Nikhil, I'll give you that–' Rich smiled wryly.

'There's one bad thing about this story–' Nikhil was sullen.

'What's that?'

'Nobody believes it.'

'I do,' Angie had come up with Nina.

'Is it any wonder?' Rich scoffed. 'You were gone for over an hour - under water, Dinesh says.'

'Children have the ability to see all kinds of different types of reality,' Angie said.

'Now you really do sound like that medicine woman of yours,' Nina wrinkled her nose. 'I need a drink.'

'Are you singing tonight?' Rich shifted in his chair.

'You believe me then?' The boy accosted Angie, who nodded. 'You all believe me –'

Rich looked down on him: 'It can't be proved –'

'It happened. I was there,' Nikhil protested.

'Yeah.'

Angie looked the boy in the eyes: 'If you say it was dolphins, it was dolphins –'

'In his dreams,' Nina's mouth curled into a sarcastic grin.

Dinesh was finishing his phone call. 'Devastated,' Rich hissed to them. 'He won't show it. But that famous grin has gone. His cousin, Babita –'

'It's shaken the town,' Angie added.

'Death – in Lemon Seas.' Nina shrugged, and looking out to sea, she laughed: 'Good title for a song. Might work on that one.'

'Everyone knows her,' Nikhil leaned on his mop.

Angie rummaged for some notes and shoved them in the boy's hand.

'You can't buy people out of bereavement, Angie,' Nina snapped. 'What's the matter with you.'

'It's how you do things round here,' Angie playfully ruffled the boy's hair with a shake of her hand and he laughed. 'Money says things. In a different way – a different language –'

'I need that drink.'

Pale yellow seas were slipping to pink.

'I'm not ready,' Rich told his callers. 'It's too early for me anyway. And I don't know where Frank is.'

'With his mythical German widow,' Nina laughed. 'Anyone actually met her?' Silence. 'I bet she doesn't even exist–'

Dinesh came back for Nikhil.

'Brother?' Nina directed at him. 'What sort?' She laughed: 'Brother-brother? Cousin-brother, Cousin-cousin-brother? Or just a kid you found on the street?'

'What does it matter whether he's Dinesh's real brother or not?' Angie said. 'Dinesh looks after him anyway–'

Dinesh shepherded the boy away, and Nikhil turned as he went and waved at Angie.

'I'll meet you at The Rocking Globe–' Rich got up.

'I bet Frank's got some little chick hidden away somewhere–' Nina finished, and then: 'I'm on at nine thirty. Get there.' She wagged her finger at him.

*****

He was alone as he cut through palms at the edge of town. Frank wasn't around – he may have gone inland to Chawjim, or like Nina said, linked up with his amour. The bald electric light bulbs of the town and the fluorescent street-light strips held up at an angle sent artificial rays among palm trunks, glowing into deeper shadows and the blackness out the back which was punctuated only by the occasional light from a hut or house. As he was crossing the short bridge over the ditch he was aware of Chanda, her face only feet from his as she came suddenly out of shadows. Her eyes met his, then looked away. He said her name softly. The moon was up among the branches watching.

'Chanda,' he wanted to hug her. How many men had she warmed? He held back.

'You pay.'

He was aware now of a man's body as black and straight as the trunk of a tree.

'You pay,' Milit pushed out the words, the corners of the whites of his eyes red and sticky. 'You pay.'

Payment would confirm her status – to all.

'You find the killers.' Pushing past Chanda, Rich ran his fingers affectionately down the hairs of her arm in the darkness, then headed for the bright lights of the bars and restaurants. Milit's stare and pointing finger following him and the moon tracked him through the trees.

Nina was already rocking when he arrived, standing behind black tables and silhouette people in candlelight before the lighted shrine of stage. Black top and black skin-tight jeans she had on, and a red neck scarf, scarlet-black lipstick and heavily shadowed eyes, rouged cheeks, and with her rich flat false-blond hair her face was ghostly warm.

He could not see Angie or find an empty chair, and stood in the background leaning on one leg with arms folded. He hated love.

Nina was singing something he did not know – one of her own songs, perhaps – the beat rocking, he found he was tapping his foot in sand.

'The only cure for love,' she was singing, 'is more love. Drown past love in fast love . . . make your last lover, one who doesn't bother . . . You know how you hate the picture you have of the one you had before . . . what they were to you . . . hate them to the core . . . The only cure for love, is more love . . . more . . .'

Nina was gesturing to the audience and slyly rolling her hips, while he was yessing to her lyrics and trying to bury Chanda, and moonshine was silvering sands and making a widening cone of spangles on the sea. Somehow he had transgressed and had to pay; he had not worked out yet with what and how.

'You cannot hate the person you love . . .' Nina was singing another of her songs: 'Even if you can't own them . . . or control them . . . you gotta control desire . . . so it don't set you on fire . . .'

Aarti had to be wrong about desire – it got you places, changed things.

'Desire makes life on fire . . .' Nina gyrated her hips.

Nina found Rich after her act and propelled forward by alcohol, linked arms with him. 'What d'y' reckon?'

'Good. Good,' he found himself saying.

'Yeah. Yeah,' she raised her glass of vodka and coke to the sky and rocked: 'I've got it see. I've got those songs. I just had to get them down.'

'Good line: "Desire makes life on fire."'

'Yeah. Yeah,' she threw her mouth open in laughter. 'Man. You think you can write songs? Not everybody can, only the brave.'

'Brave, eh?'

The light of the stars was beaten back by the moon's presence.

'Yeah. The brave. You put yourself down in words so everybody can see inside you, like an X ray. Yeah. You see I'm a poet as well. It's like you know, Rich, you write yourself down and it's like you're letting them X ray right into you. I should write a song about that – X ray vision, it's my division –' She whelped into the night sky, hanging on his arm. 'No derision, in X ray vision – let's do that revision–'

'You want rap?'

'Nah. Rap is crap. Even that rhymes.' She pouted. 'You don't like Rap, Rich?' She was smiling up at him, her little warm face cheery in a line where darkness met light. 'You're the one, Rich. The clever one. Are you looking for ways of curing love with more love?' She curled her lips, dipped her finger in her drink and stuck it in her mouth and jiggled it around. 'The quiet clever one,' she ogled him a moment cheekily and laughed in his face. 'You run away from love?'

'I've got a daughter.'

'You want a medal? You ran away from her? From her mother? You're not a hard bastard, giving your woman a hard time. Nah. You're all soft and slush inside. You're hurting inside from love. You need more love to cure love –' She hung on to him, smiling up into his face. 'You like my songs, don't you?' He nodded. 'Say they're the best. The best in the world. Say that. Go on.' She prodded him. 'Go on. Say it. Say it.'

'They're good.' He was stern.

'You dipstick. They're better than good. I'm going places me. Right up there,' she pointed at the three stars that had pushed aside palm leaves to get through. 'Right, right up there.' Her finger was wobbling, 'You can't get anywhere singing covers. You've got to be a singer-songwriter. That's how you make it. Did you know that, Rich? Did you?'

He puffed and shrugged.

'Tell me I'm the best,' she poked him, then slowed: 'Those brown eyes of yours. The girls like them, don't they, lovesick Rich? Come-to-bed eyes, aren't they Rich?' She drew her face up close to his with pouted lips: 'Say I'm the best songwriter in the world, Rich–'

Angie, making her way through tables, was about to acknowledge them as Rich leaned forward letting his lips meet those of the leader of the band. Moonlight silvered palms, stilled by the night as though sleeping after a busy ruffled day in breeze. Mosquitoes ventured in spaces between flesh. Angie stopped mid-flow, watching, as though the couple were a statue, and she was like stone too for a moment taking it in before turning back into darkness.

Nina was rough with him, fast and wild, thumping her body against his until she finished herself. He was happy to supply for her, let her urge herself forward. She was active in love, not one to lie there and let it all be done for her and he liked that about her. It impressed him that she could initiate, lead him, pull him along into her extended extravagant indulgences of him. Sometimes he wondered if he could keep up, worried she would taunt him with accusations about the feebleness of his efforts and energy. He managed to hang in, holding himself back and letting her rush into herself and allowing her senses to explode on him. She was quick and he held out, managing to cling on while she shot off again, then let himself go to her, his energies blowing through her in a swift depleting suddenness.

The smell of her cigarettes afterwards was nauseating and cheapened it for him, and he could not keep back from comparing her physical athletic lovemaking to Chanda's embraces, slow and tender, drawing him into an erotic experience that seemed somehow to elevate him spiritually – after Chanda he was floating weightless. Here he was worn out.

Yet he felt a clawing need for Nina, would want her again and again, and he knew she would maintain a cold gulf between them and create an intrigue for her through that impenetrable distance.

With Chanda emotions mixed with a meeting of the core of themselves in a joined intuition of love and unity. Or was she like that with all men, a faker?

It was bodies for Nina. And he was addicted. He held her and kissed her and she sank back into pillows and he enjoyed a distaste for the distance she had created through an edge of arrogance.

Stumbling back to his chalet, he burst into his room and threw himself under the mosquito net and pulled clothes off there. He could hear nothing from Frank next door, no snoring or body noises - he must be out - and Rich quickly got lost in a doze.

Chanda was gentle with him in sleep: dressed in a fine silk sari, she poured tea for him and danced.

'Get up,' they told him inside the dream. 'Get up.'

'Get up now. Come. Come now.'

Slivers of dawn through cracks in the curtains blasted his eyes as he tried to make sense.

'You come now.'

He knew to cover his nakedness.

'Come.' A hand reached under the net and pulled his leg. 'You come. Come now.'

He leaned up, squinting to make out who was there. A torch lit up his face and he put his hand up to ward off the pain in his eyes. 'Lakshya? Lakshya? And –'

Milit was pulling his thigh.

'What is this?'

'You must come to the police station,' Lakshya boomed.

'What for?'

'His phone, look,' a third figure came out of darkness: 'Ask you question at police station.'

'I don't know anything. Get Milit off –'

The other uniformed man found his phone and handed it over to his boss, who nodded over at Rich. Milit and the policeman levered Rich out of bed.

'Are you arresting me? What is this? I haven't done anything. Frank. Frank. Are you there?'

They threw his clothes at him and he pulled on his briefs and T Shirt. No sound came from the next door chalet.

'You can't do this,' Rich protested to the police chief. 'Are you arresting me?'

Lakshya nodded to them to move him out and they escorted him to the door. 'I'm not going anywhere,' Rich pulled back. There was a crash to the back of his head.

*****

He woke when the sun was high in the cell he was familiar with, its cement walls and floor grey. Milit brought him water and a metal plate of rice and peas but he could not eat. 'What is this? You can't do this.'

Milit said nothing.

They had bandaged Rich's head. 'Let me go -' he tried to yell, but the throbbing got the better of him and he lay back in the sticky heat and lost himself in a dream world. Falling through water, he found dolphins coming for him.

It was dark when he woke to find Milit and the big man opening the cell door. The henchmen pulled him to his feet and dragged him out along a corridor, passing the pleading man still in his cell and on into a room and threw him on a chair. Looking up, he found he was facing Lakshya beyond a desk, and he was aware of Milit and the big man standing behind him like guardian angels. Rich's phone was on the table, facing the police chief.

'What is this? Are you charging me? If not I'm going,' he began to get up, but the big man pushed him back down in his chair.

'I have told you, Mister Lomas, how I run this town.'

'With rupees collected from as many as possible.'

The big man struck the side of his neck.

'Mendez here can be very hard on people, Mister Rich. Too hard I sometimes think. That is Christians for you. They seem to do it all in the name of God, you know. It makes it easier for us. If Christians are doing right then they are doing God's word. Isn't that right Mendez?' Rich did not turn, but guessed the big man was nodding. 'So do right for Jesus and you'll go to heaven. Whole World Wars have been fought on that, haven't they, Mister Lomas - everyone killing for what is right - great slaughters to prove God is right.' Lakshya paused, taking a jug and pouring water in a glass. 'I must remind you of your position, Mister Lomas.'

'What is my position?' Rich spat out.

'A glass of water, perhaps, Mister Lomas. We are very human here, as you know,' Lakshya poured another glass. Rich stared at the crystal liquid slipping in the fingered glass and when it was half full, lunged forward, grabbed it, gulped and slammed the empty thing down, nodding for more.

'We like Oliver Twist, Mister Lomas, asking for more-' Lakshya laughed alone at his own joke, as he poured. 'Ah, English Literature. The best in the world is it not - Dickens - you even have women writers - Austen, Bronte, and - hiding under a man's name of course, George Eliot. But of course, Charles Dickens was - like you, Mister Lomas - championing the poor - especially through that little hero Oliver Twist. And it is us who are asking more from you. Much more. You know Milit here is owed. You know I look after the town with all its types, even the common whore you people love to frequent. She's like Nancy, don't you think?'

Rich shook his head.

'That is a pity.'

'And you could be Fagin,' Rich growled.

Lakshya bellowed with laughter.

'I need a lawyer.'

'I'm sure that could be arranged. But if you were to play ball with us, that may not be necessary.'

Rich took another gulp: 'What ball?'

'I have said, Mister Rich.'

'I don't owe you anything. I haven't done anything wrong.'

'If you use our services, you must pay, Mister Lomas, that is how it is all round the world.'

'You make Chanda do it.'

Lakshya laughed, nodding at the big man whose whack knocked him sideways.

'I do not think Milit would like to hear you say that, would you, Milit?' Lakshya shifted in his seat, nodding to the two men, who seized him and pulled him back along the corridor. The cell mate who had called for his help with a lawyer days earlier came to watch through bars: 'You.' He grinned. 'You did it. They will let me go now.'

Rich struggled, pulling away and immediately felt Mendez's arm round his throat, glanced down and saw red patterns across his wrist. He and Milit threw Rich back in his cell.

Rich slept.

12

He awoke sitting upright in front of Police Inspector Lakshya's desk, shocked at having been dressed up by them in blue T shirt and cotton beach trousers. Milit sat to his left and Mendez to his right.

'I do not want to make this hard for you, Mister Lomas. We have a friendship, after all. I am sure you have all the knowledge as an English teacher that I want to know about English Literature–'

'Try Russian: Crime and Punishment.'

Lakshya laughed again: 'But there, you see, Mister Lomas - an interesting point - did not Raskolnikov commit murder simply for the sake of it?'

'It was a bit more complicated than that -'

'He wanted to know what it was like - murder I mean - and in the end he wanted what we all want, Mister Rich - Power. Killing someone gives you immense feelings of power and grandeur - over others -'

'You should know better than me–'

'One thing I do not admire about you, Mister Richard Lomas, is your stubbornness.'

'If being not guilty is stubborn.'

'But that is for you to prove to me.'

'In my system you are innocent until proved guilty.'

'It doesn't always work that way. And from where I am standing, Mister Lomas, I think you've got a lot of convincing to do.'

'I don't have to convince you of anything.'

'Assuming you want the very thing all men want - even more than Power: Freedom. I think you need to do a lot of convincing.' He paused, smoothing down his already smooth moustache. 'You see, being in the position I am Mister Lomas I get to know the psychology of the murderer –'

'An Indian cop who reads Dostoyevsky - must be a one off,' Rich tried to laugh, but it made his head pound.

'You think we're all inferior dimwits, Mister Lomas, dark skinned little people who scamper about worshipping idols. I had a good education, Mister Lomas. Thanks to school systems set up in colonial times. You people might have had power over us once, Mister Lomas, but reflect now on who has power over you.'

Rich shrugged.

'You could go easily, Mister Lomas. And be my friend again in the community.'

'I'll go free. It might take a little time.'

'Think of the danger you might be in for that time.'

'Are you threatening me?'

'Mister Lomas, you can see how big and uncontrollable people like Mendez are.'

'You want an Englishman to die in custody in Bagolem. I don't think so - international news, *Mister* Lakshya –'

'Europeans who die here, Mister Lomas, are found in their chalets rock hard from drug overdoses,' Lakshya pondered, rubbing his chin, 'The last one's name was Gerry, I think.'

Rich was silent.

'Of course, the sensible ones confess.'

'I've got nothing–'

'I think you have, Mister Lomas–' Lakshya nodded to Milit. 'What did you see?'

Milit cleared his throat, letting out a croaky trail of words:

'He pay her.'

'Who?' Lakshya clicked his fingers impatiently.

'Rich here–'

'Mister Lomas–' Lakshya corrected him.

'Mister Lomas here pay her–'

'Pay who?' Lakshya clicked again. 'Tell me when and where.'

'I see Mister Lomas with dead girl. Babita. He pay her money. In shadows. Under palm tree.'

'I was with Babita and Lalima. I gave them money for dancing, idiot. They fixed my cut foot -'

Lakshya drew up his belly: 'But you gave money. To the dead girl.'

'I told you. They were dancing. That's what you do.'

Lakshya scowled at Milit.

'He pay big money to girl, under palm tree. Big, big money.'

'I'm a teacher, I–'

'Even in your country men go with girls, Mister Lomas, you know that - even teachers –' Lakshya mocked.

'I found her. I didn't –'

'You found her alone, Mister Lomas. So, you say. It is easy for you to confess. This big thing on your heart–'

'No, No–' Rich slumped forward, holding his head.

Mendez yanked him back in the chair.

'Shall we go on?' Lakshya breathed the rhetorical question: 'What is it to be, Mister Lomas? Surely you can see we are at a crossroads. They are always dangerous. You can sell your soul there,' he laughed. 'One way is the path to confession. I stand there waiting for you. The other - Mendez stands with arms folded. Perhaps there is yet another, Mister Lomas. You will know that–'

'You pay her,' Milit shook his fist. 'You pay her. You kill Babita. You kill girl.' He rushed at Rich and punched his chest;

Lakshya was slow to gesture to Mendez to pull him off, by which time Rich had fallen from the chair. Mendez heaved Rich back on.

'Perhaps you need another night to think about it, Mister Lomas.' Lakshya nodded to the men and they lifted him away.

'You had sex with the girl. You killed her.' Mendez whispered smiling in Rich's ear.

*****

Nightmares were punctuated with patches of lucidity: he stared out of the bars at the dying moon and thought of Jeanette, of being held by Chanda, then gasped back into the darkness of girls chained up by men.

'Rich. Come on Rich. Wake up.'

He knew the voice.

'Rich,' Frank whispered. 'Come on. Come back to us.'

'They say I did it, Frank.'

'Yes, yes, but -- have a glass of water. They've left food and –'

The high sun was baking the building.

Frank made him gulp water and held up a spoonful of rice and tuna for him, but he pushed it away.

'Frank. Frank,' Rich fell into tears. 'They say I did it, Frank. I didn't do that, Frank. I couldn't. You know that, Frank, don't you?'

Frank held Rich's head in his hands while he wept. The faint cawing of crows outside drifted in the concrete room.

'Frank, Frank,' Rich wailed as his mate rocked his head.

'Listen to me, Rich. Listen now,' Frank calmed him. 'You've got to be strong, right.' He pulled Rich's face up to him. 'You've got me, right? Strong, Rich. Can you do that?'

Rich turned away, smearing wetness across his cheeks.

'You've got me, Rich. I know. They've all gone – your mum, your wife – but you've got me, Rich. You've got your daughter. You've got to find it in you, man. You've got me with you.'

'Get me a lawyer, Frank.'

'Do it for your daughter, Rich. Do it for me.'

'Help me, Frank.'

'I'm with you. I'm here. Get your strength back. Have some food.' Frank sat him up, and spoon fed him. 'Just like I did with my own kids,' he laughed, 'years back–'

'You've got to help me, Frank,' Rich lightly chewed, bits of rice spilling from his lower lip.

'There's only one way out, Rich. I think you know that.'

'Frank?'

His mate spooned him another mouthful and he turned it over.

'What do I do, Frank?'

'How much have you got?'

'Frank?'

'Cash. How much can you get hold of?'

'Is it that bad, Frank?'

'How much? Come on, eat up – another spoonful.'

'You're a great bloke, Frank –'

'You sound like you're a Friday night drunk,' Frank pooh-poohed.

'You are. Getting me out.'

'We need the dosh, Rich. I've got so much, but –'

'You *are* a great bloke –'

'Shut it will you.'

'They're not having any of it.'

'Rich. Stop being so stubborn and pay up.'

'I give them money and they drop the charges? What kind of system is that?'

'You owe them. Chanda.'

'If I give them money, then she is a whore.'

Frank rolled his eyes at the ceiling: 'But she is, Rich.'

'Not to me–'

'Romantics, you're all the same–'

Rich stopped chewing and looked out of the window. The free world, sunny bright with the distant laughter of children, lay through the bars.

'You want to get forgotten inside here for the rest of your life because you won't pay off a tart you had your fun with? You want that, Rich? You want your daughter back home to know her dad was a paedophile murderer? That's how they'll make it, Rich – that's who you'll be for the rest of your life – if you've got much of one left by the time they've finished with you.'

Rich looked him in the eyes: 'Who did it Frank?'

Frank looked down at the remains of the breakfast, spooned up another mouthful and held it up, but Rich gently pushed his arm away: 'Frank? Who?'

'They've got their guy in the next cell.'

'He was inside when Babita –'

'He must have contacts.'

'You think–'

'You can't tell if he's innocent just by looking at him. Where are you from, Rich? You need to do some growing up. Fast.'

'Something about the way he talks, Frank.'

'Eat, you stubborn - Eat.' He thrust the spoon ahead and Rich took it. 'This is serious, Rich. Your daughter – everything's on the line here –'

Rich chewed.

'Are you just going to sit here? Do nothing? Denying it all and feeling sorry for yourself?' Frank's temper was rising. Rich gulped. 'To hell with you, Rich.' He threw the spoon in the remainder of the rice. 'I'm done with you.' He stood. 'If you won't help yourself. Be a Martyr. Be honest - a man of principle. See what good it'll do you-' He headed for the cell door and banged on it. 'You'll rot. You have a daughter, Rich. Jeanette, isn't it? Don't you owe it to her?'

Mendez was peering through the barred window of the cell door.

'Frank,' Rich called him back.

'You've got to mean this.'

'I said you're a good bloke, didn't I?'

'And I told you to shut up.'

'What have I got to do?'

Mendez's hand was holding the door, the red patterns just visible under his cuff.

'Give me something.'

'Get rid of him,' Rich nodded at the jailer, 'I don't like him,' he whispered. 'Milit is stupid. He's vicious.'

Frank waved at Mendez and the man retreated, although Rich was unsure how far away he had gone, so kept his whispering going: 'Vicious.'

'We need cash, Rich.'

'In my chalet. Bottom draw of the chest-thing - you've got to go through my dirty socks. You'll find one with some cash. Couple of hundred quid in rupees –'

'We'll need more than that–'

'These bent coppers–'

'Give me something else, Rich. You've got money coming from your mum, right?'

'I can't get hold of it yet, mate.'

'I'll put in a couple of hundred I can get hold of.'

Rich hugged him. Frank held himself straight, but Rich hung on as though he had found a new father.

'We need five hundred more.'

'You're joking.'

'We've got to get them off your back for good, Rich. We've got to offer them something real.'

Rich bent forward and whispered again: 'In the dirty laundry basket. Wrapped up in a pair of dirty shorts - in the back pocket you'll find a plastic debit card. It's all I've got, Frank. It should cover it. It's all I've got–'

'The number?'

Rich leaned his mate over and whispered digits in his ear.

Frank called Mendez back.

'You'll get me out, Frank?'

'Promise,' Frank eyed him and Rich drew him back into a hug.

'Great bloke. You're all I've got.' Then he lost his confidence: 'You will come back? Get me out?'

'You'll be okay. You've got to trust me now.'

'You've saved my life, Frank–'

Mendez rattled the keys and Frank was gone.

13

Rich dozed for the rest of the afternoon on a wicker chair on the veranda, a bottle of vodka and a can of coke nearby. Beach vendors with spangle coloured scarves trundled from one likely customer to another, flowing out sales mutterings and beaming as the sea shimmered imperceptibly from white to lemon in the sun's blast.

His slumber was interrupted by the occasional sound of a distant click. Makeshift stumps of branches and sawn-off poles had been forced into the hard flat sand near the reaching waters, and the cry of bowler, batsman and fielders rose with the occasional flick of bat against ball. Through half closed eyes he watched them: small kids with hand-me-down khaki shorts so big their thighs never seemed to touch the sides even when they ran, and tall bossy kids with dirty T Shirts with slogans – 'Live now, pay later'; 'I caught crabs at Bagolem'; 'If being sexy is a crime, arrest me'. A couple of German lads who had joined the league were fielding. Good bowlers were particularly welcomed it seemed, there being a plethora of wannabes who found it difficult to let the ball go at the top of the arc of the circling swing, instead converting the final action into an elbow bent chuck which batsmen relished with lofty swishes of the long bat at the slowly pinking sky in wild hopes of connecting with the missile. Nine times out of ten the batsman's lunge missed and the wicket keeper – never it seemed to Rich, selected for his ability to catch – found himself heading down the beach to retrieve the dirty little brown centre piece of action which he then hurled in the rough direction of the others. When batsmen did connect, the weighted tennis ball was scooped in a high arc above enthusiastic fielders who ran with cupped hands grasping at air, and who sometimes ended up colliding. A six rarely went in the sea – it was up to the bowler to bowl well enough not for the ball to end up in the water, for it was the bowler's job to wade in and get it, and by the time it reached the batsman again it was almost unrecognisable – the bowler having accidentally dropped the soggy lump in loose sand – it was a flying rock which on impact caused a spray of grains.

As pink skies mellowed to mauve, heaps of smoke from fires out the back flowed with straight plumes which expanded outwards and filtered through windless palm branches, stringing themselves out in long bulges which lingered overlong before dissipating in evening air.

The first mosquito of dusk nipped Rich's arm and he swatted lazily, missing the intrepid insect – for there was no bloody-black smudge on his skin where it had been.

When the sun had dropped behind the sheet of sea and pink darkness slipped in, cows ambled in corners, crows went quiet and black pigs snuggled up in grunting family bundles. Chatter seemed subdued at twilight, as though the world thought something holy was happening as light closed itself up and greyed itself into starry skies. Then when blackness fully opened its feelers to each corner, talk got louder and excited, shop lights flicked on and women called out to passers-by to come and get a cheap bargain.

'It's good you're so strong,' Angie assured him when they came.

'Oh, he can take it, can't you Rich?' Nina supped a vodka and coke which Rich had supplied, while Angie kept to the coke.

'I can't believe sometimes that it happened,' Rich said.

'Why would they do that?' Angie touched something in him.

'Wanted to set me up. Somehow I've upset them.'

'But how?' Angie persisted.

'Leave him alone.' Nina said.

'When I took my mum's ashes I said things to the police chief–' Rich evaded their glances. 'I think he got offended.'

'That all?' Nina crossed her legs. She had on black shorts.

'I was only joking.'

'They would lock you up for that?' Angie was incredulous. Her eyelids were painted powder blue, matching her blue slacks. 'You must have done something.'

Rich shrugged away ideas of having been set up and stuff about his involvement with Chanda.

'He told you, didn't he?' Nina blurted to her mate.

'If the police are that touchy–'

'They're like that everywhere, Angie. You're so naïve sometimes,' Nina smiled at Rich: 'She needs to be thankful she's got me around to look out for her–'

'She'll write a song about it,' Angie fired.

'Yeah. Best idea you've had all night, Angie. "The night of nights" –'

'Poor you, anyway, Rich,' Angie went on. 'Nobody deserves that.'

'He's a poor boy, aren't you, Richie-Rich,' Nina grabbed his nose and twisted it.

'Ow.'

'He likes a bit of torture, don't you Richie-boy?' She play-slapped his cheeks.

Angie looked away, sipping.

'Aren't you going to that bar?' Nina directed at Angie.

Angie shrugged, 'It all seems so strange.'

'What?' Nina was short.

'Why they would really try and pin that on you, Rich.'

'Leave it alone, will you.'

Rich shrugged: 'They can't find the real one.'

'They must be useless,' Nina kept in.

'Maybe they need somebody to load it on,' Angie speculated.

'Obviously,' her mate said. 'You know Angie, you just won't take the hint. You know what I'm after, but you won't take the hint–'

'Or they're hiding something, Rich,' Angie tried to ignore her.

'You do it on purpose, Angie.'

'If they could put in it on you, someone else gets away with it.'

'Just to wind me up. You do, Angie.'

'She could be right,' Rich's words got between them.

'So what?' Nina uncrossed her legs and crossed them the other way. 'You do it on purpose, Angie, I swear it. Just to rile me, get my temper up.'

'Get a life, Nina.'

Nina swallowed, smiled, then turned to Rich: 'Richie-Rich. We have a surprise. Just you and me. Little you and little me. A special beach. Miles away. Miles and miles and absolutely miles away from everyone,' she scowled at her best friend, then got back in his face, 'and we can do what we like there. Piles and piles of sand. Piles and piles of love.' She threw her lips at him.

He crumpled under the weight of the kiss.

Angie grabbed her bag and got up.

'Going then, Angie?' Nina pulled away and smiled up at her. 'What a shame.'

Angie forced a smile at Rich: 'Sorry what happened. If I can do anything . . .'

'You can go – that's what you can do.'

'Thanks Angie,' Rich smiled at her, rolling his eyes while Nina was looking away.

Nina caught him looking at Angie's back and half smiling: 'Bitch. Such a bitch sometimes.'

*****

The road was full of holes and bumps, the bus driver forever thumping the horn with his hand through villages. Dogs ran aside, monkeys skipped across. 'This was your idea?' Rich holding a half smile kept in his breakfast.

'I told you, it's good,' Nina scowled. 'I told you.'

The bus ploughed through more holes, then picked itself up and evened its trajectory.

'You never wanted to be a singer, Rich?' she pulled his arm. 'You've got the looks.' He shook his head. 'Just as well - I don't want any competition, do I?'

'This beach. It had better be worth it,' he joked at passing palms and roadside houses.

'I told you,' she smiled impishly. 'Deserted. Palm trees and beach and one little hut. Nobody.'

'I believe you. Thousands wouldn't.'

'You better had,' she was terse.

A group of people got on - a couple of old men and some chattering women with bags of shopping.

'Of course I believe you,' he laughed, teasing. 'You've got talent, Nina. Your songs -'

She sent out a half smile to him: 'I've got it all, haven't I? I've got new songs, Rich - you'll love them. I'm going to be out there, Rich. I am-'

'Yeah,' he liked her ambition, but was scared of it too.

Rich relived the smell of the inside of the cell, Mendez's words to him, and was not sure how free he felt.

He found the white shore short but spectacular. Cliffs shallow enough to support palm trees that climbed their sides surrounded the north end, while the crescent of the small bay was overrun with the trees. At the south end a stream linked with the sea. Lines of white surf poured in, each endlessly overrunning its predecessor. The fear would not go.

'Marty wants to help me work through them,' Nina said. Dark leaves crept from her wrist to her shoulder.

'Marty?'

'Geezer with a guitar. New bloke in the band.' She was sexy in her black bikini.

'Yeah?' Rich thought he should fly back home – get tickets, scoot. It would be safer. 'I'm sure you'll make it.' He knew the words did not sound sincere. Frank had persuaded him to stay.

'You keep saying that and you'll stay part of the inner circle.'

And Nina was fun. There wasn't anything to be afraid of now. He enjoyed the blast of her white-blond hair in the sun.

'Good?' she snorted. 'He's brilliant. Marty. Laid back but talented. This guy can play anything. I mean anything – picks up any song, just like that. But he can compose too. There's not many like that about, Rich, I'm telling you. Lots of bods can play any tune. World's full of them, but guitarists who've got real song writing skills - And. And. Get this: he gets to rehearsals and meetings on time. Must be a first for a musician–'

'He sounds a good guy.' Images flashed through him: the men, the cell, Babita's smile up at him from the mud. He should run.

They ambled along the silver shore: he pulled her to him and made her hold hands.

'What's this?' she sniggered.

'What lovers do.'

'Oh.'

'Get close and all that.'

The sea was warm on his feet.

'All that sloshy stuff – you're too soft, Rich. A damned romantic–'

'Maybe,' he shrugged.

She lit up a cigarette – as if to antagonise him – so he pulled it from her and threw it in the waves and kissed her before she could howl.

'Bastard. My cigarette.'

He could see she was holding back a cynical smile as she tried to whack him, but he fell away laughing, so she chased him through low waves and catching him pulled him down in the water and thrust her mouth to his as they rolled. She had his T shirt off and then his shorts, and pulling her black bikini aside thrust herself on him.

'Is this beach deserted, or what?' He mumbled before a mouthful of saline.

She laughed, ploughing through him and chancing herself on.

Her fulfilment was paramount he knew as they poured on to breaking point and he expired.

'Go on,' she banged his chest with her fist. 'Go on. Go on.'

But he was spent.

'Selfish bastard,' she shouted and muttering to the sea, pulled away from him: 'You blokes are all the same – you want one thing, and when you've got it, you don't care.'

Leaning up and spluttering through low waves he was aware of a couple of figures up the beach. His shorts were sliding up and back the shoreline along with her bikini parts and he ran to them, aware of the boys pointing. His first grab missed, as the sea drew them back, and he stumbled to more laughter, but clutched his shorts and pulled them on.

'Cover yourself,' he told her.

'They can do one -'

'You can't do this in India. They don't like it–'

'Who cares?' Her slim body was silver-naked in the sun, breasts bright.

He got her top and waded in for the bottom, but it rolled under and he had to fumble around beneath the surface. She was laughing now as he darted this way and that as if trying to catch a fish. Scooping it up he flung it in one movement towards her and it slapped in her face.

She stamped. 'I need a fag.' And still bare she strode off to their bags and towels. It was only because the inquisitive boys were heading her way that she pulled on her wet bra and bottoms, and scowled at them and told them to get off.

He found rock formations near the estuary with a warm pool that he dipped into, enjoying himself alone for around an hour.

She was smoking again when he got back, and looking out determinedly to the horizon.

'Have you got another song going on in there?' he nodded towards her head.

'What's it to you?'

'Tell me the words. I can help. English teacher and all that–'

'You don't know music. You couldn't do it.' She blew smoke out then buried the thing in sand, screwing it in maliciously.

Leaning over, he kissed her cheek, but she pulled away. 'Tonight,' he said. 'Tonight –'

'Tonight I'm at the Rocking Globe. With Marty.'

'I'll make it up after–'

She headed back to the bus stop, way up a long track through trees and gorges.

*****

As he sat on the veranda in the evening, a figure was out of shadows, rushing to him, her green dupatta scarf flowing behind her with her hair.

'Lalima.' It brought memories of someone he'd taught before. A Somali boy with limited English – the big smile on his face when he came to him of expectation and hope.

'My name is Lalima,' she knelt in the sand and wrote it.

Abshir had been sent over by his mother from Mogadishu, to keep him out of gangs and war. The Somali teacher who worked in Rich's school told him Abshir had seen his best friend murdered when he was eleven.

Lalima looked up at him for more.

'I come from India,' he said. 'Say it.'

She repeated. Then she was in tears again.

Abshir was late for his appointment at school on the first day and the head of year shouted at him.

'You have Aditya,' he told Lalima. She sniffled, then stopped. He wrote the words in the sand: 'I come from India.' And she began to copy.

Abshir had a temper. Kids loved to spark it, saying things about his mother. The head of year was always at him. Many times Rich had had to intervene, get Abshir working in his class as helper.

'I come from India,' she said over again.

He went inside and came out with an exercise book and pencil: 'Now write in here, properly,' he said, but her handwriting was as big and sloppy as a little child's, floating over the line, then beneath it.

'Here–' he wrote slowly and deliberately for her along the lines and she began to copy.

One day a big kid put a little kid up to say some insult to Abshir about his mother and the Somali boy beat hell out of him in the toilets one dinner hour. Parents came up – 'What are you going to do about it?'

'This is my sister,' he wrote, 'and this is my mother.' He tutored Lalima with his lips, then got her to write, encouraging her to keep to the lines, but the words wobbled up and down again. He gave her a line of 'a's to copy and join up, and then a line of 'b's and she had her head down keenly on the table outside his room.

The head of year wasn't going to consider provocation, this was bullying: Abshir was permanently excluded for fighting, left to drift with an anger problem through a society he did not understand.

Rich put Lalima on 'c's. He remembered Abshir doing the same, head down scribing.

Lalima smiled up at him and he set her on 'd's, showing her to keep to the line, join them up, keep the perpendicular line high and clear, and she copied.

He wrote: 'This is my sister Aditya and this is my mother Jyothi.'

Abshir got seven years and ended up in some prison up north. What he had done rumour did not cover. He never smiled much – never had much of an occasion to do so – but when he did look up and smile at Rich it was wide and genuine.

Aditya appeared at her sister's side, on tiptoe trying to see what she was writing. Pink-mauve sky was faltering to purple as darkness slowly moved in.

'I am a dancer,' Rich wrote for Lalima. 'Every day I dance on the beach. Link the letters nicely.' While she began writing, Rich darted inside, came back with a parcel wrapped in pink paper and handed it to Aditya. Brushing strands of hair from her eyes, she held it up in front of her amazed.

'Don't forget, Lalima – the 'a' – I am *a* dancer.'

She squeezed it in as Aditya tore at the paper. Inside, within a cellophane box, a girl doll in bright Rajasthani dress smiled back at Aditya. Rich had to open it for her, giving over the plaything to grabbing fingers.

As Lalima wrote, Aditya kissed her new friend and played with her hair. Nothing could take her gaze from the new addition to her family as she turned her over and round, looked up her skirts, adjusted her plastic jewellery, and hugged her.

Jyothi approached from the beach and stood watching the class.

'Come,' Lalima's mother ordered her youngest daughter who held the doll up in praise, 'Come,' her grey eye watching space. 'Lalima.'

'They need school,' Rich's words seemed useless.

'Lalima. Come. Challo.'

Lalima finished her line, handed it to her teacher and stood.

He nodded: 'Very good. Remember 'the': "Every day I dance on *the* beach."'

'Every day I dance on *the* beach.' She copied while Aditya pulled the doll to her side in a carrying hug.

'Box,' Jyothi pointed at the crumpled cellophane thing–'

Then Frank was on the scene: 'What are you doing, Rich? Rich?'

'Get box, Lalima,' the mother insisted.

'We don't want them round here, Rich. We'll never get rid of them.'

Lalima collected the wrapping as Jyothi scowled at Frank.

'Get -' Frank waved his arm at them. 'Go on, get–'

'Come on, Frank–'

'I don't want them here. The beach is their place.'

Jyothi pulled Aditya away, spitting on the sand at Frank's feet as Lalima gazed at the man as she set off. Turning and waving, Aditya held the little Rajasthani girl tight to her waist with the other hand.

Rich never did get to hear what happened to Abshir. He must not lose anybody else.

14

He had to admit Nina sang well that night – maybe it was the edge of things that day, or maybe she needed some conflict to fire up her creative energies on stage. She curled across the space, gyrating up to the new guitarist he concluded was Marty, a tallish guy with long black hair who stared over the crowd to a nowhere space. The two worked well together, if too erotically at times, he considered, pushing it aside: it was all part of the act.

Her song: 'Fire of Desire' burst off stage, getting everyone on the move. Putting everything into it, she was selling her song to them and they were loving it, her voice rocking the thin wooden walls half enclosing the stage. Women everywhere were chucking up sand with their bare feet as they rounded and shook to the sounds. She was good all right – lots of potential – if she didn't burn herself out or drift into self-destruction.

A short slip of silence after was filled with applause. Nina put in a slow number to round off, hugged Marty, jumped out of the lime light and headed for the candlelight of their table.

Frank had already had several whiskies and was nursing another half empty glass while spilling yarns.

'That was so good, Nina–' Angie stood and hugged her mate.

'Yeah. Great stuff,' Rich raised his glass to her.

'We can really make a sound, eh?'

Frank raised his glass to her.

'Me and Marty. We can go places, eh?'

The new guitarist was in the background sipping beer with the drummer.

'We can make it, eh?'

'Of course you can,' Angie said.

'I was saying,' Frank rambled, 'you won't believe it, but it is true. In those days there were cheap flights on Russian airlines – planes the size of skyscrapers and guys as big as bouncers flying them–'

'Shut up, Frank,' Nina yawned.

'I'm telling you – I was flying from Amritsar to Birmingham, like. Lots of Sikhs on board – elderly pilgrims to the Golden Temple and all that. Wonderful building – goldfish in the waters. You know the in-flight entertainment – for elderly orthodox Sikhs – films with half-dressed dancing girls and pop singers and simulated love making – just what they want –' They all laughed. 'Well, that's not all. We glide over the snows of Afghanistan, and then at two thirty in the morning there's this scheduled stop at some place called Ashkebad. Lovely name – rolls round your mouth – Ashkebad.' The crowd laughed again. 'In Turkmenistan. Refuelling? Who knows. Huge men in caps exit the cockpit and then, what do you know, rotund women in bandana-like headscarves with mops and buckets and brushes come on board for cleaning up – two thirty in the morning – they whistle and laugh. It could be Russia in the Nineteen Fifties. Amazing.' Frank had their attention now. 'I'm walking across the runway to a concrete airport made in Stalin times. And not another building in site for hundreds of miles – only a thin ripple of mountains on the horizon are a slightly pinked grey under edging dawn –'

'Very poetic, Frank,' Rich smirked.

'It was, it was,' the storyteller continued: 'No sign of a town. Just an airport in a vast plain where planes land for work for bandana ladies with buckets.'

'You said that,' Nina snorted.

'I followed the train of people through Nineteen Sixties glass and concrete to a bar busily empty with blaring disco music –

just what aging half asleep Sikh ladies and gentlemen want at two thirty in the morning - Kylie Minogue and all that. And they edge in uneasily, not ready for the invitation to get dancing and groove–'

'Where does this go, Frank?' Nina was getting bored.

'Leave him,' Angie laughed. 'It's funny.'

Nina rolled her eyes.

'It gets better,' Frank's words began to get slurred. 'I'm lying on the seats under these bright lights, and I'm dreaming the KGB come and haul me away to a gulag. The unshaven man at the bar tries to sell alcopops to teetotal Sikhs. Funny that.'

'Then what?' Nina pushed him again.

'Come on Frank–' Rich encouraged.

'Two hours later. Two long hours. This is half four, man. The bandana ladies are walking down the corridor with empty buckets. We're allowed back on.'

'Were you with your German widow then, Frank?' Nina made them laugh.

'Then, we're waiting another half hour, sitting in the cabin in rising dawn. Nothing happening. I say to a hostess who comes by: "Five in the morning. We want to go home. What's happening?" She doesn't say anything, but clears off up front to the cockpit, tries the door, but it's locked, and calls through. Absolutely nothing. Hostess looks awkward, doesn't she. Then. You're never going to believe this. Then. The cockpit door flies open and a flush faced woman comes out smoothing the red skirt of her uniform down and tucking in a stray blouse and laughing–'

'No,' Angie laughed. And as it sank in the others were propelled into giggles. Even Nina was upstaged a moment and trapped with chuckles: 'You don't say, Frank.'

'Then we're up and away,' Frank hushed them. 'Up in the skies, now the commies have learned our capitalistic ways. The sun's got away from the mountains and fans of light push out into stars and we rise over the pale horizon over the Caspian Sea–'

'You don't say, Frank. You don't say–'

'Of course this one,' Frank laughed over to Rich, 'this one takes pity on them all, don't you Rich?'

'Haven't found any Russians to rescue yet.'

'Brings them round our place.'

Nina interrupted: 'What does he do, Frank?'

'All the waifs and strays. I've told him. I've said. Don't bring them to your front door. I'm right, aren't I?'

Nina nodded: 'You don't want beggars knowing where you live. Never get rid of them.'

'Exactly, Nina. Exactly. You tell him. I can't get it into him. I don't want them pestering me.'

'I just teach Lalima a bit of English.'

'Do it somewhere else, if you must do it. You shouldn't be encouraging them. Isn't that right, Nina?'

'Dead right, Frank.'

'I think it's nice he does it,' Angie said.

'You *would*.' Nina snapped back. 'One thing you haven't learned, Angie, is you don't encourage them.'

'They deserve an education, Frank. And that girl has got something. If I can help–' Angie sipped her coke.

'How is helping giving them a doll–' Frank fired.

'Rich–' Nina gasped.

'You gave her a doll, Rich?' Angie's voice was soft.

'To little Aditya. You should have seen her face.'

'Mug,' Nina lit up.

'I only ever see her with a basket collecting money. What else has she got in her life? What sort of life is she going to have?' Rich went on.

'That's nothing to do with us,' Nina blew out smoke.

'Nina knows, Rich. You can't be soft here, you'll be taken for a big big ride. Don't say I haven't warned you,' Frank wagged a finger from side to side.

'It was a lovely gesture, Rich,' Angie smiled at him.

'Nina's right,' Frank threw out: 'It's nothing to do with us. They've got to find their own way out of it.'

'Which they are doing.' Rich stiffened his shoulders.

'Without us,' Frank looked at Nina: 'We keep to ourselves, right?' And she nodded. 'Anyway, he gives the doll and lets them take away the wrapping as well. Soft-head. You'll never learn.'

'So?' Rich's fingers were tense.

'You don't do that. Everybody knows that. Don't they Nina?'

Nina nodded and Rich looked to her.

'The mother will sell the doll in the original box, duffer.'

'Nah,' Rich looked away.

Frank smiled: 'It's been done before. All the time. You people will never learn.'

'You're drunk, Frank,' Angie said.

'No he isn't,' Nina snapped.

'Rich's trying to do something,' Angie persisted.

'No he isn't,' Nina was sharp. 'He's doing nothing - only raising their hopes. It's them, and it's us, That's how it is. Through time–'

'Well said Nina,' Frank raised his glass to her and gulped. 'Some have it and some don't in the world. Them that have it have to hang on to it–'

Nina nodded.

Rich endured the silence that followed and was glad when Angie changed the subject: 'There's a place,' she said, 'somewhere inland. It's called Lamilgusma –'

'And?' Nina was curious.

'There's supposed to be some prehistoric carvings there.'

'We should go,' Frank was loud.

'Where?' Nina was direct.

'I dunno,' Angie said. 'I saw it in some guidebook. It's somewhere inland. A good way - Aarti thought it might be interesting. She wanted to go.'

'We should definitely go,' Frank hectored.

'What is it?' Nina persisted. 'Rocks and things? Is it worth it.'

'Animals and people - cut in rock -'

'Like cave paintings in Europe?' Rich ventured to her.

'Yeah, I guess,' Angie replied.

'We go.' Frank was heavy with drink.

Marty came to them, a slim man in his early twenties wearing a jean jacket. Stooping to Nina he talked low to her. Rich watched as Frank raised his voice: 'Who's for it then?'

Angie and Rich raised their hands and Angie nudged Nina who lazily shouted a drunken: 'Yeah, Lami –what-ever-the-hell-it's-called –'

She irritated Rich, making up to this guitarist, and it made him want her more.

'Taxi?' Frank threw in.

'Scooters,' Rich said.

Angie was keen: 'Take two, two and a half hours on scooters -'

Nina was still engrossed in music talk with Marty.

Frank shrugged his shoulders.

'I want Aarti to come,' Angie piped. 'There's four of us - and Aarti. We'd have to get someone to take Aarti–'

There was silence except for distant waves.

'Nina?' Angie had become project leader. 'Frank and Rich on one, Nina and me, and Aarti - who can we get?'

Rich watched Nina, half her face in candlelight, half in shade. Light flickered off her stooping friend's nose and cheeks.

They were close. He wanted to break that. She turned to her posse in high tones: 'I don't know,' and was back with her new friend: 'What about you, Marty. Can you drive a scooter?' She shouted impressively so everyone could hear even though, Rich reasoned, she already knew the answer. He nodded. 'Want to see some art? With Aarti. Aarti-farty. Angie says it is. Got her head in the clouds that girl. But she says it, so it must be true. Always after these mystic things. You won't get anywhere with that,' she yelled. 'We'll come though, won't we Marty?' Nina threw her arms around Marty and pulled him into a kiss: 'You're a darling, a real darling. Would you do that for me? A girl like me? A girl like me could fancy you, Marty–' she yelled with laughter. Then: 'You coming, Marty?'

'Yeah,' Marty looked over at Rich and Rich looked away, regretting his move instantly – he should have held Marty's gaze, held on and stared him out, held on to his woman.

'Marty and Aarti,' Nina screamed to the sky: 'Marty and Aarti. I'll write a song. About Aarti-farty and Marty–'

An hour later Rich pulled Nina aside in darkness under palm trees and a half moon, the black rim of surf behind them. Marty was hanging around over near the bar somewhere putting gear away.

'Come on,' Rich pulled her. 'Come back.' He wanted to kill the addiction.

'Get off–'

He could feel her sweatiness, smell the liquor and he wanted more.

A hog out the back grunted.

'Early start. So we can get there. We all agreed–' she pushed him away.

He let her go in the direction of the bar which she had to pass on the way back to her place. Through the black shadows he saw her in the light, her face close to Marty's.

15

'You think this place is worth it?' Rich quizzed Angie about Lamilgusma. They sat on a low wall outside Aarti's grotto while she finished meditating.

'It looks interesting - you know, images cut in rock,' Angie said. 'Like the rock paintings in France and Spain, only carved rather than painted. That's what the book says. The river flooded a couple of years ago and dragged a pile of silt off a flat bed of rock - and there it was-'

He looked into the gloom of Aarti's place: 'She won't be long?'

They had all agreed to start out around half ten so they could rest in the shade by the river when they got there and not have to drive through the midday heat. Rich and Angie said they would pick up Aarti and meet the rest at his and Frank's place.

Angie shrugged, 'Nina said you've got a daughter. What's her name?'

'Jeanette,' he did not want to discuss it.

'How old?'

'Four now.'

'You must miss her.'

'Like not having an arm.'

'You've got a picture? Most people do.'

Reluctantly he took out his phone and poked it: 'There. That's her.'

'She's gorgeous. Got your eyes.'

'Nah.'

'She has.'

'I wanted to get her a little elephant–'

'I heard about that. The police and all that. Bad, Rich. They're after you all the time. But you'll get her one and she'll like that. You can get to see her?'

'Tina doesn't make it easy. You know how it goes: for a couple of years after she was born I couldn't do anything right. Told to stay away a while. Then this new bloke is knocking around.'

'Do you get to see her often – Jeanette?'

'Her mum's in control. What can I do?'

'Set up a cosy place at home where your daughter can come and stay.'

'I keep saying I'll do that.'

'Funny how the very thing we want in life sometimes eludes us.'

People were bending in hazy distance to the emerald of a rice field. 'What do you most want in life?' he said and she shrugged. 'Bloke? Money? Kids?'

'All my things with blokes go pear shaped.'

'Can't see why. You've got it all.'

'Can get 'em, but can't keep 'em. Nina says.'

'Don't listen to her,' he rolled his eyes.

'You don't love her then?' she laughed.

'Do I want to be caught up with a superstar?'

They laughed together. She eyed him carefully, then looked out across green rice fields.

'She'll be finished soon? We've got to go,' Rich hummed, but Aarti was still in pose among the purple shadows of her retreat.

Rich picked up a pebble and turned it over in his fingers: 'You never talk much about yourself, Angie.' She laughed. 'Always the quiet one.'

'What's to say about me?'

'I don't know – where you come from and all that. How you got here. I mean – you and Nina – a bit of an unlikely link up, isn't it?' He tossed the stone in the air and caught it.

'Suppose it is.'

'Suppose? The girl's a nutter,' he joked and they both laughed again.

'You said it.'

'So why her?'

'We've known each other since school. She was coming over, I needed a break to get away from it all – some bloke and all that –'

He nodded: 'We're all running from something.'

'Nina more than others.'

'Yeah?' Rich picked up another pebble. 'You're both London, then?'

She nodded: 'I don't know, Rich. I had everything at home – good parents, a boyfriend who adored me, a fairly good job in HR. I could have built a career–'

'So?'

'It wasn't enough.'

'Why not?' he pushed her, tossing the stone around.

'I kept feeling this pull. I was going to yoga classes, and it seemed right – I sort of felt myself becoming interested in that. I read up on it, got into meditation. The trouble is you then begin to feel there's something missing in your life – that life isn't all about making as much money as you can and being better than others. Then you look at your own life, and it sort of pans out ahead of you in a road that is entirely predictable – job, marriage, babies, middle age, grandparenthood, death – I know it sounds depressing but – it seems that way to me. Or does it? I mean, there has to be something more to life than getting on a treadmill and turning your feet, doesn't there?'

'What about the boyfriend?'

'That's it, isn't it? He was good to me. I couldn't fault him. Then I started talking like this, and suddenly this anger comes up from nowhere: he doesn't like yoga and meditation, he doesn't want to go to India. And suddenly he wants to control everything–'

'And this makes you even more determined?' Rich threw the pebble at a can and missed.

'Sort of makes up my mind for me. Do I want that sort of life? Do I want babies with this man? Then Nina comes along – hadn't seen her for years – says she wants someone to go to India with her so she can get into some bands. She's running away from stuff too. And that's it. I'm here.'

Rich smiled, picked up another stone and fired: 'Yeah, I guess. So we sort of came over for similar reasons. And your folks?'

'They didn't like it in the beginning. They've never been big fans of Nina – she got us in lots of trouble in school. So they weren't that keen. It was mum really – I suppose it's like that for mums – although she doesn't worry so much about my brother. It's the girls again – can't look after themselves. She grew up in a strict family – church going Jamaicans. But even she had to break away to marry my dad – your regular Londoner. They were brave getting it together – took a lot of stick down some of the roads we lived – black and white together. I admired them for that. My dad got a good job in engineering – design or something – so we ended up in St Albans – you know, posh. Not quite London. Too posh for that,' she laughed.

'She must have been a determined woman.'

'She was. I can see that now. She must have really loved him. Her folks didn't talk to her for years – there are some who still don't. I guess I've got some of that rebel in me,' she laughed.

He fired another pebble, hit the can and raised a fist in victory: 'Yes.'

They were quiet for a moment: Aarti was stirring.

'My mum told me to keep clear of the quiet ones, they're the worst,' he mocked.

'I had it all: "You don't know what's going on in her head" and: "Still waters run deep" and all that - "The dark horse of the family". I always felt at the time, not knowing what the words meant, that it'd got some racial slant to it, do you know what I mean? Like, the other one was: "She's the black sheep of the family." You can't win.'

'This yoga stuff helps then?'

'It opens things out for me. Made me realise there's more to life than arguing your point with people because you're not getting what you want –'

'I'm stuck on that,' he confessed. 'Desire seems to be here to stay–'

She said nothing, getting up slowly and walking over to the Buddha by the door. As she did so, Aarti came out: 'Are we ready?' she smiled.

'We're meeting the others at mine,' Rich checked his watch. 'We ought to go.'

*****

Frank was in his wicker chair on his veranda reading a paper: 'We said half ten,' he poked his head over the pages. 'I make it quarter to eleven now.'

'Nina's not here?' Angie said.

'I haven't seen her,' Frank was back among the pages.

Rich got a chair from inside for Aarti, and he sat on the low wall around the veranda: 'We've just got to wait then.' He caught sight of Jyothi in the distance, little Aditya holding her hand but there was no sign of Lalima.

'We should just wait,' Aarti settled herself.

'The thing is,' Frank lowered his paper again, 'we want to get back before dusk – all those insects come out – it's murder driving – they get in your mouth, your eyes – can't see where you're driving –'

'Frank is right,' Aarti said.

Angie tried to ring her: 'Nothing. Her phone's off.'

'Where is she?' Rich growled.

'Can you drive, Aarti?' Frank said.

Rich interrupted: 'We should go up and get her.'

'I can drive,' Aarti nodded.

'What are we waiting for,' Frank slammed his paper down. 'Rich on the back with me, and you with Angie on the back. We don't need them. If they can't make it, let's go.' He stood, brushing his hands together.

'We could go up past her place on the way,' Rich was adamant. 'Couldn't we, Angie?' He sought her support and she nodded.

It was quarter past eleven by the time they got to Nina's: 'Give me a minute,' she yelled at them as she brushed her hair and slapped lipstick on.

'Where's Marty?' Angie approached her.

'I don't know, do I?'

Rich stood around, not ready to step near her.

'He'll be here,' Nina hissed. 'He said he would, didn't he?'

'We said we'd leave at ten thirty,' Angie said.

'Don't go on about it,' Nina admired the colour of her lips in a compact mirror.

Rich kicked dust, anticipating the arrival of his love rival.

'What's his number?' Angie reached for her phone.

'I said he'll be here,' Nina finished with the lipstick, curled her lips and let them out.

'Let's go,' Frank was still on his scooter. 'They can follow.'

'You're not leaving me,' Nina roared at Angie.

'Where is he, Nina?' Frank yelled.

'Go then. Get off.'

A scooter pumped into view through palm trees, bunches of smoky sand bursting up around the thing.

'See,' Nina was in triumph.

Marty rolled into view, hair trailing in wind, jumped off smiling at the group and pecked Nina on the cheek.

Three scooters pelted down badly tarmaced roads through savannah, a couple of small towns, by three temples and one church, and a roadside image of Hanuman the wily monkey god. After two hours of bum-crippling bumps Nina hailed to them and they glided to a stop near the dry rocks of an old waterfall.

'This would be gushing in the monsoon,' Aarti observed. 'Everything's bright and green then.'

Smooth dark rocks with white streaks gave evidence.

A couple of monkeys were gambolling in tree tops, and two more ran across the road. So few vehicles traversed the back ways they could play long and hard, make it their own.

Without shade the sun beat the riders so they huddled under the speeding shadows of trees keeping away from the middle of the road and they were grateful when they got deeper into the forest to find the sun almost entirely blocked out.

Rich enjoyed the warm breeze as landscapes flicked past. Aarti was right: vegetation was brittle and parched, hanging on to its last green before its faded yellow died days before the monsoon.

Rich was not worried about Frank at the controls - he never took risks and missed potholes most of the time; his mind was on Marty ahead, with Nina holding on to him behind.

The snake was out quickly: as though recently tightened up like a squeezed rubber band, the reptile sprung out of undergrowth and swirled its way from one side of the road to the other seconds before the scooter could get to it. One side of the forest was connecting with the other. Out of its undergrowth it scored its silver trails over the hot road and dived back into the underworld. The lads shouted and pointed, but it was gone before the others could see.

'Guy ran over a snake in Oz once,' Frank yelled to Rich over his shoulder, his words catching the wind to him. 'Ran right over it with a motorbike. You know what? The thing flipped up with the motion of the blow and bit the bloke in the leg.'

'What happened?' Rich shouted back.

'Poor fella died, didn't he?'

'Your German widow wouldn't come then?'

Frank kept his eyes ahead: 'Useful info for pub quizzes that–' he laughed.

They stopped while Angie looked at a map as she tried to find the track off the road that led down to the site. Nina would not look at Rich. He wanted more of her, felt a vain dart of malicious desire to own her.

Tipper lorries with red dusty ore slammed past them. The sky had gone from blue to white.

A narrow track led down a sharp valley, through a gorge, alongside a small lake and disappeared into open ground with shrubs.

He could hear Angie say: 'It must be here.'

And as they dismounted Aarti ran ahead pointing at the river and the broad flat base of rock that ran alongside it. Angie followed: 'It is. It's here. We've found it.'

Nina was slow to get off, took up a bottle and swigged, then consulted Marty on the time: just after three. She looked at Marty: 'What is this place anyway?'

Frank joined Aarti and Angie and Rich tagged on. The sun would be down around seven: they would have to leave by four to miss the insects. He cursed Nina in his mind for delaying their start, adding an inward sneer for Marty; he would push for four thirty at the earliest – give people a chance.

'I can't see nothing,' Nina shouted down the platform of grey-white rock. Angie was stretching while Aarti was scouring the ground for images. Nothing seemed to stand out, just bumps and crannies.

The slow moving river was only four metres wide and a shallow curve was bridged by wooden planks and branches. A path on the other bank led through tall trees that guarded the river. The group were standing on a platform of thick laterite rock with a gentle slope towards the water.

'There's nothing here,' Nina dragged herself to the water's edge. 'I can't see nothing. Can you Marty? You got the wrong place, Angie. This is useless–'

Rich observed Marty: he seemed out of place without a guitar round his neck, and it appeared he had come along as taxi driver without much interest in art or sculpture or anything ancient. Or he had come to entangle himself with the singer of his band.

Frank disappeared behind bushes for a pee, and Rich took off his sandals and dipped his feet in the cool water. Leaves were motionless; trees strung up to the heavens were reflected in lines. The roar of scooter engine music was replaced by whispers. He wished he was alone with Nina for a moment. Chanda would have liked it here, but that was not possible – he could not think that way. Everywhere there was reddish dust on the ground: the river flowed through earth's iron.

'Here,' Aarti cried.

'Yeah. Right here. Under our noses,' Angie was pointing at the ground. The rock face they were standing on was punctuated with grooves and lines and gaps, although the grooves were deep, with the sun high and little shadow, these indentations seemed two dimensional – almost invisible in the bubbly surface of rock.

'Is that it?' Nina looked over without moving.

Rich danced his feet a moment in the water and wondered how Lalima was. He would worry about her if she was his daughter.

A boy of about ten appeared from inside bushes as though he had grown up out of the ground and sprouted from the forest, and nodding at the images said: 'Look.' He took half an empty coconut shell, scooped water and carefully streamed it along grooves: the shape of a bull a metre long leapt out of the flatness, the black water lines emboldening it.

'Come on Frank,' Rich waved him over, and the small crowd gathered for ritual sharing.

'The sacred bull,' Aarti said, 'appears on tablets in Harappan culture in the Indus Valley, two to three thousand years BCE. An image of virility and fertility. One horned. This is exciting.'

'Very,' Nina sniffed.

'This site could be older than that - even ten thousand years old.'

'Monsoon come,' the boy said, 'mud wash away. Animal and dancer –' And held out his hand to Rich for gratuities. This was an undeveloped and unofficial tourist site, but it needed to be managed by someone with entrepreneurial skills.

Angie dived in her purse and passed on a few notes, a move which pleased the guide and prompted him to move on enthusiastically to other images. His next water shape appeared roughly to be a human standing on one leg, the other bent at an angle.

'It could be a dancer,' Rich said to nods.

'Or someone standing in a yoga position,' Aarti added. 'Or, Krishna standing playing his flute - he leans his body weight on his left foot and bends his right leg in front resting it on the tip of his toes. It's so fascinating how these images continue through mythology, right down to the temple art we see now. And the Yakshis - ancient female earth spirits as depicted in ancient statues - are sometimes seen in a similar pose. They guard the precious metals and rocks and gemstones in Mother Earth. Like the goddess Laxmi in later Hindu mythology, they can bring wealth and prosperity. So in times gone by they might be found at the sides of front doors assuring good fortune. This is marvellous –'

Rich provided the guide with his next handful of coins which he quickly stubbed in his pocket.

There were more cattle, a deer, and a crudely shaped peacock with a train of feathers. He thought of his mother, then Jeanette older, like Lalima. He must find her, teach her more. Nothing must happen to her, not like Babita. There were human stick people and a standing man with arms and legs out making an X shape. A newly born child lay in a trail of afterbirth.

'Images often concern two things,' Aarti commented for them while Nina rolled a cigarette, lit and blew blue smoke out. 'Fertility and food. Humans build rituals around both. We shall never know why exactly they carved them – I mean we know there are cave paintings both in India and in Europe. Carvings are more unique. But they must have enjoyed rituals – dance, singing, painting, to celebrate those things that move earth and sky spirits to ensure food was always in supply and that they had healthy sons and daughters to continue community life. Were they so different from us? Trying to get through the struggles of everyday life –'

'We've got more stuff than them,' Nina chucked in. 'Phones and computers and stuff.'

'And we lack real symbols and images in our lives to give us meaning.'

'What do we want them for. Religion is dead. God is dead. Somebody said.'

'Nietzsche probably,' Rich laughed.

'Doesn't he know it all?' Nina scoffed at Rich and he wondered what drew him to her.

The boy guide again appealed for remuneration, Aarti gave him some notes, and he led the tribe a few steps up to the north end of the rock platform. Although the water in some of the outline grooves was already evaporating behind them, it was clear that the whole was covered in images. The next burgeoned before them: the tracks of a great labyrinthine circle of about two metres diameter with around seven concentric circles was soon blackened by the boy's dribbling water as he guided his hand as though drawing the shape out for the first time himself.

'Oh my god,' Aarti lost herself. 'This is just wondrous.'

Nina was smoking and chatting with Marty now while the others stood around Aarti anticipating her guidance, although for a time she was too moved to talk.

'This . . . this, I think they call a triskelion . . . three heads like serpent hoods in the middle. Look. You get images like this in the Celtic Tradition. And they used the swastika – which we see as an image in Hinduism – like the mandala, the image of the cosmos, and the image of the individual in the cosmos. The whole thing, the triskelion, might also be a sun image with rays coming out to serve the earth. So it might, as is supposed for similar shapes found in America, be used to measure time and the seasons? We don't really know – and can only speculate –'

Frank was engrossed along with the others, his shadow long over the leaping forms. Angie was watching Rich watching Nina who was twirling on one foot in front of Marty by the river in a sort of dance for him.

Fertility.

'Is that it, then?' Nina called to them. 'I'm hungry.'

Food.

'All that driving for a bunch of scratchings they say is thousands of years old,' Nina let go. 'You could have fooled me. It might be a tourist set up, eh Marty?' He nodded. Rich thought he was good at nodding. 'We should get back.'

'Look at this though,' Angie tried to get her involved, taking photos of the carved labyrinth sun disc with its rings blackened now with the darkness of water.

Out of the shade the sun hammered heads. The river was cool and slow with silver reflections. He saw Babita under the surface. A chill went through him. Where was Lalima?

'Nah. Seen it Ang. We should get back: insects. Marty's got to play tonight. Needs to rest first.'

'You never said that before,' Angie challenged. 'His gig and all that –'

'Never asked, Ang.'

'Aarti wants time here, we've only had half an hour.'

Nina pouted and shrugged, drawing on a cigarette and blowing out a plume of blue-grey smoke. She shared it with Marty who was kicking the ground.

'They truly are amazing,' Aarti kept her gaze on them.

Nina mimicked her and Marty laughed. The river was slow behind. The boy was after more rupees and Aarti paid up.

'She's stupid,' Nina hissed in hush to Marty, starting them giggling.

'More mud,' the boy pointed upstream at a bank of silt. 'Flood come and more picture . . . Nobody see before . . .'

'Yeah,' Marty could not resist: 'Or you made them, little boy. And your mates. To make a bit of dosh–'

Finding a spot near the triskelion Aarti sat in lotus position and closed her eyes, and as Angie was making moves to join her, Nina strode over.

'Nah. Nah. There's no time for that. We're not meditating now. We're going home.'

Aarti was about to get up but Angie motioned her back: 'Aarti wants to–'

'You can be so selfish sometimes, Angie. You must have been spoilt as a kid. You don't think of the needs of the group.'

'The needs of you, you mean.'

'There you go again–'

Rich tensed his shoulders. Frank was poking about on the bridge, dipping his foot in the flow like a kid. The sun was behind the trees.

'Marty's got to get back,' Nina had a hand on her hip.

'You turned up really late,' Angie held her gaze, 'so we left late. Now we have to leave early.'

'I don't know what I'm doing with you, Ang. I don't.'

Aarti was getting up: 'We can go. It's all right.'

'It's not all right, Aarti,' Angie insisted.

Frank was out of shadows: 'You two go ahead.' He nodded at Marty and Nina.

'We don't know the way.'

'Take the map. We'll work our way back ourselves,' Angie took papers from her bag and handed them to her.

'We should all go back together,' Nina turned away.

'I've got to play tonight,' Marty rolled his eyes.

Rich stared at Marty: 'He's got to get back. We've got to go.'

'Rich?' Angie scowled.

'Thank you, Rich-boy.' Nina laughed in triumph, 'Let's go.'

'Aarti and me are staying,' Angie held on, and they stood around the rock cut platform like statues that had grown up from it.

'I don't believe you, Angie. You're a little - When I need your help you're never there.'

'We all go,' Aarti was on her feet.

'No,' Angie was finding something inside herself: 'We stay. You want time here to meditate and take it in.'

'The others go then,' Aarti tried.

'Listen,' Frank gesticulated, 'I'll show you the way on the map Marty, and you two can go ahead. If you get lost wait, and we'll catch you up. You've got phones, what's the problem?'

Rich frowned at Nina.

'We should all go together. It's safer,' Nina attempted.

'We're in the outback forest in Goa, Nina, it's all villages,' Frank laughed, 'Who's going to get you? A monkey swinging from the trees.'

Angie choked a laugh; Nina slapped her thigh.

Frank came over and muttered a route through with Marty, the men nodding.

'What are we waiting for?' Nina headed for the shade of the scooters, her sandaled feet crunching over carvings along the way.

'We could go with them,' Rich tried Frank.

'Leave these two women on their own, Rich? Anyway I want to hang around longer myself. We've only just got here.'

Guitarist and singer mounted. Rich's gaze was on her, remembering her breasts silver under his hands, as he wondered what her real motive was for going early.

'You can be a real pain, Angie,' Nina left the words for her to meditate on as the scooter disappeared in a pile of red dust.

Words stopped echoing through trees and the river rolled on like silk. Rich avoided Frank's eyes, carelessly kicking the sun-greyed rock and aimlessly gazing at the trees on the other side of the river while the two women immersed themselves in another world. Placing themselves on either side of the triskelion, they sat in lotus position with closed eyes.

At first Rich found himself angry that he had been ineffective in letting Nina go. But as the water sluggishly idled by he found himself envying the calm decisiveness of the women and the quietness they brought to the place. Without Nina even the trees seemed relaxed, and as he stood with his back to the river and faced the rock carvings the labyrinth seemed slowly to roll clockwise, a cosmic wheel revolving through dimensions and transgressing barriers of space and time. Cattle etched in rock motioned steadily, turning this way and that. A peacock raised its tail and spun a fan, rippling for its mate. Men danced. A woman stood on one leg, the other crossed in front of her; she danced letting her costume twirl and flow.

Men came, and women, with sharp stones, blocking out in rock communities, marking out history, celebrating existence; they painted stories with grooves, everyday occurrences that tracked the journey through physical experience, the everyday, the joys and lows of working through life and surviving – carved roughly by ordinary folk. Not artisans or priests, but people directed by ideas that seemed to be taking on some sacred significance; images that attempted to visualise and symbolise mysteries hidden in life, and exploring timeless questions: where do we come from? Why are we here? Where are we going? Where does death take us?

Yet there seemed to be a peace in that for him, an uprising through his body of an acceptance of all that in an easy manner, without tension and fear, a place where he could feel conscious yet be unafraid, a coolness of mind and purpose, that little mattered except resolution of consciousness and an acceptance of the being of all things and all situations – that nothing was an obstacle – all things being a test of the individual's being and creative ability to overcome and thus achieve personal spiritual greatness through maturity and wisdom.

The flick of eternity he experienced seemed to last for hours, but when he looked at his watch only minutes had passed. The earth came up to him again, raising pulses from its core. The rumble of the planet's being seemed to shake him a moment and thrill him with a whorl of timelessness. For a flash he could see himself chiselling at rock, and he did not feel alone for a moment but connected to wider consciousness – the eye of the planet as it gazed out of the realms of the vacuum of space and on in and back into itself. He was on the verge of the carvings and close to falling in, but was buoyed up by energies bulging upwards from the earth's entrails, and had to give in to that.

Sitting near the labyrinth in lotus pose with straight back and closed eyes, Angie had a pious look about her face. Yet he couldn't help but like her. She took herself too seriously he thought, and needed a lot of reassurance and humour to bring out a cheerful, playful side to her, but she was a good mate, and he wondered why he could not fall in love with her instead of prickly Nina who dipped in love but was afraid to stay with it and go under. She who had to be in control. She whose coldness and physicality stimulated him.

Things had changed in him when he stumbled on the thirteen-year-old girl lying in mud like a log and staring up at the stars. One day he would bring Jeanette here, keep her safe. He was troubled about Lalima.

'Rich,' Frank was already on the scooter. 'Rich.'

All things stopped dancing.

Frank's face was ashen: there were things he never shared - you couldn't get in that deep with him.

Aarti was starting the other one up and Angie was getting on. He was shaken back into other worlds.

They spun through trails of forest: trunks and branches and leaves became blurred lines of green and yellow. Rich threw his head back to watch the stationary sky.

After an hour and a half as they approached the dry waterfall he could see a scooter ahead by the side of the road, and they cruised towards it to meet up with Marty and Nina. Sitting on the ground in the shade the pair were laughing and smoking. Rich jumped off and gobbled down some water. They looked to him like a couple who had been together for a time. They'd been sexing it up in the undergrowth, he knew it. They should be far ahead of them by now. And it made him want her more, and he hated himself for it.

16

Shouts and bangs woke Rich early. The white of morning light on the beach was blinding his half-awake eyes still tight from sleep as he stretched on the veranda in his shorts. Light mist drifted over the river. A few fishermen were pulling a craft from the surface tension of the sea, its turquoise movement lapping and sucking in an attempt to draw it back, but the sodden hull dragged itself up exhausted, half a dozen men hauling with rigid arm muscles and taut backs and bulging calf and lower muscles. Every so often it paused, more wooden runners were placed ahead of the bow and painted with an oily black lubricant so the cherished creature could ease its way over sand without digging itself in.

Satisfied, the men stopped for breath, muscles relaxed, and poked nets about, lit cigarettes, while others pulled up bulging baskets of silver and white sea life.

Women came out of trees, propelling their bodies on legs hidden under purple, red and green, their expressions set for business. Some brought lined faces and widening midriffs, others were thin and undernourished, a few had young smiles.

Rich watched the bartering: money for fish - star-like creatures that seemed to have fallen out of the night of the sky's ocean to fill the purses of women who would sit cross-legged on streets with their dead wares assisted by dancing flies.

The sound of Frank stumbling in next door had woken him.

In the distance he could see a woman and girl holding hands and a man approaching from mists. Rich dashed inside, pulled on a T shirt, and ran up the beach.

Milit met the woman and gave her something – money perhaps – as vapour billowed round his body. He was gone by the time Rich was in shouting range: 'Lalima. Where's Lalima?'

Jyothi turned to him and Aditya smiled.

'Lalima?' he smiled, trying to bridge the gap between himself and Lalima's mother.

'Go. She go,' Jyothi waved her hand sharply.

'Where?'

Aditya looked up at him with big eyes.

'Go. She go.' The mother's fingers were trembling.

'She will come back? I want to teach her – more English. It's good for her – will help her –'

Jyothi's grey eye stared at him.

'Where? She's all right? How can she be all right? Is she missing? Do you know where she is?' he tried to push down new fears with smiles, but was aware that they must look fake.

'She go,' Jyothi turned away and shivered.

'She's all right?' Rich found himself shaking her arms but the woman looked down.

Aditya pulled on his shorts.

'Aditya. Your doll. Where is it?' The child kept her smile. 'Where's her doll?' he addressed Jyothi as though she were a negligent adult at a parents' evening in school.

The mother pulled her daughter away.

'You didn't sell it?' he called after them as Aditya dragged on by her mother stared back at him. 'You sold it off. The doll. Like Lalima?'

'Go. She go. Marry.' Jyothi turned to him, a tear falling from the grey eye.

'Where? Who? You got money for her, didn't you?'

Jyothi said nothing.

'Where is she then? Where's her husband?' Rich stood, hands on hips watching Jyothi pull Aditya away, the little girl hanging back looking at him.

*****

'What did you feel, Aarti?' Angie asked when they had got back from Lamilgusma. Rich had agreed to go along with Angie for another session. 'I mean, I don't know, am I doing it right?'

'You just relax into it.'

'What happened to you at Lamilgusma?' Rich blurted suddenly at the teacher. 'You were far away – what happened?'

Aarti smiled: 'It is only love and the vibrations of love that hold the universe together. Everything else is an illusion.'

Snake lines of incense smoke twisted up towards the ceiling. Rich was not sure of things when people spouted the hippy sort of stuff.

'We're just experiencing that illusion through five sense reality – a reality that is fragile and holographic. It was clear to me then in Lamilgusma, the words coming from somewhere deep in me – almost like they were spoken by somebody else, but somehow they were my words, if you know what I mean.' She poured them all a glass of water from a jug. Angie had managed to sit in lotus position opposite her teacher, while Rich was propped up by cushions. 'The Hindu mystics and the Buddhists taught that we are travelling through a great illusion – Maya – a dream, that is what life is. When you die it's like waking from a dream, and you go back to that part of consciousness that you belong to, for beyond the illusion is consciousness. And consciousness responds to vibrations of love–'

He did not see Jeanette as an illusion. Nor Lalima – the sort of child Jeanette would grow into. A cow was lowing in the distant rice fields out the back as if in agreement.

'Which is why we have to wake up and stop killing one another. It creates low vibrations, thoughts of morbidity, revenge, hatred and the lower emotions that brood for centuries. Non-violence must be the next stage of human evolution that we aspire to.' She paused. A baby was crying somewhere. The smell of Indian food being cooked - onions, garlic, ginger - came through walls and he was fascinated by the fabric of illusion she spoke of, yet stumbled.

'We have to rise from that and see that walking away from killing requires greater spiritual energy than giving in to it.'

'All that revenge out there,' Angie was nodding all the time and following Aarti's eyes. Maybe Angie would fall in love with her she was so enamoured. Yet when he looked up again, Angie's eyes were on him. Aarti's ideas were fascinating on one level, but seemed wildly impractical on another.

'At Lamilgusma I glimpsed something of a world where people had come to terms with the pointlessness of killing. Of the need for peace and spiritual growth–'

Lines of incense wavered. Monkeys and kids played outside. The baby cried. Aarti made it sound too easy for Rich.

'An easy ability to see the right path in complex times.' Aarti finished.

'You saw all that at Lamilgusma?' Angie raised her brows.

'Feelings like that have hovered round me for years,' Aarti gave a nervous laugh. 'Even as a child. It's just that it woke up in me and found words to express itself. The important thing is to find that love–'

'It's just that the word is so clichéd,' Rich intervened.

'I'm sure you don't see your love for your daughter as a cliché, Rich,' Angie prompted him.

Aarti sipped from a glass. 'Unless we want to destroy ourselves completely, we must find a way of expressing it as a form of giving, forgiving and understanding. Letting go of our own way. If we can do that we can see there is nothing to fear. Fear is our greatest threat - the antithesis to love - fear of what others think. What a big one that is.' She laughed, then: 'Fear of death. Even bigger. Through meditation we can free ourselves.'

The child had stopped crying.

After a few yoga positions Aarti left them in their own worlds. As he meditated, Rich tried to envisage a unified earth, but it disintegrated and fell apart into violence. He was searching mountains and deserts for a key to that unity, but ended up finding Lalima dancing on a beach. She span, twirling her skirts like a courtesan in a Mughal court, round and round; dervish-like she swayed, laughing. She delighted him with nimble steps and flying hands, as though conjuring up some goddess from the depths of time: dancing a dance of life and profundity. With a shake of his body she was gone. As he flipped his eyes open a shiver ran across him: where was she?

*****

He strode through palm groves in search of her, going to the places she danced: near the estuary, under the cliffs on the other side of the river, down the south end of the beach near the restaurant that hung out over the sea. Each beach vendor that approached him with scarves and trinkets he asked for knowledge about her but received only head shakes, or advice to try other places. He checked waiters at restaurants, and when he came across tourists he had seen watching her, accosted them. He walked through the village at the back of the main street, asking women. Nothing. One sent him up river. A track led through shrubs and thorny bushes alongside muddy waters. A heron looked over at him and stalked off.

The way opened to a sandy grove under palm trees abreast of the river, their reflections perfect in its stagnant flow. Fifteen or so abodes had been crudely handmade: plastic sheets draped and tied or weighted down over branches. Two girls of around four or five were playing with a ball; women were carrying pots of water or tending to fires, making roti on pans, or stirring pots of fish and vegetables. The smell perked up his appetite.

'Lalima. You know Lalima?' he looked down at a squatting woman who was working dough for chapattis. She looked up at him blankly, then back down.

'Do you know her? Jyothi, her mother, and little Aditya?'

She would not raise her head to him again, but looked to the side.

'Does she live there? In that one?' He had hands on hips.

A man was behind him: 'Go.'

Rich turned to his grimace: 'I'm looking for Lalima.'

'You go now.' The man waved a stick.

Rich had been over eager to find her, not thinking about how it would look – a European man searching for an Indian girl: 'I can give you money.' He poked around in pockets coming out with a couple of notes and handing them out to the man.

'Go,' he raised the stick and Rich stepped back, showing his palms.

'Okay. Okay,' Rich was about to put the money away but looked down again at the woman working.

'Lalima, Lalima,' One of the little girls danced around her mother. 'Auntie Lalima. Aditya. Aditya.'

'They live in that hut?' he pointed.

The girl nodded, then: 'Gone.'

'Go. You go,' the man whacked the ground with his stick.

Stooping, Rich gave the notes to the girl who took them quickly, rolled them round and slipped them in a secret pocket.

'Okay. I'm going,' Rich told the man, moving towards the other tent-like structure, and bending – the man still behind him – looked in.

The girl had followed too, and bent sideways along with him to gaze inside: 'Aditya have doll.' She crawled inside the home, rummaged through bedding, came out with a small drawing and handed it to him. A stick girl holding a doll in Rajasthani dress – red and gold, with earrings.

'Where is Lalima?' he whispered, then endured the crack of the stick on his arm. 'Hey. Hey.'

'Go. Go.'

'I'm going, I'm going,' Rich yelled, then in hushed tones to her: 'Did she get married?'

The girl shrugged her shoulders. He found another two notes, gave her one, and her staring mother another. The mother snatched, clicked her fingers for more, which he found, and nodded towards her daughter.

'No marry,' the girl said, 'no marry,' shaking her head wildly.

*****

On the way back Chanda appeared through the gap in the trunks of palm trees and he did not recognise her at first, the light being behind her. Carrying a plastic bag of coconuts, she was following a path that rounded territory run by hogs, a bunch of snorters rustling through undergrowth and rubbish, tails wagging. She would have kept her head down and passed him like passing any other European man, but he stopped beside her and she looked up in his eyes and jerked back.

'Chanda?' he wanted to hold her jaw softly between fingers and thumb and kiss her.

She looked down, was about to go, but he touched her arm gently.

'Chanda.' His desire now was to get some sort of reassurance from her, that what they had had was genuine, not sordid.

'I must go,' she looked around anxiously. Sea breeze puffed up through palm leaves, and the cries of cricketing boys wafted up from the beach.

He wanted to say what she had meant to him. Not the money – he hated that. But he ached and could not find words: 'You are beautiful,' he fumbled. 'Really.' And it all sounded forced and fake.

She flicked a glance in his eyes and he thought she had an urgency for him too. He wanted to sum up the impossibility of their love, if she really felt that too, the irresistible tide of it as it surged through them, drawing their bodies into something they could not deny. Or was that stuff he had made up inside himself in an effort to concoct a story in his mind of how she felt for him, when he did not really know. Yet her eyes seemed to say that. 'Men are useless at reading female body language,' he ended up thinking.

'I want him to go,' Chanda said with quiet determination. 'Go, I say. Go now.'

Rich shook his head, not understanding.

'His brother in Bangalore, he has a business. He has many shops. If he goes there he will get a good job. Not this. Not here. This–' she spat out the last of it.

'Milit?' he quizzed. 'He will not let you go?'

'Go, I say,' she stamped her foot. 'No. Lakshya. He will not let him go.' She flung her arm out. 'He could be a businessman and no drinking. No–' Rich watched the frustration line her face. 'There is a good man there, somewhere, in him. Deep. When he was a young man, he was so brave. Handsome. All girls like him.' He observed the tearful frustration in her expression. 'Lakshya. He holds men in chains.'

'And women, it seems– ' Rich whispered in the breeze. The sea was pouring itself over the line of beach behind. Tourists lay on lounge beds with lines of cocktails by them while uniformed waiters shifted with made up grins: nothing was too much trouble.

'Lakshya,' she hurled the word out, 'took my husband, make him a crook. Drunk and - crook –' She shook her head and tears flowed over her cheeks leaving glossy lines.

He bent forward and kissed her cheekbone, but she quickly stepped away, looking round for eyes among trees, but then quickly she squeezed his wrist. If only the wheels could run right and they could have each other. Nina did not exist at that moment.

He watched her drifting through palms, past hogs, and a rat on its way to a pile of wasted food at the back of a restaurant. A man met her by a stone bridge over a dry stream of detritus. There was agitated talk: Milit was yelling and pointing in Rich's direction. The blow he landed powered her to the ground. Coconuts rolled from her bag across grassy sand. Rich was on the run. He would have dived at Milit but Chanda scrambled up and got in the way and kept pushing Rich off.

'They will get you,' she screamed at Rich, 'Lak's men. Get you –'

She would have a swollen bruised eye. She heaved at Rich.

'Bastard. Bastard.' Rich tried to swing a fist, but Chanda stopped it by yanking back his shirt sleeve.

'My wife. *My* wife,' Milit yelled.

'Where's Lalima?' Rich shouted, 'You paid Jyothi. Where is she?'

'Go find her.'

'Go to Bangalore,' Rich could not control his words: 'Get a proper job. You've got a brother in business. Get out of here. Be somebody –'

'You tell him?' Milit fired at Chanda who was bending to retrieve the coconuts. 'You tell him?' His fist was ready again, but Chanda, rising, saw it coming and ducked and Rich caught his arm.

'Pissed again, Milit. Always drunk.'

Milit spat in his face and pulled his arm from Rich's grip. Rich was ready to strike again, but Dinesh's hand intervened: 'Come Rich. Come now.' Rich would not move until he was sure Milit would not hit her again. Milit laughed at Rich, but something of what Aarti was going on about seemed to have come out in him and he surprised himself.

'Tell her to go ahead. Keep him here,' Rich urged Dinesh.

'The motor on the boat is not working,' Dinesh was quick to respond, 'Milit –'

Chanda was along the path near the old gate to the village, her shape covered in green and yellow blended with the foliage and she was gone in shadow.

'Come Milit. Help,' Dinesh stood between the men. 'Help us fix the boat.'

Milit spat at Rich's feet and pointed in his eyes: 'You go. Out of here. You go. Home.' He nodded smiling. 'Or Red Hand man. Red Hand man will get you–'

'He knows where Lalima is. He's in on these disappearing girls,' Rich yelled.

'Come Mil,' Dinesh led him.

'Where is she, Milit? You know –' Rich scowled at the backs of the men.

17

Nina rocked through a couple of numbers she had written with Marty that pleased the crowd at The Rocking Globe, one about a woman divided between several men. Angie nodded a wry smile across the table at Rich who shrugged and looked away: 'Personal experience,' Angie said, 'we assume.' Rich shifted in his chair. The second song was about a woman searching to find someone she could really rock with and apparently failing. 'Words tell a lot about us,' Angie whispered.

'Don't they,' Rich kept his eyes on the stage. Nina was cocksure, flinging her arms out to the moonlit sky and yelling into the mic. His shoulders tensed.

Frank was supposedly off with his German widow - still nobody had met her yet and people could only guess at her wealth, or lack of it.

'Marty's in one,' Angie observed and Rich looked from singer to guitarist. 'He's all stiff and - not his usual self - they must have had a bust up, or something.' She was smiling in candlelight. 'If he doesn't write songs how she likes them–'

Nina pushed through the crowd to their table afterwards in her black get-up - leggings and bomber jacket, bleach-blonde hair, pierced nose, ears, eyebrow - dumped her arms around his neck and slammed her lips on his cheek. Angie leaned out of the light.

'Come on Rich. I want to sit on your knee,' Nina laughed, pushing him to pull out his chair and let her dive on. He was aware of Marty's edgy scowls in distance on stage as she clung onto him. 'Good or what?' She smiled her beer stained breath in his face.

'You're always the best Nina,' Rich supplied.

'Ye-es,' she jeered at the night, 'the be-est,' bunching her fist. 'Marty's got the hump, mardy so-and-so. I told him how I wanted the guitar licks. "What you don't understand Marty is this is *my* song, not yours. I'm the writer. You just do the backing–"'

'He is a good guitarist,' Angie ventured out of shadows.

'Only because of me. I do all the hard work.'

Angie sent a look at Rich and he looked away.

'You don't understand what it takes to make a good song, Angie. You've got no idea. What people don't get is *I'm the one*.'

'If you say so,' Angie managed.

'You really don't get it Angie, I don't know why I bother.'

'You want another drink?' Rich tried to defuse the tension.

'Don't get her any worse,' Angie fiddled inside her bag.

'Come on lover,' Nina leered at him loudly, 'I can see you need me.'

'Don't make a show of yourself, Nina,' Angie said.

'Who cares? I'm here. It's me,' she leaned back and yelled. 'Let everybody know – I'm a singer-songwriter. Get it.' She shouted to the crowd. 'Why do you come along if you're so jealous?' She pulled her man close. 'Jealous of my talents, jealous of my men. Get a life, Angie. Or get a man. If you can.'

Angie clipped her bag shut and stood: 'There's some girls I met at a bar, I'll go and find them.' She sent a strained half smile at Rich.

'Or if you can keep them–' Nina called to the darkness after her, then pushed her lips on Rich's.

Rich pulled away: 'She means well,' he found himself saying, 'looks out for you–'

'What's the matter with you? In love with her? Another git to write a song about.' Nina poked her finger along his lips. 'Thing is though, you can't get enough of me, Richie-boy, can you? I know you. What you need. Come on–' She jumped up and pulled him out of his chair.

Tugging his hand she let night envelope them on dry sandy flats by the river. She wanted him up against a tree and tiring of that pulled him on the ground, urging him faster. The moon was between branches. He seemed alone, detached from her enjoyment and kept thinking of Chanda. She breathed on, yelling for more pace, but there was nothing for him, his mind weighted by memories of Jeanette, Tina, his mother, and he was sweating and weak at the knees and lost it.

'What are you doing? Bastard.'

It had gone from him and he could not work it.

'I didn't come. I didn't come,' she yell-hissed. 'Make me come. Make me come.'

He turned away.

'You're all the same. Useless. Who cares about me?'

He tried to pull her into a glorious hug but she threw him away.

'I can't wait for you,' she pulled clothes together and was off, stomping through sand. He hugged a palm trunk, gaining breath, and slipped down in sand.

When he walked back home by The Rocking Globe Nina was curling her body round Marty.

*****

Turtle Beach was long and straight and wide with heavy rollers packing themselves in from the Arabian Sea. A line of pine trees backed smooth sands and down the south end a wide river estuary opened its mouth to the ocean. Marty and Nina had been playing in the lagoon of the estuary but had now retreated to the waves, pushing each other under.

Angie led Rich to a square of sand fenced off: a rectangle the size of a grave with big 'Do not disturb: Turtle eggs,' signs around it. 'They crawl up, the mothers,' she told him, 'on certain full moon nights, hundreds of mothers, dig holes and bury their eggs. Then head back to the sea. Ages later, they hatch, their little ones, motherless and fatherless, and scurry to their home at high tide – in the hope that dive bombing seagulls and kites don't get them. What mothers will do, eh? How life must go on.'

'We've looked and we still can't find her,' Rich scowled to the horizon.

'We've tried, Rich. That's all we can do. You said she comes here sometimes.'

'I feel as though I'm doing nothing.'

A wave pounded in behind them.

'You see Lalima like your own daughter, don't you?'

'All grown up, and–' he pushed aside tears. 'It's as if I could find her, I could make things right again.'

She held his arm gently. 'That's a great thing to feel, Rich.'

'I know it's stupid, but–'

'No. How many guys do I know who wouldn't even know where to begin with that–' She filled the silence that followed with more facts: 'Some turtles live to make a hundred and fifty.' She laughed.

'Not me,' Rich joined her. Nina and Marty flicked spray at each other and yelled. Rich curbed his laughter: 'They're having fun.'

'She can't help it Rich. I've seen a lot of blokes hurt–' She glanced over at him.

'You're so different.'

'She's not the touchy-feely type, that's for sure. Scared of real affection. Scared of being loved, probably.'

'You know all this stuff?' he grinned.

Angie had a yellow bikini on and she looked good; he should say so.

'Abusive childhood, Rich. You know what it does. Uncles and uncle's friends, all wanting a piece of her. Messes you up.

It's hard to get out of that and find out who you are. She's doing her best at that. Thinks sex will heal the wounds, but all it does is open them wider –'

They ambled to the wave line and waited for waves to suck at their feet.

'How long can you be her friend?' he said.

'How long can you be her lover?'

Marty was holding Nina in waves. A roller burst in and knocked them over.

'We're both hanging on,' Rich's laugh was uncertain.

'But you want her,' she said and he felt her reading his eyes. 'There's always something intriguing about something you can't have, can't get and hold, eh?' The sea crashed over their feet and up to their knees and Angie yelled, pulling back: 'She could never handle other people's kids.'

'Are you trying to get rid of me,' he laughed.

'I've seen too many sensitive guys hurt. She's rock and roll, Rich. You have to take that on board. What's the words to her song: "I take all, and all takes me . . ." She's going to take everything, because when she was a kid everyone took everything from her. You've got to understand, Rich. She wouldn't want me to say – but her step dad, he was as bad. It was awful. And before she came here, the previous boyfriend. She did have feelings for him, but he couldn't handle her drinking, they had a fight, he drove off and smashed the car into a tree. Dead and gone forever. She's getting over that, Rich.'

'Why doesn't she tell me, let me share something of that?'

'Too proud. We are who we are, Rich. And she's locked in herself. All that talent she's got – and, she can't show love.'

'Who can?'

She looked at him.

'You think anyone can?' Rich spoke his challenge softly: 'Show love and you get hurt. We've all been through it. What about you?'

'Me and Les didn't connect. I had to own up to that, he never would. We wanted different things. He was into making as much money as fast as he could by all means possible. You end up feeling you're just another prop they use to get them down the line.'

Nina had pushed Marty in and he was rising from waves, his jeans and T shirt soaked. She was bent double laughing, her slim body blushed by weeks of sunshine, in a black bikini.

'He'll get hurt and move on,' Angie was looking at Marty. 'I don't want to sound bitchy, Rich, but you do know what you're doing?'

He looked away. The sky was white. In the distant north the island near Bagolem was a hazy bud out of the ocean. Nina was leading her soaked man to a bar under the trees. Rich picked up a shell, 'how do you know what real love is anyway?'

'That's easy,' Angie laughed: 'Mother turtles braving all to come up a beach and lay.'

'It all gets mixed up with other stuff.' She was quick to perceive, so he had to pick his words carefully: 'Life's confusing; love's worse sometimes.' Finding the shell plain, he dropped it.

She kicked sand. 'What do you mean?'

'Someone. Oh, a long time ago. You meet up. There's immediate attraction. You sleep with her–'

'Not your wife then?'

'How can you tell – I mean what she feels -?'

'Who can read other people's feelings?'

He searched the horizon. A couple of trawlers were crawling over. 'Some guy appears from nowhere and wants me to pay.'

'Oh.'

'She was so convincing – I –'

'We find out in the end, don't we? Something in them makes us know.' She paused, letting a wave warm itself over her feet. 'It was here, right?' She kicked up flicks of surf. 'Would you go back to her?'

He pouted his lips and turned away to the trees.

'Maybe she did, Rich. Who knows. Some women are imprisoned. Men think these women are in it for real – can get out any time they choose. I wonder if that's true. So many women are still enslaved by men.' She smiled at him: 'If you can't do anything about it, just remember her as someone who loved and understood you. It's the understanding part that's so missing in love–'

'You could be right, Angie,' he nodded. 'Where's your nice young man?'

She smiled at him and turned away.

The other two were wet silhouettes in shadow against the brightness of the river behind: the slender curving estuary had opened out from the forest, its waters dawdling to the sea. Up the river a diesel locomotive wailed over a bridge that looked as though it was made of matchsticks, hauling its thundering multitude behind in an endless train that heaved out of jungle one side of the bridge and back into jungle the other side. Nina and Marty had swapped glasses and were leaning over to each other with straws crossed, grinning.

'You didn't find her,' Nina told them when they came in the shade of the beach bar. 'I told you. Didn't I Marty? She won't be here.'

Marty nodded: 'Girls like that trawl all the beaches. It's like finding a needle in a haystack.'

'Girls like what?' Rich blurted.

'She's a dancing girl, Rich. She could be anywhere. Getting money–' Nina sucked her straw.

'You think she's a whore?'

'They live on the edge. That's all I'm saying,' Nina said.

'So she's not worth bothering about, then?'

'She's not your daughter, Rich,' Nina flung at him. 'Kids in India move about all the time.'

'Round here girls her age end up dead.' He strode off.

'You're up yourself, Rich,' Nina called after him. 'Lalima can look after herself.'

'I bet that's what they said about the others,' Rich threw over his shoulder.

'The police'll sort it,' Marty added.

Rich stopped and turned: 'Will they? What have they done so far?'

'Maybe you ought to check with them.'

'Maybe I should.'

Angie came after him: 'You can't, Rich. The Police Chief won't take any notice of you–' She pulled at his top, trying to stop him from going: 'They'll do things to you, Rich–'

'They can't stop me now.'

'Then I'm coming with you.'

'No, Angie. No.'

'You need help.'

'They know my face. They don't know yours. Keep it that way.'

'If they know there's more people asking questions. If we can get the press–'

'You've seen what they're writing. They're on the side of the police – photos of policemen lined up behind humiliated criminals.'

'I'm coming.'

'Me and Lakshya have something – I don't know what – some, I don't know – there's some link somehow –'

'He's the one with the power.'

'Aarti knows her way around this place. Go and see her.'

Angie gave a reluctant nod: 'Don't get angry and blow it.'

*****

'You don't come in here shouting about what I should be doing, Mister Lomas,' Lakshya was at his desk. The cranky fan overhead no longer stirred up the air, its blades stationary. 'I decide how this case should proceed.'

'You haven't got anybody. '

'Mister Lomas, if you have nothing sensible to say I shall ask you to leave.'

'What are you doing?'

'Or have you removed.'

'Nothing.'

'Or worse.'

'You're very good at framing people up, that's for sure. That guy you had banged up.'

'And you think your embassy would help you in charges of murder?'

'I'm the one who's trying to find things out.'

'And becoming - what do you say - a thorn in my side. Perhaps it is you who really know what happened to Babita? And you persist in looking for another girl, I hear. But perhaps it is you who know where Lalima has gone–'

'You know she is missing?' Rich was incredulous. 'Or perhaps *you* know where she has gone.'

'Married, I understand.'

'Then where is she?'

'In her husband's house somewhere, I imagine. That's how it's done here.'

'But where?'

Lakshya shrugged: 'I have other important matters. As you see my fan is broken. I am waiting for Milit to bring me one for my desk.'

'Because you do nothing, Mister Police Chief, makes it look bad–'

'How, Mister Lomas–'

'I don't have to spell it out.'

'What you don't understand Mister Lomas, is that I can only

do so much. It is chaos here. Bagolem. All of India is chaos. The world is chaos. Life comes out of chaos. And that is what we are here for, all of us, don't you think, Richard Lomas, to put order to the chaos around us.' His moustache remained a straight line above his half smile. 'Even the lotus grows out of the chaos of mud, and look how beautiful it is. Siva dances so ignorance and chaos evaporate from the cosmos. You see that don't you, Richard Lomas? – Where is that damned man with the fan? – In fact Siva when he dances stands on a little monster that signifies ignorance? Did you know that? I don't think you did.' He took up a glass and sipped water. 'Do you think I care? Of course I care. But in India there are many ways of caring. For each individual consciousness there is a way of caring, for each of the million million gods of Hinduism there are a million million ways of caring. Each different.' He laughed. A fly traced zig-zags through space.

'You must have a plan of some kind then.'

'You do not think what I do is good.' He took out a bleach-white handkerchief and flicked at the fly. 'Look, Mister Lomas, there is cruelty and corruption wherever you look in the world. Wherever there is a beautiful landscape there is a cess pit. Life is like that – it's the condition of the universe. Do you think I can reverse that?' He pumped his forehead with his handkerchief. 'Do you think I can make all the nasty things that go on in my block go away? Can I stop prostitution and drugs and people buying and selling favours and bodies and bank notes and pills? Can I, Mister Lomas? Do you think so?'

'It's what you're supposed to do.'

'With little resources? This is a village that has grown because people like you have come here. When I grew up it was fishermen and farmers.'

'It's a village on fire now.'

'You are an intelligent man, Mister Lomas,' he smoothed down his moustache with his handkerchief, 'You know I am right. I cannot make it all go away and turn Bagolem into what it once was. I must work with it. I must protect its inhabitants, I must look after the poor and humble–'

'Like Babita?'

'I must work with the tools I've got.' He waved his hand at the fly but it took no notice. I must manage the cess pit in front of the beautiful mountain. Manage, Mister Lomas. I must manage and work with it, make it safe, keep its boundaries–'

'The deaths of two girls then, Mister Police Chief, are just collateral damage?'

'It will not change, so I must limit its dangers. Do you understand? I must protect all who are in my care–'

'Including those that pay you?'

'India pays me. Tax pays me. I would not think of you, as a clever and intelligent man, to insinuate anything other.'

'Of course not,' Rich stared in his eyes.

'You want me to come up with something right away? You think we are not working on it? Do you think I am going to reveal my investigations to you?'

Fed up with the Police Chief the fly turned on Rich: 'You're still holding that innocent man.'

'Him in the cells? Oh no, Mister Lomas. He is a free man now, but he gave us very useful information. I can assure you that we have other more important leads now. And you will have to leave that with us. I have important paperwork to be getting on with, if you please, Mister Richard Lomas. It is always good talking with you.' He pulled a pile of papers over and picked up a pen. 'If you were to think that there was anything else or anybody else behind all this . . . then I would have to take that very seriously Mister Lomas–'

'Is that a threat?'

'Do not go looking for missing girls, Mister Lomas. It will only come out bad.'

'You are, aren't you? Threatening me--'

'There are murderers out there. I would not want you to come to any harm.'

'Do your job. Find them then.'

'She is married, Mister Lomas.'

'No she isn't. You know where she is.'

Milit came in with a fan. 'Thank god.'

The fly landed on Lakshya's moustache and he violently flicked it off: 'Get it going Milit.'

The man set it up, plugged it in and the new draft spilled papers on the floor. 'Stupid,' Lakshya barked at his assistant who was now grovelling on the ground picking things up. 'Show this man out, Milit. He has been of great help. But my patience is running out.'

Rich got up. The fly had already beaten him to the open door.

18

The hardened tennis ball zoomed past Dinesh's hands as he stumbled trying to catch it, and thumped itself into a footprint in the sand. The boys were out early evening on the beach. Dinesh picked it up and threw it back to the bowler, a ten-year-old who had been insistently trying to get the little kid out. The batsman's head appeared to leer over the handle of the bat, and it seemed he would never be able to lift it let alone score, yet according to Dinesh he was well known for his sixes. Sometimes they had to make up a rule that if anyone hit a ball into a bar or café they were out, hoping that would curb him, but it didn't, Dinesh had laughed, it only made him hone his skills further and pay attention to exactly where he wanted the ball to go.

In the corner of his vision Rich thought he saw Jyothi with a man along the edge of palm trees.

They let Dinesh bowl and made Rich field on the bowler's right, near low lapping waves yellowed by sun.

The little batsman got another couple of sixes, but in a slack moment the ball clipped the edge of the bat as he lunged upwards and span out towards Rich who dived over dramatically, putting a sensational turn to the move, and cupped the ball in his left hand as he rolled through sand. Crowds in a Mumbai stadium never cheered louder. Not only were the dozen or so players dancing ecstatically, even bar staff and waiters were applauding with smiles, shouts and claps.

He was sure Jyothi was arguing with the man.

The reward was that he must bat next. The last time he did this was at his last school: staff versus imminent school leavers.

Year 11s played regularly, staff, once a year, so the scores usually reflected that. Rich had got promise they said, and he chalked up twenty nine that last time he had played - and Year 11 had some hot bowlers who had grudges to settle with him or ego points to make off him. But here, where sea met land, the wicket was a single piece of driftwood six inches wide stuck up like a miniature obelisk behind him, the tennis ball taped up to give it weight and solidity - a dirty brown mass which bowlers had long given up illegally trying to score with their fingernails to make it swing. This thing would never swing, it would only bolt straight down on you.

Gripping the bat, which to Rich was a bit low and small, he readied himself for the bowler who had made himself a pumped up speck miles away, such was the run up this 'fast man' required. Rich had hoped Dinesh might have urged them to put in a couple of spinners first that he could lick at, but this little mad thing hurtling down the sands towards him turned out to be the same little batsman he had just caught out. Jerking himself to a halt at the other wicket - a pile of flip-flops and T shirts - the bowler stunned the ball forward, nearly tripping himself with the motion of breaking his long run up, a sight amusing enough for Rich that he nearly laughed as he swung confidently out at the missile as it powered towards his legs. This would surely be a six. The ease with which his body flung itself round and the lack of sound from contact signalled something was wrong, the rocket whizzed past his legs and knocked the obelisk flat.

Silence. Then a roar. Jumping bodies. Applause. Laughter. Cheers. Even the blasted crows with their grey helmets were mocking in the trees.

The woman by the palm trees was trying to hit the man.

The only thing he could do was laugh with them, and surrendering his bat he let his shoulders down and guffawed to the sky. It was a good laugh, one he had needed for a long time - that threw him and shook things free. Then the gush of freedom inside came welling up, the loss, the grief, the tension, fell away, were washed aside in the way the tide flows in and sucks back the debris of shells and stones and jellyfish.

His mother seemed to be watching from the pink shadows of fishing boats as the sun, unable to hold itself back from the horizon, slipped down to the sea.

Dinesh was bent double with laughter. A boy took the bat from Rich. His mother faded. The bowler was striding to his starting point. Jyothi and the man had gone.

*****

Dinesh laughed with him when he got up next morning: 'In England they talk about weather every day. What is to talk about weather here?'

Frank was already reading his paper on the veranda and Rich, let out from his dark cell, allowed the whiteness of daylight to burn his eyes and eased himself into life with a coffee brought to him from the bar next door. He fancied he might do some drawing later, but knew the tension around Lalima's disappearance would distract him. There were other things to think about: finances weren't good. If his back pay didn't arrive soon in his account he would be on the breadline. Mother's estate would be sorted, but he had to go home to do it. He must know about Lalima before he left.

'Did you see Jyothi in the trees last night, Dinesh?'

Dinesh shook his head.

'You know when we were playing cricket.'

'You got a duck,' Dinesh grinned.

'Did you though.'

'You seeing things again, Rich?' Frank spoke over the top of his paper.

'Something's wrong.'

'Girls go missing all the time around here, don't they Dinesh?' Frank muttered.

'And end up dead on the beach.'

'She's all right,' Frank did not look up from reading.

'As if you'd know,' Rich blew his coffee.

'Take it from me. She's safe,' Frank pulled down the wall of paper a moment and put it up again.

'You sound like the police.'

'Give up, Rich. What good's it doing?'

'You know Lakshya and all that lot – what do they know, Frank?'

'I'd keep out of their business. Isn't that right, Dinesh?'

Dinesh looked over: 'Milit says they will get someone soon for Babita.'

'But are they looking for Lalima?'

'She's married, Rich. Safe in the arms of her husband,' Frank rustled his paper. 'Does that make you jealous?'

Rich laughed, spluttering coffee.

'You know Rich, you need to be careful,' Frank continued. 'People might get the wrong idea.'

'Wrong idea?'

'A grown up man searching for a thirteen-year-old girl.'

'That's just stupid.'

'People can turn into an avenging mob at the drop of a hat – and there's no convincing them then.'

'Is that a good reason to stop looking? She may be in danger, Frank.'

'Leave it to the police.'

'You think they'll really do anything, unless they're given piles of cash?'

'What I have heard,' Frank eyed him firmly, 'is that they've had it with you kicking off over her. You can't go around saying things like that and getting away with it. The way I see it, if you carry on, if the mob don't get you the police will.'

'Lakshya's already pointed the finger at me.'

'Well then. Take that as a warning. Keep out.'

'You sound like you're warning me too.'

'For your own good, Rich. Believe me. Stop now.'

Rich slurped the end of his coffee. 'Or they'll get me. Thanks, Frank.' He looked up at Dinesh, but he was about to make a call.

It was a long day – he swam, paced the beach, tried to paint but couldn't, and as the sun went down he went looking for Dinesh in the village – just talking with him would make him feel better. Tourists were ambling in and out of open shops examining fabrics and boxes and images of Siva, Ganesh, little camels and elephants, and roads were busy with taxis, scooter rickshaws, scooters, motorbikes and pedestrians. Dinesh was not around. Rich sat in a bar, ordered Calamari and tested a lager as night pulled itself over Bagolem. Fluorescent tube lighting came on along roads. Traffic became sparse. Shopkeepers called to tourists: 'What price will you give me for that?' Shaking heads; nodding heads. Stars were sprinkled over the tips of palm trees. It was as though in Lalima he had lost his own daughter again, and no one seemed to bother. Everyone had a world that mattered only to them and they spent the day's energy maintaining and protecting that world.

Ambling aimlessly back, hands in pockets, he entered the dark area of palm trees behind the row of chalets. A figure on a scooter passed him along the path, the cone of light shivering side to side until the driver stopped and turned and everything was dark again.

Someone hissed.

There was only the dark, and a rim of waves beyond the trunks.

Another hiss.

They had come for him, would roll him and leave him crumpled.

'Hst.'

He made out a female shape, and as the moon eased itself out of cloud and poked through palm leaves he saw her face.

'Go with him,' Chanda said.

'Who?'

'He will take you.'

'Chanda?'

She had a baby in her arms: 'Go with him. He will take you.'

A twelve-year-old boy came forward, nose and forehead in moonlight.

'Chanda–' he struggled inside. It was too far to cross, yet he would not admit it.

'Go,' Chanda urged. The light of another scooter was finding its way through trunks. 'Nikhil will take you.'

'Where?'

'Go.'

The light was heading towards them, soon they would be onstage in the limelight. She was gone. Nikhil pulled Rich's arm towards town.

The scooter rickshaw bounced through a blackness he thought he had never before experienced. Deeper they went, bouncing over pot holed tracks, Rich's head smacking the roll bar above.

The boy was mute.

Nearly an hour of back roads, the occasional village and sometimes the comet lines of a roadside fire. They finished at the end of a winding lane at a squat building. Two lights hung around the open doorway. A statue of Siva dancing, a couple of feet high seemed to guard the veranda, and although the sounds of pre-recorded sitar music drifted out, there was no sense of any activity going on.

'What is this place, Nikhil?'

The boy was telling the driver to wait and the motor chucked to a stop.

'Nikhil?'

Rich was pulled on. Low sounds of Indian music flowed out along with jasmine incense trails and there were muffled cries and laughter from the back. Nikhil pulled him deeper, past a woman leading a man in a room. Nikhil stopped and waited.

'What is this place, Nikhil? Is it what I think . . . ?' He felt disappointed in Chanda for a moment – maybe she did think love was linked to cash. 'I don't want this, Nikhil,' Rich started pulling the boy back but he stood firm, his eyes searching.

A door opened.

'Frank,' Rich yelled excitedly as though bumping into an old friend. 'Frank. Is this your German widow?' Rich was laughing, thinking now that Nikhil had brought him here to meet his mate.

Frank had his arm round a small female who held her head down under the shadow of a Kashmiri shawl.

'Frank? Who is that, Frank? That's not your German widow–' Rich stepped forward and the figure stepped back.

'Pick a woman, Rich,' Frank edged him back, but he got round him. 'Pick one.'

'Or a kid?' Rich eased the shawl from the girl's face.

'Pick a woman or get out,' Frank railed.

Lalima lowered her face from Rich and pulled away, her shoulders shaking with sobs.

'We're going, Lalima,' Rich grabbed her arm.

'You don't know them round here, Rich,' Frank pulled him round. 'You don't know what they'll do.'

'Get off me.' He grabbed Lalima again. 'Come on.'

She did not seem able to move. Nikhil was shaking his head fearfully.

A fist came out of a doorway and flattened Rich, then multiple kicks pelted his stomach. A man with a red hand stood over him. Looking up in a daze later he saw Nikhil. The boy helped him back to the rickshaw. He was sure as he went he passed Milit.

19

A day and night passed as he lay in a stupor in his room. Dinesh brought him tea and fruit. Angie came by and finding him wounded went up the town and got him takeaway rice and vegetables. When he asked where Nina was she said: 'Probably where you think.' So he assumed a relationship with Marty was in full swing.

The helicopter blade above his head hushed air round the room – the weather was sticky, the breeze had dropped. Palm trees were stationary, held to attention by the heat.

'You mustn't worry,' Angie mopped his brow and attended to bruises and cuts. 'You need to rest.'

'I've got to get her out, Angie,' he was mumbling half conscious. 'Got to get her out –'

Angie poured him water from a bottle, hoping to contain his delirium, and softened his sweating forehead with a cold damp flannel.

'Lalima, Angie. They've got her. Sex slave – and that Frank – of all people. Frank-'

'You've got to rest, Rich. Or we take you to the hospital – you know how you hate them.'

'You're such a good friend, Angie. Where's Nina. She can help–'

Angie was shaking her head.

'Angie. Angie,' he beckoned her close and she shuffled her stool nearer the bed. 'I've got to tell you this – I've got to–'

'I'm listening.' She held his hand.

The story came out jumbled and unclear and then he said: 'I've got to do something, Angie. I can't leave her there. She's a kid. They'll kill her if she runs. And Frank–'

'Frank?'

'He goes there, Angie. I'm telling you. Who do you think his German widow really is now? Lalima. That's who. Little Lalima. I don't know who he had before she disappeared to this brothel place. Babita perhaps – or some other kid. That's who his German widow is – different thirteen-year-old girls in that place. Taken off the streets and used as sex slaves, Angie-'

There was no breeze or swishing of branches to fill the gap between words, only the distant roll of the sea like sounds inside a shell.

'Nina will help,' he said again, letting the words echo in the little room. Angie looked away. He let out a strangled laugh: 'You didn't want me to get hurt. I always get hurt–' Before he was ready for it he wept.

She nursed the ball of his head in her arms and stroked his hair like a child as he bawled into her breast. When he had finished she dried his eyes with tissue and pushed his hair back with the comb of her fingers.

'She'll help. I'll make her.' He fisted the mattress.

'You can't make her do anything, she follows her own song.' Angie paused. 'We'll do something, Rich.'

'What?' he enjoyed the self-pity a moment: 'We can't leave her there. We can't. She's a little kid – wait till I catch up with Frank–'

'You can't do anything,' she laughed. 'You need to rest, get your strength back before you go after people. Anyway, we need to think this out before you go seeking revenge. We'll do something, I promise. Aarti–'

'What can she do?'

'She's got her own contacts.' She squeezed his hand before she went. 'We'll do something. Just get yourself better–'

The sun did its daily thing, plundering the sky with a whiteness that palled to lemon and pink and purple twilight.

The next day he was fit enough to go down town and eat. When he came back the dark hinterland behind the chalets was populated with night shapes: a one horned cow, a bevy of hogs muttering in darkness about interrupted sleep. The real dangerous critters you never heard: scorpions and snakes cool in the sticky quiet heat of the night. As he turned the corner at the end of the line of huts he found him, sitting on the veranda drinking from a bottle. The men looked through the murk at each other. The moon was a crescent shaped blade in the void. The light from the bare electric bulb could not reach the full features of Frank's face.

'Ah,' Frank waved a half drunk bottle of whisky at him. 'You don't know what it's like. You don't know. You smart college boy. You go to college and you don't know nothing–'

Rich stood above him: 'What I know is - I could kill you, Frank.' He pulled him off his chair by his shirt. 'Dump your body out the back here and feed you to the pigs and nobody would know the difference. Nobody would even care. Who would mourn for you, Frank, your kids?' Rich threw him back down on his seat.

'My kids.' He swigged, 'Them? To hell with them.'

'You're only saying that because you do care – somewhere – inside –'

'I don't care about anything, college boy. Don't you try and tell me what's right and wrong. What do you know? High and mighty – and off screwing Chanda and paying for it. Are you any better?'

'She wasn't a kid.'

Lights from the restaurants were in among palms like stars.

'So it's just all me. Like old times. Frank's to blame for everything-' Frank waved his bottle.

A couple with a child were lighting a candle inside a paper lantern by the sea.

'How long has it been, Frank?'

'Get out of here.'

'Girls, I mean. How many have there been? Sunita, Babita, and now Lalima – all posing as your German widow – And they all end up dead –'

The man held the lantern waiting for it to fill with hot air, its star inside firm without breeze. The little girl was jumping up and down.

'You don't even think you've done anything wrong Frank. You're just bothered about getting found out–'

'What's it to you? She's off the streets and off the sands.'

Rich's fist tensed: 'As a dancing girl, at least she had a mother and a sister, there was some hope–'

Frank did not answer for a time. The sky drew the lantern and it faltered, heading out for sea.

'You reckon? You don't know nothing of what goes on around here.'

'I should beat you to pulp.'

'Go on. Take a swing. If that'll make you feel better.'

'It won't get her back–'

'Your precious little girl–'

Rich whacked him across the cheek and he reeled off his seat.

'You don't get it–' He stood over him again as he crawled on his knees. 'You get locked up for this back home. You get on a list.'

'You don't know nothing.' Frank spat out a glob of blood. 'Paedophiles go for tiny kids. Now that *is* sick–'

'She has a chance of a life – not in there with men like you drooling over her –'

'They know what they're doing. She knows what she's into.' Frank rolled into his wicker chair and swigged again.

Rich threw back his head. 'She was forced into it Frank. They all are –'

'Does her mum care?'

'She's in tears, man – what is it with you? '

'They pay them enough–'

The night was silent but for the cries of a child with hands up to the drifting lantern.

'What are you talking about?'

'Everyone gets something out of it. The mother gets a load–'

The lantern struggled upwards away and finding a plateau hung twenty feet above the sea.

The thump of bruises ached throughout Rich's body. He should just bash Frank, have done, but it didn't seem enough: 'Somewhere inside you know what you're doing. Give the poor girl a future.' He paused, watching the lantern will itself up to the other stars, the girl urging it with outstretched arms, then: 'You can get her out of there, Frank. You could. You know people.'

'What do you think happens to girls who run away?' Frank sounded suddenly lucid.

'What, Frank? Spell it out.'

Frank had his head in his hands, shaking.

'Babita? Is that what you're saying. And the other girl, Sunita?'

'You don't understand, Rich.'

'What is to understand about girls forced into brothels to serve men like you? Or be murdered if they run away. What is to understand?' he yelled in his face.

'What do they teach you in books?' Frank flared.

'You're telling me you're innocent in all this?' Rich was looking towards the south end of the beach. Lights flipped off and restaurants and bars became invisible, as though an earthquake had come and folded them up in darkness. One by one they vanished, the power cut reaching quickly towards them. The bulb was out. Moans came up from bars, candles appeared. The two men kept apart in their new gloom. The lantern hung still, alone among stars.

'I'll get her out,' Rich mumbled, tensing his fist again.

'You're naïve. '

'We need your help, Frank–'

'They'll replace her with somebody else. You know that–'

'So we just leave her?'

The child was singing to her light in the sky as it fizzled star-like over the Arabian Sea and snuffed out.

Then he knew: 'How deep in are you, Frank?'

Frank held his head down and shook it.

'How many?'

The black sea brought its black foam up the black sand.

'I tried to get Babita out. I left the door unlocked that night you were with Chanda. I gave a her a way out – I thought she'd get away, I didn't know they would–'

'You want me to believe that?'

'Believe what you like.'

'How deep? What is all this?'

Frank raised his head: 'They set me up.'

'Oh. A victim, then Frank?' Rich cut the words out.

'You don't understand. Your sort never do.'

'My sort?'

'Your sort,' Frank wagged a finger. 'I made a mistake. Like you. A mistake. You with Chanda. They got me drunk. I woke up with a ten-year-old girl next to me. They got me, Rich–'

Candles were aflame in bars and restaurants. Rich heard the faint trail of the girl singing to her dead star. 'You want me to believe that?'

'Believe what the hell you like. It's true. Right. They've got the pics. I've seen them. I didn't know she was ten, I was drunk, she came on to me – they showed me the pics after–'

Rich was silent.

'I was right in,' Frank railed, 'How was I going to get out? They'd got a hold on me.'

'They make you keep going back to the girls?' Rich screeched.

The little dark figure of the girl disappeared into the night.

'You men of principle. You think Gerry was an accident? His body all choked up with drugs. You think that?' Frank yelled.

'What then?'

'Gerry knew about it. Everything. Just like you. A man of principle. Hah. What good does it do you in the end? Look what they did to him. They can do anything.' Frank took a breath. 'They got to him first before he could expose the set up.' He paused, his voice cracking to a groan: 'I can't get out, Rich. I can't.' Frank was in tears. 'They make you do things -'

'You were the one who set up the deal to get Lalima?'

'I had to, Rich, you've got to see that. You can't mess with these people-'

'Who?'

'Who do you think? For a college boy you can be naïve and thick all in the same breath.'

'Who?'

'Lakshya. The lot of them. Mil-'

'They run the place?'

'Paid off, Rich. This is India. Money buys everything. Even-'

'Children-' Rich finished for him. 'And?'

'That's it-'

'Come on Frank. What are you really scared of?'

'I've told you-'

Rich reached through the night and pulled him close with his shirt: 'You set foot off a plane in England and I'll have you, Frank -'

'Figure it out. There's places all over. Mobs - like the mafia - all over, running the show behind. The police are part of that, they have to be. I've seen politicians in there - with really young girls. Not just Indian ones - English and Russian ones.

There are hives with hierarchies - special set ups for the rich and famous. Once in, you never get out – an elite club - Gives them power see – they can control laws and all sorts–'

'Who are they, Frank?'

'Don't hit me again.'

They sat in silent blackness.

'Tell me one reason?'

'I saved you once,' Frank's voice quavered in the darkness and Rich felt the man's body crumble back in his chair. 'I got you out. You could have rotted and died in that cell.'

'For what?'

'I tried–' The man was choking.

'You tried?'

'You don't know.' There was sudden anger in Frank's tone: 'People have been saving you.'

'You've been looking after me?' Rich laughed.

'They wanted you in.'

'They were never going to get me,' Rich spluttered in disbelief, then thinking back, checked himself: 'You took me to Chanda. You set it up. It was a trap. To get me in.'

'No. Rich. They made me. I'd end up like Gerry: a block of dead rock. I had to, you've got to understand–'

'It was nothing personal you had against me?' Rich scoffed ironically.

'It wasn't. That night, I got Babita out. I didn't know what they would do if they caught her–' Rich could hear him choking back tears. 'Not till you found her–'

'And I believe that?' Rich rattled.

'I got Chanda to step in.'

'Chanda? '

'They wanted you in, like me, saw you as a soft target, got me to set it up. They wanted pictures of you with a twelve-year-old girl. Like they did with me. Spiked your drink. But

Chanda heard about what they were going to do and got in and got the girl out and – Chanda's got a big heart. She saved you Rich. And the girl. The girl was so afraid she didn't want to go, but Chanda pushed her out. It turns out that particular girl was related to Chanda in some way – niece or something. Chanda took big risks pretending she didn't know what the blokes were setting up and told them that she would get loads of money out of you – that didn't work, of course because Mister High and Mighty here is too proud to pay for an honest lay with a whore. Chanda got away with a few shouts and a slap and lots of threats, thank god, it could have been so much worse for her when I think, but while Chanda's useful to them, she stays in their grip. Like everybody.' Frank paused and Rich heard a guzzle. 'You don't go there. You don't mess with them.'

'How do they enforce it? Who does the dirty work? Who killed Sunita and Babita, Frank?'

'Red Hand. I like you, Rich. You're a good bloke. Get out of it now. Get on a plane while you still can.'

'Who are Red Hand?'

'Blokes who put henna patterns on their hands so they can disguise themselves as women in saris with covered heads. They're the real police. The protective wing of Siva Sect. You don't mess with them or that's it–' Rich saw Frank's arm move in the dark as he drew it across his throat.

'Like thugs?

'Yeah thugs – stranglers – just like that – as long as the girls stay, they are safe. They run – and that's it--'

'Mendez?'

'They're psychopaths, Rich. They'll do anything without thinking and follow orders like zombies, like they've been hypnotised. Mendez is a respected member – and feared all over India.'

'You recruit people,' Rich said, 'and they own you for life.'

Frank pulled out a small torch and fired it at his wrist,

illuminating a tattoo the size of a ten pence piece. Crudely done, it showed an image of Siva dancing in a circle of flames.

'I've seen that. On the dead girl when I came - Sunita - and on Babita's arm.'

'A sign. They own you. Part of Siva Sect. You never get out.'

'Lalima?'

'You see why we can't get her.'

'She has that on her arm?'

'If she has then she is part of their property. You do what you're told and they keep you safe. Whatever it is–'

'She'll have to hide it when we get her out.'

'In your dreams, Rich. You'll never do it – you can't.'

'Would you like that for your own daughter?'

'Where would Lalima go?'

'We'll find a place. Until we can blow this thing open.'

Frank laughed into his bottle: 'You'll never do that – they're all in it – politicians, the press , the media – the lot of them – Siva Sect owns them all –'

'They wanted me too,' Rich laughed cynically. 'I messed it up for you all then.'

'You know how it is. The web has to expand outwards forever drawing new people in so it can keep growing. Like a cancer, Rich. I know. I made mistakes, I–'

'They made you have Lalima?'

Frank was silent in darkness and Rich could not see his expression. Rich smiled wryly: 'You pay them, big time then, and they've got you but you can enjoy all the nice little seedy things they've got to offer–'

'Get a life–'

'Lakshya and the lot of them then, paid off. Told to do things. All his bull about power and chaos and managing. He's just a bent copper overseeing child prostitution–'

'The world's full of them,' Frank's words popped out of his dark shape in the chair. 'When you get to know him, he's quite clever really. You shouldn't take him too seriously. He likes you, Rich. He really does–'

Lights flashed on in distant restaurants, like little theatres their stages burst up into limelight one by one.

'Enough to set me up–' Rich let out a cynical laugh.

'He's a family man, like millions round the world. To keep his family he has to do what he's told.'

'Give me the hard luck story.'

'They're better off there, Rich, that's the truth of it - and safe. What else is there for the likes of Lalima? A life on the beach as a tart–'

'You made her that–'

'Wake up, Rich. She'll get looked after, get money, food shelter–'

'Until she's too old and nobody will want her. She could be a dancer–'

'That'll never happen. She came on to me, Rich–'

The bulb pinged on. Rich could hold his fist back no longer and leaning forward let fly. Frank's head shook with the blow, but he did not retaliate, nursing a cut lip with a handkerchief that he pulled from his pocket, a white little square with an image of Siva dancing through a circle of flames at its corner, once carefully folded and now crumpled and bloodied.

A bat swirled through space.

'You could get her out.'

'She can have a good life there. Her mother knows it–'

'Did Jyothi have a choice?' Rich said. 'Selling her daughter?'

'She laughs, seems happy. Got the cash–'

'She didn't Frank. They made her. She was in tears. There was no jumping for joy over money.'

'You never know with them–'

'It's slavery, Frank.'

'Better than begging.'

'How? Kids going with clapped out old fogeys like you? What a life.' Rich shook his head in anger. 'They can get Aids, the lot–'

'They're all in it,' Frank leaned back, curling down the sides of his mouth, 'all of them. Milit. He's so deep in debt, he has to do everything Lakshya tells him. Even that - yeah - putting his wife on the game, his precious wife. He thinks the world of her, does Milit. You wouldn't think it, but - he loves her, you know. It kills him when she's with another man. You've seen him gambling and drunk on the beach. That's after some guy like you has had his wife. It goes round and round for him, the more he sells his wife the more he gets into debt. That's how they want it - they've got you that way. You ever been got, Rich? Held? We're all bought in some way or another. You've got to keep out of it. Get a flight home and get out of it. These people are bigger than us, they've got more guns, bigger guns. You've got to do what they tell you or you're done for. You don't want to end up washed up on the shore, Rich–'

'You too? Warning me again?' Rich snatched the whisky bottle from his mate, gulped, then smacked it on the little round table. Insects danced round the bare light bulb.

'Advising, Rich-boy. I like you. Always have. I wanted to be like a father to you - like I never was to my own kids. Or maybe it's that blind stupid youthful honesty and integrity I like about you - you still believe in the world. I lost that decades ago.' He laughed into the bottle and leaned over clumsily to hug Rich, but he pulled away.

A hog in the dark out back grunted.

'You think I'll let go?'

'You'll have to.'

'Will I?'

'You're so much trouble to them now - If they can't get something big on you you'll disappear. Go home, Rich. Now.

You've got a little girl of your own. Watch her grow up–'

'How can I turn my back on Lalima and bring up my own daughter?'

'Easy. Just do it. Walk away,' Frank paused, slapping insects aside: 'You know there comes a point where youthful honesty and integrity become stupid destructive things. No one really likes someone of principle – it's so boring. Everyone has their price.'

They let the sound of the waves break the rhythm of their words.

'Be a father to your own child, Rich.'

'We have to be fathers to all children.'

'He's off again. Fantasy world philosopher.'

'We've got to change. If there's any hope of anything.'

'Don't give it to me now, Rich. You are one of the good guys, the rest of us are–'

'We've got to make breaks – nothing happens without it – awareness and change –'

'That Aarti's been mind-bending you again–'

'You don't think we are what we make ourselves?'

'We're what the world makes of us,' Frank rattled the last juices of whisky in the bottle at him, 'That's all–'

'We're all victims then.'

'You know it.'

'And being victims we make others victims.'

'Got it in one, clever college boy.'

'I don't know that place.' Rich sniffed and the moon seemed to come out of shadows. Rows of palm trunks with lights coiled round them hung out to the beach. It could be paradise, it could be hell, it depended on the way you looked at it.

'You know that place. It's here. In paradise,' Frank paused, taking another gulp. Rich wanted to run and leave the man with the darkness of his thoughts, but held himself back with a desire to win him. 'You had all you wanted when you grew up, Rich. You were lucky. Most of us don't get that–'

Rich detected a fall in tone to his voice and turning saw moonlight sparkling from tear lines: 'What do you mean?'

'You go from woman to woman, sex to sex. And what you don't see is all you're trying to do is find love. The love you never had – the love I never had–'

'You're not going to give me a hard luck story –' Rich's temper rose.

'It was no different from millions of others,' Frank considered. 'That's true. Even in rich homes – the search for love, acceptance and approval from both parents. You realise when you're in your forties or fifties that all the successes you were going for were to prove yourself to your parents and be loved by them. It's a thing inside your head. Without realising you're searching for people who can give love without judgement, without chiding–'

'Girls, Frank – too weak to hurt back –'

'Then you wonder in the end,' Frank seemed to be talking to himself, 'after all this, are you really worthy of love? Are you so far down that it's impossible for you to be loved. You think that can change, Rich?' Frank's eyes were lined with rims of water.

'You can change, Frank. You can get up and throw that bottle away and come with me now Frank, and we can get her–'

'Just like that? They'll let us. And where will you take her?'

'Aarti. She'll know what to do.'

'Her? Grow up man. It's a lost cause.'

Rich paused, thinking about his words: 'You'll keep going to Lalima then?'

'I won't go to her. Not her.'

'But others.'

Tears brimmed in Frank's eyes. 'When I was a kid–'

'What?' Rich was direct.

'The man next door was a good babysitter. Real good. A teacher, like you. You think they don't exist among teachers and social workers and lawyers and politicians and policemen? You think that? Oh everyone loved Noel, such a trusted figure. They went out at night - and he brought his lot in–' His head was in his hands as his body convulsions echoed the sound and rhythm of waves on the beach.

'We need help to change–' Rich's voice quavered. 'You need that, Frank. Go back home and get it–'

'You're in a childhood prison. And the prison never goes –'

'If you can't come and get her with me, Frank, go home and find a way. Get it. Before it gets you–'

Rich left him in darkness and paced the beach. As he walked the reflected moonlight across the sea and along the beach moved ahead of him. There must be a way of getting her out. When he turned back to look at Frank the blade of the moon hung over the chalet like a sickle.

*****

'Rich,' Dinesh was calling him but he did not turn to him and carried on walking, 'Rich? Where are you going?'

'I've got to get her out, Dinesh.' He hurried.

'What ploy you have?'

He was heading towards the arch where the road ended at the beach. A few taxi drivers and rickshaw fellas were hanging about in the pool of floodlight that brightened the sandy car park. Few tourists ambled up the road now, so several shops were shutting up.

'He won't let her go, Rich–' Dinesh pulled his arm and stopped him. 'Not him.'

'Everyone's scared of Lakshya. I'm not.' Rich snapped away and approached the tall light over the archway. The men traversed the car park like actors across a brightly lit stage, the one trying to catch up with the other. Hills were black over the back. The beauty and charm of the place had receded for Rich, he saw nothing now except a cause, and smiling to himself he realised that that was what he had wanted for a long time – something to get him away from himself: a cause. 'I'm getting her out, Dinesh.'

'How?'

'I'll make him.'

'All his men are round him,' Dinesh said. 'Mendez – they'll get you –'

'Not at his house.'

'Rich. What can you do?'

'I can make him–'

'No, Rich.'

Rich hurried up the street, the tarmac greying deeper away from the floodlight at the arch.

'The things the Police Chief can do. It's too–' Dinesh persisted, but Rich strode on. 'I will come.'

They paced through the back paths under palms, then out onto the beach again. Lights still held on for late drinkers and patient waiters who slipped around surrounded by laughter and shouts. Then turning again into the dark palms they walked inland for a kilometre, crossing a road, then into deeper darkness. A dog loped in the path ahead of them, its limp frame stiffening as the men approached. They stopped, a signal for it to bark, and the pair stood blocked a moment, the creature heaving sounds at them.

'There must be another way,' Rich urged Dinesh who had picked up a brick and hurled it at the cur, striking its back, and it whelped miserably in defeat and slunk off into murky hinterlands.

As they approached the house the sound of raised voices hit the air. The place was brightly lit and Lakshya's car was on the driveway. They stopped in shadows near a wall.

'What's going on?' Rich hissed.

'Fight with wife–' Dinesh put his finger to his lips.

'We go in–'

'Not now,' Dinesh pulled his arm.

'What's he saying?'

Dinesh sniggered, his teeth bared white as they caught the light: 'Lakshya and his wife fight all the time. She says: "Before me, you wanted to marry her. Not me. She was Christian. Hindu will not marry Christian. You – want her. But she finds a better man, rich man, marry rich man, have his son." And she laughed at him. He says she's a stupid idiot, she doesn't know him. She says: "You must respect me." He says: "You give me no son." All girls he's got. He wants a son.' Dinesh giggled. "Chanda gave Milit a son," he says. "What's wrong with you?"'

Rich chuckled: 'The male chromosome decides the sex of kids. It's all down to the man. Lakshya, himself–'

A door slammed, then all was quiet. Lakshya was in the garden, lighting up, puffs of smoke clouded into night and whiffs of tobacco came to them. It was the time to take action.

'This is no good, Rich. If you go in the garden – The police are like spiders – they jump and sting. He will get men.'

Rich's fists were clenched.

'If he know Chanda helped you – he can smash Milit's house. All gone. I have seen houses burned down, people inside–'

'I've got to–' Rich was nearly at the gate.

'They will put you away, Rich. You will not get out. You don't want to be inside Indian jail. Bad, bad place. You will not survive. Then Lalima is lost. Forever–'

Rich froze, fists still in balls.

'Another way: you talk with your friends, Angie and Aarti. They will help. And your friend Nina – she will help. Not this way, Rich–'

The angry police chief was striding his empire, puffs of smoke following him. Alone, he was a man caught in the snare of past decisions. He seemed strangely vulnerable to Rich now, a family man making the best of what he had got - yet another being dissatisfied with how the cards had fallen for him, a man struggling to hold a family together, to give them the best, someone under the control of others, having to do what he was told and hemmed in by forces greater than himself. A man trying to come to terms with those forces and compromise with them.

'I didn't see a policeman, Dinesh,' he whispered as they turned back: 'I saw a human being.'

20

Sleep could not compete with images of flaming houses as he rumbled under nets, and waking at daybreak in a sweat with Lalima in his vision, he jumped up without washing, threw on T shirt and shorts and headed up the beach.

Angie was already up, drinking coffee on the veranda of her chalet hut, hair unkempt, no make-up, and when she saw Rich she yelped, apologising for not being 'up' and presentable. Quickly laughing it away with compliments about her looking cute and being a good friend, he gave her a hug causing her to look disarmed and embarrassed.

'Is she up yet?' Rich ventured, dreading Nina appearing from bed with Marty.

'You know these rock and rollers, Rich. You want coffee? I'll get you one. That bar over there. Anil is very good, he'll get me anything.' She pointed over to a small bar hidden among palm trees where the silhouette shapes of waiters moved.

'Nah.'

'Big rumpus,' Angie sipped.

'Last night?'

'I knew that Marty fella wasn't on her level,' Angie said.

'Yeah?'

A breeze was coming in from the sea, tempering the sun's blast on open sands.

'She didn't turn up to sing till real late. Drunk as a soldier on leave and he dumped her out of the band. Big scenes in front of the audience, effing and blinding, she was. Are you sure you won't have a coffee?'

'Is that a smirk on your face, Angie–'

'No–' She play slapped him. 'She's my mate. I had to drag her away–'

Rich failed to suppress part of himself feeling smug.

'That idiot – calls himself a guitarist.' Nina appeared at the chalet door, rubbing her eyes. 'You can't trust the quiet ones. I always said that. Get us a coffee Ang–' She seemed to ignore Rich while she yawned, then: 'What are you doing here?'

Angie yelled to Anil for another coffee and a figure hailed back.

'I need help.'

'Not another bloke wanting something out of me?' She rubbed her eyes fearlessly. 'You didn't help, Angie–'

'If I hadn't dragged you away they would have sent for the police–'

'Let them. Jerk. Marty thinks he's it–'

'You don't want the police involved. Believe me–' Rich said.

'Them. To hell–' Nina waved him away with her hand.

'She saved you–'

'She was just embarrassed – me shouting and stuff. That Marty is a jerk. Anyway.' She turned on Rich. 'I ain't helping you – so get off.'

'It's a good cause.'

'There's no such thing.'

'I'll tell you about it. You want a meal tonight?' Rich tried tenderness, holding on to an image he had of her the first night onstage, black outfit, smacked down blonde hair, her hips gyrating as she made love to the mic stand.

She shrugged her shoulders.

'Unless anything better comes up–' he tried to camouflage the sarcasm but it came out anyway.

Shrugging her shoulders again, she lit up: 'Where's that coffee? That Anil's useless. Anil –' her yell faltered to a croak.

'Get here.'

The lad smiled over with a steaming glass, placing it on the table for her, then glided away unflustered.

'You do have your hands full in the mornings, Angie,' Rich could not hold back.

'Go back to your little school room.'

'You've got no band now, then?' Rich retorted.

'What's it to you?' She sipped the coffee and burned her tongue. 'Damn. Why does he make it so hot?'

'I had something with you once.'

'Did you? I didn't notice.'

'Maybe you weren't there at the time,' Rich looked out to sea.

'No. Maybe I wasn't.'

Angie shifted in her seat.

'I'd like us–'

'Us? What "us"?'

'There was once.'

'Could have fooled me,' she pecked at the steaming fluid again.

Angie got up.

'I'm forming a new band.'

'Good for you,' Rich said.

'As if you care.'

'I do care,' Rich glared at her. 'That's the point. I do. I want you to get on. I want something for you. And Angie does – she really cares for you. It's a bit difficult to show any affection to someone who throws it back all the time.'

'What you don't know. Any of you. Is I'm going to get there. I'll show you all. I write all my own songs. Even Marty can't write songs like me – with edge – he just added licks. People like my songs, people want me. Why do you think I was late.

Talking to another guitarist. Someone who can really play and write. I was dumping Marty anyway–'

'And the band played: believe it if you like –' Angie threw aside.

'What do you know, Angie. Nothing. You flip around with a daft smile on your face and–'

'Pick up the pieces. Everybody likes you, Nina. But you mess up. Every time.'

'I don't need this in the morning.'

Crows were cawing in the trees.

Angie was about to go back in but Rich lightly tugged her sleeve to stay. 'We need you, Nina,' Rich tried.

'People need me all the time, dear. That's talent for you.' She smirked, blowing steam from the glass and slurped. 'Always too hot. You should tell him, Angie.'

'You should tell him,' Angie was bitter. 'Anil's a good kid.'

'There's no such thing.'

'Lalima,' Rich got there. 'A cause.'

'Who wants a cause?'

'I need help getting her out.'

'A thirteen-year-old caught up in some sort of sex ring,' Angie toyed with the towel.

'I know, I know. You told me. What can I do?'

'Come with us,' Angie said.

'Where?'

'I've talked to Aarti–'

'*That* woman.'

Angie turned away from her mate and carried on with Rich: 'Aarti wants to help–'

'She *would*. Full of herself. All her naff ideas–' Nina rocked her head.

'We're going now. Me and Rich.'

'I got plans,' Nina blew her coffee again.

Rich stared at his amour, wanting to smooth away the prickliness, love the misused bit of her and heal it: 'Come with us, Nina.' He was gentle with his words, but knew it was a final demand.

'Got to see a bloke about a band. We're going up north.'

'Not with me,' Angie was firm.

'Suit yourself.'

Rich was standing: 'Come with us, Nina. If we can help stop some abuse – you know what I mean. Lalima's a kid. Come with us.'

Nina stood up, left her coffee and stormed back inside, throwing herself on the bed.

*****

Rich and Angie rushed into Aarti's grotto, Angie pulling him back to take off his shoes. Aarti was meditating so the pair sat with fidgety feet nearby, silently urging her to come out of trance. To one side of Rich was a small shrine with a goddess with four arms, the slim smoke of incense encasing her.

'We need your help,' Rich gabbled when Aarti opened her eyes, and gasped out the story.

'It won't be easy,' Aarti rubbed her chin.

'We've got to get her out,' Rich insisted.

Aarti stood, turned towards the shrine and took two small candles in leaf shaped pottery holders, and giving one to Angie and one to Rich, lit them with a match.

'Place them before her,' she nodded to the image of the goddess. 'Think of your intentions. They are very powerful – we underestimate the power of thought. From thought comes will. Ask the goddess Laxmi to send good fortune and prosperity, to reinforce your will. In your mind imagine Lalima free and happy and dancing – this is your intention.'

They took their quivering flames to the goddess.

'Diwali is for her: goddess of light–' Aarti whispered.

The flame-light flickered round the icon, two arms up, two pointing down.

'Laxmi is a giving goddess in tradition, one who oversees wealth. She gives to the needy, but has the power to take from the greedy.' She laughed. 'A goddess of great beauty, she holds a lotus flower in one of her hands – the lotus grows out of mud, an image of beauty rising out of the chaos of the world. She was born at the Churning of the Sea of Milk – a creation story. Let's meditate on that a moment – then discuss the chaos of the world.'

She taught them to breathe, told them of prana, the inner breath, the life force, and they drew in air steadily and with purpose.

At first he shook with the desire to get up and run and do something, but soon Rich was lost, his mind swimming with angry images of Frank, and of all the men who had stood in his way, from an ineffective father to Lakshya, Milit, and back to Frank. His own father had left when Rich was about five and only once or twice come back into his life – he was always chasing money or women or both so his mother had said. Rich's father had turned up when Jeanette was born with a load of new promises, but they had faded as usual as seasons came and went, his father having things more important in his life it appeared. Rich did not want to emulate him in any way and as he slipped into drowsy meditation it was obvious to him what he was really trying to do: to be the father his father was not.

Aarti's hands were on his shoulders, massaging, helping him release the whirlpool in his head. Lalima was dancing for him, her feet kicking up a little sand, her ankle bells jingling. She span and twirled, throwing out her arms and pushing her head back. The Sea of Milk churned in vast eddies. He looked away from Lalima, saw his mother watching, then back to Lalima, who was now a thirteen-year-old Jeanette spinning.

Aarti's fingers worked his muscles until there was a feeling of release, a popping noise as he moved to a plain of stillness. Feelings of contentment filled the vacuum, and ahead a light glowed. Travelling close he found the Buddha seated in meditation, his aura giving out miles of rippling colours that seemed to energise those in its radius. The cosmos span in a timeless void, the animals of Lamilgusma grazed, a one horned cow wandered in search of its missing part, a woman gave birth, Krishna played his flute and the great labyrinth opened in a kaleidoscope of exploding colour.

'Touch the ground now, Rich,' Aarti breathed in his ear. 'We must ground ourselves after our cosmic journeys. Images of the Buddha have him with one hand touching the earth - he is of the skies and the world, as we all are, and draws graces from the spirit of the universe to inform and invigorate the material world, for it is clouded in Maya: illusion–'

Rich and Angie waited for their teacher's instructions while monkeys were chattering outside. A child was laughing in the distance and out the back, through the open door, emerald-white rice fields spread themselves in front of mauve-pink forest-covered mountains. Women and a couple of men had backs bent across the flat green. A narrow path led through the rice, over ditches and channels, to a road that wound to the hills.

'I know people who might help,' Aarti told them. 'If we can get her out–'

'What about her mother, Jyothi?' Angie watched her.

'There's lots of problems - if her mother's been paid,' Aarti reflected.

Rich was getting himself back to earth: 'If we get Lalima back and she stays here, she's not safe.'

Aarti nodded: 'We have to get her away somewhere. But how do we get her out of that place?'

'I go in as a customer,' Rich ventured.

'That's very bold, Rich,' Aarti smoothed his enthusiasm, 'but they know you. And anyway, there'll always be men there in case of trouble, so if they got an idea you were going to get her out they'd be on to you right away. It's got to be something clever – we'll have to think –'

Aarti rose from the matting and poured three glasses of pineapple juice, and handing them out carried on her thoughts: 'We'll do something.' She pursed her lips. 'Lakshya comes to me sometimes. Did you know? He searches for peace, he says, for remedies to cope with stress. '

'Should you be working with him?' Rich could not hold back.

'We can't always work with the converted. We live in the hope of change.'

'Can you talk to him then?' Rich was quick. 'You've got a route.'

'I try to ease him with massage and meditation. He has many problems that block his body. Very much into Siva worship. Would he listen? We are not close, he does not confide in me. Would he do anything? I'm not sure that's the right way for us.'

Angie sipped her nectar: 'It's sort of funny him coming here. The local gang leader looking for some kind of peace.'

'He's trapped. Like all of us,' Aarti looked at Rich who was recalling images of the police chief being shouted at by his wife, 'in his own bubble. What he's created for himself. But you know, Lakshya's friends want me out of here. They want to make it into a bar. The world does not like people who talk about peace and non-violence.'

They were standing ready to go, Rich's expression revealing gloom at the lack of any agreement on action, when Chanda entered with brush in hand.

He wanted to look in her eyes, but she kept her gaze downward, bending and brushing in repeated ritual movements, sweeping tiny bits of the world towards the door.

'Chanda helps out now and again–' Aarti told them as they nodded to the goddess Laxmi again and made their way out.

*****

Rich ate alone at the Blue Planet, trying some vegetarian dishes of aubergine baked in tomato and mushroom sauce with sweet potatoes. He had not seen Frank for over twenty four hours and did not know what he would say to him. Angie was off trying to make peace with Nina. Siva oversaw a world of permanent chaos it seemed, with factions ever at war, and he imagined himself imploring the god to dance into the brothel and send her out. But however hard he pushed his mind he could not see any solutions.

Heading back through the black of palm trunks, the moon skimming above him, he could see a flickering light on the beach and curiosity drew him there. The family had lit a candle for another paper lantern, and as a little girl sent it off it wavered, the man caught it and launched it up like a shimmering flower through the sticky windless air, spirit-like. Aarti would have said it was like a soul released from its worldly body.

He was smiling at them when a blow hit the back of his head. There were punches to his face and ribs, pummelling old wounds and he felt cold on wet sand.

Rich lost consciousness, then rolling through a tunnel into a vast brightness, struggled up for air. Gravity seemed to fall away, as though he was suspended deep in the ocean, his body hanging weightless and his mind neutralised, yet with the glimmerings of awareness of his state, yet unable to move his limbs and escape. He was gagging for air, but his body was dragged down deeper. He would have to give in to drowning unless he could turn things lucid and find a way out. He thought it was a shark at first, but the dolphin's nose checked him out, turned itself round and round him. Grabbing the dorsal fin, he was away, sliding upwards to the ripples of moonlight that flashed near the surface. He opened his eyes in an effort to breathe and bring himself alive and aware in the reality that was emerging out of his unconscious state as he lay half in the low waves that lapped over his legs and occasionally reached up to his chest and lips.

'Rich. Rich. You must come,' Dinesh's voice echoed through the trees. 'Rich. You're soaking wet. What's happened. You've been for a swim in your clothes? You must come.'

Dinesh got him to his feet and drew him forward.

'Dolphins, Dinesh. Dolphins–' Rich was struggling to work out what had happened.

They mounted the steps up to the row of chalets. 'The electric is off. Power cut,' Dinesh said.

His attackers must have beaten him, thrown him in the sea and left him, but he was uncertain whether the dolphins that came to his aid were real, or creatures his mind had made up in order to get him to wake and save himself.

A pack of stray dogs had got together on the beach for a howl. There were no lights along the north end of the beach.

'Rich. Rich,' Dinesh was shaking him: 'Rich. Rich.'

He wanted to lie down and sleep.

'Rich. Rich,' Dinesh pulled him to a door and pulled it open. Dogs roared. It was like dark matter inside. Rich kicked something on the floor. 'Rich. Rich.' It took time for his eyes to adjust and bending found a small brass icon of Siva. Nothing else was out of place, but as he looked up a large shape loomed. A human shape, long – and feet – trousers – shirt – high up –

'Frank,' Dinesh was gabbling. 'Frank.'

The rope was tight from the beam to the man's head. Lights popped on. They stared. Frank's bulging eyes stared back down at them, his tongue folded out.

Rich threw the statue of Siva at the swinging punch-bag. Frank's shirt sleeves were rolled up, and on the left wrist Rich saw the Siva Sect brand.

Dogs were yelling the news outside.

21

Dinesh bandaged his head and fed him some vegetables and chapattis his wife had made while Rich lay in bed. There was no chance of sleep for Rich – police were everywhere. They shuffled next door and Rich could hear them cutting down the torso, talking aloud, laughing and joking about the stiff they were handling. Before Dinesh left, Rich made him leave his door half open and he watched while Frank's long body came out feet first next door as the sun was coming up, the moon an upturned crescent floating above a silver line reflection. A crowd was drawn in: fishermen and women fish vendors, children, a couple of early morning joggers, taxi drivers, rickshaw men and other town workers – jabbering or reaching long necks to peer over shoulders and heads, then the silence of gawps and gasps as the covered body was hauled away on a stretcher, several children running behind.

Lakshya's voice boomed orders as men ushered the body out into the first rays of sunlight, then one staggered and slipped. A couple of men from the crowd jerked forward to catch the faller and hold his place up, but the corpse rolled down, pulling two other pall bearers with it. The crowd gasped again as Frank's bloated face smacked into sand, the bloody-deep strain marks of the ropes around his neck exposed, his trousers soaked and stained round the crotch. Women put hands up to cover their mouths, men had the cold staring eyes of creatures afraid of death. The laughter of two lads started the children pointing and laughing along with them. Lakshya was chiding Mendez for his stupidity, aiming his baton at the pallbearer.

Dogs were quiet, several of them sneaking through the legs of the crowd to get a look. A couple of crows bobbed their heads. The sea flamed in.

When it was quiet, the tall big man blocked the daylight out of Rich's doorway as he came in, and sitting on the edge of Rich's bed let his baton go slack at his side.

'Your friend,' Lakshya said. 'You are sad, perhaps?' Rich watched his lips push up the moustache as he spoke. 'Or perhaps happy?'

Rich waved him aside: 'Pooh.'

'Your friend does things you disapprove of.'

'So do you,' Rich was pleased he found some quick impertinence to throw at him.

A dog stood at the doorway looking in.

'You will be pleased to know, Mister Lomas, that we now have the killer.'

'Good. Who – No –'

'Your friend confessed all, Mister Lomas.'

'He did things wrong, but he wasn't a killer.'

'He left a note.'

'Let me see it,' Rich was lucid again.

'My officers have taken it. But I can assure you he confesses to the murders.'

'No.'

Sniffing the air, the dog stepped in.

'We know he had an accomplice–'

'One of your lot?'

'We are closing in on him.' The big man whacked his baton on the sheets. 'We will have him when everything is in place – all the evidence –'

'You're letting the real killers get away.'

'No, Mister Lomas. We know who they are. We have one, your friend Frank. And now the other,' he paused, the stray dog at his knees. 'You did say didn't you, Mister Lomas, that when you paid the girls – the dead girl Babita, and the other girl, Lalima – it was for dancing services? Nothing else?'

'Frank tried to get Babita out–'

'But we have the suicide note, Mister Lomas. Or should I say, confession.' Lakshya held a hand out to the cur and stroked its head.

'This is a cover up, *Mister* Police Chief,' Rich sneered.

'What did you say to him, Mister Lomas?'

'What do you think? I told him to get out.'

The dog leaned against his new master and trod on his feet.

'I think it was more than that, Mister Lomas. I think you scared him so much he took his own life. I think you are responsible for his death, and I know why.'

'I told him to change and get out of it.'

'You filled his head with ideas. Big ideas. He was scared of you. You were scared of him.'

'Why should I be?'

'Things that would incriminate you.'

Rich shivered. He had to hold his cool.

'I think, Mister Lomas,' Lakshya spoke quietly, 'what you said and did - your cruelty, how you harmed a poor man, led him to take his own life. You have a case to answer in that, if nothing else. I hold you responsible for his death. He had an accomplice. Someone depraved who had him in their power–'

'Unless it was you,' Rich stared in Lakshya's eyes: 'Unless he was no longer any use to you. Unless he was a liability - he might say something and blow all this open –'

Lakshya laughed, then petted the dog: 'Now here's a new recruit. I must tell my men to train this dog –' he laughed again.

'It might sniff out the truth,' Rich could not help himself.

'You English. You think you know it all–' Lakshya pulled himself up. 'But any sniffing this dog does will lead to one criminal, and I will catch him. In the meantime, Mister Lomas, in the event that you think you might be going somewhere while we deal with this matter, I will leave one of my men outside your door. We are not unreasonable men, Mister

Lomas, we will allow you time to recover, get some rest. Then my man will escort you to the police station so you can help us with our inquiries. Come on–' the big man motioned to the panting dog. 'It is best that the guard is armed, you understand, for your safety and security. We do not want anything bad happening to you.' He got to the door, laughter on his lips and his new friend in tow. 'And who knows, Mister Lomas, it might give you time to reflect on what you will tell us when we next meet, and whether that will be sufficient for the judiciary to look sympathetically on you–'

His shape filled the door frame, the dog at his heels, and turning he tossed the icon of Siva from Frank's room on Rich's bed where it bounced then stilled.

The police chief's shape was replaced by shafts of sunlight a second, then as quiet as if by a carer's hand, he shut the door on Rich.

There was peace in oblivion for some time, so that the dreams that filled him mixed with reality and Lakshya brought men to capture him and throw him in a cell with Lalima.

When he opened his eyes darkness had come and he wondered for a second if the figure at the end of his bed was from dreams.

'For you,' she was unfurling a smudged tea towel revealing a couple of slices of papaya.

'Chanda?' He shook himself from sleep.

A thin shaft of light from the outside light bulb lit him.

'Eat,' she said through darkness, although her features were becoming clearer to him.

He stuffed them in, their juices dribbling down his chin. She leaned forward with a tissue and wiped them from him. 'You must come.' She looked nervously at the door.

'I can't,' he shook his head.

'You must come. Now.' She took the tea towel from him and folded it.

He nodded at the door, but she shook her head. 'Chanda?'

'I know guard. David. He's a Christian boy. Grew up next door. He ran on a bike and got bananas for me when he was a boy–'

'Yeah? But–'

'He likes the girl in the shop near me. She is beautiful. She likes him. She is Christian, so very good match–'

'But–'

She put her finger to her lips for him to quiet.

'I bring her in the trees, in the dark. I tell him she wants him. He goes. Quickly. Jeldi.' She chuckled uncontrollably for a moment and he smirked.

'What a matchmaker, Chanda–'

'Men do all for love–'

'You're wicked, Chanda.'

She came forward and kissed him gently on the cheek, running her fingers through his hair: 'You must come. Quick.'

The fan was beating grimly above them.

'Rest Chanda. I'm bruised and–'

She grabbed his arm and leaning back on one leg tried to pull him out of bed, but he groaned with aches. 'Chanda–'

'Come. Quickly come–'

'Chanda, I–'

'Lalima. Quick. Lalima–'

His legs and arms creaked with the effort and his head was banging as though in a hangover. He still had on a dirty T-shirt with blood smears and denim shorts streaked with sandy mud from the night before and he yearned for a shower, but she was pulling him through the door and out into the bright wash of dawn. Tugging his hand, she dragged him like a reluctant plodding boy towards a couple of waiting figures.

'We've got to do it now, Rich,' Angie welcomed him, and taking in his demeanour: 'What happened? Are you all right?'

'What are we doing?' he shrugged.

'It's got to be now. Now or never,' Aarti was serious. The sun would be high in a couple of hours and the town in full flow. 'I know you need help, Rich,' Aarti held his hand, 'I know this is hard for you. But we need you with us.'

'Come on,' Angie was short with him.

'I got beaten up, Angie–'

'Just a scratch,' Angie sent her sympathy with a wry look: 'That's what you always say, isn't it?'

They stood under palm trees. A couple of women with baskets were walking towards the sea, ready to scoop fish from trawling boats.

'Chanda says we have to do it tonight. The police are busy with . . .well, other important things that have just happened . . .' Aarti let her words trail. Then: 'Nobody will come after us for a few days while they sort things out about Frank. It's all so bad - what happened.'

'Come after us?' Rich wanted bed.

Aarti held his arms and looked in his eyes: 'Chanda can get to Lalima. She can get inside and get her out,' she instructed him.

'We can do it, Rich,' Angie encouraged him. 'Rich?'

'Yeah?' he was still dazed, 'And then?'

'We hide,' Aarti said.

'You can't hide forever round here,' Rich mumbled.

'We'll see,' Aarti dismissed him. 'Taxi is waiting.'

'You must come, Rich. Challo,' Chanda scowled.

He looked to her and she turned away: 'Let's go, then.'

Aarti hurried them to the car park under the floodlight near the arch. An old Ambassador car waited, engine chugging, its huge front wing shivering with the tick-over.

'Get in,' Dinesh hushed a yell, looking nervously around. There were only a few taxi drivers about.

'Are you a taxi driver now?' Rich nodded.

'Man of many trades,' Aarti laughed: 'You want son done discreetly – Dinesh is your man.'

Dinesh gave a big smile of gums and uneven tablets of

When Angie and Rich were in, Aarti slammed the dc them from the outside.

'Aarti?' Rich cried as they pulled away from her.

'She'll meet us later,' Angie assured him, but he troubled.

The taxi parted piles of excited dogs and smoothed d tarmac under lines of night lights hanging on into com daylight. Shops and stalls were still shuttered, and a station bus appeared under a row of trees as though stirring fr slumber. A one horned cow was lying in shadows. There w not much of night left to do this in – if it was possible.

'Who will be there?' Rich worried. 'If the police get me – I done for.'

'No one.' Chanda held his hand in darkness. 'Only gi Men drunk. All the police are at the police station.' She held hand through bumpy roughness, the warmness of her agai his warmness. She kept it from Angie. So did he.

'They won't get you,' Angie told him.

'We've got to have a plan–' Rich worried.

The blurry light of early dawn seemed endless. The road into jungle, trees flicking by as Dinesh pressed the old car flinging it round bends and urging it over potholes and ro dogs and cows and the occasional rat.

As they passed a hut with a statue of Siva outside Di slowed and turned off the lights and let the car purr up track and round a long bend until they were as close to the building ahead as he dare, and braked gently. The lone storey house was hidden in shadows under stars that were in fading in the western sky. They entered the thick air, A and Chanda getting out quietly, with Dinesh preventing door slamming by hushing them with a finger to his lips.

Rich was following them, but Dinesh held him back: Woman's job now.'

Rich sat back in the car. They had to be quick: dawn was rushing to its deadline.

Chanda and Angie had reached the door. Several lines of electric lights outside the building were still alive, but competing now with rising daylight. Chanda stooped to a figure of the goddess Laxmi and bent with prayed hands a second to her, then looking up at Angie, took her hand and led her in.

Rich tapped the bonnet of the car with his fingers, Dinesh paced.

'How fast does this thing go?' Rich was imagining a car chase.

Dinesh shrugged: 'Fast as a thirsty camel looking for water –'

'Camels don't get thirsty.'

Dinesh shrugged again and smirked.

The sound of voices came from inside. 'Come on,' Rich led.

Angie was out first, then Chanda.

'Where is she?' Rich yelled.

'Run away,' Angie pushed past him.

'Not now,' Rich slapped his thigh with his fist, and looked towards Chanda. 'She can't have.'

'An hour ago. She's gone,' Chanda said.

'Where?' He got no answer.

A phone rang in the house.

'First girl, Sunita, she ran away,' Chanda carried on, 'then Babita – run away –'

'They're all right if they stay where they are,' Angie spelled it out, 'but if they run away – we know what happens–'

'We've got to find her then, before they do.'

The noise of whispered voices echoed from the house.

'Where though?' Angie looked at him. 'At least the police are too busy to worry–'

'Or they just send someone like Mendez. It only takes one–'

Chanda had drifted back to the statue of Laxmi by the front door.

'I know where she lives–' Rich screwed up his lips.

'Would she go back there? It's so obvious,' Angie quizzed him.

Whispers inside continued.

Chanda ran back to them: 'Police are coming–'

Dinesh herded them in the car.

'This had better go faster than a thirsty camel, Dinesh. Get us up the track before they meet us coming the other way–' Rich dived in the Ambassador.

More than once Rich's head bounced against the roof of the car as they rode a track rockier than the bed of a river. Headlights to the right were scouring the forest.

'They're coming,' Angie hissed.

They watched the headlights skimming towards the bend the police car would swing round bringing them face to face with the Ambassador.

'Hide Rich,' Angie yelled. 'Get him out.'

'If they find Chanda–' Dinesh shouted. 'And they find me – no job –'

'Drop me,' Rich said, 'I'll give myself up–'

'No Rich.' He felt Angie's fury.

'We all get caught then,' Rich shouted.

Dinesh flung the car to the left through a gap in trees, bumped it over boulders and logs until it stopped and flipped off the lights. Turning, he motioned them to get their heads down. As they did so the headlights of the other car pierced the main track and opened up shadows, leading the car past them and on towards the brothel.

Gaps between forest trees were mellowing from blacks to greys.

'I must go home,' Chanda trembled.

'If we don't get her back soon, Milit will find out,' Angie said.

Dinesh called Rich over: there were rocks and branches to clear before he reversed out.

'Home. I must go home,' Chanda shivered.

'We'll get you there,' Rich called.

'I said I am with my baby with my sister. If Milit finds out–'

As Rich and Dinesh laboured they could hear the other car on its way back. Dinesh hissed for them to get down again. Daylight was nearly fully open – there was a danger the boot of the Ambassador would be seen, but the other car flashed by, apparently in chase of them.

'Wait,' Dinesh said.

'I must go home,' Chanda was crying now. 'Milit was in the car.'

'We don't know that, Chanda,' Angie reassured her. 'Come on Dinesh.'

'Wait,' Dinesh held up his finger. 'Wait for the car to go.'

'We arranged to meet Aarti,' Angie's voice pierced the silence and she pulled her phone out and dialled: 'No answer.' She punched a text. 'All we need is her being picked up. She had a plan, Rich. She knew what she was doing.'

'Where is Lalima though?' Rich sat back in the car.

Chanda had her head on Angie's shoulder, weeping.

'We've got to risk it Dinesh,' Angie instructed. Dinesh pumped the car into action, reversing gingerly to the main track, then slowly urged the motor forwards.

'Faster, Dinesh,' Angie held on to Chanda.

'They might be waiting,' Rich hissed.

When they had turned the bend they could see the rest of the empty track up to the road. Dinesh put his foot down allowing the car to glide through lines of trees.

They dropped Chanda at the end of the road from her sister, near the shop, and after a hug with Angie she ran.

'I hope Chanda will be all right,' Angie told Rich. 'But I'm scared. Anything could happen to her. Or you – You can't go back to the chalet –'

'Will you check on her?' Rich faced her, hoping his expression would not betray his feelings for Chanda.

'I'll do what I can. You need rest, Rich. Get yourself patched up. I need to get to Aarti – work something out –'

'Come to mine,' Dinesh led Rich back to his house, making up his own bed for him. Rich lay down and closed his eyes while Dinesh quietly shut the door. It was no good though, he knew he could not sleep. He had to get up and do something. The first thing was to convince Dinesh that he needed a shower and persuade him to lend him some clothes. He ended up with baggy trousers and a T-shirt. While he was changing, Dinesh was in the kitchen with his wife, chatting about food for him, no doubt. Rich got to the front door and was away.

Aditya was playing with water when he arrived: a stream ran near the back of her settlement where she was making boats out of dried leaves with the little girl he had seen a few days before. 'Lalima?' he whispered, turning now and then to see if the man with the stick was around, or others.

'She go,' the other girl said.

'I know.' He took off his sandals and paddled with them. 'Where did she go?'

The little girl put her finger to her lips and went: 'Shush.'

'Aditya?' She looked up at him. 'I'll get you another doll. And you can keep it. And one for your friend. Aditya?'

The girls exchanged glances.

'Aditya?'

The other girl pointed to the hills.

'Is she safe?'

'In hut.'

'Where?'

They pointed at the mauve hills. When he turned back Jyothi was standing over her daughter: 'Go.'

'Jyothi. We've got to get her out–'

'Go.'

'If we don't–' He pulled on his sandals.

'She go back to work.'

'No, Jyothi.'

'She go back to work. Or–' Jyothi shouted through tears.

'That's why we've got to help her. She's not going back there. How many daughters are you going to sell?' He looked down at the girls and the mother came over and picked up her child. 'Are you going to sell Aditya to them as well?'

Jyothi cradled her smiling daughter.

'We can get Lalima away–'

'Away from me?' Jyothi shrieked.

'We can sort something out–'

'They will think I do–' Jyothi finished, 'then big trouble for me – go to jail. Lose children.'

The man behind Rich had a baseball bat, scuffed and notched.

'No, no, I –' Rich could not find words.

'Go–' the man said.

'Nice baseball bat. Where did you get it?' Rich sent the man a fake smile.

'Took from American,' the man laughed. 'He would not go. Me and–' He glanced over his shoulder at a couple of men and a boy over the back, staring at him.

'On my way–' Rich put his hands up in resignation. 'She is safe? Lalima?' he asked Jyothi in passing.

'She go back. Do work.'

Rich ran back among the trees, hearing the sound of men and dogs in pursuit.

He was losing the race against the men with sticks when he heard his name being called. Nikhil ran up puffing. 'Is that you, Nikhil?' Rich stopped. The boy watched him, as though waiting for some kind of confirmation: 'I believe in dolphins,' Rich said.

'Come.' Nikhil led him along tracks to a scooter.

22

Rich reckoned they must be close to Lamilgusma when Nikhil turned the scooter off the road near a man herding goats and headed up a narrow track – they had been going for almost two hours through tall hills heavy with forest, along solitary back roads devoid of traffic, and Rich was saddle-sore and suffering shoulders aching from hanging on his small driver. They had passed one truck, but no buses. He had an image of his phone and wallet in the cabinet by his bed. The track narrowed among trees and shrubs and wound up a narrow craggy gully, so it was no longer possible to drive the scooter on. Nikhil gestured for them to get off, and taking a bag from the compartment under the seat and putting it aside, heaved the machine - with Rich's help - behind a line of shrubs, and gathering dead palm branches and loose foliage camouflaged it.

'Good,' Rich said, trembling a little with anticipation as Nikhil grabbed the bag and headed up the gully. They trekked uphill in the afternoon heat for over half an hour, the only company being a couple of monkeys annoyed with the intrusion on their territory, until the land flattened. A shallow plateau spread out under an outcrop of rock in the middle of which stood a rough stone and wood hut with a roof of plastic sheeting supported by dry branches. The door opened a few centimetres while Nikhil was recognised, then widened. A woman with a leathery skinned face came out into sunlight, straggly hair frosted with white hung to her shoulders, the corners of her mouth were down, but she smiled at Nikhil and took the bag. Muttering something to her, he turned to Rich: 'Food. Fish and rice – chapatti – This is Parmita–'

Lalima stood in the doorway. She ran to him, held his hands, then fell into tears. He took her in a long hug while she sobbed, thinking to himself that he was stupid and mad: 'You're all right?' She nodded with a tearful smile up at him although there was fear in her eyes. 'They won't hurt you again.' He let clichés take over for him, took on the hero-teacher role, never allowing his realisation of his own powerlessness and the hopelessness of the situation seep into his words.

'My mama?' Lalima was still choking on tears.

'We will get you together somehow,' Rich carried on his feigned leadership.

Her glance at him seemed to indicate she believed him, but it was quickly replaced by a look of panic and the shaking of her head: 'That place. Bad–'

Rich had not known his father, and Lalima had not known hers he surmised, for Dinesh had told him begging women often went with many men, sometimes for money, and had their children without the men knowing they were fathers, that mostly it was not possible to tell who the real father was. Lalima clung to him. Neither of them had had a male figure to nurture their growing up, and he realised the role of father had to be learned and that that was what he was doing now.

'You won't be going back there,' he told her, although he did not know how he could enforce his promise. They held on to each other a long time, until Nikhil, laughing called him over.

'Look,' Nikhil directed Rich before they went inside, pulling him out to a rocky edge: they were high enough to see over the tops of trees down to a short section of the road they had climbed from.

Parmita heated the food on a gas ring and they ate cheerfully, the sun still high, then rested, men in one room, women in the other. He worried about Lalima and turning to Nikhil whispered: 'Where do we go?'

But Nikhil shrugged: 'Stay here. No one come.'

The men lay side by side on faded red and gold fabric.

'How long?'

'Nobody know.'

'Parmita will look after her forever?'

'Lalima work for her.'

'What sort of a life is it?'

'Parmita - Dalit.'

'Dalit?'

'Low class–'

'Bottom?'

'Bad caste,' Nikhil whispered. 'You Brahmin, you not come here,' Nikhil grinned, 'not stand in her shadow. Dog go in Brahman house, not Dalit–'

'No husband?' Rich tapped him.

'Husband die. Work in town, he carry thing, he help build thing, work in field, take dead cow away–'

Rich got up and strode to a shelf: 'There's books.'

'He think if he can read he can get good job. He try to teach self to read–'

Rich flipped through pages of a children's book with crudely drawn pictures and Hindi letters. 'He must have been a clever man. Forward thinking–'

'He say all must go to school. Send son. But he–'

'What?'

Nikhil shook his head.

'What happened to her husband?'

'He start big strike in town. All Dalit. Want good job, want school. One day he disappear. Not come back.'

'Anything to do with Lakshya's gang?'

'Nobody know. Police say he run away. He never run away. He love wife, love son–'

Rich fingered the books, the tops with lines of dust, and was filled with emotion a moment.

'She never chuck out.' Nikhil laughed, 'Never. Think of him.'

'He knew things, could see a way forward,' Rich pondered Parmita's misfortune, then quickly said: 'Lalima will now be a

Dalit for the rest of her life?' Putting the book back in its special place he wandered back to his friend.

'Better than–' Nikhil drew his fingers across his throat. 'Better than house of men–'

'What sort of a life, though –' he muttered. 'What work will she do?'

'People not like Dalit. Keep away. Parmita work in town - get waste and tip away.'

'Lalima will do that for the rest of her life? Getting rid of–'

'She alive–'

'From one prison to another–'

'Where you go?' Nikhil looked up and across at him, his dark pupils searching him, the whites of his eyes dull. He had worked too much for a boy, was a man too soon, Rich concluded.

Rich shrugged.

'You – prison to prison too –' Nikhil scratched his neck.

Rich looked up at the branches holding up the ceiling. It was a fragile building and like most things: easily pulled down.

Nikhil stared up with him as he spoke: 'They say you kill girls, then kill best friend–'

'The police say that?' Rich was no longer surprised by what he heard.

'All people – Bagolem. Now you and Lalima run away.'

'You believe that?' Rich looked at him and he stared back steadily.

'I believe in dolphin.'

'Good. I have a daughter back home–'

'I see you help Lalima. Teach–'

Rich nodded.

'I know Mendez,' Nikhil hissed. 'He Red Hand. Kill girl who run away. '

'And police do nothing.'

'Red Hand part of Siva Sect. Siva Sect pay police. They must do thing for them. You must have plan, Rich. They catch you, easy. They come here, and find Lalima too. Bad - '

Rich screwed up his lips: 'Try to get to Paniji, that's the best bet for me. There must be an embassy there. I could take Lalima with me – tell them everything. They would protect her.'

'How you travel?'

'On a bus.'

Nikhil pulled his arms around himself laughing, his body shaking in convulsions.

'Nikhil?'

He took time to shake himself sane again: 'White man and Indian girl on bus. Everybody see –' He was back into laughter.

'We sit on different seats.'

NIkhil could not stop giggling: 'They look for you and girl. Everybody think you murder – all paper say – ' Then he was serious: 'You need disguise–'

'What?'

'Good disguise. Then you go to Paniji, then you tell about Lalima–'

Rich yawned at the ceiling. A lizard crept out of a crevice, ran across the wall and froze. Rich could not stop his eyelids drooping.

In the early evening Rich and Nikhil and Lalima sat on a bench out the front of the hut while Parmita cooked rice and aloo gobi. The sun had edged behind the rim of forest casting purple shade across the yard in front of the house. Mosquitoes would soon be out for lunch. A lonely motorbike skimmed along the road a mile away.

'You come to give me lesson?' Lalima joked.

'Yes, Lalima,' Rich laughed.

'Rich go to Paniji tomorrow,' Nikhil told her. 'We get disguise.'

'You can't stay here forever, Lalima. Not in this kind of life.

Afraid all the time someone will be hiding behind a tree for you.'

She turned away.

'I will get help.'

'They get you –' she bunched her hands.

'Nikhil will help me.'

The light beyond forest shadows was slipping from white to soft lemon.

'They catch you–' She held on to her teacher.

'They want us both, Lalima – Just like in the movies –' he laughed, and she smiled. 'Dance for us. Cheer us up–'

Rich banged two sticks together in a crude beat, and Nikhil joined him whacking a bit of tin with a stick.

Lalima, in orange and blue salwar kameez, span for them, flipping up her fingers, her feet swirling in semi circles, her legs in sudden leaps, her dupatta streaming with her as she turned. Parmita clapped a beat from the doorway.

A sound came from the distance, as though at first in tune with the melody they were bashing out. Rich looked around at the smiling faces, remembering the mental journey he had travelled to get here. Ties to criminal labels put on him seemed to dissolve: she danced and the world was all right, and everybody loved her. Lalima's dance drew in all her onlookers, working her charisma with them, so that their inner crises were suddenly stilled, washed away with a joy in her art, and her ecstatic movements raised spirits and offered healing solace to their everyday troubled minds. They clapped and banged. She danced. The world was good.

The sound came again from the distance.

Nikhil threw down his instruments and rushed to the edge of the cliff, pointing.

Lalima carried on twirling, her face beaming.

'There– ' Nikhil pointed to the road.

Rich joined him. A horn sounded. The truck wound into sight along the road a mile away, headlights flashing, horn buzzing again.

'They come–' Nikhil scowled, afraid. 'They come –'

'How do they know?' Rich yelled.

'Police Chief have spy,' Nikhil said as they charged inside, as though the building would hold back the police onslaught.

'We have to go into the jungle,' Rich was uncertain, and bunched his fingers, his teacher powers of decision making seeming to desert him.

'We go–' Lalima stood with him.

'Where you go?' Nikhil insisted.

'There's a town?'

'Twenty mile through jungle – bad jungle. You go in town, they see white man with Indian girl – police come quick –'

'You take us, ' Rich reasoned with Nikhil, 'You go into the town when we get there and I'll wait in the forest–'

'No good,' the new leader emerged. 'I go back to Bagolem, get Aarti and Chanda, they get help – you find cheap hotel in town – Rajput Dream - meet you – then all escape –'

'If I'm seen, Nikhil?'

Parmita was pulling his shirt and when he turned she had green material draped over her arm: 'Nikhil?' Nikhil told him to get his clothes off so Parmita could begin. Puzzled at first, Rich froze and Nikhil helped Parmita and Lalima pull his shirt off. Shuddering, he understood their intent and backed away in rebellion: 'No.'

'Good disguise, Rich. Very good,' Nikhil hissed. 'They come. Must not find you. Must find old lady. Get trouser off –'

Rich jumped like a machine to his young mentor's instructions, pulling down his slacks as Lalima turned away coyly as he began to cast things off down to his under-shorts, but Nikhil pushed her into helping and told them to get their fingers going. First the under petticoat, tied and knotted around the waist, then the blouse, which he had to squeeze his shoulders into.

Lalima could not stop giggling as she and Parmita quickly wound the fabric round him, pleating and tucking in his navel with a safety pin here and there to hold in folds. Parmita wound the thick coloured end, the pallu, over his left shoulder and around his head, so his features were half in shadow.

'You should wear sari every day,' Lalima laughed. 'Green and yellow - good colour for you.' She covered her grins with her hands.

'No,' Nikhil was agitated, pointing at Rich's hands: 'People know. See face, people know. Keep head down under headscarf of sari, keep pallu down over eye - you old auntie to Lalima -'

Rich felt mummified, 'I'll have to keep away from people-' he said. 'I can't do this. I'm too big.'

'You keep hand covered,' Lalima offered. 'No one see.' She allowed herself another giggle. 'No one see this.' She jabbed the bare skin above his hips, and pulled the sari right over so it was covered. 'Anyway, pale colour good in India. People like pale skin colour, not dark-'

'You bend down. Walk like old woman-' Nikhil said and Rich stooped, but Nikhil pushed his back, 'Go. Like old woman- ' Rich tried a few steps across the room and Lalima laughed. 'Hand not right. See your face - then all done -'

'We've got to go-' Rich snapped.

Parmita stood by him, throwing over his head a Kashmiri shawl of pink and purple Paisley, pulling it round the globe of his cranium, then down over his shoulders like a large headscarf leaving a narrow oval space so he could see through the tunnel of material. Quickly she taught him how to hold the shawl tight and close to his body without showing too much of his hands so the shawl would not slip and his facial features would remain in shadow.

No,' Rich gasped. 'I can't do this. No-'

'You want to escape?' Nikhil yelled.

'Is this how the women feel - looking out at the world through blinkers?' Rich straightened, staring out from the gap for his face through the shawl and Parmita whacked his back with a stick, making him stoop in reflex, and laughed. 'Now you old woman.'

They gazed a moment, Lalima hiding smiles behind her hands, Nikhil anxious but bemused and Parmita with crossed arms.

'You have to go, Nikhil - hide in the jungle until they've gone and double back to your scooter.' The boy nodded. 'What about Parmita?'

'She come with me. We hide. When they go, she come back. You must walk like woman, Rich. Stoop.' Nikhil ordered again while Parmita gathered Rich's clothes, put them in a plastic bag with a tin of rice and a bottle of water and handed them to Lalima. Then she noticed his sandals. 'Must walk slow, not show big feet.'

Their laugher was halted by the sound of cries down the cliff.

The back door opened to the darkness of forest. The moon was high. 'There is track.' Nikhil led the troupe and they ran into hiding as torches way below sent their beams searching. Rich was surprised that the sari allowed his legs freedom to move quickly as Lalima pulled him up and away.

Nikhil raced them along a track for half a kilometre, then stopped and whispered instructions to his followers: 'Me and Parmita go here–' He pointed at a narrow track that branched away to the left: 'You,' he faced Rich, 'Lalima and you. Go there. You run. They not find you, they come in forest–'

'You will be all right?' Rich wanted reassurance. 'And Parmita–' Rich hugged the little woman and while he was kissing her cheek, she slipped a small torch in his hand. 'Go –'

They could hear excited cries at Parmita's house. The track was wide and the moon lit the route as they cantered for ten minutes. The cries were fainter now but a muffled boom filled the sky behind with a glow.

'Parmita's house–' Lalima shouted as the sky above the forest sparkled lemon-gold. 'Her house.' Lalima's panic returned. 'She will be all right?' Lalima threw herself at him, clutching leach-like to his strangely attired body, and he held her: 'We have to hope. She is with Nikhil. He will look after her, take her back–' He doubted his own words, but hoped by the saying of them that they would prove true. If Nikhil failed to get back and get help the future would look grim. He held her, thinking of Jeanette, ran his fingers through her hair and kissed her forehead. They rushed on.

Lalima jumped at the echo of a creature's bark way inside the forest, and they hurried on, but stopping, looked back. Although the flame-glow in the sky was fainter now, the flicking blades of torch beams were cutting through forest. They ran until Rich stopped them by a boulder, and pulling her they crouched behind it waiting, Lalima's trembling knee knocking his side. Gasping, they squatted. The wait was long, but enabled them to stop panting. Lalima looked up at him and he eased down the shawl.

'No need yet. If someone come. Pull over head,' she told him.

Two men, talking loudly, strolled to the other side of the rock and stopped, lit cigarettes and talked on. Rich held back a cough as a whiff of tobacco came to him, pulling the shawl back over his head, his nose poking out.

Then finishing their smokes, they headed on, leaving their hidden assailants. Rich kept holding Lalima back from going out and looking, and in whispers he said: 'What did they say? Could you understand, Lalima?'

'Talk about girl. Stupid talk,' she screwed up her nose in disgust. 'Dirty.'

'Is that all?'

'They say they have to find me–' she was in tears. 'If they don't find–'

He held her to him again while she cried: 'Nothing's going to happen.'

'Red Hand. They kill me–'

'No they won't.'

'They kill. Mendez. Kill Babita–'

'But not you.' He made her drink water from a bottle Parmita had put in the bag along with a tin of food. Remembering some of Aarti's teachings, he took deep breaths to calm his body and fill his awareness with intelligent choices, and feeling eased, encouraged her to breathe into her fears.

'The trouble is, if we go ahead along the main track, as we were, we might catch them up. Or worse, they'll turn back.'

'Or other police will follow–' Lalima was clearer now.

'And we'll be caught between the two lots.' Standing away from the boulder he looked around. 'There must be other tracks – They talk about me? Do they know we're together?'

'They say you disappear with Nikhil on scooter. Man see you near my home–'

'Someone must have followed Nikhil and I on the scooter, or seen us stop and go up the track, or something – so they'll guess you and me are together–'

'You must be woman.' She pulled his sari into shape, straightening ruffles. 'You must be woman–'

'Your old auntie,' he laughed. 'Come on, there's a way down–' although fear was tightening his stomach and he could not tell how effective he was at playing a female. A part of him that had been dormant since birth was excited by it, but the thought was lost in a flash: the need was to survive.

A narrow path led through bushes down the side of the hill. Rocks, dry branches, and the inclination downwards made movement slow for them. Lalima slipped several times so they had to use the torch for some stretches.

They heard voices again, above them and stilled themselves against a rock-face as men passed overhead. They seemed to stop, chat again, laugh and then move on.

Lalima would not tell him what they said at first, but he said she must. 'They find you with me, that prove you kill Babita and other girl–'

'And?'

'"Maybe you and Lalima girl have accident - fall off cliff -" they laughed. They think up plan - say you were beating me so they have to beat you. Then both dead, falling off cliff. Mendez have bad laugh–'

'Yes. And Milit?'

'Not Milit. Milit too scared and not proper police,' she told him. 'Someone different with Mendez.'

They drank more water and headed downwards for half an hour until the track evened out, although the moon had fallen low taking away its guiding light. Stumbling, they reached the silver swirling blackness of a river with a bridge of planks and branches.

'I know this place,' he guided her over the shaking structure to a flat bed of rock. The moon had found its way between trees on either side of the river. 'Lamilgusma.'

He took her to the dancer, took palmfuls of water and scooped them in the gouges round the figure barely lit by fading moonlight and the first washes of dawn in the eastern sky. She smiled at the black outline. He figured the one horned bull with water, and they stood around the triskelion.

'An outline of the cosmos–' he said.

'I like dancer–' She went back and sat with it.

Stars were fading with slow sunlight.

'We should rest,' he said, but she was already asleep, head on hands, by her favourite image.

He sat next to the triskelion looking out at the slowly passing water, and tried meditating in the way Aarti had instructed. The triskelion seemed to revolve, dragging all life with it, inspiring it to further and further consciousness, and his little spike of awareness was drawn in its whirlpool as the wheel surged upwards gaining in its journey to heights of understanding and perception.

He woke with a dry mouth, sunlight pounding his uncovered head, with whispers behind him. Rising himself on an elbow he looked over: two men were chatting and pointing at him. It could be all over now.

23

Pulling the Kashmiri shawl over his head, he leaned towards Lalima and shook her. Waking, and taking in the observers, she got up, walked to them and started talking, while he turned to the river crouching and held his hands in prayer position, hoping he would look convincing.

Talk went on for some time, until finally the men crossed the river and headed into the forest.

'What did they want?'

'They say "why old woman and girl here?" I tell them this is holy place and figure in rock here is of Krishna. Auntie worship Lord Krishna. They say: "Why in night?" I say early morning is holy time here, best time for prayer. And you put hands up to pray. You know right time.' She laughed. 'They farmer. Get coconut from forest and betel.' She was serious. 'But police look for Englishman and girl, they say – we must be careful, he dangerous – they say.'

Rich smiled: 'We've got to go though. Did you ask them which way to the town?'

'They say: "How you get here? On bus up road?" I nod. Must be road–'

'Of course,' Rich remembered, 'up there – a mile or so - Wait. No money -' The wallet was still in his cabinet.

Lalima pulled a small roll of notes from her bra.

'Enough for a hotel?'

She nodded.

'Clever girl – never run away without money –'

'I take. They owe–' she smiled. 'Now you be proper old woman–'

He bent over at the bus stop, the shawl pulled over his eyes. Nikhil had to have got through. Rich let Lalima get on and pay first, following her as though he had failing eyesight and trying to make his gait less obviously a male swagger. Walking with mini steps helped, but he was sweating and worried that it might be noticed and commented on. The full bus had only standing room and as they shuffled to fill two tiny standing spaces at the front a couple of women said something to him, but keeping his head down, he just nodded lightly muttering the greeting: 'Namaste-ji', leaving Lalima to chat, hoping she was telling them her old aunt was hard of hearing as well as poor sighted. The other sitting man was more of a problem, his loud voice haranguing Rich, to which he pulled his shawl down a centimetre further, then embarrassed by the size of his exposed hand, found a place to hide it in folds. He nudged Lalima's leg with his own to get her to do something about him, and she smiled at the male passenger. Rich sneaked a look from the corner of his eye beyond the edge of his pink and purple Paisley shawl - it would be - a policeman. It was a fair cop at last: the man again shouted, pulling himself abruptly up from his seat as Rich was about to hold up his arm to be handcuffed.

'He wants you to have his seat, auntie,' Lalima hissed in his ear.

Rich nodded to the man and thought about how he was going to sit ladylike on a vehicle now bumping through a series of potholes, but the sudden breaking of the bus to avoid a cyclist threw him into the arms of the police officer, who muttered something, held Rich's arms gently and lowered him onto the seat. The policeman's teeth were bloody red from chewing betel nuts. Rich nodded again while the man stood over him for mile after bouncing mile, expecting any moment to be frogmarched off to a police station, never to be seen again. The top of his T-shirt was just visible in the plastic bag.

Much horn work by the driver progressed the bus to the local town where it spluttered to a halt in a market square busy with fruit and veg vendors. The policeman was not going to go off it appeared and stood talking with Lalima for some time. Rich heard him mention the Rajput Dream, and repeat it back to her while Rich stuffed his T-shirt down in the bag. He must burn his old clothes soon and completely cut himself off from his identity and fully immerse himself in womanhood. He had to admit part of him felt awkward, but part felt strangely relaxed in the role.

After a minute's talk the policeman started beckoning them and Lalima grabbed Rich's arm and led him on, his temper rising – what was this idiot doing? Why didn't he just go?

'He wants to take us to hotel,' Lalima hissed in his ear when the policeman turned to lead the way.

He just happened to be a one in a million good cop who wanted to do his duty. Rich bit his lip and bent over in a hobble. Fortunately the walk was shorter than he had anticipated, for the policeman took them to a scooter rickshaw, saw them in, saluted and went on his way to find more criminals and old ladies.

Rich coughed with the fumes, Lalima gave her dear auntie tissues to stifle the male throatiness he was sending out, but it was lost in traffic noise. The town was small, dusty, but being way back from the sea, had no tourists – without disguise he would be noticed right away.

The Rajput Dream had long drifted into nightmare, its faded façade of yellow greyed with age and neglect, and somehow it seemed to lean a little to the left, as though brutes had come alongside and heaved at it. Or perhaps it was his imagination.

Reception smelled of jasmine and disinfectant, but the lad there was full of smiles and when booked in under names Rich hoped Lalima had made up, he was relieved when a bell hop bounced over, an old fella it seemed with a crouch like Rich, so they could walk together in rapport. He showed some surprise at their lack of luggage, but Rich assumed from Lalima's instructions to the bell hop that she'd given him a good line, for he led them to a lift that seemed to have a life of its own, swinging first up past them, and then back down past them, until finally coming to their level.

The room was large, musty with a double bed. He thought Lalima might recoil, but she held her cool, turning and giving the old boy a few rupees which he turned over in his hand ungratefully, looking up for more, but she dismissed him with a wave of her hand to the door.

'Lalima, at last–' he sighed openly.

She whipped her fingers up to her lips for him to hush, and tiptoeing to the door, slung it open. The old boy nearly fell in, recovered himself, smiled at them, touched his cap and left.

'I'm so stupid, I – and you're so clever,' he kept his voice low.

'Little money,' she said. 'Can't pay them to shut up.'

'Was it a good idea to tell Mister Plod where we're staying?'

'Plod?'

'Policeman.'

'He keep on. I have to say. Make up story about you visit Siva temple in town. For special puja. He say you must stay at Rajput. Rickshaw driver his friend.'

Rich looked for quick ways out. The window at the back led onto a balcony overlooking an overgrown garden at the end of which stood a line of houses with outside toilets. They could scramble down in an emergency, get across the overgrown garden and out through an alley – or even hide in a privy – if need be.

'How much money, Lalima?' he quizzed.

'Let's eat,' Lalima said, getting tins out of the bag. 'We not go out yet.'

'Lalima?'

'A little–'

'Show me–'

'We eat–'

'For one night?'

She nodded – probably lying.

Evening was setting in.

'Yes, best not go out much. Only for necessities,' he reiterated. 'Stay safe until they arrive –' If Nikhil gets through, he kept from her.

'Aarti and Chanda?'

'Angie too. She'll help. Then we can tell all at the embassy and get you properly protected. Easy–' He scoffed the cold fish and rice Parmita had packed for them and tried to make his expression look like he was enjoying it and that the hard part of their adventure was over.

'I can sleep in the chair,' he nodded to a high backed wicker chair that looked as comfortable as a bed of nails, 'but let me get a lie down for an hour or so on the bed first.'

She stopped him lying on the bed with a wave of her hand, and pulling off the bedclothes revealed it was two single frames put together which they divided. They shared covers out and lay until it was dark.

A tapping on their door woke him. His watch said ten past eleven. Aarti had found them, or the police. He shook Lalima and she jumped up, ran to the door and asked who it was, then pulling it open a little to check, let Parmita in.

Agitated the woman gave a half smile to Rich while Lalima hugged her, sat on the edge of her bed and talked with her.

'Tiny English,' Lalima apologised on her new friend's behalf. 'Just little –'

'Her house?' Rich was anxious.

'Not her house on fire,' Lalima corrected him.

'What then?' Rich boomed, and Parmita laughed at the male voice sounding from the female clothes.

'Nikhil's scooter. They find, set fire, blow up–'

'What about Nikhil, he's all right?'

Lalima quizzed her, then turned back: 'She doesn't know.

They both ran in the forest, but she lost him. Then bang - his scooter -'

'He must have got away?'

Lalima shrugged her shoulders. The best vision he had of little Nikhil in his mind was of him getting a lift in a truck along the back roads to Bagolem and alerting his friends, but that would take at least a day; the worst image, and the frighteningly more likely one, was he was caught and was suffering a beating - or worse. Hopefully the dolphins would help him resurface. Rich shivered.

Without Aarti and Angie's help, the chances of getting to the embassy at Paniji were slim - they would surely be discovered in the hotel in a matter of days if they waited. It seemed they had no money either. Tomorrow they would have to get buses and go, he decided.

'They wrecked Parmita's home, trying to find us - or clues we had been there, but nothing -'

'She was not hurt?'

Parmita had brought okra and rice with some curried fish with chapattis and they ate heartily in silence. Then more chat, until Lalima turned to him with a grin and said: 'She wants to henna your hand, says it will look good and make it like you are a real woman.' The two women sniggered behind hands while the older of the two pulled his right hand to her and opened it. 'She says we need cheering up.'

He spread his palm to her and she oozed the earthy brown sludge from her conical cardboard squeezer in lines across it. Paisley drops she formed and flowers in swirling shapes, leaves in filigree patterns and curlicue. Lalima took over and guided patterns over his wrist and the two women admired their work and talked and laughed over it, discussing various patterns. When they were happy with the shapes they made him lie back and wait while the mixture dried.

'Must pull shawl right down-' Lalima smiled. He was glad she looked relaxed now, and nodded.

Parmita found gulab jamun in a cardboard box in her bag and they sucked on the sweets. He wanted to hold the moment in his memory - a woman as he was now, with two other women, sharing something of their bond with each other, knowing in a flash the link they enjoyed. The thought of Jeanette brought tears to his eyes.

They made him rest and brushed away the henna, leaving strands of yellow-gold patterns across his palm and over his wrist and he could not stop looking at the shapes, turning his hand round this way and that, following the sepia imagery. The women laughed. They made up his eyes, put dark lines of kajal around the rims.

'Get marry–' Parmita bent double with laughter, and they joined her.

'Yes,' Lalima screamed with laughter. 'You are ready to get married–'

'Very good hijra,' Parmita clapped her hands. 'Dance at wedding –'

'Hijra?' he recalled something.

'And bless baby boy–' Lalima adjusted his sari.

'Hijra?' he sounded the word again.

'Man who is woman.' Lalima stood back and viewed him.

'Transgender?'

'Eunuch,' Parmita said.

When they had finished their jokes he handed Parmita his bag of clothes. He had to give up being who he was and his old togs were dragging him back; without them he could grow fully into his new identity, could explore what being a woman was. Although he was acting, he was going deeper into the part and must let go of all past traces if he was to survive; he had to be fully female, or nothing. 'Burn them, Parmita,' he said, and she took them without a murmur or look of uncertainty, knowing what he wanted.

Parmita left, telling Lalima she was staying with a friend overnight, but would be back the next day after work.

When he lay waiting for sleep, still in the green and yellow and white sari, he noticed Lalima turning restlessly. 'We will find your mother and your sister,' he sent words quietly to her that he hoped he could make true. 'It will be all right.' But her eyes were still open when he drifted off.

*****

Sunlight through the back window woke him and he was alert in a second. Something was different. He sat up. Lalima was not there. He shouted to the shower. No reply. He pulled the sari into creased shape as he jumped up deciding whether to wait - maybe she had gone to reception for something - or whether to go out and look. The latter idea being the most risky, he would have to wait. But as the minutes ticked by the realisation came that if she was picked up it was only a matter of time before they came for him. He braved the door, having no plan, and no idea how he would communicate, and pulling the edge of the shawl down as far as he could and still see the ground in front of him, headed for the stairs. First he ran, then hearing a door open along the corridor remembered to get into character: a crouching old lady.

The first steps down led to a platform with doors opening onto a balcony facing the street. A couple of male guests were heading down the corridor towards him - a woman on her own - surely they would question him. He hobbled to the balcony, and turned along its little length.

A street burbled busily underneath - rickshaw, bus and taxi horns blaring in a jam along a road full of shops that had tumbled their goods onto pavements. There seemed to be a crowd up one end which was blocking traffic. In the circle - a girl dancing.

'Stupid girl. This is not the way to get more money now-'

Twirling and spinning with big smiles Lalima had entranced her audience. And it was working. Men were dropping notes at her feet which she gathered, stuffing them in her bag. Perhaps she had made it, the crowd was dispersing. Rich smiled.

He did not notice at first a couple of blokes pushing through the mingle. Police. He dare not call, the cry would be lost in traffic noise or draw attention to him. He watched as they came in to her, and another two appeared from an alley grabbing her arm and folding it behind her back. They hustled her to a waiting car and two of them shoved her in. The other two chatted a second, turned looking up his end of the street and one of them pointed at the hotel. As the car pulled away the other two started running towards reception.

Rich headed back to his room. The lift was on its way up – that could not be them yet. There was a way out, but surely they would catch up with him. The lift stopped and Parmita ran to him: 'Jeldi, Jeldi –' she yelled for him to get to his room and they piled in panting.

Flinging open the windows, she pushed him onto the ridge. He could jump onto the flat roof just below. They could hear shouts. He leapt, bracing himself back from the edge as he landed and looking back, uncertain, saw Parmita jump and he half caught her. They would have to climb down the next bit over broken brickwork. He found a foothold and was on his way. More shouts from inside. Only twelve feet above ground, he lost his grip and fell back, his landing broken by shrubs. He pushed back the pain and jumped up to help his friend who was also running out of footholds.

'Fall back,' he cried, 'I will catch you.' His back hurt. She did not understand or was too scared, frozen twelve feet above him. 'I will catch you.'

Her face was taut with fear.

'Come, come. Challo. Challo,' he remembered the Hindi word for 'let's go.' She turned to look down, the movement shaking one hand free, enough to send her plummeting. He had her waist in his hands as she came to him, but they both fell back, her heaviness winding him. She was the first up: 'Jeldi. Jeldi–'

'Quick, yes?' he muttered and she nodded.

'Jeldi,' she headed through shrub land which had once been the gardens of the hotel towards the backs of houses.

He thought she knew a way through the alleys, but stopped. If the men had got to his room they would certainly see them.

Parmita was near a privy at the back of one of the houses, and finding a bucket and spade held it to him. 'Work. Work–' She nodded. 'Cover head.' She pulled the shawl edge to his eyes.

A few flies enjoyed fluttering around the equipment she had forwarded to him, but that was not unusual in this heat.

'Work. Work–' She took him to the base of the toilet, grabbed the wooden spade from him and thrust it inside. 'Head. Head –' She motioned him to keep his head and body down as she withdrew the spade but he jerked back. 'Head. Head –' She hissed.

He could hear the men talking at his hotel window and looking out at their backs.

Parmita pulled out a spade full of human waste.

'Ahh,' he sneered.

She smacked the contents into the bucket and went in for more.

The smell was so powerful it threatened his ability not to pass out, his legs faltering.

When they had told him her work as a Dalit meant dealing with waste his naïve mind had envisaged piles of discarded fruit and veg peels.

She plopped more of the stuff in the bucket, scraping the spade along the edge then passed it on to him to go for a last lot, but he was unmoveable, bunching his fists and trying to stay on his feet. She prodded him twice: 'Do. Do.' He had to show he was a Dalit woman with Parmita, so grabbing the handle he thrust into the pit and pulled out the remains, retching as he did so.

The men were laughing upstairs.

Parmita nodded to a bucket of water nearby, which he hauled over to her and she sloshed it around the inside of the toilet and over the spade.

He could hear the men still there.

Parmita motioned for him to follow her to the next house and they bent there again, delving into the underneath of the toilet and pulling the stuff out and loading the bucket.

'Why don't they go?' he thought aloud, imagining she would not understand. 'What are they talking about?'

'They say you big bum–' Parmita's words echoed through the privy.

A quick burst of laughter from him sounded through the toilet - his body must not shake with it though - although Parmita was laughing too.

The men had gone. Rich and Parmita smiled at each other.

'Take to friend–' she said.

He picked up the bucket of faeces and said: 'Where?' and balanced himself by grabbing the walls of the privy.

She gesticulated to her head and he only understood when she piled the full wooden bucket onto a cloth pad on her head and strode off. He grimaced.

She motioned him to stay now the police had gone and she would go on and finish alone, but he would not, going with her to several more toilets until four buckets were full. Then they went for a hand cart at her friend's house and having loaded it rolled the lot several miles to a cess pit out of town which they could smell several hundred metres away. Rich was coughing and holding back vomit as they poured heaps of the stuff down with water. A bout of coughing and retching followed and he staggered back, supported by his new friend.

They were to eat at her friend Meena's house where he was made to have a shower during which he gathered Parmita was relating the story - no doubt with lots of embellishments, for the two could not stop laughing. Meena gave him a clean sari of blue and red and they made him up silently, wafting the material round him as they would with any other woman, straightening and tucking here and there, and then looking at him, Meena with a grin behind her fingers. She explored the henna on his hands and talked with Parmita about it, wanting her to do hers. He could tell they thought he looked good.

Embarrassed, but still queasy, Rich could not touch his food. At first his host was alarmed, but he motioned he felt ill and they seemed to understand, leading him to a bed.

He would have to go back to the Rajput Dream soon though in case his friends did arrive. Parmita and Meena left him to sleep but he spent the night awake, coughing and sweating with flu-like symptoms.

'I must go to the Rajput Dream,' he told them in the morning, but Parmita wagged her finger sideways: 'Police. Guard.'

'Then catch a bus to Paniji.'

She wagged her finger again. They thought it was too dangerous - perhaps buses were being searched. They made him wait in the house all day.

'Sick,' Meena pointed at him. 'Sick. Stay bed.'

They had taken the sari off and wrapped him in cotton pyjamas.

'Watch Rajput,' Parmita tapped her breast. 'Watch Rajput. See friend-' Parmita reassured him as he slipped out of consciousness.

When he woke, he could not remember the nightmare tussle of his coma, although the remnants of fear and tension clung to him, along with the image of his mother facing a long road, and a pile of dung in a cess pit.

'How long?' he asked the women.

'Two day.'

'Two days? Where will Lalima be now?'

They eased his confused head back on the pillows, added cold poultices to his forehead and fed him a bitter tasting herbal broth.

When he woke again Nikhil was smiling at him.

'You're safe–'

The boy nodded: 'You see dolphin in your dream?'

Rich smiled.

'Tomorrow your friends come–'

'You got through, Nikhil–'

'They come and get you.'

'Lalima?'

He shrugged his shoulders: 'Nobody know.'

Nikhil was gone like a phantom as Rich went back under.

'Nikhil came,' Rich told them when he woke again and they looked at each other. 'Nikhil–'

Parmita tapped his arm. Rich was finding it hard to establish reality.

'Tomorrow. You better.'

When he woke again Chanda was there, and Angie, with Dinesh behind them: 'We've found her,' Angie said, but he did not believe his hallucinations. 'Lalima. We know where she is.'

24

The beige Ambassador car rattled along the dark road, its fading headlights searching for potholes, Dinesh at the wheel.

'Where?' Rich mumbled, barely alert from the dragging sickness. No one replied.

They pushed through black jungle.

Angie hissed a giggle at him – made up as a woman again in his new blue and red sari with matching Kashmiri shawl. 'Very becoming. You should go into drag–'

'Where is Lalima?

'We think she's back at the brothel. Poor girl. We'll get her out, Rich.' Angie looked him up and down again with a smirk. 'And you're getting by so well, my lovely.'

'I'm a woman now, that's for sure, ' he muttered through his drowsiness. 'Got to stay that way to survive.'

'There's no future for us then,' Angie laughed again.

'I learned the work of a Dalit – a pile of filth –'

'You have to be born lucky here, that's for sure,' Angie added.

Chanda was up front, directing Dinesh.

'We can get her out?' Rich motioned.

'We're going to try,' Angie's tone sounded a little uncertain now.

'You sure she's there?'

Chanda turned to him: 'Milit says the police take her there. They don't know what to do now with her–'

'It seems like it's too risky to kill her at the moment, thank god,' Angie sighed.

'They will keep her there and then move her to some place far away. Mumbai –'

'What chance has she got there?' Rich said. 'On the game for the rest of her days.'

'We've got to get to her quickly, if we're going to do it,' Angie went on. 'And if we want to get you safe as well, you've got to put up with drag for sometime yet. Maybe later you can show us some of your courtesan skills.' She laughed. 'Dancing, reciting poetry, playing sitar.' Chanda laughed with them.

'We go to the Embassy then?' Rich wanted to know what had been decided.

'Aarti's got a plan – we're meeting with her later –'

Dinesh pulled off the main road and skimmed down the track, taking the bend too fast, skidding, then screeching towards the house.

'Stop, Dinesh,' Angie shouted. 'Stop here, they may be waiting, it might be heavily guarded.'

He pulled the car up, turned the lights off and they waited, the lamps of the place dimly visible ahead through trees and hanging forest debris.

Dinesh came to Rich's door, opened it, allowing meagre dimness from the inner car light to spread a way for him, and cheekily offered Rich a gentle hand to alight which he took playfully, and holding Dinesh's fingers stepped down in the manner of a superior lady. The women got out and readied themselves – Chanda by taking a swig of water, Angie fixing her shoes tightly.

'Women's job now,' Dinesh winked at Rich and nodded at Chanda and Angie.

'I'm a woman too,' Rich insisted, but Dinesh pulled him and Angie back. 'Only Chanda. People inside know her.'

Rich stood by the car. They would have to be quick – dawn was rushing to its deadline. When Chanda reached the door several lines of electric lights were still alive but would soon be competing with daylight. Chanda acknowledged the statue of Laxmi with a short curtsey with praying hands and went inside.

The others waited in the car, tapping hands and feet, breathing on windows and rubbing them. 'Something's happened,' Rich said and before the other two could stop him he was heading up the track towards the house. Angie ran behind him, but stopped at the edge of the pool of light around the building. The sight of Rich as he began to hobble shocked her - somehow he was an old Dalit woman - and she threw her fingers to her mouth with a gasp.

Rich hesitated at the icon of Laxmi, thinking it good to imitate Chanda's ritual actions before it in case anyone was looking and stooped with praying hands a moment. Then, approaching the open doorway, and catching his breath, he stepped forward, suppressing feelings of fear - he was used to this now. A thick blade of light from a doorway to the right of the corridor he entered was an obstacle. This place would not be unguarded. He could hear chattering women's voices up the end as he edged towards the open door and shuffled by - two men, one with his head down on a table, the other in shadow with a bottle of whisky lying asleep in a chair, his back to Rich.

He eased past.

The first room he entered had several sleeping figures, some half croaking with dreams, some snoring, some half aware of his female shape in the light of the corridor. Chanda was not there, neither was Lalima, and he feared for a moment that the girl might be in a back room sleeping with a man - a guard even, but turned and moved on towards the whispering voices which were now agitated. Half way along a candle was burning in a holder on a small ledge next to a miniature image of Siva dancing in a circle of flames, and taking the flame he rolled his old body forward, covered head down, feet shuffling.

Chanda was in the next room talking quickly to a woman in her forties while Lalima was sitting on the edge of a bed behind them, but Rich dare not show signs of glee. The woman pointed at him and hissed at Chanda, to which she replied. He guessed the woman was aggressively asking: 'who is she?' And Chanda was giving her some line. Rich sensed the awkwardness of the moment: he would have to play hard of hearing, but by doing that Chanda couldn't tell him what was going on. He stood by her and held her arm in what he imagined was a womanly way. The woman was shaking her hand in a 'no' gesture. This had to be sorted or the guards would wake up and sort it for them.

Lalima broke the silence: 'Auntie. Auntie.' She came to Rich, half bent and touched his foot in the Hindu manner of respect for elders.

'No take–' The other woman broke into English. 'No take girl–'

'She needs her mother–' Chanda insisted.

'No take–' The woman was almost in tears.

Candlelight flickered over the woman's head - perhaps actually she was in her late thirties it seemed to Rich, but she looked much older - lines had compressed and distorted her face, and what had once been beautiful features were now lost except for deep brown eyes that shone out with vivacity.

'Auntie, auntie,' Lalima clung to him. A couple of other women were stirring in their sleep. Lemon dawn was pushing aside shadows.

Lalima whispered to him: 'Woman say: "Lalima must stay. I must go. They take new girl here. Get rid of old. I am free then." Chanda say: "She young, sister. Need mother. She can have life."'

The woman stared.

Chanda searched for a little cotton bag in the folds of her sari and shoved notes in the woman's hand.

'Chanda say she help her get out one day–' Lalima said, and then quickly: 'But woman say: "No. Lalima not go."'

'Lalima,' Rich hissed.

'They kill me–' Lalima was hooked in fear.

'We've got to run–' he could not disguise his voice.

'Man. Man,' the woman screamed. 'Guard. Get guard.' She pulled Rich's shawl back and shouted in his face: 'Man.'

The two security men were in the doorway, then rushing to him, one grabbed his arm and dragged him down the corridor, the other kicking him from behind. Reaching the front office, the one holding his arm looked down at his grip and suddenly let go: 'Red Hand,' he shouted. 'Red Hand,' and the other looked down at the henna lines across Rich's palm and up his wrist and gasped.

'Sorry sir,' the first said.

'We are very sorry, sir.'

'We did not know you are Red Hand, sir–'

'Idiots,' he shouted, resuming his old woman pose and pulling his Kashmiri shawl back down to eye level, pushed them aside.

'Red Hand want the girl,' Chanda nodded at Lalima. The men looked at each other and backed away.

'Yes miss–' they pointed in unison to the door. Before he went Rich snatched the whisky bottle for a swig and banged it down on the table - he needed the kick - the men jumped.

Chanda had got Lalima to the edge of the veranda, the dreamy girl in flower covered pyjamas was still rubbing her eyes and walking heavy footed, so that Chanda had to coax her.

'They will kill me–' Lalima sounded hysterical a moment.

'We have a plan, Lalima. Challo–' Chanda reached to the girl gently and held her hand, leading her into the rising light. 'Aarti will take care of you and your mother.'

Lalima stepped towards the track home. Dawn was up, no stars, only the bright of the relentless sun.

Rich held her hand: 'We ran before, Lalima. Now we have to run again–'

Headlights were pushing down the track towards them as they hastened towards Dinesh's Ambassador. An old Jeep screeched and stopped, disgorging its driver.

'Take her back,' Milit roared, running to Chanda. 'Back. Back –' She shook her head, and Rich could see she was flinching ready for a blow, and stepped ahead.

'We must go, Mil,' Chanda said. 'We must go.'

Dinesh and Angie had come up from the car.

'She not go–' Milit yelled towards Lalima.

There was a short silence before a couple of crows croaked.

'Milit,' Chanda dropped her hold of Lalima and went to her husband, 'if you had a daughter, Milit,' she held his gaze, 'would you do this to her? I see hurt in your eyes when men look at me. She is just a girl, Milit–'

The crows listened for the outcome.

'Let Lalima go, Mil,' Cousin Dinesh piped.

'You can change things, Milit,' Chanda put her hand on his arm, 'make things go right –'

He pulled away.

'Is this the Milit I married?' she carried on in front of the audience. 'Is he the young man who cared about me, brought me flowers and kissed my lips in the morning? The Milit who held me when the moon was up? That Milit was a good man – a man who hated people cheating. Where is that Milit? He has gone. I knew him once, he was my husband. How can this be my husband if he says a girl can stay here? He is not Milit at all. He does not know love–'

A crow squawked, then silence.

'She stay here,' Milit waved his arm angrily.

Dinesh came forward and hissed to his cousin: 'You let them go, Milit. Let Chanda make her safe.'

'They will kill me.'

Chanda interrupted: 'Your brother in Bangalore. He will give you a job.'

'They will kill me. All of you.'

'Always I looked after you, Mil,' Dinesh said as rays of sun burst through trees and monkeys started sharing details.

'Always - drunk, gambling - I looked after you. I have a story. Lalima ran out, you chased her, but she disappeared like spirit in forest. Yes, tree spirit - Yakshi - you try and try, but-'

Chanda touched Milit's arm but he waved her away, his face distorted.

'The gods will bless you, husband,' she said, leading the young one to the car. 'Bhagavan will bless you -' Chanda looked back on him as she took Lalima, and when the girl was inside the car she went back to Milit: 'We can go to your brother in Bangalore. New life. With baby. Your boy. New life, Milit-'

The man fell on his knees in tears and held her legs and she put her hand on his hair.

Chanda looked back on him as the car headed down the track. Rich nodded to her while Angie had Lalima in her arms, asking for her mother.

'The plan?' Rich threw the question out. 'Where do we go?' But no one answered.

Dinesh took them into daylight, whisking the car through forest and hills, while they bumped along silently, and Chanda and Angie took turns in stroking Lalima's forehead and telling her not to worry.

Rich kept looking over his shoulder, ready for police cars or jeeps in chase. His 'red hand' would not work again.

Dinesh drew them to a stop under a banyan tree at a crossroads and they got out for water and a stretch. Rich needed a pee, and headed behind the tree, but it was a job getting to his equipment through rolls of fabric - he fumbled and flapped and resorted to a female stooping stance and let out a gush. The tree's branches hung as tough fronds, sometimes as thick as a man's arm, in tangled masses to the ground, rooting themselves, greedy for earth's juices.

'Very old tree,' Dinesh smiled as he readjusted Rich's dress and Chanda helped him make it look realistic again. 'Thousand years old. More, maybe-'

'Before 1066, then–' Rich laughed, 'and Henry the Eighth and Cromwell and Margaret Thatcher even –'

They laughed. 'You make a good woman,' Dinesh said. 'Very good –'

'I can't wait to get back to who I am,' he muttered, 'and not look over my shoulder –' Yet some secret part of him enjoyed the pretence.

A scooter rickshaw waddled into view, stopped and tipped out its occupants: Jyothi rushed out to hug Lalima, followed by Aarti. Rich imagined himself holding Jeanette. Jyothi's arms were bandaged, her eyes weary looking, cheeks stained with old tear tracks. A male passenger stepped out of the rickshaw and stood in the background.

Having greeted Aarti and Jyothi, Rich was agitated: 'Where do we go, Aarti?'

The woman was searching Lalima's wrists: 'No sign.' Her cry of joy rose to the rafters of the banyan tree. 'No little circle on her arm of Siva dancing. She is not part of Siva Sect. Thank god.'

'The gods you mean,' Rich said as Aarti looked up at him and examined her new female friend.

'Jyothi has been harming herself with anxiety and grief,' Aarti whispered to him. 'She will be all right, but we must be careful with her, she is confused and worried.' She raised her voice: 'Let me introduce Charles.' Aarti waved a finger for the young Indian man to come to the fore. He had on a worn suit and a shirt with a collar too big and wide for the tie that tried to trap his throat. 'Christian and Hindu work together. Charles is a reporter for Bagolem Herald. He wants to make a name for himself. A good story will get him a job on a national paper–'

'What better story,' Angie was fired, 'than corrupt police and underage girls in sex slavery.'

'Exposed by a man in drag–' Rich could not help adding.

'Charles will take it all down, won't you Charles?' Aarti said, and the young man pulled a notebook from his pocket: 'All the details.' She turned and continued in leadership: 'Now, Rich and Chanda you join me in the rickshaw. Charles, you get your story from Lalima and Jyothi with Dinesh. Angie, you go with them too.' And turning back to Rich: 'Old ladies get in first.'

The back of the rickshaw loaded with three bodies along uneven roads was torture for Rich, still groggy from his fever, they had to stop a couple of times for Chanda to give him water. Their eyes met when he took the bottle from his mouth, she screwed the top on, smiling at him, before Aarti pushed them on: 'We have to get them out quickly,' Aarti urged the driver and then spoke quietly to Chanda. 'You need to go with Jyothi and Lalima.'

Chanda did not speak.

'Chanda?' Aarti frowned at her.

'You must go,' Rich held Chanda's hand. 'Get out now.'

'My husband-'

'Lakshya has him chained,' Aarti called over traffic noise. 'We do not know what he will do. We don't know what Milit will have to do to save himself. It's too dangerous for you to stay, Chanda-'

'When the newspaper comes out,' Chanda stalled, 'all will be sorry.'

'No Chanda. It takes time. Lakshya and the Red Hand mob will be on the loose for god knows how long - if you go on to Bangalore, Mil's got a reason to follow you - he can make himself safe that way -'

She was still shaking her head: 'My baby.'

'We'll get him now,' Aarti directed the driver to Chanda's house.

'My sister is looking after him—' Chanda said, and turning to Rich and holding his hand: 'Where will you go?'

*****

The horn of a diesel train broke the silence of early dawn. The young reporter was still busily trying to scribble notes in a bumpy car, while Angie was telling him to emphasise Lalima's age and how she'd been forced into prostitution – spelling words for him, the paper being printed as usual in English – while Lalima and Jyothi rolled out details faster than his pencil could keep up.

The train was coming out of the forest, a long creature meeting dawn by hauling itself up a gradient, over a river, along a cutting, lizard-like in its desire to warm itself in a sun that was now rising to scorching heights.

Chanda and her baby, Rich and Aarti tipped themselves out of the rickshaw and hurried to the platform, Rich in a fast shuffle, shawl still low over his eyes.

'Lalima,' Aarti came to her and Jyothi as the train, still a spot at the end of converging lines, wobbled in haze towards them. 'My Auntie Jaina in Bangalore. You will stay with her. Little Aditya will stay with me for a few days, and I will come down with her to you and arrange things–'

'What things?' Angie could not help herself.

'I have contacts in Bangalore. And Auntie Jaina,' Aarti watched as the train eased its way into the long north end of the platform. 'A dance school for Lalima. We will get her in. She must learn to dance for her food, not beg. Indian classical dance. And her mother – Jyothi – my aunt knows co-operative ventures for women making crafts. No more cutting herself–'

Angie hugged Aarti. The diesel rumbled by them, thudding its bulk along the platform and drawing its great load of carriages past them, its wheels with heavy metallic sounds grating along the track.

Lalima and Jyothi climbed on, and Aarti turned to Chanda with her baby: 'You must go now–'

'I will take care of Mil–' Dinesh came to her.

Chanda handed the baby to Angie a moment and went to Rich: 'Where will Rich go?'

'We'll hide him until the story breaks,' Aarti told her.

'They will believe it?' Chanda sounded uncertain.

'An Englishman in a sari,' Rich laughed. 'They're bound to believe it – Top story – yes, Charles? '

The reporter laughed.

Holding his hand, Chanda looked in his eyes. Angie turned away to the baby. Quickly searching a little bag Chanda brought out a shining shape and slipped it in his hand. He laughed – an elephant with upturned trunk – and kissed her cheek.

The diesel's horn warned the locality again. Chanda was on the carriage steps, while Angie handed back the baby, and the great shape gradually started easing its way out, rolling itself southwards. Tearful, Lalima pushed past Chanda, stepping down from the sluggishly moving carriage and before anyone could hold her back threw herself at Rich. Struggling anxiously to free her hold on him before the train picked up speed, he yelled: 'Auntie will come and see you.' And lifting her from her feet sped her to the crawling thing and put her back on, but she did not want to let go and he had to run with her a time until Jyothi grabbed her and Lalima's hands turned from holding him to waving to him.

Chanda was waving from the windows as dawn came up fully in lemon streaks and the thundering locomotive urged its load away from the little crowd. Charles the reporter shook a handkerchief to the heads and hands that hung out of windows and doors and disappeared in daylight.

The train parted the forest with a final cry and was gone.

25

The shack Dinesh had found for him with the help of Parmita was half a mile from where she lived. Dinesh had insisted that it was too dangerous for him to stay with her, but in the makeshift cabin in the forest a short distance away he would be safe at night. Daytime, he could go to her for meals. Rich had made sure that Dinesh would bring his wallet, remaining clothes and belongings - especially his painting gear - he would be here a while and needed something to do. Besides, he wanted to give money to Parmita for food. And he spent some time in the evenings when the heat had dimmed, patching holes in her roof; he collected water from the stream nearby and did the washing up. She scolded him for doing the chores in a way that made him know she had actually enjoyed him helping.

It was good to be back in men's clothes - Parmita had saved his togs from burning - but he admitted to himself he had enjoyed the experience and promised himself to do it again: he had seen women's things, been down their paths, learned of their restrictions, glimpsed the captivity some were held in, but more than that, he had found a woman inside himself and scared of her at first, had ended by embracing her. Bundling the sari in a bag, he made a note not to let it go.

Days moved slowly - repairs, walks through the forest - he spent an hour each morning sitting in meditation in the shade, allowing his mind to relax and sift through images of Lamilgusma, although he reckoned it was still too risky to go there. Aarti's techniques for breathing into meditation seemed to click for him as he allowed his mind to travel, settling back with images of Jeanette. If this took him to the heart of something peaceful, a place of balance and non-violence, he was happy. His inner circles led him to plateaus away from the noise of life, where he could feel the resonance of a restful aware existence, where ego needs seemed to drip away to be replaced by alert perceptions. The triskelion wheel turned like the great Wheel of India, a slow juggernaut in motions of life-force, energy and consciousness, like spiral galaxies opening out to the wideness of the cosmos - a great sense of consciousness he wished he could hold on to when he came back down to ground to the microcosm around him.

Discovering the forest, watching lines of soldier ants, following monkeys through trees, eyeing bright birds, he was no longer worried about having no one to talk to or afraid of being alone for long periods, the chatter of his own inner dialogue subsided after a time, leaving him a pool of quietness in its place.

He did enjoy seeing Parmita in the evenings though, like a boy waiting for his mum to come home from work, even though they could only converse through crazy gesture and terse phrases. They laughed a lot. She brought him oranges and pineapples and coconuts. He carved funny faces on the coconut shells that made her laugh.

At first he had thought he would not be able to sleep alone in a shack covered with dried branches that harboured spiders, snakes even, or perhaps a scorpion, but it was the mosquitoes on the first few nights that were the most bothersome - he must get Dinesh to bring the nets.

It was a few days before Dinesh arrived, bringing Aarti, who was carrying Aditya the last few metres up the track. Rich took the child from her and showed her the funny faces he had made and they sat together drawing detail on them, and sticking coconut strands as hair around them.

'Nothing then?' Rich asked. It was late afternoon and Parmita was still at work.

'News has not broken yet,' Aarti pulled her lips in.

'How much is the media controlled?'

'We don't know,' she said.

'We wait.' Dinesh dumped Rich's bag outside the door.

'Mosquito nets?'

Dinesh nodded.

'Thank god for that.'

'I have to get Aditya to her mother,' Aarti looked sternly to him. 'She's not safe here until this is over. I'm going down tomorrow.'

'What else?'

'Frank,' Dinesh shuffled.

'They burned his body by the estuary,' Aarti told him, 'on a great funeral pyre of driftwood. It was what he wanted: he had told his daughter, and she came over and organised it. I don't think it was easy, there was a lot of red tape, and in the end she just went ahead and did it–'

'Like father, like daughter,' Rich laughed cynically.

'It was all done properly, Hindu style,' Aarti explained. 'Men carried his wrapped body on a wooden stretcher on their shoulders up to a pyre of logs they had prepared earlier, set his body there and put flames to it. The pyre and the body are doused in sandalwood, so the aroma trails pleasantly down the beach, and his soul slips off to other realms – we did a puja for him: short prayers. It was the place he loved most in the world. Dinesh helped. We watched the smoke of him rise to future lives, until the pile of him fell apart in flames and ash as he disintegrated into warm dust to the sound of his daughter's muffled tears–'

'He was some mate,' Rich looked at the ground. 'Someone I liked and hated. But I couldn't forget what he did–' Rich shook his head.

'Too late,' Dinesh said.

'Too late to change. I wanted that for him – but it was too late –' Rich nodded.

Dinesh handed Rich his old peacock box half full of coarse grey powder:

'They let me take some of him, the last ashes,' he said. 'The last bit of Frank – we put it in the sea, Rich. Good ploy?'

'Very good ploy, Dinesh.' Rich was in thought a moment. 'What we don't know though for certain is – whether he took his own life, or whether Red Hand finished him – either for helping me, or because he was no use to them and was a liability, someone who might talk –'

'Will we ever know?' Aarti asked.

'Easy,' Dinesh interrupted. 'When Red Hand kill a traitor - a Red Hand who betrays them - they get a big knife and cut out the Siva Sect circle on their arm and leave a big red hole. Then everyone knows Red Hand has killed a traitor. It's a warning –'

'I saw his wrist and lower arm.' Rich thought back to the hanging man. 'The Siva Sect badge was still there–'

'He took his own life, then?' Aarti concluded and Dinesh nodded.

'Maybe a realisation did come then and a change – and he couldn't face up to what he had done?' Rich pondered. 'If only I could have talked him round to help us.'

'Some things we can't change, Rich,' Aarti assured him.

Rich got them juices and nut snacks and they sat on the bench in the shade facing the openness of forest, cut open in a short stretch by the road below.

'I will be free soon?' he asked Aarti.

'The news goes local first – and big stories like this are picked up nationally – you'll be safe, but I don't know when. There'll have to be a massive inquiry. You can talk to your embassy then–'

'It'll expose everything, and everybody?'

'We can hope. These things are never straightforward, and Lakshya is slippery. So we have to keep you in hiding.'

The sun was going down when they left. Aditya hugged and kissed him: 'Give me doll,' she laughed in his ear.

'I will get you a new one. We will come and see you.'

There were hugs from Aarti, and he assured her he was using her breathing method for meditation.

Rich gave Dinesh his last cash from his bag and told him to bring them provisions when he next came.

'In two days,' Dinesh shook his hand.

'We'll get your cousin's killers, Dinesh–'

He watched them down the track and stood at the ridge half an hour later, waiting for Dinesh's Ambassador to come out of the tree line below for seconds and disappear round a bend. Another car emerged from the forest seconds after, heading in the same direction.

He got Parmita to show him how to make dhal that night, and she laughed while they worked together on a gas ring the size of a camping stove in light from solar lamps, chopping onions, garlic, ginger and chilli for the tarka, sprinkling in turmeric, cumin, masala.

'You have no children, Parmita?'

She looked away.

'Do they come and see you?'

'Son. No come.'

'Where is he?'

She pointed at the faded brown henna on Rich's arm.

'He's Red Hand?'

She nodded, chewing.

'Red Hand is not just here - in other parts of India?'

'Big. They get boy, make join.'

'I've got no mother now,' he smiled, 'and you've got no son–'

She smiled.

'You're my mother now–'

In the yellow spread of candlelight he held the garment to her, its tones golden and red and blue in the windless line of flame. She searched his eyes and he knew something deeper in her then, a knowledge through suffering, a wisdom that transcended pleasure and contentment. She would not speak of what she had seen in any language, except in the silent language of eyes. She was a new mother to him, and understood dimensions of manhood he had only glimpsed at so far, and taking the material she let its folds fall out gently as she wrapped it ready for him. Like a son he stripped to his shorts and held his arms up ready for the little blouse, then out again as she plied the red and the gold and the blue and the white round him, straightening, tucking in, adjusting. And she took him to the small square mirror with a corner missing and put lipstick on and kajal round his eyes. She had gold for his earrings, did final touches to the sari. And staring back at himself was a person he was coming to know. No longer did he need to run from himself, for that's what the running had been for him, he realised. He stood, finding himself complete.

'Hijra,' Parmita laughed, pointing at him. 'Hijra.'

He remembered they had talked before of transgender females who blessed little boys and attended weddings - hijra - and laughed with her.

Parmita sang, her notes filling the shadows of the room, and although he could not understand the words they brought images of his daughter along with tears at the edges of his eyes. They clapped and laughed and sang together, and she taught him dance steps, until they fell back on cushions with laughter. Until now he had missed the woman in himself, but she was alive and certain and would not be dismissed and must be integrated into his being. It was like a great wheel turning and bringing change; with change new awareness was inevitable, he reflected. He had moved on. Tina was in the past, Jeannette, the future. The turning wheel expanded consciousness.

The next morning he pulled out his drawing things and sat by the ridge in jeans and T-shirt. A huge beam of sunlight fanned out behind the edge of a forested hillside. Sketching in tree-lines faintly with a hard pencil, he soon took out his small pack of watercolours and washed in watery greens and yellowy lemon sunlight.

As the sun moved overhead he went into the forest and sat on the rock Lalima and he had hidden behind days before. Tree trunks, the fronds of creepers, shrubs, rocks he outlined and experimented with using pen and brush.

The following day he did more studies of trees and light, but found his mind drifting and doodled images of Lalima dancing on sand. He tried to hold what he remembered of Jeanette still while he drew, but it was hazy and faded and he was not happy with the attempt - it only made the hurt for her a deeper groove of pain inside than before. Quickly he tried to push them aside with memories of others - Aarti meditating, Nina singing, and Angie in her big sun hat - that last one was better - he caught her shy expression in the shade of the brim; he liked her calmness, and the wide sphere of caring she seemed to bring with her.

Clearly he needed a lot more practise with figure drawing and faces - and it was a lot easier when you had them there. He could start with Parmita.

Being alone, his mind was free to dabble with myriads of ideas, images and memories and he found himself sitting on top of the rocks at the south end of Bagolem, the blazing white sand of the bay shaping out in a long tree lined crescent ahead, dotted with the movement of people. Their cries and laughter came up to him as he spread colour on his pad. Others lunged in low waves that fed themselves on sands and washed back into the swell they came from - as though waves were only lent to the beach and must be returned so that the great globe of water could contain itself and continue to dominate.

The brush eased itself over the paper freely in a way he had not experienced before, as though his hand was doing the thinking for him and he became lost in its movement, unaware of thoughts for a time as it seemed colours were described for him and images rose effortlessly. He no longer felt his mother at his shoulder; she had left ten pounds and was gone. The sun was off-white, dimming to lemon.

Dinesh bashed the horn in three long blasts in the evening and Rich ran to the ridge and watched the car slow down along the bit of tarmac he could see. Dinesh would park it in trees off road and be up within half an hour. Rich helped Parmita get juices and pakora snacks ready for the guest and brought them out on plates as Dinesh came to the top of the track, a figure trailing him a few metres behind.

'Dinesh,' Rich greeted him with a handshake and hug: 'News?'

Dinesh looked down, shaking his head.

'This is never going to break, Dinesh. I'll always be seen as guilty of the murders – the papers are corrupt – they won't print it - I can't stay here forever –'

'Siva Sect have big power–'

'I'll go to the Embassy–' Angie offered as she came forward and pecked his cheek. He loved her warmness close to him.

'If you make it, if they don't find something to put on you, Angie. Your best bet is to get on a plane home–'

She lowered her head and shook it.

'You've got to–'

'She won't leave you,' Dinesh spelled it out.

'You can't stay for me,' Rich laughed nervously. 'It's a great idea, but – and very – you're just very caring – too caring. You've got to go home. Do you think they would believe you at the Embassy? Tales of an English child killer on the run is bound to have got to them. Will they believe you and me – or Lakshya?'

Dinesh was nodding.

'So what do we do?' Angie insisted.

'They've got to catch me. India is a big place, lots of people, lots of places to hide. I've got contacts now – Aarti in Bangalore –'

'You can't run forever, Rich.'

'Watch me.'

'I'm going to write it all out,' Angie challenged. 'Everything. A copy for the papers and a copy for the Embassy.'

'You can try.'

They sat and ate in silence with Parmita in the shade. She brought out some of the dhal with rice that Rich had made, and showed it off to them.

'What about Rita?' Angie asked Dinesh. 'Did you hear from Mumbai?'

'She is safe,' he nodded while loading his mouth. 'She got a job helping in a school and got a place for daughter and granddaughter to live. One day she will visit again, she says.'

'It's good you are staying in touch, Dinesh,' Angie spooned the dhal to her mouth. 'And this is very good dhal, Rich.'

Dinesh approved too: 'You can work in a restaurant – a chef,' he laughed.

'Yes, Dinesh,' Rich said. 'You looked after Rita, didn't you? She was special to you.'

They ate for a time before Rich asked about Nina and Angie told him she had disappeared for a time with a drummer.

'Another one?' he laughed, getting Angie going too.

'You have let go of her?'

'I guess I have–' He rooted about for his pad and showed her his drawing of her onstage, prancing in black.

'You've caught the melody–'

'I don't know,' Rich said, 'I'm never happy with what I do – I always think it should be better –'

'I'm sure that's what makes artists improve.'

'You reckon?'

Flipping over a page she found Lalima dancing. 'Rich, that really is her – and the movement –'

Dinesh said, 'Very good.' And Parmita was chuckling in agreement.

'That's it?' Angie turned a few more leaves: 'No – this must be Bagolem beach – yes, I can see, and –' She turned another: 'And this is me?' she laughed, 'In that stupid hat. You should throw that away, Rich–'

'Wouldn't dream of it.'

Parmita pointed a gnarled index finger at the picture, then up at Angie: 'This her. Good. Good.'

'See. It's you, Angie–' Rich smiled and Dinesh nodded.

The sun was behind a ridge when they finished eating and chatting.

He looked at Angie, not wanting her to go: 'You came to say goodbye, then?'

'You men,' she laughed, 'think you're the centre of the world. There were other reasons.'

'Oh.'

'I want to see it again.'

'What?'

'Lamilgusma.'

'It takes at least an hour through the forest, and by then it'll be dark,' Rich said.

'Another day then?'

'Tomorrow, Dinesh? Here, Dinesh. My phone needs charging, can you do it and bring it back? I need to get hold of Aarti -' Dinesh was wringing his hands. 'Dinesh? Last time.'

'I will come early, leave Angie here, and come back in two more days. I have big work to do on the beach, very busy. And the more times I come here, more risk–'

'He's right, Angie. You wouldn't want to stay up here for two nights with a killer, would you?'

'Parmita? I can stay?' she nodded over, and Parmita nodded back.

When they had gone Rich got Parmita to sit for him and he outlined her face, her ruffled clothing, her hands folded on her lap. After ten minutes he was having to work by solar lamp, and rounded it off casually. She looked at it when he had finished, chin in hand, and laughed, then he tore it carefully along the bound edge out of the pad and put it on a shelf for them to admire: 'Parmita,' he said.

*****

The river had gone down further than when he had been here last, but there was enough of a slow swell to be deep in places. Peacocks and bullocks, deer and lions, gambolled in an astrological extravaganza. Rich got water from the river in an empty bottle and outlined the figures for Angie, as though like the prehistoric ancestors he was marking it out for the first time. A mother giving birth, a figure with one leg crossed in front of the other - Yoga practitioner, or Siva dancing, or Krishna playing his flute. He made the great triskelion, the three hooded snake-head, burn into life with streams of water turning the grey rock black as graphite, and remembering his mother he made the peacock come to life. The world seemed to swirl in the vortex of the universe, time collapsed, all things were shaken up - like the Churning of The Sea of Milk. It was as though he could see things there that had been previously hidden, as though truths opened out perceptions, intuition and further understanding.

The wheel moved in circles of life and death and rebirth and the energy that turned it was from the heart chakra as it opened to knowledge and consciousness.

Things buried came up from the past - mother with father. There was a raging argument, ending in him hitting her, like Milit had hit Chanda. In his mind Rich found pictures of himself pulling Chanda to her feet after the blow, and as she stood - she was his mother. In that world his mother had protected him from his father, but in that protection had loaded all her love on him as a child, so that when his father went Rich became his substitute.

It made sense: her possessive love would not let him go, so that as he grew older he was not free in his heart to break away from her and make love relationships of his own, his unconscious yearnings for mother drawing him back from handing over his heart fully to another woman. So every encounter was one of bodies, but not of a deeper consciousness shared mutually and given over in the trust of love. Even to Tina he could not give everything of himself, and unconsciously, because she could, it frustrated her and she was not fulfilled by him.

Wheels turned wheels.

He had taken from Chanda too, yet with her he had got deeper and closer to awareness of his giving potential. They had touched in a communion, yet the abyss between cultures and family ties would always keep them separate. He had transgressed that - had gone in selfishly with her, not understanding the consequences to her.

Wheels turned more wheels - consciousness revolved. 'All we can do is know ourselves better,' he thought, 'in the chaos - as Lakshya had said - manage the chaos - learn and move on -'

He was unsteady by the river: perhaps he could do it all better now, live better, give better. If he was given the chance, if he was allowed to live longer. He saw himself pouring his mother in the sea, spangles of her dust flickering in the evening light, a Brahminy Kite with its crisp white underbody and chestnut brown wings, circling above, and he let the waste of her drift on dusted waters as she disintegrated and resurrected herself in rebirth in the lemon seas that embraced her.

He said to Angie: 'Aarti says Buddha says: "There's only one certainty. That is change." I understand a bit of that now–'

Her eyes were on him, and the dance of the animals and creatures in the laterite rock below seemed to slow for him and fade. Wind ruffled trees. He heard Jeanette call: 'Dada.'

'The Wheel of India,' Angie said: 'Change. Consciousness.'

'You know all that - all that giving in your heart, Angie -'

'A cow with one horn,' she pointed down at an indolent creature in rock. 'No. A bull I think.' She laughed. 'It's curious you know. Aarti was telling me, on tablets found in Harappa - the most ancient site ever found in India - there's a one horned bull - prehistoric. The same as here.'

'The same as down town, in Bagolem.'

'Only that's a cow.'

'They scared me then. I admit it–' he held his hands up and she smiled. 'I understand a bit of that now – the animal side of ourselves. It's in us and we have to see it and tame it. Everything seems to make sense when I'm here by these figures. I can see that all things we do are somehow triggered by desire. And what Aarti says about non-violence. All that came from India. We have to understand the killing gene in us, but turn its energy positive.'

'Gandhi's belief in non-violence did that.'

'So our teacher Aarti says live a life of–' he began.

'Laughing and loving, maybe–' she ended it and they stared at their reflections in the sheen of water.

'It begins to make sense, all of it–'

'It gives us something to work on about what we're doing here,' she let out again with a laugh. 'Isn't that what the people who made these images were trying to work out: what they were doing here? And what this short cycle of consciousness means?'

They looked in the slow moving water and their reflections shimmered.

'You've got to get back to Jeanette, Rich,' she tapped him, bringing him back to earth and he turned to her, eyes welling. 'I could come with you.' She squeezed his hand, looked in his eye and brought her lips close to his lips. She kissed him and he held on to her.

'Bangalore,' he said after she had pecked his face with little kisses and stroked his hair. 'Will you come?'

'Run with a serial killer? That's better than a Bollywood movie.' She laughed and kissed him again. Then, breaking away she pulled off her top, slipped off her jeans and knickers, howled with joy, ran and jumped in the river. 'Come on, Rich, come on.'

His kit was off and he was in the air, his spread eagled shape lunging in beside her and they splashed and laughed like a couple of kids.

She drew him to her on a towel on the rock of dancing animals, and he pulsed on with her, their bodies rolling freely near the spiralling labyrinth, while animals mated, gave birth, danced. They rocked, kissing and pulling themselves in the swirl, and gasping and laughing, until he could release himself with her and take her to her own completion.

They laughed and then slept in each other's arms for what seemed to Rich like hours, until a shadow was over them: 'So, Mister Lomas - you like our prehistoric sites.'

Angie was up pulling clothes to her, while Rich gathered the towel and draped it round her.

'And you bring a new friend for your sordid rituals,' Lakshya pointed a hand gun loosely towards them, casually waving the barrel in circles. 'Perhaps I should shoot your balls off now, Mister Lomas, while I have the chance.' He pointed his weapon at Rich's penis. Rich made to get his shorts, but Lakshya nailed him again: 'We'll leave you as you are. For the moment. Let my men see you like this when they get here, it will be amusing for them.'

'The story will break,' Rich flung out.

'You think so, Mister Lomas. The fingers of the Siva Sect go deep in the pockets of all the media. And if they do not do what they are told, there is always a Red Hand somewhere who will encourage them.'

'The truth will get out,' Angie tried. 'It always does.'

'Only our truth gets printed. '

'There's always people who really know what's going on.'

'Your optimism is misguided, Richard Lomas. And unfortunately you have compromised us somewhat - kicked up too much fuss. But it ends here. There's no way out, miss, I'm afraid. When my truck arrives you will be bundled off and the murderer and his assisting moll will be up for media grabs, as you say - and Bagolem will once again become a good place to stay–'

Rich flinched.

'It's not a good idea for you to run, Mister Lomas, nothing would give me greater pleasure than to say I had to shoot a fleeing criminal. And a naked one at that,' he laughed. 'Or perhaps you would like that. Who wants a child killer in the world–'

'You know it wasn't me. The Red Hands–'

'Who you seem to have joined,' Lakshya glanced at Rich's wrist. 'We cannot have trouble from them, can we?'

'You need someone to blame and cover up–'

'Yes, Mister Lomas. We do. And you will do nicely. And our prisons for women are very friendly, miss. Like I said, Mister Rich. Nothing personal. I have to do my duty to the community and manage the chaos that reigns there–'

Rich could find no more words. It was over and he had to give in. Men were shuffling down a track over the back of the platform of rock. Two policemen in khaki uniforms bounded in the scene with semi-automatics, followed by Milit in shirt and trousers. The three sniggered at his nakedness.

'You can't let this happen, Milit. You can be free–' Rich cried, his shoulders baking in the sun.

'I do this,' Milit threw at him as the men raced to the group, one with a hennaed hand around a trigger.

'You see, Mister Lomas–' Lakshya shrugged.

Milit pulled out handcuffs, and resigned, Rich held out his hands, but the Red Hand policeman pulled the gun from Lakshya's hand and drew his wrist out while the other pointed his gun at the police chief and Milit clipped the cuffs on him.

Lakshya yelled, pulling away, but a gun was poked into his belly. The policemen shouted something to him and jerked him away and Lakshya yelled and heaved, cursing his captors and swearing at Rich.

'The news?' Rich shouted to Milit. 'The story is out?'

Milit came to him, half smiling and nodding at the police chief: 'Soon, soon, news will come. Siva Sect don't like him. Say he makes big trouble–' He drew his hand across his throat. Lakshya's screams and curses echoed through the trees as he was taken, his struggling body restrained by the men he once controlled. 'Siva Sect unhappy Lakshya did not shut you up, Rich. Now everything will go open in newspaper with people's names – and big people. Newspaper will say many big and rich people are in Siva Sect, even politician. Then everyone knows about Siva Sect and about Red Hand. It will be big news. Siva Sect says Lakshya is to blame – even though Big Man in Siva Sect tell Lakshya to set you up.' He paused for breath, then: 'Nobody know what they will do with police chief, cut Siva from his arm, maybe.'

Silence followed Milit's explanation for a time as warm breeze tripped through tree tops. The river slipped on its silvery way, gloss black in the shadow of trees, gloss blue in the light by the platform of rock.

'Does that mean we're all right?' Angie asked Rich, but he could not answer. She came to him for hugs.

'I don't know anything, anymore,' he half smiled after a time. 'It's all so big – they get Lakshya, but what about the rest, people like Mendez – the real killers –'

'Many Red Hand people go and hide,' Milit informed them. 'They all disappear. But Siva Sect still has big power and many people who hide in secret. So Red Hand still are dangerous. You hide.'

Milit turned and ran after his comrades and the dust settled as Angie pulled Rich along the track back to the hut in the forest. As stars came out they slept in each other's arms under the net.

In the morning they decided they would get Dinesh to take them to the Embassy in Paniji. 'There's police all round, maybe waiting for you–' Dinesh scowled.

'But it's in the news, Dinesh? Milit said.'

'It must get bigger first, before you are safe. If you get seen by Red Hand policeman in Paniji - you will not like Indian prison - it will take a long time to get you out.' Dinesh looked up at Angie.

'We have to go to Bangalore then. Keep on the move,' Rich said. 'They can still get us here, and Parmita will get caught up in it. But-'

'What?' Angie said.

'All my money's gone. I may have a trickle at the ATM, but-'

'I've got it,' she said.

'And we must leave some for Parmita-'

'I can cover it, Rich. The thing is to get you out of here-'

*****

They waited for a train south, bags packed at their feet, Rich and Angie clinging to each other like first lovers afraid that without permanent touch they would expire. Dinesh and Nikhil waited with them near a begging woman hovering in the background and propped up with a stick. Dinesh handed over the new doll he had found for Rich to take to Aditya and he and the lovers cuddled it as though it was their child.

'You've got some money for the begging woman over there?' Rich fussed his new girlfriend.

'I might have something-'

As Angie was searching her purse another figure approached.

'Where are you going?' Nina had walked up the platform, and stopped, staring at Angie: 'With him? Always was more your type - gooey Rich -' She paused a minute: 'I'm going north, Rich. Mumbai. Some band wants a singer.' She paused again: 'You want to come, Rich?'

Angie glowered at her old friend.

Rich laughed: 'I've moved on-'

'Did you get her out?' Nina snapped. 'That kid? You get her?'

'Yeah.'

'No thanks to you,' Angie put in.

'It's a long story. Go and play some blues, Nina,' Rich told her: 'It's what you do best.'

The beggar advanced on them, palm in an open cone, her head covered with a Kashmiri shawl.

'You rescued Lalima,' Nina yelped. 'Good one. High fives.' She held up her hand for him to smack. 'Good one, Rich. We had some times, didn't we? You can have him babe,' she laughed to Angie, 'but he ain't no good–'

Angie and Rich laughed. 'That could be a line from one of your songs,' Angie said.

The train had reached the top end of the long platform. The beggar was rocking her hand. The diesel blared its way in, sliding along the platform's far end. 'A strange hand.' Rich thought as he waved to Nina as she bound off to the footbridge. The engine thudded heavily, rippling the platform. 'More like a man's hand,' Rich mused. The machine's relentless rattle pumped towards them. The begging woman was crouched, her hand trembling.

'That is strange, Angie.'

She looked at him and across at the poor figure.

'I could swear that was a man's hand –'

The locomotive was metres away, blaring.

Rich pulled Angie back: 'A man's hand. Henna. It's a Red Hand.'

The stick fell away as the beggar stuffed his fist in folds of material.

'Red Hand–' he shouted again in shock.

A spangle of sunlight burst from the blade, over the attacker's head.

The train was nearly up with them.

Dinesh picked up the stick and smacked the beggar's arm, sending the knife spinning. Then he and Nikhil were on him, pulling back the shawl.

'Mendez,' Rich shouted as the diesel bore down on them. 'Mendez.'

Mendez broke free, chasing his blade, but tripped over Rich's feet, rolled a foot or two and bounced off the edge of the platform.

The man's screams were drowned by the diesel's horn as the train smoothed slowly over his flesh.

*****

There would be fuss, police, Dinesh told them - he would have to drive them south thirty miles to the next station where they could board, and urged them back to his car, but they were stopped by Charles waving a newspaper, along with Milit.

'The Times of India. National Paper.' Charles kept saying: 'Headline: Man in Sari Foils Bent Cops. Police Cover Up Child Murders–'

Angie held Rich close.

The trip to Bangalore would have to wait - police interviews, statements, talk with the press, the Embassy. It would all take time. Rich looked at Milit, his face drawn by years of bad stuff - booze, gambling, pimping - he had lost himself, the youthful yearning to be somebody in the world and achieve something caged; all it needed was a stronger man to take him under his control and use him like a robot. Rich was reminded of the weeping Milit on his knees holding Chanda's legs; of how he had let them go and the risk to himself. Rich stuffed his rail ticket in Milit's shirt pocket and told him to be in the train when it set off again. The man retreated, shocked, but Dinesh nodded and they bundled him on.

*****

After letting Frank's ashes drift in the sea with Dinesh and Nikhil, Rich sat with Angie on the rock – somehow he had pulled her up with him, and they sat while he painted. The sea's sparkle echoed back sunlight in the mid-afternoon, the moment when white light mellowed to pale yellow. When you walked along the beach, he remembered, that shaft of the sun's reflection over the waves travelled along with you, as though it was a fan of light especially for you, so that everyone, wherever they stood, was served with a line of lemon sea that faded as the ball of light dragged itself to its pink demise.

Smoke from burned rubbish lumped in breathless air and rode behind palms along the tide drained river. From thunder earlier without rain, the atmosphere was charged. Fires hid under smoke, the stuff so heavy it would press down and smother the flame that created it and swamp figures. The land thirsted; cloud cover would not crack, the monsoon still weeks away. Fires burned along the back of the beach – like the beginnings of life, Rich imagined – like from Lamilgusma times, he thought – fires for families, communities, nations; and then fires for wars even; smoke pasting itself past crags and palms and dissipating over the sea. Then the time of mosquitoes.

'Frank said:' Rich told her, 'An hour or so before the sun goes down, just for a few seconds before it goes rosy pink, there's a quick moment – very quick – you have to be so quick to see it. Now. There. You get it? You see it, Angie? Lemon Seas . . .'

About Neil Beardmore

Leaving school early to work in a factory to buy an electric piano, Neil joined a band and that paid off as today he still enjoys playing the Blues. He continued to get pleasure from writing as it initially grew from writing songs, poetry, then plays. Later on teacher training opened up the world of literature. He won the Sussex Playwriting competition and the Richard Burton Poetry competition. An MA in Creative Writing followed and as a published poet he performs regularly. Pristine In Blue was professionally staged as part of the Milton Keynes Fringe and received critical acclaim.

His dearest friend and wife Ashra gives him much support, inspiration and laughter. She has opened up the doors to India, her country of birth, which continues to intrigue, fascinate and mesmerise Neil. Lemon Seas is the result. He is fortunate still to share his work and facilitate writing workshops.

Connect with Neil Beardmore

Via author's website: www.neilbeardmore.com

Lightning Source UK Ltd.
Milton Keynes UK
UKOW02f0416131116
287491UK00001B/9/P

9 781782 284239